fishermen's village

ale house

fezzick's cave

the farm

the armada

pursuit ship

high wall

golden carriage

lombardo's castle

great square

miracle max

florin

zoo of death

wheelbarrow

humperdinck

TABLE OF CONTENTS

Introduction to the Twenty-fifth Anniversary Edition   iv

The Princess Bride   1

Buttercup's Baby: An Explanation   321

Buttercup's Baby: Chapter One

    Fezzik Dies   349

A Ballantine Book
The Random House Publishing Group

www.ballantinebooks.com

Library of Congress Cataloging-in-Publication Data
Goldman, William, 1931–
The princess bride : S. Morgenstern's classic tale of true love and high adventure :
the "good parts" version, abridged / by William Goldman.—1st Ballantine Books
hardcover ed.
p. cm.
ISBN 0-345-43014-X (alk. paper)
I. Title.
PS3557.0384P7   1998
813'.54—dc21   98-39556
                                                                                    CIP

This edition published by arrangement
with Harcourt Brace Jovanovich, Inc.

Manufactured in the United States of America

Book design by Fritz Metsch

First Ballantine Books Hardcover Edition: December 1998

11 13 15 17 19 20 18 16 14 12

ALSO BY WILLIAM GOLDMAN

FICTION
The Temple of Gold (1957)
Your Turn to Curtsy, My Turn to Bow (1958)
Soldier in the Rain (1960)
Boys and Girls Together (1964)
No Way to Treat a Lady (1964)
The Thing of It Is . . . (1967)
Father's Day (1971)
Marathon Man (1974)
Magic (1976)
Tinsel (1979)
Control (1982)
The Silent Gondoliers (1983)
The Color of Light (1984)
Heat (1985)
Brothers (1986)

NON-FICTION
The Season: A Candid Look at Broadway (1969)
The Making of 'A Bridge Too Far' (1977)
Adventures in the Screen Trade: A Personal
View of Hollywood and Screenwriting (1983)
Wait Till Next Year (With Mike Lupica) (1988)
Hype and Glory (1990)
Four Screenplays (1995)
Five Screenplays (1997)

SCREENPLAYS
Masquerade (with Michael Relph) (1965)
Harper (1966)
Butch Cassidy and the Sundance Kid (1969)
The Hot Rock (1972)
The Great Waldo Pepper (1975)
The Stepford Wives (1975)
All the President's Men (1976)
Marathon Man (1976)
A Bridge Too Far (1977)
Magic (1978)
Mr. Horn (1979)
Heat (1987)
The Princess Bride (1987)
Misery (1990)
The Year of the Comet (1992)
Maverick (1994)
The Chamber (1996)
The Ghost and the Darkness (1996)
Absolute Power (1997)

PLAYS
Blood, Sweat and Stanley Poole (with James Goldman) (1961)
A Family Affair (with James Goldman and John Kander) (1961)

FOR CHILDREN
Wigger (1974)

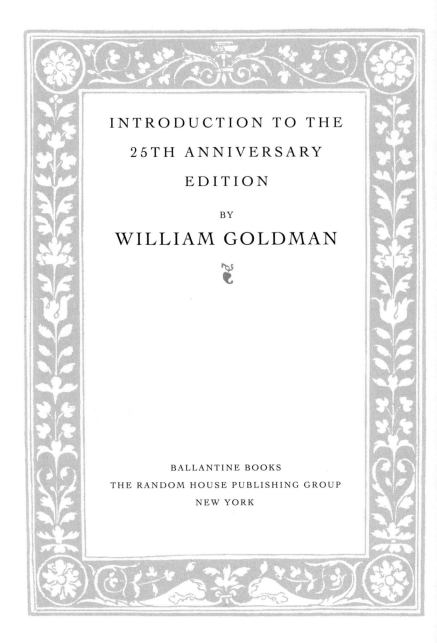

INTRODUCTION TO THE 25TH ANNIVERSARY EDITION

BY

WILLIAM GOLDMAN

BALLANTINE BOOKS
THE RANDOM HOUSE PUBLISHING GROUP
NEW YORK

T'S still my favorite book in all the world.

And more than ever, I wish I had written it. Sometimes I like to fantasize that I did, that *I* came up with Fezzik (my favorite character), that *my* imagination summoned the iocane sequence, the ensuing battle of wits to the death.

Alas, Morgenstern invented it all, and I must be contented with the fact that my abridgment (though *killed* by all Florinese experts back in '73—the reviews in the learned journals brutalized me; in my book-writing career, only *Boys and Girls Together* got a worse savaging) at least brought Morgenstern to a wider American audience.

What is stronger than childhood memory? Nothing, at least for me. I still have a recurring dream of my poor, sad father reading the book out loud—only in the dream he wasn't poor and sad; he'd had a wonderful life, a life equal to his decency, and as he read, his English, so painful in truth, was splendid. And he was happy. And my mother so proud . . .

But the movie is the reason we're back together. I doubt that my publishers would have sprung for this edition if the movie hadn't happened. If you're reading this, dollars to donuts you've seen the movie. It was a mild success when it first hit theaters, but word of mouth caught up with it when the videocassette came out. It was a big hit in video stores then, still is. If you have kids, you've probably watched it with them. Robin Wright in the title role began her film career as Buttercup, and I'm sure we all fell in love with her again in *Forrest Gump*. (Personally, I think she was the reason for that phenomenon. She was so lovely and warm, you just ached for poor dopey Tom Hanks to live happily with someone like that.)

Most of us love movie stories. Maybe back when Broadway held sway, people loved theater stories, but I don't think anymore. And I'll bet no one begs Julia Louis-Dreyfus to talk about what it was like shooting Seinfeld episode number 89. And novelist stories? Can you imagine cornering Dostoyevsky and begging him for funny stuff about *The Idiot*?

Anyway, these are some movie memories pertaining to *The Princess Bride* I thought you might not know.

I had taken time off from writing *The Stepford Wives* screenplay to abridge the Morgenstern. And then someone at Fox heard about it, got hold of a manuscript copy of the book, liked it, was interested in making a movie out of it. This is early '73 we're talking about. The "someone" at Fox was their *Greenlight Guy*. (Referred to hereinafter as the GG.)

You will read in such magazines as *Premiere* and *Entertainment Weekly* and *Vanity Fair*, endless lists about the "100 most powerful" studio figures. These various idiots all have titles: Vice President in charge of this, Chief Executive in charge of that, etc.

The truth: they are all oil slicks.

Only one person per studio has anything resembling power, and that is the GG. The GG, you see, can make a picture happen. He (or she) is the one who releases the fifty million bucks—if your movie is aimed for Sundance. Triple that if it's a special effects job.

Anyway, the GG at Fox liked *The Princess Bride*.

Problem: he wasn't sure it was a movie. So we struck a peculiar arrangement—they would buy the book, but they would not buy the screenplay unless they decided to move forward. In other words, we both owned half the pie. So even though I was tired from finishing the abridgment, I went on nervous energy and did the screenplay immediately after.

My very great agent, Evarts Ziegler, came to town. Ziegler was the one who orchestrated the *Butch Cassidy* deal, which, along with *The Temple of Gold*, my first novel, changed my life as much as anything. We went to lunch at Lutèce, chatted, enjoyed each other, parted, me to my office on the Upper East Side in a building that had a swimming pool. I used to swim every day because I had a very bad back then, and the swimming eased things. I was heading for the pool when I realized this: I didn't want to swim.

I didn't want to do anything but get home *fast*. Because I was shivering terribly now. I made it home, got to bed, the shivering replaced by fire. Helen, my superstar-shrink wife, came in from work, took one look at me, got me to New York Hospital.

All kinds of doctors came in—everybody knew something was seriously wrong, nobody had a guess as to what it might be.

I woke at four in the morning. And I *knew* what was wrong. Somehow, the awful pneumonia that almost killed me when I was ten—the reason my father read *The Princess Bride* to me in the first place was to get me through those first woeful posthospital days—well, that pneumonia had come back to finish the job.

And right then, in that hospital (and, yes, I expect this will sound nutty to you) as I woke in pain and delirium, somehow I *knew* that if I was to live, I had to get back to that place where I was as a child. I started yelling for the night nurse—

—because somehow my life and *The Princess Bride* were forever joined.

The night nurse came in and I told her to read me the Morgenstern.

"The what, Mr. Goldman?" she said.

"Start with the Zoo of Death," I told her. Then I said, "No, no, forget that, start with the Cliffs of Insanity."

She took one close look at me, nodded, said, "Oh, right, that's exactly where I'll start, but I left my Morgenstern at the desk, I'll just go get it."

The next thing I knew, here came Helen. And several other doctors. "I went to your office, I think I picked up the right pages. Now what is it you want me to read?"

"I don't want *you* to read anything, Helen, you never liked the book, you don't want to read to me, you're just humoring me, and besides there's no part for you—"

"I could be Buttercup—"

"Oh, come on, she's twenty-one—"

"Is that a screenplay?" this handsome doctor said then. "I always wanted to be a movie star."

"You be the man in black," I told him. Then I pointed to the big doctor in the doorway. "Give Fezzik a shot."

That was how I first heard the screenplay. These medicos and my genius wife struggling with it in the middle of the night while I froze and sweated and the fever raged inside me.

I passed out after a little while. And I remember thinking at the last that the big doctor wasn't bad and Helen, miscast and all, was an OK Buttercup, and so what if the handsome doctor was a stiff, I was going to live.

Well, that was the beginning of the life of the screenplay.

The GG at Fox sent it to Richard Lester in London—Lester directed, among others, *A Hard Day's Night*, the first wonderful Beatles film—and we met, worked, solved problems. The GG was thrilled, we were a *go*—

—then he got fired, and a new GG came in to replace him.

Here is what happens Out There when that happens: the old GG is stripped of his epaulets and his ability to get into Morton's on Monday nights and off he goes, very rich—he had a deal in place for this inevitability—but disgraced.

And the new GG takes the throne with but one rule firmly writ in stone: *nothing* his predecessor had in motion must ever get made. Why? Say it gets made. Say it's a hit. Who gets the credit? The *old* GG. And when the new GG, who can now get into Morton's on Mondays, has to run the gauntlet there, he knows all his peers are sniggering: "That asshole, it wasn't his picture."

Death.

So *The Princess Bride* was buried, conceivably forever.

And I realized that I had let control of it go. Fox had the book. So what if I had the screenplay; they could commission another. They could change anything they wanted. So I did something of which I am genuinely proud. I bought the book back from the studio, *with my own money.* I think they were suspicious I had some deal or plan, but I didn't. I just didn't want some idiot destroying what I had come to realize was the most important thing I would ever be involved with.

After a good bit of negotiating, it was again mine. I was the only idiot who could destroy it now.

*   *   *

I READ RECENTLY that the fine Jack Finney novel *Time and Again* has taken close to twenty years and still hasn't made it to the screen. *The Princess Bride* didn't take that long, but not a lot less either. I didn't keep notes, so this is from memory. Understand, in order for someone to make a movie, they need two things: passion and money. A lot of people, it turned out, loved *The Princess Bride*.

I know of at least two different GGs who were mad about it. Who shook hands with me on the deal. Who wanted to make it more than any other movie.

Who both got fired the *weekend* before they were going to set things in motion. One studio (a small one) even *closed* the weekend before they were going to set things in motion. The screenplay began to get a certain reputation—one magazine article listed it among the best that had never been shot.

The truth is, after a decade and more, I thought it would never happen. Every time there was interest, I kept waiting for the other shoe to come clunking down—and it always did. But, without my knowledge, events had been put in motion a decade before that eventually would be my salvation.

When *Butch Cassidy and the Sundance Kid* was done, I took myself out of the movie business for awhile. (We are back in the late '60s now.) I wanted to try something I had never done, nonfiction.

I wrote a book about Broadway called *The Season*. In the course of a year I went to the theater hundreds of times, both in New York and out of town, saw everything at least once. But the show I saw most was a terrific comedy called *Something Different*, written by Carl Reiner.

Reiner was terribly helpful to me, and I liked him a lot. When *The Season* was done I sent him a copy. A few years later, when *The Princess Bride* was finished, I sent him the novel. And one day he gave it to his eldest son. "Here's something," he said to his boy Robert. "I think you'll like this."

Rob was a decade away from starting his directing career then, but in '85 we met, and Norman Lear (bless him) gave us the money to go forward with the movie.

Keep hope alive.

*   *   *

WE HAD OUR first script reading in a hotel in London in the spring of '86. Rob was there, as was his producer Andy Scheinman. Cary Elwes and Robin Wright, Buttercup and Westley, were there. So, too, were Chris Sarandon and Chris Guest, the villains Prince Humperdinck and Count Rugen, and Wally Shawn, the evil genius Vizzini. Mandy Patinkin, who played Inigo, was very much there. And sitting by himself, quietly—he always tried to sit quietly—was Andre the Giant who *was* Fezzik.

Not your ordinary Hadassah group.

Sitting suavely in a corner was *moi.* Two of the major figures of my years in the entertainment business—Elia Kazan and George Roy Hill—said the same thing to me in interviews: that by the time of the first cast reading, the crucial work was done. If you had gotten the script to work and cast it properly, then you had a chance for something of quality. But if you had not, it didn't matter how skillful the rest of the process was; you were dead in the water.

This probably sounds like madness to the uninitiated, and it should, but it is very much true. The reason it sounds like madness is this: *Premiere* magazine isn't around when the script is being prepared. *Entertainment Tonight* isn't around for casting. They are only around during the shooting of a flick, which is the *least* important part of the making of any movie. Remember this: *shooting is just the factory putting together the car.*

*   *   *

A. R. ROUSSIMOFF was our biggest gamble that rehearsal morning. Under the name of Andre the Giant, he was the most famous wrestler in the world. I had become convinced that if there ever was to be a movie, he should be Fezzik, the strongest man.

Rob thought Andre might be good for the part, too. The problem was, no one could find him. He wrestled 330 plus days a year, always on the move.

So we went ahead trying to find someone else. Strangest casting calls I ever saw. These big guys came in—we are talking immense here—but they weren't giants. Occasionally we would find a giant—but either he couldn't act or he was skinny, and a skinny giant was not at all what we needed.

Still, no Andre.

One day Rob and Andy were in Florin doing final location scouting when a call came—Andre would be in Paris the next afternoon. They flew over to meet him. Not easy, since Florin City has zero nonstops to any of the major capitals of Europe. Not to mention that their scheduling depends on load—all Florin Air's flights are jammed because they wait until they are before they'll take off. They even allow people to stand in the aisles. (I had only seen that myself once, in Russia, on a nightmare jaunt from Tblisi to Saint Petersburg.) Eventually, Rob and Andy had to charter a tiny propeller plane to make the meeting. They got to the Ritz, where the doorman said, in a weird voice, "There is a *man* waiting for you in the bar."

Andre, for me, was like the Pentagon—no matter how big you're told it's going to be, when you get close, it's bigger.

Andre was bigger.

His listed size was 550 pounds, seven-and-a-half-feet tall. But he wasn't really sure and he didn't spend a lot of time fretting on the scale each morning. He was sick once, he told me, and lost 100 pounds in three weeks. But other than that he never talked about his dimensions.

They chatted in the bar, then went up to Rob's room where they went over the script. A couple of things were clear: Andre had a clock-stopping French accent and, worse, his voice came from the subbasement.

Rob gambled, gave him the role. He also recorded Andre's part on tape for him—line for line, inflections hopefully included—so Andre could take it with him on the road and study it in the months before rehearsal began.

Rehearsal that London morning was intentionally light: a couple of readings of the script, few comments. It was a beautiful afternoon when we broke for lunch, and we found a nearby bistro with outside tables. It was perfect except the chair was far too small for Andre—the width was for normal people, the arms way too close. There was a table inside that had a bench, and someone suggested we eat there. But Andre wouldn't hear of it. So we sat outside. I can still see him pulling the metal arms of the chair wide apart, squeezing in, then watching the arms all but snapping back into place where they pinioned him for the remainder of the meal. He ate very little. And the utensils were like baby toys, dwarfed by his hands.

After lunch we rehearsed again, doing scenes now, and Andre was working with our Inigo, Mandy Patinkin. Andre had clearly studied Rob's tapes—but it was undeniable that his readings were slow, with more than a little rote quality.

They were doing one of their scenes after they have been re-united. Mandy was trying to get some information out of Andre and Andre was giving one of his slow, memorized readings. Mandy as Inigo tried to get Fezzik to go faster. Andre gave back another of his slow, rote responses. They went back and tried it again and again. Mandy as Inigo asked Andre as Fezzik to go faster—and Andre came back at the same speed as before—

—which was when Mandy said, "Faster, Fezzik!" And with no warning he slapped the Giant hard in the face.

I can still see Andre's eyes go wide. I don't think he had been slapped outside the ring since he was a little boy. He looked at Mandy . . . and there was a brief pause. A very dead silence filled the room.

And then Andre started speaking faster. He just rose to the occasion, gave it more pace and energy. You could almost see his mind: "Oh, this is how you do it outside the ring, let's try it for awhile." In truth, that slap was the beginning of the happiest period of his life.

It was a wonderful time for me, too. After the decade plus of waiting, the most important book of my youth was coming to life in front of me. When it was finished and I saw it finally, I realized that, in my entire career, I only really loved two of the movies I've been involved with: *Butch Cassidy and the Sundance Kid* and *The Princess Bride*.

But the movie did so much more than just please me. It brought the book back to life. I began getting these wonderful letters again. Got one today—Scout's honor—from a guy in L.A. who had been dumped by his Buttercup and, after a decade of separation, heard she was in trouble. So he sent her a copy of the novel and, well, obviously they are together now. You think that isn't wonderful—especially for someone like me who spends his life in his pit, writing—touching another human? Can't get better.

Of course, along with the good, I have regrets. I'm sorry about the legal troubles with the Morgenstern estate, about which more later. I'm sorry Helen and I went *pffft*. (Not that we both didn't know it was coming—but did she have to leave the very *day* the movie opened in New York?) And I'm sorry the Cliffs of Insanity have now become the biggest tourist attraction in Florin, making life hell for their forest rangers.

But this is life on earth, you can't have everything.

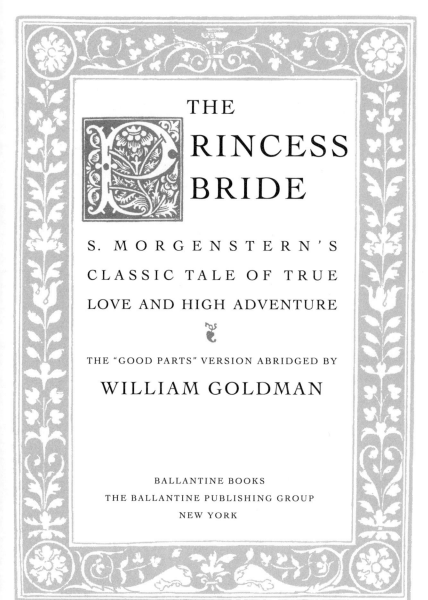

THE PRINCESS BRIDE

S. MORGENSTERN'S CLASSIC TALE OF TRUE LOVE AND HIGH ADVENTURE

THE "GOOD PARTS" VERSION ABRIDGED BY

WILLIAM GOLDMAN

BALLANTINE BOOKS
THE BALLANTINE PUBLISHING GROUP
NEW YORK

HIS is my favorite book in all the world, though I have never read it.

How is such a thing possible? I'll do my best to explain. As a child, I had simply no interest in books. I hated reading, I was very bad at it, and besides, how could you take the time to read when there were games that shrieked for playing? Basketball, baseball, marbles—I could never get enough. I wasn't even good at them, but give me a football and an empty playground and I could invent last-second triumphs that would bring tears to your eyes. School was torture. Miss Roginski, who was my teacher for the third through fifth grades, would have meeting after meeting with my mother. "I don't feel Billy is perhaps extending himself quite as much as he might." Or, "When we test him, Billy does really exceptionally well, considering his class standing." Or, most often, "I don't know, Mrs. Goldman: what *are* we going to do about Billy?"

What *are* we going to do about Billy? That was the phrase that haunted me those first ten years. I pretended not to care, but secretly I was petrified. Everyone and everything was passing me by. I had no real friends, no single person who shared an equal interest in all games. I seemed busy, busy, busy, but I suppose, if pressed, I might have admitted that, for all my frenzy, I was very much alone.

"What *are* we going to do about you, Billy?"

"I don't know, Miss Roginski."

"How could you have failed this reading test? I've heard you use every word with my own ears."

"I'm sorry, Miss Roginski. I must not have been thinking."

"You're always thinking, Billy. You just weren't thinking about the reading test."

I could only nod.

"What was it this time?"

"I don't know. I can't remember."

"Was it Stanley Hack again?" (Stan Hack was the Cubs' third baseman for these and many other years. I saw him play once from a bleacher seat, and even at that distance he had the sweetest smile I had ever seen and to this day I swear he smiled at me several times. I just worshipped him. He could also hit a ton.)

"Bronko Nagurski. He's a football player. A great football player, and the paper last night said he might come back and play for the Bears again. He retired when I was little but if he came back and I could get someone to take me to a game, I could see him play and maybe if whoever took me also knew him, I could meet him after and maybe if he was hungry, I might let him have a sandwich I might have brought with me. I was trying to figure out what kind of sandwich Bronko Nagurski would like."

She just sagged at her desk. "You've got a wonderful imagination, Billy."

I don't know what I said. Probably "thank you" or something.

"I can't harness it, though," she went on. "Why is that?"

"I think it's that probably I need glasses and I don't read because the words are so fuzzy. That would explain why I'm all the time squinting. Maybe if I went to an eye doctor who could give me glasses I'd be the best reader in class and you wouldn't have to keep me after school so much."

She just pointed behind her. "Get to work cleaning the black-boards, Billy."

"Yes, ma'am." I was the best at cleaning blackboards.

"Do they look fuzzy?" Miss Roginski said after a while.

"Oh, no, I just made that up." I never squinted either. But she just seemed so whipped about it. She always did. This had been go-ing on for three grades now.

"I'm just not getting through to you somehow."

"It's not your fault, Miss Roginski." (It wasn't. I just worshipped her too. She was all dumpy and fat but I used to wish she'd been my mother. I could never make that really come out right, unless she had been married to my father first, and then they'd gotten divorced and my father had married my mother, which was okay, because Miss Roginski had to work, so my father got custody of me—that all made sense. Only they never seemed to know each other, my dad and Miss Roginski. Whenever they'd meet, each year during the Christmas pageant when all the parents came, I'd watch the two of them like crazy, hoping for some kind of secret glimmer or look that could only mean, "Well, how are you, how's your life been going since our divorce?" but no soap. She wasn't my mother, she was just my teacher, and I was her own personal and growing disaster area.)

"You're going to be all right, Billy."

"I sure hope so, Miss Roginski."

"You're a late bloomer, that's all. Winston Churchill was a late bloomer and so are you."

I was about to ask her who he played for but there was some-thing in her tone that made me know enough not to.

"And Einstein."

Him I also didn't know. Or what a late bloomer was either. But boy, did I want to be one.

*　　　　*　　　　*

W HEN I WAS twenty-six, my first novel, *The Temple of Gold,* was published by Alfred A. Knopf. (Which is now part of Random House which is now part of R.C.A. which is just part of what's wrong with publishing in America today which is not part of this story.) Anyway, before publication, the publicity people at Knopf were talking to me, trying to figure what they could do to justify their salaries, and they asked who did I want to send advance copies to that might be an opinion maker, and I said I didn't know anybody like that and they said, "Think, everybody knows somebody," and so I got all excited because the idea just came to me and I said, "Okay, send a copy to Miss Roginski," which I figure was logical and terrific because if anybody made my opinions, she did. (She's all through *The Temple of Gold,* by the way, only I called her "Miss Patulski"—even then I was creative.)

"Who?" this publicity lady said.

"This old teacher of mine, you send her a copy and I'll sign it and maybe write a little—" I was really excited until this publicity guy interrupted with, "We were thinking of someone more on the national scene."

Very soft I said, "Miss Roginski, you just send her a copy, please, okay?"

"Yes," he said, "yes, by all means."

You remember how I didn't ask who Churchill played for because of her tone? I must have hit that same tone too just then. Anyway, something must have happened because he right away wrote her name down asking was it *ski* or *sky*.

"With the *i*," I told him, already hiking through the years, trying to get the inscription fantastic for her. You know, clever and modest and brilliant and perfect, like that.

"First name?"

That brought me back fast. I didn't know her first name. "Miss" was all I ever called her. I didn't know her address either. I didn't even know if she was alive or not. I hadn't been back to Chicago in ten years; I was an only child, both folks gone, who needed Chicago?

"Send it to Highland Park Grammar School," I said, and first what I thought I'd write was "For Miss Roginski, a rose from your late bloomer," but then I thought that was too conceited, so I decided "For Miss Roginski, a weed from your late bloomer," would be more humble. Too humble, I decided next, and that was it for bright ideas that day. I couldn't think of anything. Then I thought, What if she doesn't even remember me? Hundreds of students over the years, why should she? So finally in desperation I put, "For Miss Roginski from William Goldman—Billy you called me and you said I would be a late bloomer and this book is for you and I hope you like it. I was in your class for third, fourth and fifth grades, thank you very much. William Goldman."

The book came out and got bombed; I stayed in and did the same, adjusting. Not only did it not establish me as the freshest thing since Kit Marlowe, it also didn't get read by anybody. Not true. It got read by any number of people, all of whom I knew. I think it is safe to say, however, no strangers savored it. It was a grinding experience and I reacted as indicated above. So when Miss Roginski's note came—late—it got sent to Knopf and they took their time relaying it—I was really ready for a lift.

"Dear Mr. Goldman: Thank you for the book. I have not had time yet to read it, but I am sure it is a fine endeavor. I of course remember you. I remember all my students. Yours sincerely, Antonia Roginski."

What a crusher. She didn't remember me at all. I sat there

holding the note, rocked. People don't remember me. Really. It's not any paranoid thing; I just have this habit of slipping through memories. It doesn't bother me all that much, except I guess that's a lie; it does. For some reason, I test very high on forgettability.

So when Miss Roginski sent me that note making her just like everyone else, I was glad she'd never gotten married, I'd never liked her anyway, she'd always been a rotten teacher, and it served her right her first name was Antonia.

"I didn't mean it," I said out loud right then. I was alone in my one-room job on Manhattan's glamorous West Side and talking to myself. "I'm sorry, I'm sorry," I went on. "You got to believe that, Miss Roginski."

What had happened, of course, was that I'd finally seen the postscript. It was on the back of the thank-you note and what it said was, "Idiot. Not even the immortal S. Morgenstern could feel more parental than I."

S. Morgenstern! *The Princess Bride*. She remembered!

Flashback.

1941. Autumn. I'm a little cranky because my radio won't get the football games. Northwestern is playing Notre Dame, it starts at one, and by one-thirty I can't get the game. Music, news, soap operas, everything, but not the biggie. I call for my mother. She comes. I tell her my radio's busted, I can't find Northwestern–Notre Dame. She says, you mean the football? Yes yes yes, I say. It's Friday, she says; I thought they played on Saturday.

Am I an idiot!

I lie back, listening to the soaps, and after a little I try finding it again, and my stupid radio will pick up every Chicago station except the one carrying the football game. I really holler now, and again my mother tears in. I'm gonna heave this radio right out the window, I say; it won't get it, it won't get it, I cannot make it get it.

Get what? she says. *The football game,* I say; how dumb are you, the *gaaaaame.* Saturday, and watch your tongue, young man, she says—I already told you, it's Friday. She goes again.

Was there ever so ample a dunce?

Humiliated, I flick around on my trusty Zenith, trying to find the football game. It was so frustrating I was lying there sweating and my stomach felt crazy and I was pounding the top of the radio to make it work right and that was how they discovered I was delirious with pneumonia.

Pneumonia today is not what it once was, especially when I had it. Ten days or so in the hospital and then home for the long recuperating period. I guess it was three more weeks in bed, a month maybe. No energy, no games even. I just was this lump going through a strength-gathering time, period.

Which is how you have to think of me when I came upon *The Princess Bride.*

It was my first night home. Drained; still one sick cookie. My father came in, I thought to say good night. He sat on the end of my bed. "Chapter One. The Bride," he said.

It was then only I kind of looked up and saw he was holding a book. That alone was surprising. My father was next to illiterate. In English. He came from Florin (the setting of *The Princess Bride*) and there he had been no fool. He said once he would have ended up a lawyer, and maybe so. The facts are when he was sixteen he got a shot at coming to America, gambled on the land of opportunity and lost. There was never much here for him. He was not attractive to look upon, very short and from an early age bald, and he was ponderous at learning. Once he got a fact, it stayed, but the hours it took to pass into his cranium were not to be believed. His English always stayed ridiculously immigranty, and that didn't help him either. He met my mother on the boat over, got married later and, when he thought they could afford it, had me. He worked forever as the number-two chair in the least successful barbershop in Highland Park, Illinois. Toward the end, he used to doze all day in his chair. He went that way. He was gone an hour before the number-one guy realized it; until then he just thought my father was having a good doze. Maybe he was. Maybe that's all any of this is. When they told me I was terribly upset, but I thought at the same time it was an almost Existence-Proving way for him to go.

Anyway, I said, "Huh? What? I didn't hear." I was so weak, so terribly tired.

"Chapter One. The Bride." He held up the book then. "I'm reading it to you for relax." He practically shoved the book in my face. "By S. Morgenstern. Great Florinese writer. *The Princess Bride.* He too came to America. S. Morgenstern. Dead now in New York. The English is his own. He spoke eight tongues." Here my father put down the book and held up all his fingers. "*Eight.* Once, in Florin City, I was in his café." He shook his head now; he was always doing that, my father, shaking his head when he'd said it wrong. "Not *his* café. He was in it, me too, the same time. I saw him. S. Morgenstern. He had head like this, that big," and he shaped his hands like a big balloon. "Great man in Florin City. Not so much in America."

"Has it got any sports in it?"

"Fencing. Fighting. Torture. Poison. True love. Hate. Revenge. Giants. Hunters. Bad men. Good men. Beautifulest ladies. Snakes. Spiders. Beasts of all natures and descriptions. Pain. Death. Brave men. Coward men. Strongest men. Chases. Escapes. Lies. Truths. Passion. Miracles."

"Sounds okay," I said, and I kind of closed my eyes. "I'll do my best to stay awake . . . but I'm awful sleepy, Daddy. . . ."

Who can know when his world is going to change? Who can tell before it happens, that every prior experience, all the years, were a preparation for . . . nothing. Picture this now: an all-but-illiterate old man struggling with an enemy tongue, an all-but-exhausted young boy fighting against sleep. And nothing between them but the words of another alien, painfully translated from native sounds to foreign. Who could suspect that in the morning a different child would wake? I remember, for myself, only trying to beat back fatigue. Even a week later I was not aware of what had begun that night, the doors that were slamming shut while others slid into the clear. Perhaps I should have at least known something, but maybe not; who can sense revelation in the wind?

What happened was just this: I got hooked on the story.

For the first time in my life, I became actively interested in a *book*. Me the sports fanatic, me the game freak, me the only ten-year-old in Illinois with a hate on for the alphabet wanted to know *what happened next.*

What became of beautiful Buttercup and poor Westley and Inigo, the greatest swordsman in the history of the world? And how really strong was Fezzik and were there limits to the cruelty of Vizzini, the devil Sicilian?

Each night my father read to me, chapter by chapter, always fighting to sound the words properly, to nail down the sense. And I lay there, eyes kind of closed, my body slowly beginning the long flow back to strength. It took, as I said, probably a month, and in that time he read *The Princess Bride* twice to me. Even when I was able to read myself, this book remained his. I would never have dreamed of opening it. I wanted his voice, his sounds. Later, years later even, sometimes I might say, "How about the duel on the cliff with Inigo and the man in black?" and my father would gruff and grumble and get the book and lick his thumb, turning pages till the mighty battle began. I loved that. Even today, that's how I summon back my father when the need arises. Slumped and squinting and halting over words, giving me Morgenstern's masterpiece as best he could. *The Princess Bride* belonged to my father.

Everything else was mine.

There wasn't an adventure story anywhere that was safe from me. "Come on," I would say to Miss Roginski when I was well again. "Stevenson, you keep saying Stevenson, I've finished Stevenson, who now?" and she would say, "Well, try Scott, see how you like him," so I tried old Sir Walter and I liked him well enough to butt through a half-dozen books in December (a lot of that was Christmas vacation when I didn't have to interrupt my reading for anything but now and then a little food). "Who else, who else?" "Cooper maybe," she'd say, so off I went into *The Deerslayer* and all the Leatherstocking stuff, and then on my own one day I stumbled onto Dumas and D'Artagnan and that got me through most of February, those guys. "You have become, before my very eyes, a novel-holic," Miss Roginski said. "Do you realize you are spending more time now reading than you used to spend on games? Do you know that your arithmetic grades are actually getting worse?" I never minded when she knocked me. We were alone in the schoolroom, and I was after her for somebody good to devour. She shook her head. "You're certainly blooming, Billy. Before my very eyes. I just don't know into what."

I just stood there and waited for her to tell me to read somebody.

"You're impossible, standing there waiting." She thought a second. "All right. Try Hugo. *The Hunchback of Notre Dame.*"

"Hugo," I said. "*Hunchback.* Thank you," and I turned, ready to begin my sprint to the library. I heard her words sighed behind me as I moved.

"This can't last. It just can't last."

But it did.

And it has. I am as devoted to adventure now as then, and that's never going to stop. That first book of mine I mentioned, *The Temple of Gold*—do you know where the title comes from? From the movie *Gunga Din*, which I've seen sixteen times and I still think is the greatest adventure movie ever ever ever made. (True story about *Gunga Din*: when I got discharged from the Army, I made a vow never to go back on an Army post. No big deal, just a simple life-long vow. Okay, now I'm home the day after I get out and I've got a buddy at Fort Sheridan nearby and I call to check in and he says, "Hey, guess what's on post tonight? *Gunga Din*." "We'll go," I said. "It's tricky," he said; "you're a civilian." Upshot: I got back into uniform the first night I was out and snuck onto an Army post to see that movie. *Snuck* back. A thief in the night. Heart pounding, the sweats, everything.) I'm addicted to action/adventure/call-it-what-you-will, in any way, shape, etc. I never missed an Alan Ladd picture, an Errol Flynn picture. I still don't miss John Wayne pictures.

My whole life really began with my father reading me the Morgenstern when I was ten. Fact: *Butch Cassidy and the Sundance Kid* is, no question, the most popular thing I've ever been connected with. When I die, if the *Times* gives me an obit, it's going to be because of *Butch*. Okay, now what's *the* scene everybody talks about, the single moment that stays fresh for you and me and the masses? Answer: the jump off the cliff. Well, when I wrote that, I remember thinking that those cliffs they were jumping off, those were the Cliffs of Insanity that everybody tries to climb in *The Princess Bride*. In my mind, when I wrote *Butch*, I was thinking back further into my mind, remembering my father reading the rope climb up the Cliffs of Insanity and the death that was lurking right behind.

That book was the single best thing that happened to me (sorry about that, Helen; Helen is my wife, the hot-shot child psychiatrist), and long before I was even married, I knew I was going to share it with my son. I knew I was going to have a son too. So when Jason was born (if he'd been a girl, he would have been Pamby; can you believe that, a woman child psychiatrist who would give her kids such names?)—anyway, when Jason was born, I made a mental note to buy him a copy of *The Princess Bride* for his tenth birthday.

After which I promptly forgot all about it.

Flash forward: the Beverly Hills Hotel last December. I am going mad having meetings on Ira Levin's *The Stepford Wives*, which I am adapting for the Silver Screen. I call my wife in New York at dinnertime, which I always do—it makes her feel wanted—and we're talking and at the close she says, "Oh. We're giving Jason a ten-speed bike. I bought it today. I thought that was fitting, don't you?"

"Why fitting?"

"Oh come on, Willy, ten years, ten speeds."

"Is he ten tomorrow? It went clean outta my head."

"Call us at suppertime tomorrow and you can wish him a happy."

"Helen?" I said then. "Listen, do me something. Buzz the Nine-nine-nine bookshop and have them send over *The Princess Bride*."

"Lemme get a pencil," and she's gone a while. "Okay. Shoot. The what bride?"

"Princess. By S. Morgenstern. It's a kids' classic. Tell him I'll quiz him on it when I'm back next week and that he doesn't have to like it or anything, but if he doesn't, tell him I'll kill myself. Give him that message exactly please; I wouldn't want to apply any extra pressure or anything."

"Kiss me, my fool."

"Mmmm-wah."

"No starlets now." This was always her sign-off line when I was alone and on the loose in sunny California.

"They're extinct, dummy." That was mine. We hung up.

Now the next afternoon, it so happened, from somewhere, there actually appeared a living, sun-tanned, breathing-deeply starlet. I'm lolling by the pool and she moves by in a bikini and she is gorgeous. I'm free for the afternoon, I don't know a soul, so I start playing a game about how can I approach this girl so she won't laugh out loud. I never do anything, but ogling is great exercise and I am a major-league girl watcher. I can't come up with any approach that connects with reality, so I start to swim my laps. I swim a quarter-mile a day because I have a bad disc at the base of my spine.

Up and back, up and back, eighteen laps, and when I'm done, I'm hanging on in the deep end, panting away, and over swims this starlet. She hangs on the ledge in the deep end too, maybe all of six inches away, hair all wet and glistening and the body's under water but you know it's there and she says (this happened now), "Pardon me, but aren't you the William Goldman who wrote *Boys and Girls Together*? That's, like, my favorite book in all the world."

I clutch the ledge and nod; I don't remember what I said exactly. (Lie: I remember *exactly* what I said, except it's too goonlike to put it down; ye gods, I'm forty years old. "Goldman, yes Goldman, I'm Goldman." It came out like all in one word, so there's no telling what language she thought I was responding in.)

"I'm Sandy Sterling," she said. "Hi."

"Hi, Sandy Sterling," I got out, which was pretty suave, suave for me anyway; I'd say it again if the same situation came up.

Then my name was paged. "The Zanucks won't leave me alone," I say, and she breaks out laughing and I hurry to the phone thinking was it really all that clever, and by the time I get there I decide yes it was, and into the receiver I say that, "Clever." Not "hello." Not "Bill Goldman." "Clever" is what I say.

"Did you say 'clever,' Willy?" It's Helen.

"I'm in a story conference, Helen, and we're speaking tonight at suppertime. Why are you calling at lunch for?"

"Hostile, hostile."

Never argue with your wife about hostility when she's a certified Freudian. "It's just they're driving me crazy with stupid notions in this story conference. What's up?"

"Nothing, probably, except the Morgenstern's out of print. I've checked with Doubleday's too. You sounded kind of like it might be important so I'm just letting you know Jason will have to be satisfied with his very fitting ten-speed machine."

"Not important," I said. Sandy Sterling was smiling. From the deep end. Straight at me. "Thanks though anyway." I was about to hang up, then I said, "Well, as long as you've gone this far, call Argosy on Fifty-ninth Street. They specialize in out-of-print stuff."

"Argosy. Fifty-ninth. Got it. Talk to you at supper." She hung up.

Without saying "No starlets now." Every call she ends with that and now she doesn't. Could I have given it away by something in my tone? Helen's very spooky about that, being a shrink and all. Guilt, like pudding, began bubbling on the back burner.

I went back to my lounge chair. Alone.

Sandy Sterling swam a few laps. I picked up my *New York Times*. A certain amount of sexual tension in the vicinity. "Done swimming?" she asks. I put my paper down. She was by the edge of the pool now, nearest my chair.

I nod, staring at her.

"Which Zanuck, Dick or Darryl?"

"It was my wife," I said. Emphasis on the last word.

Didn't faze her. She got out and lay down in the next chair. Top heavy but golden. If you like them that way, you had to like Sandy Sterling. I like them that way.

"You're out here on the Levin, aren't you? *Stepford Wives?*"

"I'm doing the screenplay."

"I really loved that book. That's, like, my favorite book in all the world. I'd really love to be in a picture like that. Written by you. I'd do anything for a shot at that."

So there it was. She was putting it right out there, on the line.

Naturally I set her straight fast. "Listen," I said, "I don't do things like that. If I did, I would, because you're gorgeous, that goes without saying, and I wish you joy, but life's too complicated without that kind of thing going on."

That's what I *thought* I was going to say. But then I figured, Hey wait a minute, what law is there that says you have to be the token puritan of the movie business? I've worked with people who keep card files on this kind of thing. (True; ask Joyce Haber.) "Have you acted a lot in features?" I heard myself asking. Now you know I was really passionate to know the answer to that one.

"Nothing that really enlarged my boundaries, y' know what I mean?"

"Mr. Goldman?"

I looked up. It was the assistant lifeguard.

"For you again." He handed me the phone.

"Willy?" Just the sound of my wife's voice sent sheer blind misgivings through each and every bit of me.

"Yes, Helen?"

"You sound funny."

"What is it, Helen?"

"Nothing, but—"

"It can't be nothing or you wouldn't have called me."

"What's the matter, Willy?"

"*Nothing* is the matter. I was trying to be logical. You did, after all, place the call. I was merely trying to ascertain why." I can be pretty distant when I put my mind to it.

"You're hiding something."

Nothing drives me crazier than when Helen does that. Because, see, with this horrible psychiatrist background of hers, she only accuses me of hiding things from her when I'm hiding things from her. *"Helen, I'm in the middle of a story conference now; just get on with it."*

So there it was again. I was lying to my wife about another woman, and the other woman knew it.

Sandy Sterling, in the next chair, smiled dead into my eyes.

"Argosy doesn't have the book, nobody has the book, good-by, Willy." She hung up.

"Wife again?"

I nodded, put the phone on the table by my lounge chair.

"You sure talk to each other a lot."

"I know," I told her. "It's murder trying to get any writing done."

I guess she smiled.

There was no way I could stop my heart from pounding.

"Chapter One. The Bride," my father said.

I must have jerked around or something because she said, "Huh?"

"My fa—" I began. "I thou—" I began. "Nothing," I said finally.

"Easy," she said, and she gave me a really sweet smile. She dropped her hand over mine for just a second, very gentle and reassuring. I wondered was it possible she was understanding too. Gorgeous *and* understanding? Was that legal? Helen wasn't ever understanding. She was always saying she was—"I understand why you're saying that, Willy"—but secretly she was ferreting out my neuroses. No, I guess she was understanding; what she wasn't was sympathetic. And, of course, she wasn't gorgeous too. Skinny, yes. Brilliant, yes.

"I met my wife in graduate school," I said to Sandy Sterling. "She was getting her Ph.D."

Sandy Sterling was having a little trouble with my train of thought.

"We were just kids. How old are you?"

"You want my real age or my baseball age?"

I really laughed then. Gorgeous *and* understanding *and* funny?

"Fencing. Fighting. Torture," my father said. "Love. Hate. Revenge. Giants. Beasts of all natures and descriptions. Truths. Passion. Miracles."

It was 12:35 and I said, "One phone call, okay?"

"Okay."

"New York City information," I said into the receiver, and when I was through I said, "Could you give me the names of some Fourth Avenue bookshops, please. There must be twenty of them." Fourth Avenue is the used and out-of-print book center of the English-speaking chapter of the civilized world. While the operator looked, I turned to the creature on the next lounge and said, "My kid's ten today, I'd kind of like for him to have this book from me, a present, won't take a sec."

"Swing," Sandy Sterling said.

"I list one bookstore called the Fourth Avenue Bookshop," the operator said, and she gave me the number.

"Can't you give me any of the others? They're all down there in a clump."

"If yew we-ill give mee they-re names, I can help you," the operator said, speaking Bell talk.

"This one'll do," I said, and I got the hotel operator to ring through for me. "Listen, I'm calling from Los Angeles," I said, "and I need *The Princess Bride* by S. Morgenstern."

"Nope. Sorry," the guy said, and before I could say, "Well, could you give me the names of the other stores down there," he hung up. "Get me that number back, please," I said to the hotel operator, and when the guy was on the line again, I said, "This is your Los Angeles correspondent; don't hang up so fast this time."

"I ain't got it, mister."

"I understand that. What I'd like is, since I'm in California, could you give me the names and numbers of some of the other stores down there. They might have it and there aren't exactly an abundance of New York Yellow Pages drifting around out here."

"They don't help me, I don't help them." He hung up again.

I sat there with the receiver in my hand.

"What's this special book?" Sandy Sterling asked.

"Not important," I said, and hung up. Then I said, "Yes it is" and picked up the receiver again, eventually got my publishing house in New York, Harcourt Brace Jovanovich, and, after a few more *eventually*s, my editor's secretary read me off the names and numbers of every bookstore in the Fourth Avenue area.

"Hunters," my father was saying now. "Bad men. Good men. Beautifulest ladies." He was camped in my cranium, hunched over, bald and squinting, trying to read, trying to please, trying to keep his son alive and the wolves away.

It was 1:10 before I had the list completed and rang off from the secretary.

Then I started with the bookstores. "Listen, I'm calling from Los Angeles on the Morgenstern book, *The Princess Bride,* and . . ."

". . . sorry . . ."

". . . sorry . . ."

Busy signal.

". . . not for years . . ."

Another busy.

1:35.

Sandy swimming. Getting a little angry too. She must have thought I was putting her on. I wasn't, but it sure looked that way.

". . . sorry, had a copy in December . . ."

". . . no soap, sorry . . ."

"This is a recorded announcement. The number you have dialed is not in working order. Please hang up and . . ."

". . . nope . . ."

Sandy really upset now. Glaring, gathering debris.

". . . who reads Morgenstern today? . . ."

Sandy going, going, gorgeous, gone.

Bye, Sandy. Sorry, Sandy.

". . . sorry, we're closing . . ."

1:55 now. 4:55 in New York.

Panic in Los Angeles.

Busy.

No answer.

No answer.

"Florinese I got I think. Somewhere in the back."

I sat up in my lounge chair. His accent was thick. "I need the English translation."

"You don't get much call for Morgenstern nowadays. I don't know any more what I got back there. You come in tomorrow, you look around."

"I'm in California," I said.

"Mashuganuh," he said.

"It would mean just a great deal to me if you'd look."

"You gonna hold on while I do it? I'm not gonna pay for this call."

"Take your time," I said.

He took seventeen minutes. I just hung on, listening. Every so often I'd hear a footstep or a crash of books or a grunt—"uch—uch."

Finally: "Well, I got the Florinese like I thought."

So close. "But not the English," I said.

And suddenly he's yelling at me: "What, are you crazy? I break my back and he says I haven't got it, yes I got it, I got it right here, and, believe me, it's gonna cost a pretty penny."

"Great—really, no kidding, now listen, here's what you do, get yourself a cab and tell him to take the books straight up to Park and—"

"Mister California Mashuganuh, *you* listen now—it's coming up a blizzard and I'm going no place and neither are these books without money—six fifty, on the barrel each, you want the English, you got to take the Florinese, and I close at 6:00. These books don't leave my premises without thirteen dollars changing hands."

"Don't move," I said, hanging up, and who do you call when it's after hours and Christmas on the horizon? Only your lawyer. "Charley," I said when I got him. "Please do me this. Go to Fourth Avenue, Abromowitz's, give him thirteen dollars for two books, taxi up to my house and tell the doorman to take them to my apartment, and yes, I know it's snowing, what do you say?"

"That is such a bizarre request I have to agree to do it."

I called Abromowitz yet again. "My lawyer is hot on the trail."

"No checks," Abromowitz said.

"You're all heart." I hung up, and started figuring. More or less 120 minutes long distance at $1.35 per first three minutes plus thirteen for the books plus probably ten for Charley's taxi plus probably sixty for his time came to . . . ? Two hundred fifty maybe. All for my Jason to have the Morgenstern. I leaned back and closed my eyes. Two hundred fifty not to mention two solid hours of torment and anguish and let's not forget Sandy Sterling.

A steal.

They called me at half past seven. I was in my suite. "He loves the bike," Helen said. "He's practically out of control."

"Fabbo," I said.

"And your books came."

"What books?" I said; Chevalier was never more casual.

"*The Princess Bride.* In various languages, one of them, fortunately, English."

"Well, that's nice," I said, still loose. "I practically forgot I asked to have 'em sent."

"How'd they get here?"

"I called my editor's secretary and had her scrounge up a couple copies. Maybe they had them at Harcourt, who knows?" (They *did* have copies at Harcourt; can you buy that? I'll get to why in the next pages, probably.) "Gimme the kid."

"Hi," he said a second later.

"Listen, Jason," I told him. "We thought about giving you a bike for your birthday but we decided against it."

"Boy, are you wrong, I got one already."

Jason has inherited his mother's total lack of humor. I don't know; maybe he's funny and I'm not. We just don't laugh much together is all I can say for sure. My son Jason is this incredible-looking kid—paint him yellow, he'd mop up for the school sumo team. A blimp. All the time stuffing his face. I watch my weight and old Helen is only visible full front plus on top of which she is this leading child shrink in Manhattan and our kid can roll faster than he can walk. "He's expressing himself through food," Helen always says. "His anxieties. When he feels ready to cope, he'll slim down."

"Hey, Jason? Mom tells me this book arrived today. The Princess thing? I'd sure like it if maybe you'd give it a read while I'm gone. I loved it when I was a kid and I'm kind of interested in your reaction."

"Do I have to love it too?" He was his mother's son all right.

"Jason, no. Just the truth, exactly what you think. I miss you, big shot. And I'll talk to you on your birthday."

"Boy, are you wrong. Today *is* my birthday."

We bantered a bit more, long past when there was much to say. Then I did the same with my spouse, and hung up, promising a return by the end of one week.

It took two.

Conferences dragged, producers got inspirations that had to carefully get shot down, directors needed their egos soothed. Anyway, I was longer than anticipated in sunny Cal. Finally, though, I was allowed to return to the care and safety of the family, so I quick buzzed to L.A. airport before anybody's mind changed. I got there early, which I always do when I come back, because I had to load up my pockets with doodads and such for Jason. Every time I get home from a trip he runs (waddles) to me hollering, "Lemmesee, lemmesee the pockets," and then he goes through all my pockets taking out his graft, and once the loot is totaled, he gives me a nice hug. Isn't it awful what we'll do in this world to feel wanted?

"Lemmesee the pockets," Jason shouted, moving to me across the foyer. It was a suppertime Thursday and, while he went through his ritual, Helen emerged from the library and kissed my cheek, going "what a dashing-looking fellow I have," which is also ritual, and, laden with gifts, Jason kind of hugged me and belted off (waddled off) to his room. "Angelica's just getting dinner on," Helen said; "you couldn't have timed it better."

"Angelica?"

Helen put her finger to her lips and whispered, "It's her third day on but I think she may be a treasure."

I whispered back, "What was wrong with the treasure we had when I left? She'd only been with us a week then."

"She proved a disappointment," Helen said. That was all. (Helen is this brilliant lady—junior Phi Bete in college, every academic honor conceivable, really an intellect of startling breadth and accomplishment—only she can't keep a maid. First, I guess she feels guilty having anybody, since most of the anybodys available nowadays are black or Spanish and Helen is ultra-super liberal. Second, she's so efficient, she scares them. She can do everything better than they can and she knows it and she knows they know it. Third, once she's got them panicked, she tries to explain, being an analyst, why they shouldn't be frightened, and after a good solid half-hour ego search with Helen, they're *really* frightened. Anyway, we have had an average of four "treasures" a year for the last few years.)

"We've been running in bad luck but it'll change," I said, just as reassuringly as I knew how. I used to heckle her about the help problem, but I learned that was not necessarily wise.

Dinner was ready a little later, and with an arm around my wife and an arm around my son, I advanced toward the dining room. I felt, at that moment, safe, secure, all the nice things. Supper was on the table: creamed spinach, mashed potatoes, gravy and pot roast; terrific, except I don't like pot roast, since I'm a rare-meat man, but creamed spinach I have a lech for, so, all in all, a more than edible spread was set across the tablecloth. We sat. Helen served the meat: the rest we passed. My pot-roast slice was not terribly moist but the gravy could compensate. Helen rang. Angelica appeared. Maybe twenty or eighteen, swarthy, slow-moving. "Angelica," Helen began, "this is Mr. Goldman."

I smiled and said "Hi" and waved a fork. She nodded back.

"Angelica, this is not meant to be construed as criticism, since what happened is *all my fault*, but in the future we must both try *very hard* to remember that Mr. Goldman likes his roast beef rare—"

"This was roast beef?" I said.

Helen shot me a look. "Now, Angelica, there is no problem, and *I* should have told you more than once about Mr. Goldman's preferences, but next time we have boned rib roast, let's all do our best to make the middle pink, shall we?"

Angelica backed into the kitchen. Another "treasure" down the tubes.

Remember now, we all three started this meal happy. Two of us are left in that state, Helen clearly being distraught.

Jason was piling the mashed potatoes on his plate with a practiced and steady motion.

I smiled at my kid. "Hey," I tried, "let's go a little easy, huh, fella?"

He splatted another fat spoonful onto his plate.

"Jason, they're just loaded," I said then.

"I'm really hungry, Dad," he said, not looking at me.

"Fill up on the meat then, why don't you," I said. "Eat all the meat you want, I won't say a word."

"I'm not eatin' nothin'!" Jason said, and he shoved his plate away and folded his arms and stared off into space.

"If I were a furniture salesperson," Helen said to me, "or perhaps a teller in a bank, I could understand; but how can you have spent all these years married to a psychiatrist and talk like that? You're out of the Dark Ages, Willy."

"Helen, the boy is overweight. All I suggested was he might leave a few potatoes for the rest of the world and stuff on this lovely prime pot roast your treasure has whipped up for my triumphant return."

"Willy, I don't want to shock you, but Jason happens to have not only a very fine mind but also exceptionally keen eyesight. When he looks at himself in the mirror, I assure you he knows he is not slender. That is because he does not *choose*, at this stage, to be slender."

"He's not that far from dating, Helen; what then?"

"Jason is ten, darling, and not interested, at this stage, in girls. At this stage, he is interested in rocketry. What difference does a slight case of overweight make to a rocket lover? When he *chooses* to be slender, I assure you, he has both the intelligence and the will power to become slender. Until that time, please, in my presence, do not frustrate the child."

Sandy Sterling in her bikini was dancing behind my eyes.

"I'm not eatin' and that's it," Jason said then.

"Sweet child," Helen said to the kid, in that tone she reserves on this Earth only for such moments, "be logical. If *you* do not eat your potatoes, *you* will be upset, and *I* will be upset; your father, clearly, is already upset. If you *do* eat your potatoes, *I* shall be pleased, *you* will be pleased, your tummy will be pleased. We can do nothing about your father. You have it in your power to upset all or one, about whom, as I have already said, we can do nothing. Therefore, the conclusion should be clear, but I have faith in your ability to reach it yourself. Do what you will, Jason."

He began to stuff it in.

"You're making a poof out of that kid," I said, only not loud enough for anybody but me and Sandy to hear. Then I took a deep, deep breath, because whenever I come home there's always trouble, which is because, Helen says, I bring tension with me, I always need inhuman proof that I've been missed, that I'm still needed, loved, etc. All I know is, I hate being away but coming home is the worst. There's never really much chance to go into "well, what's new since I'm gone" chitchat, seeing that Helen and I talk every night anyway.

"I'll bet you're a whiz on that bike," I said then. "Maybe we'll go for a ride this weekend."

Jason looked up from his potatoes. "I really loved the book, Dad. It was great."

I was surprised that he said it, because, naturally, I was just starting to work my way into that subject matter. But then, as Helen's always saying, Jason ain't no dummy. "Well, I'm glad," I said. And was I ever.

Jason nodded. "Maybe it's even the best I read in all my life."

I nibbled away at my spinach. "What was your favorite part?"

"Chapter One. The Bride," Jason said.

That really surprised me. Not that Chapter One stinks or anything, but there's not that much that goes on compared with the incredible stuff later. Buttercup grows up mostly is all. "How about the climb up the Cliffs of Insanity?" I said then. That's in Chapter Five.

"Oh, great," Jason said.

"And that description of Prince Humperdinck's Zoo of Death?" That's in the second chapter.

"Even greater," Jason said.

"What knocked me out about it," I said, "was that it's this very short little passage on the Zoo of Death but yet somehow you just know it's going to figure in later. Did you get that same feeling?"

"Umm-humm." Jason nodded. "Great."

By then I knew he hadn't read it.

"He tried to read it," Helen cut in. "He did read the first chapter. Chapter Two was impossible for him, so when he'd made a sufficient and reasonable attempt, I told him to stop. Different people have different tastes. I told him you'd understand, Willy."

Of course I understood. I felt just so deserted though.

"I didn't like it, Dad. I wanted to."

I smiled at him. How could he not like it? Passion. Duels. Miracles. Giants. True love.

"You're not eating the spinach either?" Helen said.

I got up. "Time change; I'm not hungry." She didn't say anything until she heard me open the front door. "Where are you going?" she called then. If I'd known, I would have answered.

I wandered through December. No topcoat. I wasn't aware of being cold though. All I knew was I was forty years old and I didn't mean to be here when I was forty, locked with this genius shrink wife and this balloon son. It must have been 9:00 when I was sitting in the middle of Central Park, alone, no one near me, no other bench occupied.

That was when I heard the rustling in the bushes. It stopped. Then again. Verrry soft. Nearer.

I whirled, screaming *"Don't you bug me!"* and whatever it was— friend, foe, imagination—fled. I could hear the running and I realized something: right then, at that moment, I was dangerous.

Then it got cold. I went home. Helen was going over some notes in bed. Ordinarily, she would come out with something about me being a bit elderly for acts of juvenile behavior. But there must have been danger clinging to me still. I could see it in her smart eyes. "He did try," she said finally.

"I never thought he didn't," I answered. "Where's the book?"

"The library, I think."

I turned, started out.

"Can I get you anything?"

I said no. Then I went to the library, closed myself in, hunted out *The Princess Bride*. It was in pretty good shape, I realized as I checked the binding, which is when I saw it was published by my publishing house, Harcourt Brace Jovanovich. This was before that; they weren't even Harcourt, Brace & World yet. Just plain old Harcourt, Brace period. I flicked to the title page, which was funny, since I'd never done that before; it was always my father who'd done the handling. I had to laugh when I saw the real title, because right there it said:

THE PRINCESS BRIDE
*S. Morgenstern's
Classic Tale of True Love
and High Adventure*

You had to admire a guy who called his own new book a classic before it was published and anyone else had a chance to read it. Maybe he figured if he didn't do it, nobody would, or maybe he was just trying to give the reviewers a helping hand; I don't know. I skimmed the first chapter, and it was pretty much exactly as I remembered. Then I turned to the second chapter, the one about Prince Humperdinck and the little kind of tantalizing description of the Zoo of Death.

And that's when I began to realize the problem.

Not that the description wasn't there. It was, and again pretty much as I remembered it. But before you got to it, there were maybe sixty pages of text dealing with Prince Humperdinck's ancestry and how his family got control of Florin and this wedding and that child begatting this one over here who then married somebody else, and then I skipped to the third chapter, The Courtship, and that was all about the history of Guilder and how that country reached its place in the world. The more I flipped on, the more I knew: Morgenstern wasn't writing any children's book; he was writing a kind of satiric history of his country and the decline of the monarchy in Western civilization.

But my father only read me the action stuff, the good parts. He never bothered with the serious side at all.

About two in the morning I called Hiram in Martha's Vineyard. Hiram Haydn's been my editor for a dozen years, ever since *Soldier in the Rain*, and we've been through a lot together, but never any phone calls at two in the morning. To this day I know he doesn't understand why I couldn't wait till maybe breakfast. "You're sure you're all right, Bill," he kept saying.

"Hey, Hiram," I began after about six rings. "Listen, you guys published a book just after World War I. Do you think it might be a good idea for me to abridge it and we'd republish it now?"

"You're sure you're all right, Bill?"

"Fine, absolutely, and see, I'd just use the good parts. I'd kind of bridge where there were skips in the narrative and leave the good parts alone. What do you think?"

"Bill, it's two in the morning up here. Are you still in California?"

I acted like I was all shocked and surprised. So he wouldn't think I was a nut. "I'm sorry, Hiram. My God, what an idiot; it's only 11:00 in Beverly Hills. Do you think you could ask Mr. Jovanovich, though?"

"You mean *now*?"

"Tomorrow or the next day, no big deal."

"I'll ask him anything, only I'm not quite sure I'm getting an accurate reading on exactly what you want. You're sure you're all right, Bill?"

"I'll be in New York tomorrow. Call you then about the specifics, okay?"

"Could you make it a little earlier in the business day, Bill?"

I laughed and we hung up and I called Zig in California. Evarts Ziegler has been my movie agent for maybe eight years. He did the *Butch Cassidy* deal for me, and I woke him up too. "Hey, Zig, could you get me a postponement on the *Stepford Wives*? There's this other thing that's come up."

"You're contracted to start now; how long a postponement?"

"I can't say for sure; I've never done an abridgement before. Just tell me what you think they'd do?"

"I think if it's a long postponement they'd threaten to sue and you'd end up losing the job."

It came out pretty much as he said; they threatened to sue and I almost lost the job and some money and didn't make any friends in "the industry," as those of us in show biz call movies.

But the abridgement got done, and you hold it in your hands. The "good parts" version.

*   *   *

W HY DID I go through all that?

Helen pressured me greatly to think about an answer. She felt it was important, not that *she* know necessarily, but that *I* know. "Because you acted crackers, Willy boy," she said. "You had me truly scared."

So why?

I never was worth beans at self-scrutiny. Everything I write is impulse. This feels right, that sounds wrong—like that. I can't analyze—not my own actions anyway.

I know I don't expect this to change anybody else's life the way it altered mine.

But take the title words—"true love and high adventure"—I *believed* in that once. I thought my life was going to follow that path. Prayed that it would. Obviously it didn't, but I don't think there's high adventure left any more. Nobody takes out a sword nowadays and cries, "Hello. My name is Inigo Montoya. You killed my father; prepare to die!"

And true love you can forget about too. I don't know if I love anything truly any more beyond the porterhouse at Peter Luger's and the cheese enchilada at El Parador's. (Sorry about that, Helen.)

Anyway, here's the "good parts" version. S. Morgenstern wrote it. And my father read it to me. And now I give it to you. What you do with it will be of more than passing interest to us all.

New York City
December, 1972

ONE

THE BRIDE

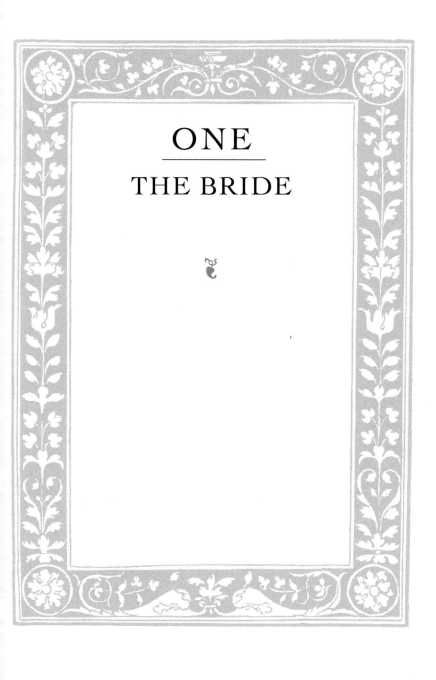

HE year that Buttercup was born, the most beautiful woman in the world was a French scullery maid named Annette. Annette worked in Paris for the Duke and Duchess de Guiche, and it did not escape the Duke's notice that someone extraordinary was polishing the pewter. The Duke's notice did not escape the notice of the Duchess either, who was not very beautiful and not very rich, but plenty smart. The Duchess set about studying Annette and shortly found her adversary's tragic flaw.

Chocolate.

Armed now, the Duchess set to work. The Palace de Guiche turned into a candy castle. Everywhere you looked, bonbons. There were piles of chocolate-covered mints in the drawing rooms, baskets of chocolate-covered nougats in the parlors.

Annette never had a chance. Inside a season, she went from delicate to whopping, and the Duke never glanced in her direction without sad bewilderment clouding his eyes. (Annette, it might be noted, seemed only cheerier throughout her enlargement. She eventually married the pastry chef and they both ate a lot until old age claimed them. Things, it might also be noted, did not fare so cheerily for the Duchess. The Duke, for reasons passing understanding, next became smitten with his very own mother-in-law, which caused the Duchess ulcers, only they didn't have ulcers yet. More precisely, ulcers existed, people had them, but they weren't called "ulcers." The medical profession at that time called them "stomach pains" and felt the best cure was coffee dolloped with brandy twice a day until the pains subsided. The Duchess took her mixture faithfully, watching through the years as her husband and her mother blew kisses at each other behind her back. Not surprisingly, the Duchess's grumpiness became legendary, as Voltaire has so ably chronicled. Except this was before Voltaire.)

The year Buttercup turned ten, the most beautiful woman lived in Bengal, the daughter of a successful tea merchant. This girl's name was Aluthra, and her skin was of a dusky perfection unseen in India for eighty years. (There have only been eleven perfect complexions in all of India since accurate accounting began.) Aluthra was nineteen the year the pox plague hit Bengal. The girl survived, even if her skin did not.

When Buttercup was fifteen, Adela Terrell, of Sussex on the Thames, was easily the most beautiful creature. Adela was twenty, and so far did she outdistance the world that it seemed certain she would be the most beautiful for many, many years. But then one day, one of her suitors (she had 104 of them) exclaimed that without question Adela must be the most ideal item yet spawned. Adela, flattered, began to ponder on the truth of the statement. That night, alone in her room, she examined herself pore by pore in her mirror. (This was after mirrors.) It took her until close to dawn to finish her inspection, but by that time it was clear to her that the young man had been quite correct in his assessment: she was, through no real faults of her own, perfect.

As she strolled through the family rose gardens watching the sun rise, she felt happier than she had ever been. "Not only am I perfect," she said to herself, "I am probably the first perfect person in the whole long history of the universe. Not a part of me could stand improving, how lucky I am to be perfect and rich and sought after and sensitive and young and . . ."

Young?

The mist was rising around her as Adela began to think. Well of course I'll *always* be sensitive, she thought, and I'll always be rich, but I don't quite see how I'm going to manage to always be young. And when I'm not young, how am I going to stay perfect? And if I'm not perfect, well, what else is there? What indeed? Adela furrowed her brow in desperate thought. It was the first time in her life her brow had ever had to furrow, and Adela gasped when she realized what she had done, horrified that she had somehow damaged it, perhaps permanently. She rushed back to her mirror and spent the morning, and although she managed to convince herself that she was still quite as perfect as ever, there was no question that she was not quite as happy as she had been.

She had begun to fret.

The first worry lines appeared within a fortnight; the first wrinkles within a month, and before the year was out, creases abounded. She married soon thereafter, the selfsame man who accused her of sublimity, and gave him merry hell for many years.

Buttercup, of course, at fifteen, knew none of this. And if she had, would have found it totally unfathomable. How could someone care if she were the most beautiful woman in the world or not. What difference could it have made if you were only the third most beautiful. Or the sixth. (Buttercup at this time was nowhere near that high, being barely in the top twenty, and that primarily on potential, certainly not on any particular care she took of herself. She hated to wash her face, she loathed the area behind her ears, she was sick of combing her hair and did so as little as possible.) What she liked to do, preferred above all else really, was to ride her horse and taunt the farm boy.

The horse's name was "Horse" (Buttercup was never long on imagination) and it came when she called it, went where she steered it, did what she told it. The farm boy did what she told him too. Actually, he was more a young man now, but he had been a farm boy when, orphaned, he had come to work for her father, and Buttercup referred to him that way still. "Farm Boy, fetch me this"; "Get me that, Farm Boy—quickly, lazy thing, trot now or I'll tell Father."

"As you wish."

That was all he ever answered. "As you wish." Fetch that, Farm Boy. "As you wish." Dry this, Farm Boy. "As you wish." He lived in a hovel out near the animals and, according to Buttercup's mother, he kept it clean. He even read when he had candles.

"I'll leave the lad an acre in my will," Buttercup's father was fond of saying. (They had acres then.)

"You'll spoil him," Buttercup's mother always answered.

"He's slaved for many years; hard work should be rewarded." Then, rather than continue the argument (they had arguments then too), they would both turn on their daughter.

"You didn't bathe," her father said.

"I did, I did" from Buttercup.

"Not with water," her father continued. "You reek like a stallion."

"I've been riding all day," Buttercup explained.

"You must bathe, Buttercup," her mother joined in. "The boys don't like their girls to smell of stables."

"Oh, the boys!" Buttercup fairly exploded. "I do not care about 'the boys.' Horse loves me and that is quite sufficient, thank you."

She said that speech loud, and she said it often.

But, like it or not, things were beginning to happen.

Shortly before her sixteenth birthday, Buttercup realized that it had now been more than a month since any girl in the village had spoken to her. She had never much been close to girls, so the change was nothing sharp, but at least before there were head nods exchanged when she rode through the village or along the cart tracks. But now, for no reason, there was nothing. A quick glance away as she approached, that was all. Buttercup cornered Cornelia one morning at the blacksmith's and asked about the silence. "I should think, after what you've done, you'd have the courtesy not to pretend to ask" came from Cornelia. "And what have I done?" "What? *What?* . . . You've stolen them." With that, Cornelia fled, but Buttercup understood; she knew who "them" was.

The boys.

The village boys.

The beef-witted featherbrained rattleskulled clodpated dim-domed noodle-noggined sapheaded lunk-knobbed *boys*.

How could anybody accuse her of stealing them? Why would anybody *want* them anyway? What good were they? All they did was pester and vex and annoy. "Can I brush your horse, Butter-cup?" "Thank you, but the farm boy does that." "Can I go riding with you, Buttercup?" "Thank you, but I really do enjoy myself alone." "You think you're too good for anybody, don't you, Butter-cup?" "No; no I don't. I just like riding by myself, that's all."

But throughout her sixteenth year, even this kind of talk gave way to stammering and flushing and, at the very best, questions about the weather. "Do you think it's going to rain, Buttercup?" "I don't think so; the sky is blue." "Well, it might rain." "Yes, I sup-pose it might." "You think you're too good for anybody, don't you, Buttercup?" "No, I just don't think it's going to rain, that's all."

At night, more often than not, they would congregate in the dark beyond her window and laugh about her. She ignored them. Usually the laughter would give way to insult. She paid them no mind. If they grew too damaging, the farm boy handled things, emerging silently from his hovel, thrashing a few of them, sending them flying. She never failed to thank him when he did this. "As you wish" was all he ever answered.

When she was almost seventeen, a man in a carriage came to town and watched as she rode for provisions. He was still there on her return, peering out. She paid him no mind and, indeed, by himself he was not important. But he marked a turning point. Other men had gone out of their way to catch sight of her; other men had even ridden twenty miles for the privilege, as this man had. The importance here is that this was the first rich man who had bothered to do so, the first noble. And it was this man, whose name is lost to antiquity, who mentioned Buttercup to the Count.

*   *   *

THE LAND OF Florin was set between where Sweden and Germany would eventually settle. (This was before Europe.) In theory, it was ruled by King Lotharon and his second wife, the Queen. But in fact, the King was barely hanging on, could only rarely tell day from night, and basically spent his time in muttering. He was very old, every organ in his body had long since betrayed him, and most of his important decisions regarding Florin had a certain arbitrary quality that bothered many of the leading citizens.

Prince Humperdinck actually ran things. If there had been a Europe, he would have been the most powerful man in it. Even as it was, nobody within a thousand miles wanted to mess with him.

The Count was Prince Humperdinck's only confidant. His last name was Rugen, but no one needed to use it—he was the only Count in the country, the title having been bestowed by the Prince as a birthday present some years before, the happening taking place, naturally, at one of the Countess's parties.

The Countess was considerably younger than her husband. All of her clothes came from Paris (this was after Paris) and she had superb taste. (This was after taste too, but only just. And since it was such a new thing, and since the Countess was the only lady in all Florin to possess it, is it any wonder she was the leading hostess of the land?) Eventually, her passion for fabric and face paint caused her to settle permanently in Paris, where she ran the only salon of international consequence.

For now, she busied herself with simply sleeping on silk, eating on gold and being the single most feared and admired woman in Florinese history. If she had figure faults, her clothes concealed them; if her face was less than divine, it was hard to tell once she got done applying substances. (This was before glamour, but if it hadn't been for ladies like the Countess, there would never have been a need for its invention.)

In sum, the Rugens were Couple of the Week in Florin, and had been for many years. . . .

*   *   *

This is me. All abridging remarks and other comments will be in this fancy italic type so you'll know. When I said at the start that I'd never read this book, that's true. My father read it to me, and I just quick skimmed along, crossing out whole sections when I did the abridging, leaving everything just as it was in the original Morgenstern.

This chapter is totally intact. My intrusion here is because of the way Morgenstern uses parentheses. The copy editor at Harcourt kept filling the margins of the galley proofs with questions: 'How can it be before Europe but after Paris?' And 'How is it possible this happens before glamour when glamour is an ancient concept? See "glamer" in the Oxford English Dictionary.' And eventually: 'I am going crazy. What am I to make of these parentheses? When does this book take place? I don't understand anything. Hellllppppp!!!' Denise, the copy editor, has done all my books since Boys and Girls Together *and she had never been as emotional in the margins with me before.*

I couldn't help her.

Either Morgenstern meant them seriously or he didn't. Or maybe he meant some of them seriously and some others he didn't. But he never said which were the serious ones. Or maybe it was just the author's way of telling the reader stylistically that 'this isn't real; it never happened.' That's what I think, in spite of the fact that if you read back into Florinese history, it did happen. The facts, anyway; no one can say about the actual motivations. All I can suggest to you is, if the parentheses bug you, don't read them.

*   *   *

"QUICK—QUICK—COME—" Buttercup's father stood in his farmhouse, staring out the window.

"Why?" This from the mother. She gave away nothing when it came to obedience.

The father made a quick finger point. "Look—"

"You look; you know how." Buttercup's parents did not have exactly what you might call a happy marriage. All they ever dreamed of was leaving each other.

Buttercup's father shrugged and went back to the window. "Ah-hhh," he said after a while. And a little later, again, "Ahhhh."

Buttercup's mother glanced up briefly from her cooking.

"Such riches," Buttercup's father said. "Glorious."

Buttercup's mother hesitated, then put her stew spoon down. (This was after stew, but so is everything. When the first man first clambered from the slime and made his first home on land, what he had for supper that first night was stew.)

"The heart swells at the magnificence," Buttercup's father muttered very loudly.

"What exactly is it, dumpling?" Buttercup's mother wanted to know.

"You look; you know how" was all he replied. (This was their thirty-third spat of the day—this was long after spats—and he was behind, thirteen to twenty, but he had made up a lot of distance since lunch, when it was seventeen to two against him.)

"Donkey," the mother said, and came over to the window. A moment later she was going "Ahhhh" right along with him.

They stood there, the two of them, tiny and awed.

From setting the dinner table, Buttercup watched them.

"They must be going to meet Prince Humperdinck someplace," Buttercup's mother said.

The father nodded. "Hunting. That's what the Prince does."

"How lucky we are to have seen them pass by," Buttercup's mother said, and she took her husband's hand.

The old man nodded. "Now I can die."

She glanced at him. "Don't." Her tone was surprisingly tender, and probably she sensed how important he really was to her, because when he did die, two years further on, she went right after, and most of the people who knew her well agreed it was the sudden lack of opposition that undid her.

Buttercup came close and stood behind them, staring over them, and soon she was gasping too, because the Count and Countess and all their pages and soldiers and servants and courtiers and champions and carriages were passing by the cart track at the front of the farm.

The three stood in silence as the procession moved forward. Buttercup's father was a tiny mutt of a man who had always dreamed of living like the Count. He had once been two miles from where the Count and Prince had been hunting, and until this moment that had been the high point of his life. He was a terrible farmer, and not much of a husband either. There wasn't really much in this world he excelled at, and he could never quite figure out how he happened to sire his daughter, but he knew, deep down, that it must have been some kind of wonderful mistake, the nature of which he had no intention of investigating.

Buttercup's mother was a gnarled shrimp of a woman, thorny and worrying, who had always dreamed of somehow just once being popular, like the Countess was said to be. She was a terrible cook, an even more limited housekeeper. How Buttercup slid from her womb was, of course, beyond her. But she had been there when it happened; that was enough for her.

Buttercup herself, standing half a head over her parents, still holding the dinner dishes, still smelling of Horse, only wished that the great procession wasn't quite so far away, so she could see if the Countess's clothes really were all that lovely.

As if in answer to her request, the procession turned and began entering the farm.

"Here?" Buttercup's father managed. "My God, why?"

Buttercup's mother whirled on him. "Did you forget to pay your taxes?" (This was after taxes. But everything is after taxes. Taxes were here even before stew.)

"Even if I did, they wouldn't need all *that* to collect them," and he gestured toward the front of his farm, where now the Count and Countess and all their pages and soldiers and servants and courtiers and champions and carriages were coming closer and closer. "What could they want to ask me about?" he said.

"Go see, go see," Buttercup's mother told him.

"You go. Please."

"No. You. Please."

"We'll both go."

They both went. Trembling . . .

"Cows," the Count said, when they reached his golden carriage. "I would like to talk about your cows." He spoke from inside, his dark face darkened by shadow.

"My cows?" Buttercup's father said.

"Yes. You see, I'm thinking of starting a little dairy of my own, and since your cows are known throughout the land as being Florin's finest, I thought I might pry your secrets from you."

"My cows," Buttercup's father managed to repeat, hoping he was not going mad. Because the truth was, and he knew it well, he had terrible cows. For years, nothing but complaints from the people in the village. If anyone else had had milk to sell, he would have been out of business in a minute. Now granted, things had improved since the farm boy had come to slave for him—no question, the farm boy had certain skills, and the complaints were quite nonexistent now—but that didn't make his the finest cows in Florin. Still, you didn't argue with the Count. Buttercup's father turned to his wife. "What would you say my secret is, my dear?" he asked.

"Oh, there are so many," she said—she was no dummy, not when it came to the quality of their livestock.

"You two are childless, are you?" the Count asked then.

"No, sir," the mother answered.

"Then let me see her," the Count went on—"perhaps she will be quicker with her answers than her parents."

"Buttercup," the father called, turning. "Come out, please."

"How did you know we had a daughter?" Buttercup's mother wondered.

"A guess. I assumed it had to be one or the other. Some days I'm luckier than—" He simply stopped talking then.

Because Buttercup moved into view, hurrying from the house to her parents.

The Count left the carriage. Gracefully, he moved to the ground and stood very still. He was a big man, with black hair and black eyes and great shoulders and a black cape and gloves.

"Curtsy, dear," Buttercup's mother whispered.

Buttercup did her best.

And the Count could not stop looking at her.

Understand now, she was barely rated in the top twenty; her hair was uncombed, unclean; her age was just seventeen, so there was still, in occasional places, the remains of baby fat. Nothing had been done to the child. Nothing was really there but potential.

But the Count still could not rip his eyes away.

"The Count would like to know the secrets behind our cows' greatness, is that not correct, sir?" Buttercup's father said.

The Count only nodded, staring.

Even Buttercup's mother noted a certain tension in the air.

"Ask the farm boy; he tends them," Buttercup said.

"And is that the farm boy?" came a new voice from inside the carriage. Then the Countess's face was framed in the carriage doorway.

Her lips were painted a perfect red; her green eyes lined in black. All the colors of the world were muted in her gown. Buttercup wanted to shield her eyes from the brilliance.

Buttercup's father glanced back toward the lone figure peering around the corner of the house. "It is."

"Bring him to me."

"He is not dressed properly for such an occasion," Buttercup's mother said.

"I have seen bare chests before," the Countess replied. Then she called out: *"You!"* and pointed at the farm boy. "Come *here*." Her fingers snapped on "here."

The farm boy did as he was told.

And when he was close, the Countess left the carriage.

When he was a few paces behind Buttercup, he stopped, head properly bowed. He was ashamed of his attire, worn boots and torn blue jeans (blue jeans were invented considerably before most people suppose), and his hands were tight together in almost a gesture of supplication.

"Have you a name, farm boy?"

"Westley, Countess."

"Well, Westley, perhaps you can help us with our problem." She crossed to him. The fabric of her gown grazed his skin. "We are all of us here passionately interested in the subject of cows. We are practically reaching the point of frenzy, such is our curiosity. Why, do you suppose, Westley, that the cows of this particular farm are the finest in all Florin. What do you do to them?"

"I just feed them, Countess."

"Well then, there it is, the mystery is solved, the secret; we can all rest. Clearly, the magic is in Westley's feeding. Show me how you do it, would you, Westley?"

"Feed the cows for you, Countess?"

"Bright lad."

"When?"

"Now will be soon enough," and she held out her arm to him. "Lead me, Westley."

Westley had no choice but to take her arm. Gently. "It's behind the house, madam; it's terrible muddy back there. Your gown will be ruined."

"I wear them only once, Westley, and I burn to see you in action."

So off they went to the cowshed.

Throughout all this, the Count kept watching Buttercup.

"I'll help you," Buttercup called after Westley.

"Perhaps I'd best see just how he does it," the Count decided.

"Strange things are happening," Buttercup's parents said, and off they went too, bringing up the rear of the cow-feeding trip, watching the Count, who was watching their daughter, who was watching the Countess.

Who was watching Westley.

*   *   *

" I COULDN'T SEE what he did that was so special," Buttercup's father said. "He just fed them." This was after dinner now, and the family was alone again.

"They must like him personally. I had a cat once that only bloomed when I fed him. Maybe it's the same kind of thing." Buttercup's mother scraped the stew leavings into a bowl. "Here," she said to her daughter. "Westley's waiting by the back door; take him his dinner."

Buttercup carried the bowl, opened the back door.

"Take it," she said.

He nodded, accepted, started off to his tree stump to eat.

"I didn't excuse you, Farm Boy," Buttercup began. He stopped, turned back to her. "I don't like what you're doing with Horse. What you're *not* doing with Horse is more to the point. I want him cleaned. Tonight. I want his hoofs varnished. Tonight. I want his tail plaited and his ears massaged. This very evening. I want his stables spotless. Now. I want him glistening, and if it takes you all night, it takes you all night."

"As you wish."

She slammed the door and let him eat in darkness.

"I thought Horse had been looking very well, actually," her father said.

Buttercup said nothing.

"You yourself said so yesterday," her mother reminded her.

"I must be overtired," Buttercup managed. "The excitement and all."

"Rest, then," her mother cautioned. "Terrible things can happen when you're overtired. I was overtired the night your father proposed." Thirty-four to twenty-two and pulling away.

Buttercup went to her room. She lay on her bed. She closed her eyes.

And the Countess was staring at Westley.

Buttercup got up from bed. She took off her clothes. She washed a little. She got into her nightgown. She slipped between the sheets, snuggled down, closed her eyes.

The Countess was still staring at Westley!

Buttercup threw back the sheets, opened her door. She went to the sink by the stove and poured herself a cup of water. She drank it down. She poured another cup and rolled its coolness across her forehead. The feverish feeling was still there.

How feverish? She felt fine. She was seventeen, and not even a cavity. She dumped the water firmly into the sink, turned, marched back to her room, shut the door tight, went back to bed. She closed her eyes.

The Countess would not stop staring at Westley!

Why? Why in the world would the woman in all the history of Florin who was in all ways perfect be interested in the farm boy. Buttercup rolled around in bed. And there simply was no other way of explaining that look—she *was* interested. Buttercup shut her eyes tight and studied the memory of the Countess. Clearly, something about the farm boy interested her. Facts were facts. But *what?* The farm boy had eyes like the sea before a storm, but who cared about eyes? And he had pale blond hair, if you liked that sort of thing. And he was broad enough in the shoulders, but not all that much broader than the Count. And certainly he was muscular, but anybody would be muscular who slaved all day. And his skin was perfect and tan, but that came again from slaving; in the sun all day, who wouldn't be tan? And he wasn't that much taller than the Count either, although his stomach was flatter, but that was because the farm boy was younger.

Buttercup sat up in bed. It must be his teeth. The farm boy did have good teeth, give credit where credit was due. White and perfect, particularly set against the sun-tanned face.

Could it have been anything else? Buttercup concentrated. The girls in the village followed the farm boy around a lot, whenever he was making deliveries, but they were idiots, they followed anything. And he always ignored them, because if he'd ever opened his mouth, they would have realized that was all he had, just good teeth; he was, after all, exceptionally stupid.

It was really very strange that a woman as beautiful and slender and willowy and graceful, a creature as perfectly packaged, as supremely dressed as the Countess should be hung up on teeth that way. Buttercup shrugged. People were surprisingly complicated. But now she had it all diagnosed, deduced, clear. She closed her eyes and snuggled down and got all nice and comfortable, and *people don't look at other people the way the Countess looked at the farm boy because of their teeth.*

"Oh," Buttercup gasped. "Oh, oh dear."

Now the *farm boy* was staring back at the *Countess*. He was feeding the cows and his muscles were rippling the way they always did under his tanned skin and Buttercup was standing there watching as the farm boy looked, for the first time, deep into the Countess's eyes.

Buttercup jumped out of bed and began to pace her room. How

could he? Oh, it was all right if he looked at her, but he wasn't looking at her, he was *looking at her*.

"She's so old," Buttercup muttered, starting to storm a bit now. The Countess would never see thirty again and that was fact. And her dress looked ridiculous out in the cowshed and that was fact too.

Buttercup fell onto her bed and clutched her pillow across her breasts. The dress was ridiculous before it ever got to the cowshed. The Countess looked rotten the minute she left the carriage, with her too big painted mouth and her little piggy painted eyes and her powdered skin and . . . and . . . and . . .

Flailing and thrashing, Buttercup wept and tossed and paced and wept some more, and there have been three great cases of jealousy since David of Galilee was first afflicted with the emotion when he could no longer stand the fact that his neighbor Saul's cactus outshone his own. (Originally, jealousy pertained solely to plants, other people's cactus or ginkgoes, or, later, when there was grass, grass, which is why, even to this day, we say that someone is green with jealousy.) Buttercup's case rated a close fourth on the all-time list.

It was a very long and very green night.

She was outside his hovel before dawn. Inside, she could hear him already awake. She knocked. He appeared, stood in the doorway. Behind him she could see a tiny candle, open books. He waited. She looked at him. Then she looked away.

He was too beautiful.

"I love you," Buttercup said. "I know this must come as something of a surprise, since all I've ever done is scorn you and degrade you and taunt you, but I have loved you for several hours now, and every second, more. I thought an hour ago that I loved you more than any woman has ever loved a man, but a half hour after that I knew that what I felt before was nothing compared to what I felt then. But ten minutes after that, I understood that my previous love was a puddle compared to the high seas before a storm. Your eyes are like that, did you know? Well they are. How many minutes ago was I? Twenty? Had I brought my feelings up to then? It doesn't matter." Buttercup still could not look at him. The sun was rising behind her now; she could feel the heat on her back, and it gave her courage. "I love you so much more now than twenty minutes ago that there cannot be comparison. I love you so much more now than when you opened your hovel door, there cannot be comparison. There is no room in my body for anything but you. My arms love you, my ears adore you, my knees shake with blind affection. My mind begs you to ask it something so it can obey. Do you want me to follow you for the rest of your days? I will do that. Do you want me to crawl? I will crawl. I will be quiet for you or sing for you, or if you are hungry, let me bring you food, or if you have thirst and nothing will quench it but Arabian wine, I will go to Araby, even though it is across the world, and bring a bottle back for your lunch. Anything there is that I can do for you, I will do for you; anything there is that I cannot do, I will learn to do. I know I cannot compete with the Countess in skills or wisdom or appeal, and I saw the way she looked at you. And I saw the way you looked at her. But remember, please, that she is old and has other interests, while I am seventeen and for me there is only you. Dearest Westley—I've never called you that before, have I?—Westley, Westley, Westley, Westley, Westley,—darling Westley, adored Westley, sweet perfect Westley, whisper that I have a chance to win your love." And with that, she dared the bravest thing she'd ever done: she looked right into his eyes.

He closed the door in her face.

Without a word.

Without a word.

Buttercup ran. She whirled and burst away and the tears came bitterly; she could not see, she stumbled, she slammed into a tree trunk, fell, rose, ran on; her shoulder throbbed from where the tree trunk hit her, and the pain was strong, but not enough to ease her shattered heart. Back to her room she fled, back to her pillow. Safe behind the locked door, she drenched the world with tears.

Not even *one* word. He hadn't had the decency for that. "Sorry," he could have said. Would it have ruined him to say "sorry"? "Too late," he could have said.

Why couldn't he at least have said something?

Buttercup thought very hard about that for a moment. And suddenly she had the answer: he didn't talk because the minute he opened his mouth, that was it. Sure he was handsome, but dumb? The minute he had exercised his tongue, it would have all been over.

"Duhhhhhhh."

That's what he would have said. That was the kind of thing Westley came out with when he was feeling really sharp. "Duhhhh-hhh, tanks, Buttercup."

Buttercup dried her tears and began to smile. She took a deep breath, heaved a sigh. It was all part of growing up. You got these little quick passions, you blinked, and they were gone. You forgave faults, found perfection, fell madly; then the next day the sun came up and it was over. Chalk it up to experience, old girl, and get on with the morning. Buttercup stood, made her bed, changed her clothes, combed her hair, smiled, and burst out again in a fit of weeping. Because there was a limit to just how much you could lie to yourself.

Westley wasn't stupid.

Oh, she could pretend he was. She could laugh about his diffi-culties with the language. She could chide herself for her silly in-fatuation with a dullard. The truth was simply this: he had a head on his shoulders. With a brain inside every bit as good as his teeth. There was a reason he hadn't spoken and it had nothing to do with gray cells working. He hadn't spoken because, really, there was nothing for him to say.

He didn't love her back and that was that.

The tears that kept Buttercup company the remainder of the day were not at all like those that had blinded her into the tree trunk. Those were noisy and hot; they pulsed. These were silent and steady and all they did was remind her that she wasn't good enough. She was seventeen, and every male she'd ever known had crumbled at her feet and it meant nothing. The one time it mat-tered, she wasn't good enough. All she knew really was riding, and how was that to interest a man when that man had been looked at by the Countess?

It was dusk when she heard footsteps outside her door. Then a knock. Buttercup dried her eyes. Another knock. "Whoever is that?" Buttercup yawned finally.

"Westley."

Buttercup lounged across the bed. "Westley?" she said. "Do I know any West—oh, *Farm* Boy, it's you, how droll!" She went to her door, unlocked it, and said, in her fanciest tone, "I'm ever so glad you stopped by, I've been feeling just ever so slummy about the little joke I played on you this morning. Of course you knew I wasn't for a moment serious, or at least I thought you knew, but then, just when you started closing the door I thought for one dreary instant that perhaps I'd done my little jest a bit too convinc-ingly and, poor dear thing, you might have thought I meant what I said when of course we both know the total impossibility of that ever happening."

"I've come to say good-by."

Buttercup's heart bucked, but she still held to fancy. "You're going to sleep, you mean, and you've come to say good night? How thoughtful of you, Farm Boy, showing me that you forgive me for my little morning's tease; I certainly appreciate your thoughtfulness and—"

He cut her off. "I'm leaving."

"Leaving?" The floor began to ripple. She held to the doorframe. "Now?"

"Yes."

"Because of what I said this morning?"

"Yes."

"I frightened you away, didn't I? I could kill my tongue." She shook her head and shook her head. "Well, it's done; you've made your decision. Just remember this: I won't take you back when she's done with you, I don't care if you beg."

He just looked at her.

Buttercup hurried on. "Just because you're beautiful and perfect, it's made you conceited. You think people can't get tired of you, well you're wrong, they can, and she will, besides you're too poor."

"I'm going to America. To seek my fortune." (This was just after America but long after fortunes.) "A ship sails soon from London. There is great opportunity in America. I'm going to take advantage of it. I've been training myself. In my hovel. I've taught myself not to need sleep. A few hours only. I'll take a ten-hour-a-day job and then I'll take another ten-hour-a-day job and I'll save every penny from both except what I need to eat to keep strong, and when I have enough I'll buy a farm and build a house and make a bed big enough for two."

"You're just crazy if you think she's going to be happy in some run-down farmhouse in America. Not with what she spends on clothes."

"Stop talking about the Countess! As a special favor. Before you drive me *maaaaaaaad*."

Buttercup looked at him.

"Don't you understand anything that's going on?"

Buttercup shook her head.

Westley shook his too. "You never have been the brightest, I guess."

"Do you love me, Westley? Is that it?"

He couldn't believe it. "Do I love you? My God, if your love were a grain of sand, mine would be a universe of beaches. If your love were—"

"I don't understand that first one yet," Buttercup interrupted. She was starting to get very excited now. "Let me get this straight. Are you saying my love is the size of a grain of sand and yours is this other thing? Images just confuse me so—is this universal business of yours bigger than my sand? Help me, Westley. I have the feeling we're on the verge of something just terribly important."

"I have stayed these years in my hovel because of you. I have taught myself languages because of you. I have made my body strong because I thought you might be pleased by a strong body. I have lived my life with only the prayer that some sudden dawn you might glance in my direction. I have not known a moment in years when the sight of you did not send my heart careening against my rib cage. I have not known a night when your visage did not accompany me to sleep. There has not been a morning when you did not flutter behind my waking eyelids. . . . Is any of this getting through to you, Buttercup, or do you want me to go on for a while?"

"Never stop."

"There has not been—"

"If you're teasing me, Westley, I'm just going to kill you."

"How can you even dream I might be teasing?"

"Well, you haven't once said you loved me."

"That's all you need? Easy. I love you. Okay? Want it louder? *I love you.* Spell it out, should I? I ell-oh-vee-ee why-oh-you. Want it backward? You love I."

"You are teasing now; aren't you?"

"A little maybe; I've been saying it so long to you, you just wouldn't listen. Every time you said 'Farm Boy do this' you thought I was answering 'As you wish' but that's only because you were hearing wrong. 'I love you' was what it was, but you never heard, and you never heard."

"I hear you now, and I promise you this: I will never love anyone else. Only Westley. Until I die."

He nodded, took a step away. "I'll send for you soon. Believe me."

"Would my Westley ever lie?"

He took another step. "I'm late. I must go. I hate it but I must. The ship sails soon and London is far."

"I understand."

He reached out with his right hand.

Buttercup found it very hard to breathe.

"Good-by."

She managed to raise her right hand to his.

They shook.

"Good-by," he said again.

She made a little nod.

He took a third step, not turning.

She watched him.

He turned.

And the words ripped out of her: *"Without one kiss?"*

They fell into each other's arms.

*   *   *

THERE HAVE BEEN five great kisses since 1642 B.C., when Saul and Delilah Korn's inadvertent discovery swept across Western civilization. (Before then couples hooked thumbs.) And the precise rating of kisses is a terribly difficult thing, often leading to great controversy, because although everyone agrees with the formula of affection times purity times intensity times duration, no one has ever been completely satisfied with how much weight each element should receive. But on any system, there are five that everyone agrees deserve full marks.

Well, this one left them all behind.

*   *   *

THE FIRST MORNING after Westley's departure, Buttercup thought she was entitled to do nothing more than sit around moping and feeling sorry for herself. After all, the love of her life had fled, life had no meaning, how could you face the future, et cetera, et cetera.

But after about two seconds of that she realized that Westley was out in the world now, getting nearer and nearer to London, and what if a beautiful city girl caught his fancy while she was just back here moldering? Or, worse, what if he got to America and worked his jobs and built his farm and made their bed and sent for her and when she got there he would look at her and say, "I'm sending you back, the moping has destroyed your eyes, the self-pity has taken your skin; you're a slobby-looking creature, I'm marrying an Indian girl who lives in a teepee nearby and is always in the peak of condition."

Buttercup ran to her bedroom mirror. "Oh, Westley," she said, "I must never disappoint you," and she hurried downstairs to where her parents were squabbling. (Sixteen to thirteen, and not past breakfast yet.) "I need your advice," she interrupted. "What can I do to improve my personal appearance."

"Start by bathing," her father said.

"And do something with your hair while you're at it," her mother said.

"Unearth the territory behind your ears."

"Neglect not your knees."

"That will do nicely for starters," Buttercup said. She shook her head. "Gracious, but it isn't easy being tidy." Undaunted, she set to work.

Every morning she awoke, if possible by dawn, and got the farm chores finished immediately. There was much to be done now, with Westley gone, and more than that, ever since the Count had visited, everyone in the area had increased his milk order. So there was no time for self-improvement until well into the afternoon.

But then she really set to work. First a good cold bath. Then, while her hair was drying, she would slave after fixing her figure faults (one of her elbows was just too bony, the opposite wrist not bony enough). And exercise what remained of her baby fat (little left now; she was nearly eighteen). And brush and brush her hair.

Her hair was the color of autumn, and it had never been cut, so a thousand strokes took time, but she didn't mind, because Westley had never seen it clean like this and wouldn't he be surprised when she stepped off the boat in America. Her skin was the color of wintry cream, and she scrubbed her every inch well past glistening, and that wasn't much fun really, but wouldn't Westley be pleased with how clean she was as she stepped off the boat in America.

And very quickly now, her potential began to be realized. From twentieth, she jumped within two weeks to fifteenth, an unheard-of change in such a time. But three weeks after that she was already ninth and moving. The competition was tremendous now, but the day after she was ninth a three-page letter arrived from Westley in London and just reading it over put her up to eighth. That was really what was doing it for her more than anything—her love for Westley would not stop growing, and people were dazzled when she delivered milk in the morning. Some people were only able to gape at her, but many talked and those that did found her warmer and gentler than she had ever been before. Even the village girls would nod and smile now, and some of them would ask after West-ley, which was a mistake unless you happened to have a lot of spare time, because when someone asked Buttercup how Westley was— well, she told them. He was supreme as usual; he was spectacular; he was singularly fabulous. Oh, she could go on for hours. Some-times it got a little tough for the listeners to maintain strict attention, but they did their best, since Buttercup loved him so completely.

Which was why Westley's death hit her the way it did.

He had written to her just before he sailed for America. The *Queen's Pride* was his ship, and he loved her. (That was the way his sentences always went: It is raining today and I love you. My cold is better and I love you. Say hello to Horse and I love you. Like that.)

Then there were no letters, but that was natural; he was at sea. Then she heard. She came home from delivering the milk and her parents were wooden. "Off the Carolina coast," her father whispered.

Her mother whispered, "Without warning. At night."

"What?" from Buttercup.

"Pirates," said her father.

Buttercup thought she'd better sit down.

Quiet in the room.

"He's been taken prisoner then?" Buttercup managed.

Her mother made a "no."

"It was Roberts," her father said. "The Dread Pirate Roberts."

"Oh," Buttercup said. "The one who never leaves survivors."

"Yes," her father said.

Quiet in the room.

Suddenly Buttercup was talking very fast: "Was he stabbed? . . . Did he drown? . . . Did they cut his throat asleep? . . . Did they wake him, do you suppose? . . . Perhaps they whipped him dead. . . ." She stood up then. "I'm getting silly, forgive me." She shook her head. "As if the way they got him mattered. Excuse me, please." With that she hurried to her room.

She stayed there many days. At first her parents tried to lure her, but she would not have it. They took to leaving food outside her room, and she took bits and shreds, enough to stay alive. There was never noise inside, no wailing, no bitter sounds.

And when she at last came out, her eyes were dry. Her parents stared up from their silent breakfast at her. They both started to rise but she put a hand out, stopped them. "I can care for myself, please," and she set about getting some food. They watched her closely.

In point of fact, she had never looked as well. She had entered her room as just an impossibly lovely girl. The woman who emerged was a trifle thinner, a great deal wiser, an ocean sadder. This one understood the nature of pain, and beneath the glory of her features, there was character, and a sure knowledge of suffering.

She was eighteen. She was the most beautiful woman in a hundred years. She didn't seem to care.

"You're all right?" her mother asked.

Buttercup sipped her cocoa. "Fine," she said.

"You're sure?" her father wondered.

"Yes," Buttercup replied. There was a very long pause. "But I must never love again."

She never did.

TWO

THE GROOM

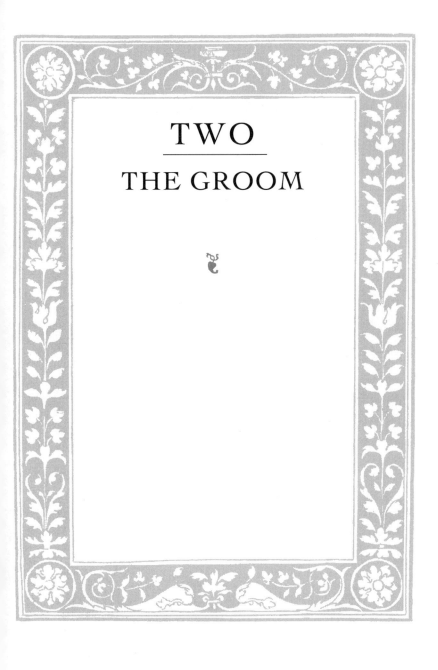

*HIS is my first major excision. Chapter One, The Bride, is almost in its entirety about the bride. Chapter Two, The Groom, only picks up Prince Humperdinck in the last few pages.*

    This chapter is where my son Jason stopped reading, and there is simply no way of blaming him. For what Morgenstern has done is open this chapter with sixty-six pages of Florinese history. More accurately, it is the history of the Florinese crown.

Dreary? Not to be believed.

Why would a master of narrative stop his narrative dead before it has much chance to begin generating? No known answer. All I can guess is that for Morgenstern, the real narrative was not Buttercup and the remarkable things she endures, but, rather, the history of the monarchy and other such stuff. When this version comes out, I expect every Florinese scholar alive to slaughter me. (Columbia University has not only the leading Florinese experts in America, but also direct ties to the New York Times Book Review. *I can't help that, and I only hope they understand my intentions here are in no way meant to be destructive of Morgenstern's vision.)*

*   *   *

PRINCE HUMPERDINCK WAS shaped like a barrel. His chest was a great barrel chest, his thighs mighty barrel thighs. He was not tall but he weighed close to 250 pounds, brick hard. He walked like a crab, side to side, and probably if he had wanted to be a ballet dancer, he would have been doomed to a miserable life of endless frustration. But he didn't want to be a ballet dancer. He wasn't in that much of a hurry to be king either. Even war, at which he excelled, took second place in his affections. Everything took second place in his affections.

Hunting was his love.

He made it a practice never to let a day go by without killing something. It didn't much matter what. When he first grew dedicated, he killed only big things: elephants or pythons. But then, as his skills increased, he began to enjoy the suffering of little beasts too. He could happily spend an afternoon tracking a flying squirrel across forests or a rainbow trout down rivers. Once he was determined, once he had focused on an object, the Prince was relentless. He never tired, never wavered, neither ate nor slept. It was death chess and he was international grand master.

In the beginning, he traversed the world for opposition. But travel consumed time, ships and horses being what they were, and the time away from Florin was worrying. There always had to be a male heir to the throne, and as long as his father was alive, there was no problem. But someday his father would die and then the Prince would be the king and he would have to select a queen to supply an heir for the day of his own death.

So to avoid the problem of absence, Prince Humperdinck built the Zoo of Death. He designed it himself with Count Rugen's help, and he sent his hirelings across the world to stock it for him. It was kept brimming with things that he could hunt, and it really wasn't like any other animal sanctuary anywhere. In the first place, there were never any visitors. Only the albino keeper, to make sure the beasts were properly fed, and that there was never any sickness or weakness inside.

The other thing about the Zoo was that it was underground.

The Prince picked the spot himself, in the quietest, remotest corner of the castle grounds. And he decreed there were to be five levels, all with the proper needs for his individual enemies. On the first level, he put enemies of speed: wild dogs, cheetahs, hummingbirds. On the second level belonged the enemies of strength: anacondas and rhinos and crocodiles of over twenty feet. The third level was for poisoners: spitting cobras, jumping spiders, death bats galore. The fourth level was the kingdom of the most dangerous, the enemies of fear: the shrieking tarantula (the only spider capable of sound), the blood eagle (the only bird that thrived on human flesh), plus, in its own black pool, the sucking squid. Even the albino shivered during feeding time on the fourth level.

The fifth level was empty.

The Prince constructed it in the hopes of someday finding something worthy, something as dangerous and fierce and powerful as he was.

Unlikely. Still, he was an eternal optimist, so he kept the great cage of the fifth level always in readiness.

And there was really more than enough that was lethal on the other four levels to keep a man happy. The Prince would sometimes choose his prey by luck—he had a great wheel with a spinner and on the outside of the wheel was a picture of every animal in the Zoo and he would twirl the spinner at breakfast, and wherever it stopped, the albino would ready that breed. Sometimes he would choose by mood: "I feel quick today; fetch me a cheetah" or "I feel strong today, release a rhino." And whatever he requested, of course, was done.

*   *   *

HE WAS RINGING down the curtain on an orangutan when the business of the King's health made its ultimate intrusion. It was midafternoon, and the Prince had been grappling with the giant beast since morning, and finally, after all these hours, the hairy thing was weakening. Again and again, the monkey tried to bite, a sure sign of failure of strength in the arms. The Prince warded off the attempted bites with ease, and the ape was heaving at the chest now, desperate for air. The Prince made a crablike step sidewise, then another, then darted forward, spun the great beast into his arms, began applying pressure to the spine. (This was all taking place in the ape pit, where the Prince had his pleasure with many simians.) From up above now, Count Rugen's voice interrupted. "There is news," the Count said.

From battle, the Prince replied, "Cannot it wait?"

"For how long?" asked the Count.

C

R

A

C

K

The orangutan fell like a rag doll. "Now, what is all this," the Prince replied, stepping past the dead beast, mounting the ladder out of the pit.

"Your father has had his annual physical," the Count said. "I have the report."

"And?"

"Your father is dying."

"Drat!" said the Prince. "That means I shall have to get married."

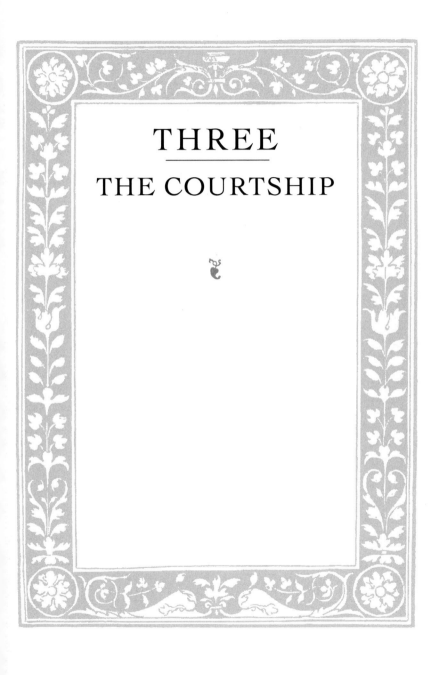

THREE

THE COURTSHIP

OUR of them met in the great council room of the castle. Prince Humperdinck, his confidant, Count Rugen, his father, aging King Lotharon, and Queen Bella, his evil stepmother.

Queen Bella was shaped like a gumdrop. And colored like a raspberry. She was easily the most beloved person in the kingdom, and had been married to the King long before he began mumbling. Prince Humperdinck was but a child then, and since the only stepmothers he knew were the evil ones from stories, he always called Bella that or "E. S." for short.

"All right," the Prince began when they were all assembled. "Who do I marry? Let's pick a bride and get it done."

Aging King Lotharon said, "I've been thinking it's really getting to be about time for Humperdinck to pick a bride." He didn't actually so much say that as mumble it: "I've beee mumbbble mumbbble Humpmummmble engamumble."

Queen Bella was the only one who bothered ferreting out his meanings any more. "You couldn't be righter, dear," she said, and she patted his royal robes.

"What did he say?"

"He said whoever we decided on would be getting a thunderously handsome prince for a lifetime companion."

"Tell him he's looking quite well himself," the Prince returned.

"We've only just changed miracle men," the Queen said. "That accounts for the improvement."

"You mean you fired Miracle Max?" Prince Humperdinck said. "I thought he was the only one left."

"No, we found another one up in the mountains and he's quite extraordinary. Old, of course, but then, who wants a young miracle man?"

"Tell him I've changed miracle men," King Lotharon said. It came out: "Tell mumble mirumble mumble."

"What did he say?" the Prince wondered.

"He said a man of your importance couldn't marry just *any* princess."

"True, true," Prince Humperdinck said. He sighed. Deeply. "I suppose that means Noreena."

"That would certainly be a perfect match politically," Count Rugen allowed. Princess Noreena was from Guilder, the country that lay just across Florin Channel. (In Guilder, they put it differently; for them, Florin was the country on the other side of the Channel of Guilder.) In any case, the two countries had stayed alive over the centuries mainly by warring on each other. There had been the Olive War, the Tuna Fish Discrepancy, which almost bankrupted both nations, the Roman Rift, which did send them both into insolvency, only to be followed by the Discord of the Emeralds, in which they both got rich again, chiefly by banding together for a brief period and robbing everybody within sailing distance.

"I wonder if she hunts, though," said Humperdinck. "I don't care so much about personality, just so they're good with a knife."

"I saw her several years ago," Queen Bella said. "She seemed lovely, though hardly muscular. I would describe her more as a knitter than a doer. But again, lovely."

"Skin?" asked the Prince.

"Marbleish," answered the Queen.

"Lips?"

"Number or color?" asked the Queen.

"Color, E. S."

"Roseish. Cheeks the same. Eyes largeish, one blue, one green."

"Hmmm," said Humperdinck. "And form?"

"Hourglassish. Always clothed divineishly. And, of course, famous throughout Guilder for the largest hat collection in the world."

"Well, let's bring her over here for some state occasions and have a look at her," said the Prince.

"Isn't there a princess in Guilder that would be about the right age?" said the King. It came out "Mumcess Guilble, abumble mumble?"

"Are you never wrong?" said Queen Bella, and she smiled into the weakening eyes of her ruler.

"What did he say?" wondered the Prince.

"That I should leave this very day with an invitation," replied the Queen.

So began the great visit of the Princess Noreena.

*   *   *

Me again. Of all the cuts in this version, I feel most justified in making this one. Just as the chapters on whaling in Moby Dick *can be omitted by all but the most punishment-loving readers, so the packing scenes that Morgenstern details here are really best left alone. That's what happens for the next fifty-six and a half pages of* The Princess Bride: *packing. (I include unpacking scenes in the same category.)*

What happens is just this: Queen Bella packs most of her wardrobe (11 pages) and travels to Guilder (2 pages). In Guilder she unpacks (5 pages), then tenders the invitation to Princess Noreena (1 page). Princess Noreena accepts (1 page). Then Princess Noreena packs all her clothes and hats (23 pages) and, together, the Princess and the Queen travel back to Florin for the annual celebration of the founding of Florin City (1 page). They reach King Lotharon's castle, where Princess Noreena is shown her quarters (1/2 page) and unpacks all the same clothes and hats we've just seen her pack one and a half pages before (12 pages).

It's a baffling passage. I spoke to Professor Bongiorno, of Columbia University, the head of their Florinese Department, and he said this was the most deliciously satiric chapter in the entire book, Morgenstern's point, apparently, being simply to show that although Florin considered itself vastly more civilized than Guilder, Guilder was, in fact, the far more sophisticated country, as indicated by the superiority in number and quality of the ladies' clothes. I'm not about to argue with a full professor, but if you ever have a really unbreakable case of insomnia, do yourself a favor and start reading Chapter Three of the uncut version.

Anyway, things pick up a bit once the Prince and Princess meet and spend the day. Noreena did have, as advertised, marbleish skin, roseish lips and cheeks, largeish eyes, one blue, one green, hourglassish form, and easily the most extraordinary collection of hats ever assembled. Wide brimmed and narrow, some tall, some not, some fancy, some colorful, some plaid, some plain. She doted on changing hats at every opportunity. When she met the Prince, she was wearing one hat, when he asked her for a stroll, she excused herself, shortly to return wearing another, equally flattering. Things went on like this throughout the day, but it seems to me to be a bit too much court etiquette for modern readers, so it's not till the evening meal that I return to the original text.

*   *   *

DINNER WAS HELD in the Great Hall of Lotharon's castle. Ordinarily, they would all have supped in the dining room, but, for an event of this importance, that place was simply too small. So tables were placed end to end along the center of the Great Hall, an enormous drafty spot that was given to being chilly even in the summertime. There were many doors and giant entrance ways, and the wind gusts sometimes reached gale force.

This night was more typical than less; the winds whistled constantly and the candles constantly needed relighting, and some of the more daringly dressed ladies shivered. But Prince Humperdinck didn't seem to mind, and in Florin, if he didn't, you didn't either.

At 8:23 there seemed every chance of a lasting alliance starting between Florin and Guilder.

At 8:24 the two nations were very close to war.

What happened was simply this: at 8:23 and five seconds, the main course of the evening was ready for serving. The main course was essence of brandied pig, and you need a lot of it to serve five hundred people. So in order to hasten the serving, a giant double door that led from the kitchen to the Great Hall was opened. The giant double door was on the north end of the room. The door remained open throughout what followed.

The proper wine for essence of brandied pig was in readiness behind the double door that led eventually to the wine cellar. This double door was opened at 8:23 and ten seconds in order that the dozen wine stewards could get their kegs quickly to the eaters. This double door, it might be noted, was at the south end of the room.

At this point, an unusually strong cross wind was clearly evident. Prince Humperdinck did not notice, because at that moment, he was whispering with the Princess Noreena of Guilder. He was cheek to cheek with her, his head under her wide-brimmed blue-green hat, which brought out the exquisite color in both of her largeish eyes.

At 8:23 and twenty seconds, King Lotharon made his somewhat

belated entrance to the dinner. He was always belated now, had been for years, and in the past people had been known to starve before he got there. But of late, meals just began without him, which was fine with him, since his new miracle man had taken him off meals anyway. The King entered through the King's Door, a huge hinged thing that only he was allowed to use. It took several servants in excellent condition to work it. It should be reported that the King's Door was always in the east side of any room, since the King was, of all people, closest to the sun.

What happened then has been variously described as a norther or a sou'wester, depending on where you were seated in the room when it struck, but all hands agree on one thing: at 8:23 and twenty-five seconds, it was pretty gusty in the Great Hall.

Most of the candles lost their flames and toppled, which was only important because a few of them fell, still burning, into the small kerosene cups that were placed here and there across the banquet table so that the essence of brandied pig could be properly flaming when served. Servants rushed in from all over to put out the flames, and they did a good enough job, considering that everything in the room was flying this way, that way, fans and scarves and hats.

Particularly the hat of Princess Noreena.

It flew off to the wall behind her, where she quickly retrieved it and put it properly on. That was at 8:23 and fifty seconds. It was too late.

At 8:23:55 Prince Humperdinck rose roaring, the veins in his thick neck etched like hemp. There were still flames in some places, and their redness reddened his already blood-filled face. He looked, as he stood there, like a barrel on fire. He then said to Princess Noreena of Guilder the five words that brought the nations to the brink.

"Madam, feel free to flee!"

And with that he stormed from the Great Hall. The time was then 8:24.

Prince Humperdinck made his angry way to the balcony above the Great Hall and stared down at the chaos. The fires were still in places flaming red, guests were pouring out through the doors and Princess Noreena, hatted and faint, was being carried by her servants far from view.

Queen Bella finally caught up with the Prince, who stormed along the balcony clearly not yet in control. "I do wish you hadn't been quite so blunt," Queen Bella said.

The Prince whirled on her. "I'm not marrying any bald princess, and that's that!"

"No one would know," Queen Bella explained. "She has hats even for sleeping."

"*I* would know," cried the Prince. "Did you see the candlelight reflecting off her skull?"

"But things would have been so good with Guilder," the Queen said, addressing herself half to the Prince, half to Count Rugen, who now joined them.

"Forget about Guilder. I'll conquer it sometime. I've been wanting to ever since I was a kid anyway." He approached the Queen. "People snicker behind your back when you've got a bald wife, and I can do without that, thank you. You'll just have to find someone else."

"Who?"

"Find me somebody, she should just look nice, that's all."

"That Noreena has no hair," King Lotharon said, puffing up to the others. "Nor-umble mumble humble."

"Thank you for pointing that out, dear," said Queen Bella.

"I don't think Humperdinck will like that," said the King. "Dumble Humble Mumble."

Then Count Rugen stepped forward. "You want someone who looks nice; but what if she's a commoner?"

"The commoner the better," Prince Humperdinck replied, pacing again.

"What if she can't hunt?" the Count went on.

"I don't care if she can't spell," the Prince said. Suddenly he stopped and faced them all. "I'll tell you what I want," he began then. "I want someone who is so beautiful that when you see her you say, 'Wow, that Humperdinck must be some kind of fella to have a wife like that.' Search the country, search the world, just find her!"

Count Rugen could only smile. "She is already found," he said.

*   *   *

IT WAS DAWN when the two horsemen reined in at the hilltop. Count Rugen rode a splendid black horse, large, perfect, powerful. The Prince rode one of his whites. It made Rugen's mount seem like a plow puller.

"She delivers milk in the mornings," Count Rugen said.

"And she is truly-without-question-no-possibility-of-error beautiful?"

"She was something of a mess when I saw her," the Count admitted. "But the potential was overwhelming."

"A milkmaid." The Prince ran the words across his rough tongue. "I don't know that I could wed one of them even under the best of conditions. People might snicker that she was the best I could do."

"True," the Count admitted. "If you prefer, we can ride back to Florin City without waiting."

"We've come this far," the Prince said. "We might as well

wai—" His voice quite simply died. "I'll take her," he managed, finally, as Buttercup rode slowly by below them.

"No one will snicker, I think," the Count said.

"I must court her now," said the Prince. "Leave us alone for a minute." He rode the white expertly down the hill.

Buttercup had never seen such a giant beast. Or such a rider.

"I am your Prince and you will marry me," Humperdinck said.

Buttercup whispered, "I am your servant and I refuse."

"I am your Prince and you cannot refuse."

"I am your loyal servant and I just did."

"Refusal means death."

"Kill me then."

"I am your Prince and I'm not that bad—how could you rather be dead than married to me?"

"Because," Buttercup said, "marriage involves love, and that is not a pastime at which I excel. I tried once, and it went badly, and I am sworn never to love another."

"Love?" said Prince Humperdinck. "Who mentioned love? Not me, I can tell you. Look: there must always be a male heir to the throne of Florin. That's me. Once my father dies, there won't be an heir, just a king. That's me again. When that happens, I'll marry and have children until there is a son. So you can either marry me and be the richest and most powerful woman in a thousand miles and give turkeys away at Christmas and provide me a son, or you can die in terrible pain in the very near future. Make up your own mind."

"I'll never love you."

"I wouldn't want it if I had it."

"Then by all means let us marry."

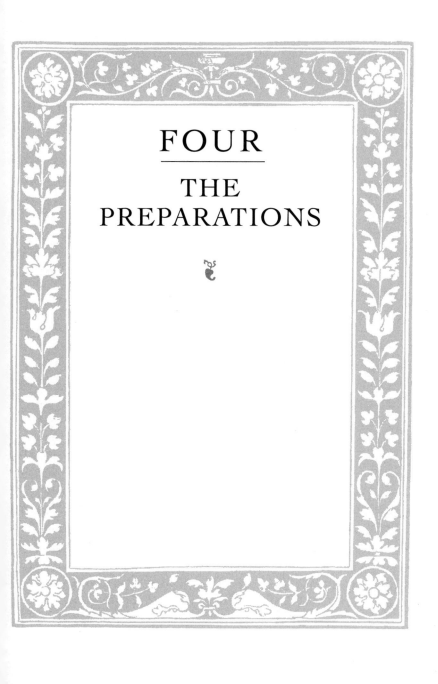

FOUR

THE
PREPARATIONS

DIDN'T even know this chapter existed until I began the 'good parts' version. All my father used to say at this point was, 'What with one thing and another, three years passed,' and then he'd explain how the day came when Buttercup was officially introduced to the world as the coming queen, and how the Great Square of Florin City was filled as never before, awaiting her introduction, and by then, he was into the terrific business dealing with the kidnapping.

Would you believe that in the original Morgenstern this is the longest single chapter in the book?

Fifteen pages about how Humperdinck can't marry a common subject, so they fight and argue with the nobles and finally make Buttercup Princess of Hammersmith, which was this little lump of land attached to the rear of King Lotharon's holdings.

Then the miracle man began improving King Lotharon, and eighteen pages are used up in describing the cures. (Morgenstern hated doctors, and was always bitter when they outlawed miracle men from working in Florin proper.)

And seventy-two — count 'em — seventy-two pages on the training of a princess. He follows Buttercup day to day, month to month, as she learns all the ways of curtsying and tea pouring and how to address visiting nabobs and like that. All this in a satiric vein, naturally, since Morgenstern hated royalty more even than doctors.

But from a narrative point of view, in 105 pages nothing happens. Except this: 'What with one thing and another, three years passed.'

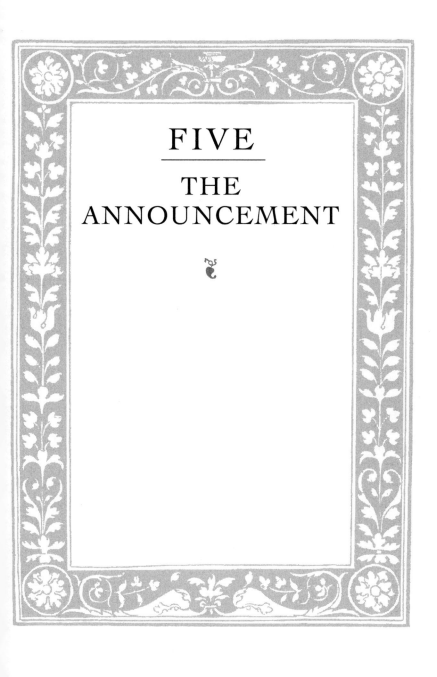

FIVE

THE ANNOUNCEMENT

HE Great Square of Florin City was filled as never before, awaiting the introduction of Prince Humperdinck's bride-to-be, Princess Buttercup of Hammersmith. The crowd had begun forming some forty hours earlier, but up to twenty-four hours before, there were still fewer than one thousand. But then, as the moment of introduction grew nearer, from across the country the people came. None had ever seen the Princess, but rumors of her beauty were continual and each was less possible than the one before.

At noontime, Prince Humperdinck appeared at the balcony of his father's castle and raised his arms. The crowd, which by now was at the danger size, slowly quieted. There were stories that the King was dying, that he was already dead, that he had been dead long since, that he was fine.

"My people, my beloveds, from whom we draw our strength, today is a day of greeting. As you must have heard, my honored father's health is not what it once was. He is, of course, ninety-seven, so who can ask more. As you also know, Florin needs a male heir."

The crowd began to stir now—it was to be this lady they had heard so much about.

"In three months, our country celebrates its five hundredth anniversary. To celebrate that celebration, I shall, on that sundown, take for my wife the Princess Buttercup of Hammersmith. You do not know her yet. But you will meet her now," and he made a sweeping gesture and the balcony doors swung open and Buttercup moved out beside him on the balcony.

And the crowd, quite literally, gasped.

The twenty-one-year-old Princess far surpassed the eighteen-year-old mourner. Her figure faults were gone, the too bony elbow having fleshed out nicely; the opposite pudgy wrist could not have been trimmer. Her hair, which was once the color of autumn, was still the color of autumn, except that before, she had tended it herself, whereas now she had five full-time hairdressers who managed things for her. (This was long after hairdressers; in truth, ever since there have been women, there have been hairdressers, Adam being the first, though the King James scholars do their very best to muddy this point.) Her skin was still wintry cream, but now, with two handmaidens assigned to each appendage and four for the rest of her, it actually, in certain lights, seemed to provide her with a gentle, continually moving as she moved, glow.

Prince Humperdinck took her hand and held it high and the crowd cheered. "That's enough, mustn't risk overexposure," the Prince said, and he started back in toward the castle.

"They have waited, some of them, so long," Buttercup answered. "I would like to walk among them."

"We do not walk among commoners unless it is unavoidable," the Prince said.

"I have known more than a few commoners in my time," Buttercup told him. "They will not, I think, harm me."

And with that she left the balcony, reappeared a moment later on the great steps of the castle and, quite alone, walked open-armed down into the crowd.

Wherever she went, the people parted. She crossed and re-crossed the Great Square and always, ahead of her, the people swept apart to let her pass. Buttercup continued, moving slowly and smiling, alone, like some land messiah.

Most of the people there would never forget that day. None of them, of course, had ever been so close to perfection, and the great majority adored her instantly. There were, to be sure, some who, while admitting she was pleasing enough, were withholding judgment as to her quality as a queen. And, of course, there were some more who were frankly jealous. Very few of them hated her.

And only three of them were planning to murder her.

Buttercup, naturally, knew none of this. She was smiling, and when people wanted to touch her gown, well, let them, and when they wanted to brush their skin against hers, well, let them do that too. She had studied hard to do things royally, and she wanted very much to succeed, so she kept her posture erect and her smile gentle, and that her death was so close would have only made her laugh, if someone had told her.

But—

—in the farthest corner of the Great Square—

—in the highest building in the land—

—deep in the deepest shadow—

—the man in black stood waiting.

His boots were black and leather. His pants were black and his shirt. His mask was black, blacker than raven. But blackest of all were his flashing eyes.

Flashing and cruel and deadly . . .

*   *   *

BUTTERCUP WAS MORE than a little weary after her triumph. The touching of the crowds had exhausted her, so she rested a bit, and then, toward midafternoon, she changed into her riding clothes and went to fetch Horse. This was the one aspect of her life that had not changed in the years preceding. She still loved to ride, and every afternoon, weather permitting or not, she rode alone for several hours in the wild land beyond the castle.

She did her best thinking then.

Not that her best thinking ever expanded horizons. Still, she told herself, she was not a dummy either, so as long as she kept her thoughts to herself, well, where was the harm?

As she rode through woods and streams and heather, her brain was awhirl. The walk through the crowds had moved her, and in a way most strange. For even though she had done nothing for three years now but train to be a princess and a queen, today was the first day she actually understood that it was all soon to be a reality.

And I just don't like Humperdinck, she thought. It's not that I hate him or anything. I just never *see* him; he's always off someplace or playing in the Zoo of Death.

To Buttercup's way of thinking, there were two main problems: (1) was it wrong to marry without like, and (2) if it was, was it too late to do anything about it.

The answers, to her way of thinking, as she rode along, were: (1) no and (2) yes.

It wasn't wrong to marry someone you didn't like, it just wasn't right either. If the whole world did it, that wouldn't be so great, what with everybody kind of grunting at everybody else as the years went by. But, of course, not everybody did it; so forget about that. The answer to (2) was even easier: she had given her word she would marry; that would have to be enough. True, he had told her quite honestly that if she said "no" he would have to have her disposed of, in order to keep respect for the Crown at its proper level; still, she could have, had she so chosen, said "no."

Everyone had told her, since she became a princess-in-training, that she was very likely the most beautiful woman in the world. Now she was going to be the richest and most powerful as well.

Don't expect too much from life, Buttercup told herself as she rode along. Learn to be satisfied with what you have.

*   *   *

DUSK WAS CLOSING in when Buttercup crested the hill. She was perhaps half an hour from the castle, and her daily ride was three-quarters done. Suddenly she reined Horse, for standing in the dimness beyond was the strangest trio she had ever seen.

The man in front was dark, Sicilian perhaps, with the gentlest face, almost angelic. He had one leg too short, and the makings of a humpback, but he moved forward toward her with surprising speed and nimbleness. The other two remained rooted. The second, also dark, probably Spanish, was as erect and slender as the blade of steel that was attached to his side. The third man, mustachioed, perhaps a Turk, was easily the biggest human being she had ever seen.

"A word?" the Sicilian said, raising his arms. His smile was more angelic than his face.

Buttercup halted. "Speak."

"We are but poor circus performers," the Sicilian explained. "It is dark and we are lost. We were told there was a village nearby that might enjoy our skills."

"You were misinformed," Buttercup told him. "There is no one, not for many miles."

"Then there will be no one to hear you scream," the Sicilian said, and he jumped with frightening agility toward her face.

That was all that Buttercup remembered. Perhaps she did scream, but if she did it was more from terror than anything else, because certainly there was no pain. His hands expertly touched places on her neck, and unconsciousness came.

She awoke to the lapping of water.

She was wrapped in a blanket and the giant Turk was putting her in the bottom of a boat. For a moment she was about to talk, but then when they began talking, she thought it better to listen. And after she had listened for a moment, it got harder and harder to hear. Because of the terrible pounding of her heart.

"I think you should kill her now," the Turk said.

"The less you think, the happier I'll be," the Sicilian answered.

There was the sound of ripping cloth.

"What is that?" the Spaniard asked.

"The same as I attached to her saddle," the Sicilian replied. "Fabric from the uniform of an officer of Guilder."

"I still think—" the Turk began.

"She must be found dead on the Guilder frontier or we will not be paid the remainder of our fee. Is that clear enough for you?"

"I just feel better when I know what's going on, that's all," the Turk mumbled. "People are always thinking I'm so stupid because I'm big and strong and sometimes drool a little when I get excited."

"The reason people think you're so stupid," the Sicilian said, "is because you are so stupid. It has nothing to do with your drooling."

There came the sound of a flapping of sail. "Watch your heads," the Spaniard cautioned, and then the boat was moving. "The people of Florin will not take her death well, I shouldn't think. She has become beloved."

"There will be war," the Sicilian agreed. "We have been paid to start it. It's a fine line of work to be expert in. If we do this perfectly, there will be a continual demand for our services."

"Well I don't like it all that much," the Spaniard said. "Frankly, I wish you had refused."

"The offer was too high."

"I don't like killing a girl," the Spaniard said.

"God does it all the time; if it doesn't bother Him, don't let it worry you."

Through all this, Buttercup had not moved.

The Spaniard said, "Let's just tell her we're taking her away for ransom."

The Turk agreed. "She's so beautiful and she'd go all crazy if she knew."

"She knows already," the Sicilian said. "She's been awake for every word of this."

Buttercup lay under the blanket, not moving. How could he have known that, she wondered.

"How can you be sure?" the Spaniard asked.

"The Sicilian senses all," the Sicilian said.

Conceited, Buttercup thought.

"Yes, very conceited," the Sicilian said.

He must be a *mind* reader, Buttercup thought.

"Are you giving it full sail?" the Sicilian said.

"As much as is safe," the Spaniard answered from the tiller.

"We have an hour on them, so no risks yet. It will take her horse perhaps twenty-seven minutes to reach the castle, a few minutes more for them to figure out what happened and, since we left an obvious trail, they should be after us within an hour. We should reach the Cliffs in fifteen minutes more and, with any luck at all, the Guilder frontier at dawn, when she dies. Her body should be quite warm when the Prince reaches her mutilated form. I only wish we could stay for his grief—it should be Homeric."

Why does he let me know his plans, Buttercup wondered.

"You are going back to sleep now, my lady," the Spaniard said, and his fingers suddenly were touching her temple, her shoulder, her neck, and she was unconscious again. . . .

Buttercup did not know how long she was out, but they were

still in the boat when she blinked, the blanket shielding her. And this time, without daring to think—the Sicilian would have known it somehow—she threw the blanket aside and dove deep into Florin Channel.

She stayed under for as long as she dared and then surfaced, starting to swim across the moonless water with every ounce of strength remaining to her. Behind her in the darkness there were cries.

"Go in, go in!" from the Sicilian.

"I only dog paddle" from the Turk.

"You're better than I am" from the Spaniard.

Buttercup continued to leave them behind her. Her arms ached from effort but she gave them no rest. Her legs kicked and her heart pounded.

"I can hear her kicking," the Sicilian said. "Veer left."

Buttercup went into her breast stroke, silently swimming away.

"Where *is* she?" shrieked the Sicilian.

"The sharks will get her, don't worry," cautioned the Spaniard.

Oh dear, I wish you hadn't mentioned that, thought Buttercup.

"Princess," the Sicilian called, "do you know what happens to sharks when they smell blood in the water? They go mad. There is no controlling their wildness. They rip and shred and chew and devour, and I'm in a boat, Princess, and there isn't any blood in the water now, so we're both quite safe, but there is a knife in my hand, my lady, and if you don't come back I'll cut my arms and I'll cut my legs and I'll catch the blood in a cup and I'll fling it as far as I can and sharks can smell blood in the water for miles and you won't be beautiful for long."

Buttercup hesitated, silently treading water. Around her now, although it was surely her imagination, she seemed to be hearing the swish of giant tails.

"Come back and come back now. There will be no other warning."

Buttercup thought, If I come back, they'll kill me anyway, so what's the difference?

"The difference is—"

There he goes doing that again, thought Buttercup. He really *is* a mind reader.

"—if you come back now," the Sicilian went on, "I give you my word as a gentleman and assassin that you will die totally without pain. I assure you, you will get no such promise from the sharks."

The fish sounds in the night were closer now.

Buttercup began to tremble with fear. She was terribly ashamed of herself but there it was. She only wished she could see for a minute if there really were sharks and if he really would cut himself.

The Sicilian winced out loud.

"He just cut his arm, lady," the Turk called out. "He's catching the blood in a cup now. There must be a half-inch of blood on the bottom."

The Sicilian winced again.

"He cut his leg this time," the Turk went on. "The cup's getting full."

I don't believe them, Buttercup thought. There are no sharks in the water and there is no blood in his cup.

"My arm is back to throw," the Sicilian said. "Call out your location or not, the choice is yours."

I'm not making a peep, Buttercup decided.

"Farewell," from the Sicilian.

There was the splashing sound of liquid landing on liquid.

Then there came a pause.

Then the sharks went mad—

*　　　　*　　　　*

"She does not get eaten by the sharks at this time," my father said.

I looked up at him. "What?"

"You looked like you were getting too involved and bothered so I thought I would let you relax."

"Oh, for Pete's sake," I said, "you'd think I was a baby or something. What kind of stuff is that?" I really sounded put out, but I'll tell you the truth: I was getting a little too involved and I was glad he told me. I mean, when you're a kid, you don't think, Well, since the book's called The Princess Bride *and since we're barely into it, obviously, the author's not about to make shark kibble of his leading lady. You get hooked on things when you're a youngster; so to any youngsters reading, I'll simply repeat my father's words since they worked to soothe me: 'She does not get eaten by the sharks at this time.'*

*   *   *

THEN THE SHARKS went mad. All around her, Buttercup could hear them beeping and screaming and thrashing their mighty tails. Nothing can save me, Buttercup realized. I'm a dead cookie.

Fortunately for all concerned save the sharks, it was around this time that the moon came out.

"There she is," shouted the Sicilian, and like lightning the Spaniard turned the boat and as the boat drew close the Turk reached out a giant arm and then she was back in the safety of her murderers while all around them the sharks bumped each other in wild frustration.

"Keep her warm," the Spaniard said from the tiller, tossing his cloak to the Turk.

"Don't catch cold," the Turk said, wrapping Buttercup into the cloak's folds.

"It doesn't seem to matter all that much," she answered, "seeing you're killing me at dawn."

"He'll do the actual work," the Turk said, indicating the Sicilian, who was wrapping cloth around his cuts. "We'll just hold you."

"Hold your stupid tongue," the Sicilian commanded.

The Turk immediately hushed.

"I don't think he's so stupid," Buttercup said. "And I don't think you're so smart either, with all your throwing blood in the water. That's not what I would call grade-A thinking."

"It worked, didn't it? You're back, aren't you?" The Sicilian crossed toward her. "Once women are sufficiently frightened, they scream."

"But I didn't scream; the moon came out," answered Buttercup somewhat triumphantly.

The Sicilian struck her.

"Enough of that," the Turk said then.

The tiny humpback looked dead at the giant. "Do you want to fight me? I don't think you do."

"No, sir," the Turk mumbled. "No. But don't use force. Please. Force is mine. Strike me if you feel the need. I won't care."

The Sicilian returned to the other side of the boat. "She *would* have screamed," he said. "She was *about* to cry out. My plan was *ideal* as *all* my plans are ideal. It was the moon's ill timing that robbed me of perfection." He scowled unforgivingly at the yellow wedge above them. Then he stared ahead. "There!" The Sicilian pointed. "The Cliffs of Insanity."

And there they were. Rising straight and sheer from the water, a thousand feet into the night. They provided the most direct route between Florin and Guilder, but no one ever used them, sailing instead the long way, many miles around. Not that the Cliffs were impossible to scale; two men were known to have climbed them in the last century alone.

"Sail straight for the steepest part," the Sicilian commanded.

The Spaniard said, "I was."

Buttercup did not understand. Going up the Cliffs could hardly be done, she thought; and no one had ever mentioned secret passages through them. Yet here they were, sailing closer and closer to the mighty rocks, now surely less than a quarter-mile away.

For the first time the Sicilian allowed himself a smile. "All is well. I was afraid your little jaunt in the water was going to cost me too much time. I had allowed an hour of safety. There must still be fifty minutes of it left. We are miles ahead of anybody and safe, safe, safe."

"No one could be following us yet?" the Spaniard asked.

"No one," the Sicilian assured him. "It would be inconceivable."

"Absolutely inconceivable?"

"Absolutely, totally, and, in all other ways, inconceivable," the Sicilian reassured him. "Why do you ask?"

"No reason," the Spaniard replied. "It's only that I just happened to look back and something's there."

They all whirled.

Something was indeed there. Less than a mile behind them across the moonlight was another sailing boat, small, painted what looked like black, with a giant sail that billowed black in the night, and a single man at the tiller. A man in black.

The Spaniard looked at the Sicilian. "It must just be some local fisherman out for a pleasure cruise alone at night through shark-infested waters."

"There is probably a more logical explanation," the Sicilian said. "But since no one in Guilder could know yet what we've done, and no one in Florin could have gotten here so quickly, he is definitely not, however much it may look like it, following us. It is coincidence and nothing more."

"He's gaining on us," the Turk said.

"That is also inconceivable," the Sicilian said. "Before I stole this boat we're in, I made many inquiries as to what was the fastest ship on all of Florin Channel and everyone agreed it was this one."

"You're right," the Turk agreed, staring back. "He isn't gaining on us. He's just getting closer, that's all."

"It is the angle we're looking from and nothing more," said the Sicilian.

Buttercup could not take her eyes from the great black sail. Surely the three men she was with frightened her. But somehow, for reasons she could never begin to explain, the man in black frightened her more.

"All right, look sharp," the Sicilian said then, just a drop of edginess in his voice.

The Cliffs of Insanity were very close now.

The Spaniard maneuvered the craft expertly, which was not easy, and the waves were rolling in toward the rocks now and the spray was blinding. Buttercup shielded her eyes and put her head straight back, staring up into the darkness toward the top, which seemed shrouded and out of reach.

Then the humpback bounded forward, and as the ship reached the cliff face, he jumped up and suddenly there was a rope in his hand.

Buttercup stared in silent astonishment. The rope, thick and strong, seemed to travel all the way up the Cliffs. As she watched, the Sicilian pulled at the rope again and again and it held firm. It was attached to something at the top—a giant rock, a towering tree, something.

"Fast now," the Sicilian ordered. "If he is following us, which of course is not within the realm of human experience, but if he is, we've got to reach the top and cut the rope off before he can climb up after us."

"Climb?" Buttercup said. "I would never be able to—"

"Hush!" the Sicilian ordered her. "Get ready!" he ordered the Spaniard. "Sink it," he ordered the Turk.

And then everyone got busy. The Spaniard took a rope, tied Buttercup's hands and feet. The Turk raised a great leg and stomped down at the center of the boat, which gave way immediately and began to sink. Then the Turk went to the rope and took it in his hands.

"Load me," the Turk said.

The Spaniard lifted Buttercup and draped her body around the Turk's shoulders. Then he tied himself to the Turk's waist. Then the Sicilian hopped, clung to the Turk's neck.

"All aboard," the Sicilian said. (This was before trains, but the expression comes originally from carpenters loading lumber, and this was well after carpenters.)

With that the Turk began to climb. It was at least a thousand feet and he was carrying the three, but he was not worried. When it came to power, nothing worried him. When it came to reading, he got knots in the middle of his stomach, and when it came to writing, he broke out in a cold sweat, and when addition was mentioned or, worse, long division, he always changed the subject right away.

But strength had never been his enemy. He could take the kick of a horse on his chest and not fall backward. He could take a hundred-pound flour sack between his legs and scissor it open without thinking. He had once held an elephant aloft using only the muscles in his back.

But his real might lay in his arms. There had never, not in a thousand years, been arms to match Fezzik's. (For that was his name.) The arms were not only Gargantuan and totally obedient and surprisingly quick, but they were also, and this is why he never worried, tireless. If you gave him an ax and told him to chop down a forest, his legs might give out from having to support so much weight for so long, or the ax might shatter from the punishment of killing so many trees, but Fezzik's arms would be as fresh tomorrow as today.

And so, even with the Sicilian on his neck and the Princess around his shoulders and the Spaniard at his waist, Fezzik did not feel in the least bit put upon. He was actually quite happy, because it was only when he was requested to use his might that he felt he wasn't a bother to everybody.

Up he climbed, arm over arm, arm over arm, two hundred feet now above the water, eight hundred feet now to go.

More than any of them, the Sicilian was afraid of heights. All of his nightmares, and they were never far from him when he slept, dealt with falling. So this terrifying ascension was most difficult for him, perched as he was on the neck of the giant. Or should have been most difficult.

But he would not allow it.

From the beginning, when as a child he realized his humped body would never conquer worlds, he relied on his mind. He trained it, fought it, brought it to heel. So now, three hundred feet in the night and rising higher, while he should have been trembling, he was not.

Instead he was thinking of the man in black.

There was no way anyone could have been quick enough to follow them. And yet from some devil's world that billowing black sail had appeared. How? How? The Sicilian flogged his mind to find an answer, but he found only failure. In wild frustration he took a deep breath and, in spite of his terrible fears, he looked back down toward the dark water.

The man in black was still there, sailing like lightning toward the Cliffs. He could not have been more than a quarter-mile from them now.

"Faster!" the Sicilian commanded.

"I'm sorry," the Turk answered meekly. "I thought I was going faster."

"Lazy, lazy," spurred the Sicilian.

"I'll never improve," the Turk answered, but his arms began to move faster than before. "I cannot see too well because your feet are locked around my face," he went on, "so could you tell me please if we're halfway yet?"

"A little over, I should think," said the Spaniard from his position around the giant's waist. "You're doing wonderfully, Fezzik."

"Thank you," said the giant.

"And he's closing on the Cliffs," added the Spaniard.

No one had to ask who "he" was.

Six hundred feet now. The arms continued to pull, over and over. Six hundred and twenty feet. Six hundred and fifty. Now faster than ever. Seven hundred.

"He's left his boat behind," the Spaniard said. "He's jumped onto our rope. He's starting up after us."

"I can feel him," Fezzik said. "His body weight on the rope."

"He'll never catch up!" the Sicilian cried. "Inconceivable!"

"You keep using that word!" the Spaniard snapped. "I don't think it means what you think it does."

"How fast is he at climbing?" Fezzik said.

"I'm frightened" was the Spaniard's reply.

The Sicilian gathered his courage again and looked down.

The man in black seemed almost to be flying. Already he had cut their lead a hundred feet. Perhaps more.

"I thought you were supposed to be so strong!" the Sicilian shouted. "I thought you were this great mighty thing and yet he gains."

"I'm carrying three people," Fezzik explained. "He has only himself and—"

"Excuses are the refuge of cowards," the Sicilian interrupted. He looked down again. The man in black had gained another hundred feet. He looked up now. The cliff tops were beginning to come into view. Perhaps a hundred and fifty feet more and they were safe.

Tied hand and foot, sick with fear, Buttercup wasn't sure what she wanted to happen. Except this much she knew: she didn't want to go through anything like it again.

"Fly, Fezzik!" the Sicilian screamed. "A hundred feet to go."

Fezzik flew. He cleared his mind of everything but ropes and arms and fingers, and his arms pulled and his fingers gripped and the rope held taut and—

"He's over halfway," the Spaniard said.

"Halfway to doom is where he is," the Sicilian said. "We're fifty feet from safety, and once we're there and I untie the rope . . ." He allowed himself to laugh.

Forty feet.

Fezzik pulled.

Twenty.

Ten.

It was over. Fezzik had done it. They had reached the top of the Cliffs, and first the Sicilian jumped off and then the Turk removed the Princess, and as the Spaniard untied himself, he looked back over the Cliffs.

The man in black was no more than three hundred feet away.

"It seems a shame," the Turk said, looking down alongside the Spaniard. "Such a climber deserves better than—" He stopped talking then.

The Sicilian had untied the rope from its knots around an oak. The rope seemed almost alive, the greatest of all water serpents heading at last for home. It whipped across the cliff tops, spiraled into the moonlit Channel.

The Sicilian was roaring now, and he kept at it until the Spaniard said, "He did it."

"Did what?" The humpback came scurrying to the cliff edge.

"Released the rope in time," the Spaniard said. "See?" He pointed down.

The man in black was hanging in space, clinging to the sheer rock face, seven hundred feet above the water.

The Sicilian watched, fascinated. "You know," he said, "since I've made a study of death and dying and am a great expert, it might interest you to know that he will be dead long before he hits the water. The fall will do it, not the crash."

The man in black dangled helpless in space, clinging to the Cliffs with both hands.

"Oh, how rude we're being," the Sicilian said then, turning to Buttercup. "I'm sure you'd like to watch." He went to her and brought her, still tied hand and foot, so that she could watch the final pathetic struggle of the man in black three hundred feet below.

Buttercup closed her eyes, turned away.

"Shouldn't we be going?" the Spaniard asked. "I thought you were telling us how important time was."

"It is, it is," the Sicilian nodded. "But I just can't miss a death like this. I could stage one of these every week and sell tickets. I could get out of the assassination business entirely. Look at him—do you think his life is passing before his eyes? That's what the books say."

"He has very strong arms," Fezzik commented. "To hold on so long."

"He can't hold on much longer," the Sicilian said. "He has to fall soon."

It was at that moment that the man in black began to climb. Not quickly, of course. And not without great effort. But still, there was no doubt that he was, in spite of the sheerness of the Cliffs, heading in an upward direction.

"Inconceivable!" the Sicilian cried.

The Spaniard whirled on him. "*Stop saying that word.* It was inconceivable that anyone could follow us, but when we looked behind, there was the man in black. It was inconceivable that anyone could sail as fast as we could sail, and yet he gained on us. Now this too is inconceivable, but look—look—" and the Spaniard pointed down through the night. "See how he rises."

The man in black was, indeed, rising. Somehow, in some almost miraculous way, his fingers were finding holds in the crevices, and he was now perhaps fifteen feet closer to the top, farther from death.

The Sicilian advanced on the Spaniard now, his wild eyes glittering at the insubordination. "I have the keenest mind that has ever been turned to unlawful pursuits," he began, "so when I tell you something, it is not guesswork; it is fact! And the fact is that the man in black is *not* following us. A more logical explanation would be that he is simply an ordinary sailor who dabbles in mountain climbing as a hobby who happens to have the same general final destination as we do. That certainly satisfies me and I hope it satisfies you. In any case, we cannot take the risk of his seeing us with the Princess, and therefore one of you must kill him."

"Shall I do it?" the Turk wondered.

The Sicilian shook his head. "No, Fezzik," he said finally. "I need your strength to carry the girl. Pick her up now and let us hurry along." He turned to the Spaniard. "We'll be heading directly for the frontier of Guilder. Catch up as quickly as you can once he's dead."

The Spaniard nodded.

The Sicilian hobbled away.

The Turk hoisted the Princess, began following the humpback. Just before he lost sight of the Spaniard he turned and hollered, "Catch up quickly."

"Don't I always?" The Spaniard waved. "Farewell, Fezzik."

"Farewell, Inigo," the Turk replied. And then he was gone, and the Spaniard was alone.

Inigo moved to the cliff edge and knelt with his customary quick grace. Two hundred and fifty feet below him now, the man in black continued his painful climb. Inigo lay flat, staring down, trying to pierce the moonlight and find the climber's secret. For a long while, Inigo did not move. He was a good learner, but not a particularly fast one, so he had to study. Finally, he realized that somehow, by some mystery, the man in black was making fists and jamming them into the rocks, and using them for support. Then he would reach up with his other hand, until he found a high split in the rock, and make another fist and jam it in. Whenever he could find support for his feet, he would use it, but mostly it was the jammed fists that made the climbing possible.

Inigo marveled. What a truly extraordinary adventurer this man in black must be. He was close enough now for Inigo to realize that the man was masked, a black hood covering all but his features. Another outlaw? Perhaps. Then why should they have to fight and for what? Inigo shook his head. It was a shame that such a fellow must die, but he had his orders, so there it was. Sometimes he did not like the Sicilian's commands, but what could he do? Without the brains of the Sicilian, he, Inigo, would never be able to command jobs of this caliber. The Sicilian was a master planner. Inigo was a creature of the moment. The Sicilian said "kill him," so why waste sympathy on the man in black. Someday someone would kill Inigo, and the world would not stop to mourn.

He stood now, quickly jumping to his feet, his blade-thin body ready. For action. Only, the man in black was still many feet away. There was nothing to do but wait for him. Inigo hated waiting. So to make the time more pleasant, he pulled from the scabbard his great, his only, love:

The six-fingered sword.

How it danced in the moonlight. How glorious and true. Inigo brought it to his lips and with all the fervor in his great Spanish heart kissed the metal. . . .

INIGO

I N THE MOUNTAINS of Central Spain, set high in the hills above Toledo, was the village of Arabella. It was very small and the air was always clear. That was all you could say that was good about Arabella: terrific air—you could see for miles.

But there was no work, the dogs overran the streets and there was never enough food. The air, clear enough, was also too hot in daylight, freezing at night. As to Inigo's personal life, he was always just a trifle hungry, he had no brothers or sisters, and his mother had died in childbirth.

He was fantastically happy.

Because of his father. Domingo Montoya was funny-looking and crotchety and impatient and absent-minded and never smiled.

Inigo loved him. Totally. Don't ask why. There really wasn't any one reason you could put your finger on. Oh, probably Domingo loved him back, but love is many things, none of them logical.

Domingo Montoya made swords. If you wanted a fabulous sword, did you go to Domingo Montoya? If you wanted a great balanced piece of work, did you go to the mountains behind Toledo? If you wanted a masterpiece, a sword for the ages, was it Arabella that your footsteps led you to?

Nope.

You went to Madrid, because Madrid was where lived the famous Yeste, and if you had the money and he had the time, you got your weapon. Yeste was fat and jovial and one of the richest and most honored men in the city. And he should have been. He made wonderful swords, and noblemen bragged to each other when they owned an original Yeste.

But sometimes—not often, mind you, maybe once a year, maybe less—a request would come in for a weapon that was more than even Yeste could make. When that happened, did Yeste say, "Alas, I am sorry, I cannot do it"?

Nope.

What he said was, "Of course, I'd be delighted, fifty per cent down payment please, the rest before delivery, come back in a year, thank you very much."

The next day he would set out for the hills behind Toledo.

"So, Domingo," Yeste would call out when he reached Inigo's father's hut.

"So, Yeste," Domingo Montoya would return from the hut doorway.

Then the two men would embrace and Inigo would come running up and Yeste would rumple his hair and then Inigo would make tea while the two men talked.

"I need you," Yeste would always begin.

Domingo would grunt.

"This very week I have accepted a commission to make a sword for a member of the Italian nobility. It is to be jewel encrusted at the handle and the jewels are to spell out the name of his present mistress and—"

"No."

That single word and that alone. But it was enough. When Domingo Montoya said "no" it meant nothing else but.

Inigo, busy with the tea, knew what would happen now: Yeste would use his charm.

"No."

Yeste would use his wealth.

"No."

His wit, his wonderful gift for persuasion.

"No."

He would beg, entreat, promise, pledge.

"No."

Insults. Threats.

"No."

Finally, genuine tears.

"No. More tea, Yeste?"

"Perhaps another cup, thank you—" Then, big: "WHY WON'T YOU?"

Inigo hurried to refill their cups so as never to miss a word. He knew they had been brought up together, had known each other sixty years, had never not loved one another deeply, and it thrilled him when he could hear them arguing. That was the strange thing: arguing was all they ever did.

"Why? My fat friend asks me why? He sits there on his world-class ass and has the nerve to ask me why? Yeste. Come to me sometime with a challenge. Once, just once, ride up and say, 'Domingo, I need a sword for an eighty-year-old man to fight a duel,' and I would embrace you and cry 'Yes!' Because to make a sword for an eighty-year-old man to survive a duel, that would be something. Because the sword would have to be strong enough to win, yet light enough not to tire his weary arm. I would have to use my all to perhaps find an unknown metal, strong but very light, or devise a different formula for a known one, mix some bronze with some iron and some air in a way ignored for a thousand years. I would kiss your smelly feet for an opportunity like that, fat Yeste. But to make a stupid sword with stupid jewels in the form of stupid initials so some stupid Italian can thrill his stupid mistress, no. That, I will not do."

"For the last time I ask you. Please."

"For the last time I tell you, I am sorry. No."

"I gave my word the sword would be made," Yeste said. "I cannot make it. In all the world no one can but you, and you say no. Which means I have gone back on a commitment. Which means I have lost my honor. Which means that since honor is the only thing in the world I care about, and since I cannot live without it, I must die. And since you are my dearest friend, I may as well die now, with you, basking in the warmth of your affection." And here Yeste would pull out a knife. It was a magnificent thing, a gift from Domingo on Yeste's wedding day.

"Good-by, little Inigo," Yeste would say then. "God grant you your quota of smiles."

It was forbidden for Inigo to interrupt.

"Good-by, little Domingo," Yeste would say then. "Although I die in your hut, and although it is your own stubborn fault that causes my ceasing, in other words, even though you are killing me, don't think twice about it. I love you as I always have and God forbid your conscience should give you any trouble." He pulled open his coat, brought the knife closer, closer. *The pain is worse than I imagined!*" Yeste cried.

"How can it hurt when the point of the weapon is still an inch away from your belly?" Domingo asked.

"I'm anticipating, don't bother me, let me die unpestered." He brought the point to his skin, pushed.

Domingo grabbed the knife away. "Someday I won't stop you," he said. "Inigo, set an extra place for supper."

"I was all set to kill myself, truly."

"Enough dramatics."

"What is on the menu for the evening?"

"The usual gruel."

"Inigo, go check and see if there's anything by chance in my carriage outside."

There was always a feast waiting in the carriage.

And after the food and the stories would come the departure, and always, before the departure, would come the request. "We would be partners," Yeste would say. "In Madrid. My name before yours on the sign, of course, but equal partners in all things."

"No."

"All right. Your name before mine. You are the greatest sword maker, you deserve to come first."

"Have a good trip back."

"WHY WON'T YOU?"

"Because, my friend Yeste, you are very famous and very rich, and so you should be, because you make wonderful weapons. But you must also make them for any fool who happens along. I am poor, and no one knows me in all the world except you and Inigo, but I do not have to suffer fools."

"You are an artist," Yeste said.

"No. Not yet. A craftsman only. But I dream to be an artist. I pray that someday, if I work with enough care, if I am very very lucky, I will make a weapon that is a work of art. Call me an artist then, and I will answer."

Yeste entered his carriage. Domingo approached the window, whispered: "I remind you only of this: when you get this jeweled initialed sword, claim it as your own. Tell no one of my involvement."

"Your secret is safe with me."

Embraces and waves. The carriage would leave. And that was the way of life before the six-fingered sword.

Inigo remembered exactly the moment it began. He was making lunch for them—his father always, from the time he was six, let him do the cooking—when a heavy knocking came on the hut door. "Inside there," a voice boomed. "Be quick about it."

Inigo's father opened the door. "Your servant," he said.

"You are a sword maker," came the booming voice. "Of distinction. I have heard that this is true."

"If only it were," Domingo replied. "But I have no great skills. Mostly I do repair work. Perhaps if you had a dagger blade that was dulling, I might be able to please you. But anything more is beyond me."

Inigo crept up behind his father and peeked out. The booming voice belonged to a powerful man with dark hair and broad shoulders who sat upon an elegant brown horse. A nobleman clearly, but Inigo could not tell the country.

"I desire to have made for me the greatest sword since Excalibur."

"I hope your wishes are granted," Domingo said. "And now, if you please, our lunch is almost ready and—"

"I do not give you permission to move. You stay right exactly where you are or risk my wrath, which, I must tell you in advance, is considerable. My temper is murderous. Now, what were you saying about your lunch?"

"I was saying that it will be hours before it is ready; I have nothing to do and would not dream of budging."

"There are rumors," the nobleman said, "that deep in the hills behind Toledo lives a genius. The greatest sword maker in all the world."

"He visits here sometimes—that must be your mistake. But his name is Yeste and he lives in Madrid."

"I will pay five hundred pieces of gold for my desires," said the big-shouldered noble.

"That is more money than all the men in all this village will earn in all their lives," said Domingo. "Truly, I would love to accept your offer. But I am not the man you seek."

"These rumors lead me to believe that Domingo Montoya would solve my problem."

"What is your problem?"

"I am a great swordsman. But I cannot find a weapon to match my peculiarities, and therefore I am deprived of reaching my highest skills. If I had a weapon to match my peculiarities, there would be no one in all the world to equal me."

"What are these peculiarities you speak of?"

The noble held up his right hand.

Domingo began to grow excited.

The man had six fingers.

"You see?" the noble began.

"Of course," Domingo interrupted, "the balance of the sword is wrong for you because every balance has been conceived of for five. The grip of every handle cramps you, because it has been built for five. For an ordinary swordsman it would not matter, but a great swordsman, a master, would have eventual discomfort. And the greatest swordsman in the world must always be at ease. The grip of his weapon must be as natural as the blink of his eye, and cause him no more thought."

"Clearly, you understand the difficulties—" the nobleman began again.

But Domingo had traveled where others' words could never reach him. Inigo had never seen his father so frenzied. "The measurements . . . of course . . . each finger and the circumference of the wrist, and the distance from the sixth nail to the index pad . . . so many measurements . . . and your preferences . . . Do you prefer to slash or cut? If you slash, do you prefer the right-to-left movement or perhaps the parallel? . . . When you cut, do you enjoy an upward thrust, and how much power do you wish to come from the shoulder, how much from the wrist? . . . and do you wish your point coated so as to enter more easily or do you enjoy seeing the opponent's wince? . . . So much to be done, so much to be done . . ." and on and on he went until the noble dismounted and had to almost take him by the shoulders to quiet him.

"You are the man of the rumors."

Domingo nodded.

"And you will make me the greatest sword since Excalibur."

"I will beat my body into ruins for you. Perhaps I will fail. But no one will try harder."

"And payment?"

"When you get the sword, then payment. Now let me get to work measuring. Inigo—my instruments."

Inigo scurried into the darkest corner of the hut.

"I insist on leaving something on account."

"It is not necessary; I may fail."

"*I insist.*"

"All right. One goldpiece. Leave that. But do not bother me with money when there is work that needs beginning."

The noble took out one piece of gold.

Domingo put it in a drawer and left it, without even a glance.

"Feel your fingers now," he commanded. "Rub your hands hard, shake your fingers—you will be excited when you duel and this handle must match your hand in that excitement; if I measured when you were relaxed, there would be a difference, as much as a thousandth of an inch and that would rob us of perfection. And that is what I seek. Perfection. I will not rest for less."

The nobleman had to smile. "And how long will it take to reach it?"

"Come back in a year," Domingo said, and with that he set to work.

Such a year.

Domingo slept only when he dropped from exhaustion. He ate only when Inigo would force him to. He studied, fretted, complained. He never should have taken the job; it was impossible. The next day he would be flying: he never should have taken the job; it was too simple to be worth his labors. Joy to despair, joy to despair, day to day, hour to hour. Sometimes Inigo would wake to find him weeping: "What is it, Father?" "It is that I cannot do it. I cannot make the sword. I cannot make my hands obey me. I would kill myself except what would you do then?" "Go to sleep, Father." "No, I don't need sleep. Failures don't need sleep. Anyway, I slept yesterday." "Please, Father, a little nap." "All right; a few minutes; to keep you from nagging."

Some nights Inigo would awake to see him dancing. "What is it, Father?" "It is that I have found my mistakes, corrected my misjudgments." "Then it will be done soon, Father?" "It will be done tomorrow and it will be a miracle." "You are wonderful, Father." "I'm more wonderful than wonderful, how dare you insult me."

But the next night, more tears. "What is it now, Father?" "The sword, the sword, I cannot make the sword." "But last night, Father, you said you had found your mistakes." "I was mistaken;

tonight I found new ones, worse ones. I am the most wretched of creatures. Say you wouldn't mind it if I killed myself so I could end this existence." "But I would mind, Father. I love you and I would die if you stopped breathing." "You don't really love me; you're only speaking pity." "Who could pity the greatest sword maker in the history of the world?" "Thank you, Inigo." "You're welcome, Father." "I love you back, Inigo." "Sleep, Father." "Yes. Sleep."

A whole year of that. A year of the handle being right, but the balance being wrong, of the balance being right, but the cutting edge too dull, of the cutting edge sharpened, but that threw the balance off again, of the balance returning, but now the point was fat, of the point regaining sharpness, only now the entire blade was too short and it all had to go, all had to be thrown out, all had to be done again. Again. Again. Domingo's health began to leave him. He was fevered always now, but he forced his frail shell on, because this had to be the finest since Excalibur. Domingo was battling legend, and it was destroying him.

Such a year.

One night Inigo woke to find his father seated. Staring. Calm. Inigo followed the stare.

The six-fingered sword was done.

Even in the hut's darkness, it glistened.

"At last," Domingo whispered. He could not take his eyes from the glory of the sword. "After a lifetime. Inigo. Inigo. I am an artist."

The big-shouldered nobleman did not agree. When he returned to purchase the sword, he merely looked at it a moment. "Not worth waiting for," he said.

Inigo stood in the corner of the hut, watching, holding his breath.

"You are disappointed?" Domingo could scarcely get the words spoken.

"I'm not saying it's trash, you understand," the nobleman went on. "But it's certainly not worth five hundred pieces of gold. I'll give you ten; it's probably worth that."

"Wrong!" Domingo cried. "It is not worth ten. It is not worth even one. Here." And he threw open the drawer where the one goldpiece had lain untouched the year. "The gold is yours. All of it. You have lost nothing." He took back the sword and turned away.

"'I'll take the sword," the nobleman said. "I didn't say I wouldn't take it. I only said I would pay what it was worth."

Domingo whirled back, eyes bright. "You quibbled. You haggled. Art was involved and you saw only money. Beauty was here for the taking and you saw only your fat purse. You have lost nothing; there is no more reason for your remaining here. Please go."

"The sword," the noble said.

"The sword belongs to my son," Domingo said. "I give it to him now. It is forever his. Good-by."

"You're a peasant and a fool and I want my sword."

"You're an enemy of art and I pity your ignorance," Domingo said.

They were the last words he ever uttered.

The noble killed him then, with no warning; a flash of the nobleman's sword and Domingo's heart was torn to pieces.

Inigo screamed. He could not believe it; it had not happened. He screamed again. His father was fine; soon they would have tea. He could not stop screaming.

The village heard. Twenty men were at the door. The nobleman pushed his way through them. "That man attacked me. See? He holds a sword. He attacked me and I defended myself. Now move from my way."

It was lies, of course, and everyone knew it. But he was a noble so what was there to do? They parted, and the nobleman mounted his horse.

"Coward!"

The nobleman whirled.

"Pig!"

Again the crowd parted.

Inigo stood there, holding the six-fingered sword, repeating his words: "Coward. Pig. Killer."

"Someone tend the babe before he oversteps himself," the noble said to the crowd.

Inigo ran forward then, standing in front of the nobleman's horse, blocking the nobleman's path. He raised the six-fingered sword with both his hands and cried, "I, Inigo Montoya, do challenge you, coward, pig, killer, ass, fool, to battle."

"Get him out of my way. Move the infant."

"The infant is ten and he stays," Inigo said.

"Enough of your family is dead for one day; be content," said the noble.

"When you beg me for your breath, then I shall be contented. Now *dismount!*"

The nobleman dismounted.

"Draw your sword."

The nobleman unsheathed his killing weapon.

"I dedicate your death to my father," Inigo said. "Begin."

They began.

It was no match, of course. Inigo was disarmed in less than a minute. But for the first fifteen seconds or so, the noble was uneasy. During those fifteen seconds, strange thoughts crossed his mind. For even at the age of ten, Inigo's genius was there.

Disarmed, Inigo stood very straight. He said not a word, begged nothing.

"I'm not going to kill you," the nobleman said. "Because you have talent and you're brave. But you're also lacking in manners, and that's going to get you in trouble if you're not careful. So I shall help you as you go through life, by leaving you with a reminder that bad manners are to be avoided." And with that his blade flashed. Two times.

And Inigo's face began to bleed. Two rivers of blood poured from his forehead to his chin, one crossing each cheek. Everyone watching knew it then: the boy was scarred for life.

Inigo would not fall. The world went white behind his eyes but he would not go to ground. The blood continued to pour. The nobleman replaced his sword, remounted, rode on.

It was only then that Inigo allowed the darkness to claim him.

He awoke to Yeste's face.

"I was beaten," Inigo whispered. "I failed him."

Yeste could only say, "Sleep."

Inigo slept. The bleeding stopped after a day and the pain stopped after a week. They buried Domingo, and for the first and last time Inigo left Arabella. His face bandaged, he rode in Yeste's carriage to Madrid, where he lived in Yeste's house, obeyed Yeste's commands. After a month, the bandages were removed, but the scars were still deep red. Eventually, they softened some, but they always remained the chief features of Inigo's face: the giant parallel scars running one on each side, from temple to chin. For two years, Yeste cared for him.

Then one morning, Inigo was gone. In his place were three words: "I must learn" on a note pinned to his pillow.

Learn? Learn what? What existed beyond Madrid that the child had to commit to memory? Yeste shrugged and sighed. It was beyond him. There was no understanding children any more. Everything was changing too fast and the young were different. Beyond him, beyond him, life was beyond him, the world was beyond him, you name it, it was beyond him. He was a fat man who made swords. That much he knew.

So he made more swords and he grew fatter and the years went by. As his figure spread, so did his fame. From all across the world they came, begging him for weapons, so he doubled his prices because he didn't want to work too hard any more, he was getting old, but when he doubled his prices, when the news spread from duke to prince to king, they only wanted him the more desperately. Now the wait was two years for a sword and the line-up of royalty was unending and Yeste was growing tired, so he doubled his prices again, and when that didn't stop them, he decided to triple his already doubled and redoubled prices and besides that, all work had to be paid for in jewels in advance and the wait was up to three years, but nothing would stop them. They had to have swords by Yeste or nothing, and even though the work on the finest was nowhere what it once was (Domingo, after all, no longer could save him) the silly rich men didn't notice. All they wanted was his weapons and they fell over each other with jewels for him.

Yeste grew very rich.

And *very* heavy.

Every part of his body sagged. He had the only fat thumbs in Madrid. Dressing took an hour, breakfast the same, everything went slowly.

But he could still make swords. And people still craved them. "I'm sorry," he said to the young Spaniard who entered his shop one particular morning. "The wait is up to four years and even I am embarrassed to mention the price. Have your weapon made by another."

"I have my weapon," the Spaniard said.

And he threw the six-fingered sword across Yeste's workbench.

Such embraces.

"Never leave again," Yeste said. "I eat too much when I'm lonely."

"I cannot stay," Inigo told him. "I'm only here to ask you one question. As you know, I have spent the last ten years learning. Now I have come for you to tell me if I'm ready."

"Ready? For what? What in the world have you been learning?"

"The sword."

"Madness," said Yeste. "You have spent ten entire years just learning to fence?"

"No, not *just* learning to fence," Inigo answered. "I did many other things as well."

"Tell me."

"Well," Inigo began, "ten years is what? About thirty-six hundred days. And that's about—I figured this out once, so I remember pretty well—about eighty-six thousand hours. Well, I always made it a point to get four hours sleep per night. That's fourteen thousand hours right there, leaving me perhaps seventy-two thousand hours to account for."

"You slept. I'm with you. What else?"

"Well, I squeezed rocks."

"I'm sorry, my hearing sometimes fails me; it sounded like you said you squeezed rocks."

"To make my wrists strong. So I could control the sword. Rocks like apples. That size. I would squeeze them in each hand for perhaps two hours a day. And I would spend another two hours a day in skipping and dodging and moving quickly, so that my feet would be able to get me into position to deliver properly the thrust of the sword. That's another fourteen thousand hours. I'm down to fifty-eight thousand now. Well, I always sprinted two hours each day as fast as I could, so my legs, as well as being quick, would also be strong. And that gets me down to about fifty thousand hours."

Yeste examined the young man before him. Blade thin, six feet in height, straight as a sapling, bright eyed, taut; even motionless he seemed whippet quick. "And these last fifty thousand hours? These have been spent studying the sword?"

Inigo nodded.

"Where?"

"Wherever I could find a master. Venice, Bruges, Budapest."

"I could have taught you here?"

"True. But you care for me. You would not have been ruthless. You would have said, 'Excellent parry, Inigo, now that's enough for one day; let's have supper.'"

"That does sound like me," Yeste admitted. "But why was it so important? Why was it worth so much of your life?"

"Because I could not fail him again."

"Fail who?"

"My father. I have spent all these years preparing to find the six-fingered man and kill him in a duel. But he is a master, Yeste. He said as much and I saw the way his sword flew at Domingo. I must not lose that duel when I find him, so now I have come to you. You know swords and swordsmen. You must not lie. Am I ready? If you say I am, I will seek him through the world. If you say no, I will spend another ten years and another ten after that, if that is needed."

So they went to Yeste's courtyard. It was late morning. Hot. Yeste put his body in a chair and the chair in the shade. Inigo stood waiting in the sunshine. "We need not test desire and we know you have sufficient motive to deliver the death blow," Yeste said. "Therefore we need only probe your knowledge and speed and stamina. We need no enemy for this. The enemy is always in the mind. Visualize him."

Inigo drew his sword.

"The six-fingered man taunts you," Yeste called. "Do what you can."

Inigo began to leap around the courtyard, the great blade flashing.

"He uses the Agrippa defense," Yeste shouted.

Immediately, Inigo shifted position, increased the speed of his sword.

"Now he surprises you with Bonetti's attack."

But Inigo was not surprised for long. Again his feet shifted; he moved his body a different way. Perspiration was pouring down his thin frame now and the great blade was blinding. Yeste continued to shout. Inigo continued to shift. The blade never stopped.

At three in the afternoon, Yeste said, "Enough. I am exhausted from the watching."

Inigo sheathed the six-fingered sword and waited.

"You wish to know if I feel you are ready to duel to the death a man ruthless enough to kill your father, rich enough to buy protection, older and more experienced, an acknowledged master."

Inigo nodded.

"I'll tell you the truth, and it's up to you to live with it. First, there has never been a master as young as you. Thirty years at least before that rank has yet been reached, and you are barely twenty-two. Well, the truth is you are an impetuous boy driven by madness and you are not now and you will never be a master."

"Thank you for your honesty," Inigo said. "I must tell you I had hoped for better news. I find it very hard to speak just now, so if you'll please excuse me, I'll be on my—"

"I had not finished," Yeste said.

"What else is there to say?"

"I loved your father very dearly, that you know, but this you did not know: when we were very young, not yet twenty, we saw, with our own eyes, an exhibition by the Corsican Wizard, Bastia."

"I know of no wizards."

"It is the rank beyond master in swordsmanship," Yeste said. "Bastia was the last man so designated. Long before your birth, he died at sea. There have been no wizards since, and you would never in this world have beaten him. But I tell you this: he would never in this world have beaten you."

Inigo stood silent for a long time. "I am ready then."

"I would not enjoy being the six-fingered man" was all Yeste replied.

The next morning, Inigo began the track-down. He had it all carefully prepared in his mind. He would find the six-fingered man. He would go up to him. He would say simply, "Hello, my name is Inigo Montoya, you killed my father, prepare to die," and then, oh then, the duel.

It was a lovely plan really. Simple, direct. No frills. In the beginning, Inigo had all kinds of wild vengeance notions, but gradually, simplicity had seemed the better way. Originally, he had all kinds of little plays worked out in his mind—the enemy would weep and beg, the enemy would cringe and cry, the enemy would bribe and slobber and act in every way unmanly. But eventually, these too gave way in his mind to simplicity: the enemy would simply say, "Oh, yes, I remember killing him; I'll be only too delighted to kill you too."

Inigo had only one problem: he could not find the enemy.

It never occurred to him there would be the least difficulty. After all, how many noblemen were there with six fingers on their right hands? Surely, it would be the talk of whatever his vicinity happened to be. A few questions: "Pardon, I'm not crazy, but have you seen any six-fingered noblemen lately?" and surely sooner or later, there would be an answering "yes."

But it didn't come sooner.

And later wasn't the kind of thing you wanted to hold your breath for either.

The first month wasn't all that discouraging. Inigo crisscrossed Spain and Portugal. The second month he moved to France and spent the rest of the year there. The year following that was his Italian year, and then came Germany and the whole of Switzerland.

It was only after five solid years of failure that he began to worry. By then he had seen all of the Balkans and most of Scandinavia and had visited the Florinese and the natives of Guilder and into Mother Russia and down step by step around the entire Mediterranean.

By then he knew what had happened: ten years learning was ten years too long; too much had been allowed to happen. The six-fingered man was probably crusading in Asia. Or getting rich in America. Or a hermit in the East Indies. Or . . . or . . .

Dead?

Inigo, at the age of twenty-seven, began having a few extra glasses of wine at night, to help him get to sleep. At twenty-eight, he was having a few extra glasses to help him digest his lunch. At twenty-nine, the wine was essential to wake him in the morning. His world was collapsing around him. Not only was he living in daily failure, something almost as dreadful was beginning to happen:

Fencing was beginning to bore him.

He was simply too good. He would make his living during his travels by finding the local champion wherever he happened to be, and they would duel, and Inigo would disarm him and accept whatever they happened to bet. And with his winnings he would pay for his food and his lodging and his wine.

But the local champions were nothing. Even in the big cities, the local experts were nothing. Even in the capital cities, the local masters were nothing. There was no competition, nothing to help him keep an edge. His life began to seem pointless, his quest pointless, everything, everything, without reason.

At thirty he gave up the ghost. He stopped his search, forgot to eat, slept only on occasion. He had his wine for company and that was enough.

He was a shell. The greatest fencing machine since the Corsican Wizard was barely even practicing the sword.

He was in that condition when the Sicilian found him.

At first the little hunchback only supplied him with stronger wine. But then, through a combination of praise and nudging, the Sicilian began to get him off the bottle. Because the Sicilian had a dream: with his guile plus the Turk's strength plus the Spaniard's sword, they might become the most effective criminal organization in the civilized world.

Which is precisely what they became.

In dark places, their names whipped sharper than fear; everyone had needs that were hard to fulfill. The Sicilian Crowd (two was company, three a crowd, even then) became more and more famous and more and more rich. Nothing was beyond or beneath them. Inigo's blade was flashing again, more than ever like lightning. The Turk's strength grew more prodigious with the months.

But the hunchback was the leader. There was never doubt. Without him, Inigo knew where he would be: on his back begging wine in some alley entrance. The Sicilian's word was not just law, it was gospel.

So when he said, "Kill the man in black," all other possibilities ceased to exist. The man in black had to die. . . .

*   *   *

INIGO PACED THE cliff edge, fingers snapping. Fifty feet below him now, the man in black still climbed. Inigo's impatience was beginning to bubble beyond control. He stared down at the slow progress. Find a crevice, jam in the hand, find another crevice, jam in the other hand; forty-eight feet to go. Inigo slapped his sword handle, and his finger snapping began to go faster. He examined the hooded climber, half hoping he would be six-fingered, but no; this one had the proper accompaniment of digits.

Forty-seven feet to go now.

Now forty-six.

"Hello there," Inigo hollered when he could wait no more.

The man in black glanced up and grunted.

"I've been watching you."

The man in black nodded.

"Slow going," Inigo said.

"Look, I don't mean to be rude," the man in black said finally, "but I'm rather busy just now, so try not to distract me."

"I'm sorry," Inigo said.

The man in black grunted again.

"I don't suppose you could speed things up," Inigo said.

"If you want to speed things up so much," the man in black said, clearly quite angry now, "you could lower a rope or a tree branch or find some other helpful thing to do."

"I could do that," Inigo agreed. "But I don't think you would accept my help, since I'm only waiting up here so that I can kill you."

"That does put a damper on our relationship," the man in black said then. "I'm afraid you'll just have to wait."

Forty-three feet left.

Forty-one.

"I could give you my word as a Spaniard," Inigo said.

"No good," the man in black replied. "I've known too many Spaniards."

"I'm going crazy up here," Inigo said.

"Anytime you want to change places, I'd be too happy to accept."

Thirty-nine feet.

And resting.

The man in black just hung in space, feet dangling, the entire weight of his body supported by the strength of his hand jammed into the crevice.

"Come along now," Inigo pleaded.

"It's been a bit of a climb," the man in black explained, "and I'm weary. I'll be fine in a quarter-hour or so."

Another quarter-hour! Inconceivable. "Look, we've got a piece of extra rope up here we didn't need when we made our original climb, I'll just drop it down to you and you grab hold and I'll pull and—"

"No good," the man in black repeated. "You *might* pull, but then again, you also just *might* let go, which, since you're in a hurry to kill me, would certainly do the job quickly."

"But you wouldn't have ever known I was going to kill you if I hadn't been the one to tell you. Doesn't that let you know I can be trusted?"

"Frankly, and I hope you won't be insulted, no."

"There's no way you'll trust me?"

"Nothing comes to mind."

Suddenly Inigo raised his right hand high—"I swear on the soul of Domingo Montoya you will reach the top alive!"

The man in black was silent for a long time. Then he looked up. "I do not know this Domingo of yours, but something in your tone says I must believe you. Throw me the rope."

Inigo quickly tied it around a rock, dropped it over. The man in black grabbed hold, hung suspended alone in space. Inigo pulled. In a moment, the man in black was beside him.

"Thank you," the man in black said, and he sank down on the rock.

Inigo sat alongside him. "We'll wait until you're ready," he said.

The man in black breathed deeply. "Again, thank you."

"Why have you followed us?"

"You carry baggage of much value."

"We have no intention of selling," Inigo said.

"That is your business."

"And yours?"

The man in black made no reply.

Inigo stood and walked away, surveying the terrain over which they would battle. It was a splendid plateau, really, filled with trees for dodging around and roots for tripping over and small rocks for losing your balance on and boulders for leaping off if you could climb on them fast enough, and bathing everything, the entire spot, moonlight. One could not ask for a more suitable testing ground for a duel, Inigo decided. It had everything, including the marvelous Cliffs at one end, beyond which was the wonderful thousand-foot drop, always something to bear in mind when one was planning tactics. It was perfect. The place was perfect.

Provided the man in black could fence.

Really fence.

Inigo did then what he always did before a duel: he took the great sword from its scabbard and touched the side of the blade to his face two times, once along one scar, once along the other.

Then he examined the man in black. A fine sailor, yes; a mighty climber, no question; courageous, without a doubt.

But could he fence?

Really fence?

Please, Inigo thought. It has been so long since I have been tested, let this man test me. Let him be a glorious swordsman. Let him be both quick and fast, smart and strong. Give him a matchless mind for tactics, a background the equal of mine. Please, please, it's been so long: let—him—be—a—*master!*

"I have my breath back now," the man in black said from the rock. "Thank you for allowing me my rest."

"We'd best get on with it then," Inigo replied.

The man in black stood.

"You seem a decent fellow," Inigo said. "I hate to kill you."

"You seem a decent fellow," answered the man in black. "I hate to die."

"But one of us must," Inigo said. *"Begin."*

And so saying he took the six-fingered sword.

And put it into his left hand.

He had begun all his duels left-handed lately. It was good practice for him, and although he was the only living wizard in the world with his regular hand, the right, still, he was more than worthy with his left. Perhaps thirty men alive were his equal when he used his left. Perhaps as many as fifty; perhaps as few as ten.

The man in black was also left-handed and that warmed Inigo; it made things fairer. His weakness against the other man's strength. All to the good.

They touched swords, and the man in black immediately began the Agrippa defense, which Inigo felt was sound, considering the rocky terrain, for the Agrippa kept the feet stationary at first, and made the chances of slipping minimal. Naturally, he countered with Capo Ferro which surprised the man in black, but he defended well, quickly shifting out of Agrippa and taking the attack himself, using the principles of Thibault.

Inigo had to smile. No one had taken the attack against him in so long and it was thrilling! He let the man in black advance, let him build up courage, retreating gracefully between some trees, letting his Bonetti defense keep him safe from harm.

Then his legs flicked and he was behind the nearest tree, and the man in black had not expected it and was slow reacting. Inigo flashed immediately out from the tree, attacking himself now, and the man in black retreated, stumbled, got his balance, continued moving away.

Inigo was impressed with the quickness of the balance return. Most men the size of the man in black would have gone down or, at the least, fallen to one hand. The man in black did neither; he simply quick-stepped, wrenched his body erect, continued fighting.

They were moving parallel to the Cliffs now, and the trees were behind them, mostly. The man in black was slowly being forced toward a group of large boulders, for Inigo was anxious to see how well he moved when quarters were close, when you could not thrust or parry with total freedom. He continued to force, and then the boulders were surrounding them. Inigo suddenly threw his body against a nearby rock, rebounded off it with stunning force, lunging with incredible speed.

First blood was his.

He had pinked the man in black, grazed him only, along the left wrist. A scratch was all. But it was bleeding.

Immediately the man in black hurried his retreat, getting his position away from the boulders, getting out into the open of the plateau. Inigo followed, not bothering to try to check the other man's flight; there would always be time for that later.

Then the man in black launched his greatest assault. It came with no warning and the speed and strength of it were terrifying. His blade flashed in the light again and again, and at first, Inigo was only too delighted to retreat. He was not entirely familiar with the style of the attack; it was mostly McBone, but there were snatches of Capo Ferro thrown in, and he continued moving backward while he concentrated on the enemy, figuring the best way to stop the assault.

The man in black kept advancing, and Inigo was aware that behind him now he was coming closer and closer to the edge of the Cliffs, but that could not have concerned him less. The important thing was to outthink the enemy, find his weakness, let him have his moment of exultation.

Suddenly, as the Cliffs came ever nearer, Inigo realized the fault in the attack that was flashing at him; a simple Thibault maneuver would destroy it entirely, but he didn't want to give it away so soon. Let the other man have the triumph a moment longer; life allowed so few.

The Cliffs were very close behind him now.

Inigo continued to retreat; the man in black continued advancing.

Then Inigo countered with the Thibault.

And the man in black blocked it.

He blocked it!

Inigo repeated the Thibault move and again it didn't work. He switched to Capo Ferro, he tried Bonetti, he went to Fabris; in desperation he began a move used only twice, by Sainct.

Nothing worked!

The man in black kept attacking.

And the Cliffs were almost there.

Inigo never panicked—never came close. But he decided some things very quickly, because there was no time for long consultations, and what he decided was that although the man in black was slow in reacting to moves behind trees, and not much good at all amidst boulders, when movement was restricted, yet out in the open, where there was space, he was a terror. A left-handed black-masked terror. "You are most excellent," he said. His rear foot was at the cliff edge. He could retreat no more.

"Thank you," the man in black replied. "I have worked very hard to become so."

"You are better than I am," Inigo admitted.

"So it seems. But if that is true, then why are you smiling?"

"Because," Inigo answered, "I know something you don't know."

"And what is that?" asked the man in black.

"I'm not left-handed," Inigo replied, and with those words, he all but threw the six-fingered sword into his right hand, and the tide of battle turned.

The man in black retreated before the slashing of the great sword. He tried to side-step, tried to parry, tried to somehow escape the doom that was now inevitable. But there was no way. He could block fifty thrusts; the fifty-first flicked through, and now his left arm was bleeding. He could thwart thirty ripostes, but not the thirty-first, and now his shoulder bled.

The wounds were not yet grave, but they kept on coming as they dodged across the stones, and then the man in black found himself amidst the trees and that was bad for him, so he all but fled before Inigo's onslaught, and then he was in the open again, but Inigo kept coming, nothing could stop him, and then the man in black was back among the boulders, and that was even worse for him than the trees and he shouted out in frustration and practically ran to where there was open space again.

But there was no dealing with the wizard, and slowly, again, the deadly Cliffs became a factor in the fight, only now it was the man in black who was being forced to doom. He was brave, and he was strong, and the cuts did not make him beg for mercy, and he showed no fear behind his black mask. "You are amazing," he cried, as Inigo increased the already blinding speed of the blade.

"Thank you. It has not come without effort."

The death moment was at hand now. Again and again Inigo thrust forward, and again and again the man in black managed to ward off the attacks, but each time it was harder, and the strength in Inigo's wrists was endless and he only thrust the more fiercely and soon the man in black grew weak. "You cannot tell it," he said then, "because I wear a cape and mask. But I am smiling now."

"Why?"

"Because I'm not left-handed either," said the man in black.

And he too switched hands, and now the battle was finally joined. And Inigo began to retreat.

"Who are you?" he screamed.

"No one of import. Another lover of the blade."

"I must know!"

"Get used to disappointment."

They flashed along the open plateau now, and the blades were both invisible, but oh, the Earth trembled, and ohhhh, the skies shook, and Inigo was losing. He tried to make for the trees, but the man in black would have none of it. He tried retreating to the boulders, but that was denied him too.

And in the open, unthinkable as it was, the man in black was superior. Not much. But in a multitude of tiny ways, he was of a slightly higher quality. A hair quicker, a fraction stronger, a speck faster. Not really much at all.

But it was enough.

They met in center plateau for the final assault. Neither man conceded anything. The sound of metal clashing metal rose. A final burst of energy flew through Inigo's veins and he made every attempt, tried every trick, used every hour of every day of his years of experience. But he was blocked. By the man in black. He was shackled. By the man in black. He was baffled, thwarted, muzzled.

Beaten.

By the man in black.

A final flick and the great six-fingered sword went flying from his hand. Inigo stood there, helpless. Then he dropped to his knees, bowed his head, closed his eyes. "Do it quickly," he said.

"May my hands fall from my wrists before I kill an artist like yourself," said the man in black. "I would as soon destroy da Vinci. However"—and here he clubbed Inigo's head with the butt of his sword—"since I can't have you following me either, please understand that I hold you in the highest respect." He struck one more time and the Spaniard fell unconscious. The man in black quickly tied Inigo's hands around a tree and left him there, for the moment, sleeping and helpless.

Then he sheathed his sword, picked up the Sicilian's trail, and raced into the night. . . .

*   *   *

"HE HAS BEATEN Inigo!" the Turk said, not quite sure he wanted to believe it, but positive that the news was sad; he liked Inigo. Inigo was the only one who wouldn't laugh when Fezzik asked him to play rhymes.

They were hurrying along a mountainous path on the way to the Guilder frontier. The path was narrow and strewn with rocks like cannonballs, so the Sicilian had a terrible time keeping up. Fezzik carried Buttercup lightly on his shoulders; she was still tied hand and foot.

"I didn't hear you, say it again," the Sicilian called out, so Fezzik waited for the hunchback to catch up to him.

"See?" Fezzik pointed then. Far down, at the very bottom of the mountain path, the man in black could be seen running. "Inigo is beaten."

"Inconceivable!" exploded the Sicilian.

Fezzik never dared disagree with the hunchback. "I'm so stupid," Fezzik nodded. "Inigo has not lost to the man in black, he has *defeated* him. And to prove it he has put on all the man in black's clothes and masks and hoods and boots and gained eighty pounds."

The Sicilian squinted down toward the running figure. "Fool," he hurled at the Turk. "After all these years can't you tell Inigo when you see him? That isn't Inigo."

"I'll never learn," the Turk agreed. "If there's ever a question about anything, you can always count on me to get it wrong."

"Inigo must have slipped or been tricked or otherwise unfairly beaten. That's the only conceivable explanation."

Conceivable believable, the giant thought. Only he didn't dare say it out loud. Not to the Sicilian. He might have whispered it to Inigo late at night, but that was before Inigo was dead. He also might have whispered heavable thievable weavable but that was as far as he got before the Sicilian started talking again, and that always meant he had to pay very strict attention. Nothing angered the hunchback as quickly as catching Fezzik thinking. Since he barely imagined someone like Fezzik capable of thought, he never asked what was on his mind, because he couldn't have cared less. If he had found out Fezzik was making rhymes, he would have laughed and then found new ways to make Fezzik suffer.

"Untie her feet," the Sicilian commanded.

Fezzik put the Princess down and ripped the ropes apart that bound her legs. Then he rubbed her ankles so she could walk.

The Sicilian grabbed her immediately and yanked her away. "Catch up with us quickly," the Sicilian said.

"Instructions?" Fezzik called out, almost panicked. He hated being left on his own like this.

"Finish him, finish him." The Sicilian was getting peeved. "Succeed, since Inigo failed us."

"But I can't fence, I don't know how to fence—"

"*Your* way." The Sicilian could barely control himself now.

"Oh yes, good, my way, thank you, Vizzini," Fezzik said to the hunchback. Then, summoning all his courage: "I need a hint."

"You're always saying how you understand force, how force belongs to you. Use it, I don't care how. Wait for him behind there"—he pointed to a sharp bend in the mountain path—"and crush his head like an eggshell." He pointed to the cannonball-sized rocks.

"I could do that, yes," Fezzik nodded. He was marvelous at throwing heavy things. "It just seems not very sportsmanlike, doesn't it?"

The Sicilian lost control. It was terrifying when he did it. With most people, they scream and holler and jump around. With Vizzini, it was different: he got very very quiet, and his voice sounded like it came from a dead throat. And his eyes turned to fire. "I tell you this and I tell it once: stop the man in black. Stop him for good and all. If you fail, there will be no excuses; I will find another giant."

"Please don't desert me," Fezzik said.

"Then do as you are told." He grabbed hold of Buttercup again and hobbled up the mountain path and out of sight.

Fezzik glanced down toward the figure racing up the path toward him. Still a good distance away. Time enough to practice. Fezzik picked up a rock the size of a cannonball and aimed at a crack in the mountain thirty yards away.

Swoosh.

Dead center.

He picked up a bigger rock and threw it at a shadow line twice as distant.

Not quite swoosh.

Two inches to the right.

Fezzik was reasonably satisfied. Two inches off would still crush a head if you aimed for the center. He groped around, found a perfect rock for throwing; it just fit his hand. Then he moved to the sharp turn in the path, backed off into deepest shadow. Unseen, silent, he waited patiently with his killing rock, counting the seconds until the man in black would die. . . .

FEZZIK

TURKISH WOMEN ARE famous for the size of their babies. The only happy newborn ever to weigh over twenty-four pounds upon entrance was the product of a southern Turkish union. Turkish hospital records list a total of eleven children who weighed over twenty pounds at birth. And ninety-five more who weighed between fifteen and twenty. Now all of these 106 cherubs did what babies usually do at birth: they lost three or four ounces and it took them the better part of a week before they got it totally back. More accurately, 105 of them lost weight just after they were born.

Not Fezzik.

His first afternoon he gained a pound. (Since he weighed but fifteen and since his mother gave birth two weeks early, the doctors weren't unduly concerned. "It's because you came two weeks too soon," they explained to Fezzik's mother. "That explains it." Actually, of course, it didn't explain anything, but whenever doctors are confused about something, which is really more frequently than any of us would do well to think about, they always snatch at something in the vicinity of the case and add, "That explains it." If Fezzik's mother had come late, they would have said, "Well, you came late, that explains it." Or "Well, it was raining during delivery, this added weight is simply moisture, that explains it.")

A healthy baby doubles his birth weight in about six months and triples it in a year. When Fezzik was a year old, he weighed eighty-five pounds. He wasn't fat, understand. He looked like a perfectly normal strong eighty-five-pound kid. Not all that normal, actually. He was pretty hairy for a one-year-old.

By the time he reached kindergarten, he was ready to shave. He was the size of a normal man by this time, and all the other children made his life miserable. At first, naturally, they were scared to death (even then, Fezzik looked fierce) but once they found out he was chicken, well, they weren't about to let an opportunity like *that* get away.

"Bully, bully," they taunted Fezzik during morning yogurt break.

"I'm not," Fezzik would say out loud. (To himself he would go "Woolly, woolly." He would never dare to consider himself a poet, because he wasn't anything like that; he just loved rhymes. Anything you said out loud, he rhymed it inside. Sometimes the rhymes made sense, sometimes they didn't. Fezzik never cared much about sense; all that ever mattered was the sound.)

"Coward."

Towered. "I'm not."

"Then fight," one of them would say, and would swing all he had and hit Fezzik in the stomach, confident that all Fezzik would do was go "oof" and stand there, because he never hit back no matter what you did to him.

"Oof."

Another swing. Another. A good stiff punch to the kidneys maybe. Maybe a kick in the knee. It would go on like that until Fezzik would burst into tears and run away.

One day at home, Fezzik's father called, "Come here."

Fezzik, as always, obeyed.

"Dry your tears," his mother said.

Two children had beaten him very badly just before. He did what he could to stop crying.

"Fezzik, this can't go on," his mother said. "They must stop picking on you."

Kicking on you. "I don't mind so much," Fezzik said.

"Well you should mind," his father said. He was a carpenter, with big hands. "Come on outside. I'm going to teach you how to fight."

"Please, I don't want—"

"Obey your father."

They trooped out to the back yard.

"Make a fist," his father said.

Fezzik did his best.

His father looked at his mother, then at the heavens. "He can't even make a fist," his father said.

"He's trying, he's only six; don't be so hard on him."

Fezzik's father cared for his son greatly and he tried to keep his voice soft, so Fezzik wouldn't burst out crying. But it wasn't easy. "Honey," Fezzik's father said, "look: when you make a fist, you don't put your thumb *inside* your fingers, you keep your thumb *outside* your fingers, because if you keep your thumb *inside* your fingers and you hit somebody, what will happen is you'll break your thumb, and that isn't good, because the whole object when you hit somebody is to hurt the other guy, not yourself."

Blurt. "I don't want to hurt anybody, Daddy."

"I don't *want* you to hurt anybody, Fezzik. But if you know how to take care of yourself, and they *know* you know, they won't bother you any more."

Father. "I don't mind so much."

"Well we do," his mother said. "They shouldn't pick on you, Fezzik, just because you need a shave."

"Back to the fist," his father said. "Have we learned how?"

Fezzik made a fist again, this time with the thumb outside.

"He's a natural learner," his mother said. She cared for him as greatly as his father did.

"Now hit me," Fezzik's father said.

"No, I don't want to do that."

"Hit your father, Fezzik."

"Maybe he doesn't know how to hit," Fezzik's father said.

"Maybe not." Fezzik's mother shook her head sadly.

"Watch, honey," Fezzik's father. "See? Simple. You just make a fist like you already know and then pull back your arm a little and aim for where you want to land and let go."

"Show your father what a natural learner you are," Fezzik's mother said. "Make a punch. Hit him a good one."

Fezzik made a punch toward his father's arm.

Fezzik's father stared at the heavens again in frustration.

"'He came close to your arm," Fezzik's mother said quickly, before her son's face could cloud. "That was very good for a start, Fezzik; tell him what a good start he made," she said to her husband.

"It was in the right general direction," Fezzik's father managed. "If only I'd been standing one yard farther west, it would have been perfect."

"I'm very tired," Fezzik said. "When you learn so much so fast, you get so tired. I do anyway. Please may I be excused?"

"Not yet," Fezzik's mother said.

"Honey, please hit me, really hit me, try. You're a smart boy; hit me a good one," Fezzik's father begged.

"Tomorrow, Daddy; I promise." Tears began to form.

"Crying's not going to work, Fezzik," his father exploded. "It's not gonna work on me and it's not gonna work on your mother, you're gonna do what I say and what I say is you're gonna hit me and if it takes all night we're gonna stand right here and if it takes all week we're gonna stand right here and if it—"

S

P

L

A

T

!!!!

(This was before emergency wards, and that was too bad, at least for Fezzik's father, because there was no place to take him after Fezzik's punch landed, except to his own bed, where he remained with his eyes shut for a day and a half, except for when the milkman came to fix his broken jaw—this was not before doctors, but in Turkey they hadn't gotten around to claiming the bone business yet; milkmen still were in charge of bones, the logic being that since milk was so good for bones, who would know more about broken bones than a milkman?)

When Fezzik's father was able to open his eyes as much as he wanted, they had a family talk, the three of them.

"You're very strong, Fezzik," his father said. (Actually, that is not strictly true. What his father *meant* was, "You're very strong, Fezzik." What came out was more like this: "Zzz'zz zzzz zzzzzz, Zzzzzz." Ever since the milkman had wired his jaws together, all he could manage was the letter *z*. But he had a very expressive face, and his wife understood him perfectly.)

"He says, 'You're very strong, Fezzik.' "

"I thought I was," Fezzik answered. "Last year I hit a tree once when I was very mad. I knocked it down. It was a small tree, but still, I figured that had to mean something."

"Z'z zzzzzz zz zzzzz z zzzzzzzzz, Zzzzzz."

"He says he's giving up being a carpenter, Fezzik."

"Oh, no," Fezzik said. "You'll be all well soon, Daddy; the milkman practically promised me."

"Z *zzzz* zz zzzz zz zzzzz z zzzzzzzzz, Zzzzzz."

"He *wants* to give up being a carpenter, Fezzik."

"But what will he do?"

Fezzik's mother answered this one herself; she and her husband had been up half the night agreeing on the decision. "He's going to be your manager, Fezzik. Fighting is the national sport of Turkey. We're all going to be rich and famous."

"But Mommy, Daddy, I don't like fighting."

Fezzik's father reached out and gently patted his son's knee. "Zz'z zzzzz zz zz *zzzzzzzz*," he said.

"It's going to be *wonderful*," his mother translated.

Fezzik only burst into tears.

They had his first professional match in the village of Sandiki, on a steaming-hot Sunday. Fezzik's parents had a terrible time getting him into the ring. They were absolutely confident of victory, because they had worked very hard. They had taught Fezzik for three solid years before they mutually agreed that he was ready. Fezzik's father handled tactics and ring strategy, while his mother was more in charge of diet and training, and they had never been happier.

Fezzik had never been more miserable. He was scared and frightened and terrified, all rolled into one. No matter how they reassured him, he refused to enter the arena. Because he knew something: even though outside he looked twenty, and his mustache was already coming along nicely, inside he was still this nine-year-old who liked rhyming things.

"No," he said. "I won't, I won't, and you can't make me."

"After all we've slaved for these three years," his father said. (His jaw was almost as good as new now.)

"He'll *hurt* me!" Fezzik said.

"Life is pain," his mother said. "Anybody that says different is selling something."

"Please. I'm not ready. I forget the holds. I'm not graceful and I fall down a lot. It's true."

It was. Their only real fear was, were they rushing him? "When the going gets tough, the tough get going," Fezzik's mother said.

"Get going, Fezzik," his father said.

Fezzik stood his ground.

"Listen, we're not going to threaten you," Fezzik's parents said, more or less together. "We all care for each other too much to pull any of that stuff. If you don't want to fight, nobody's going to force you. We'll just leave you alone forever." (Fezzik's picture of hell was being alone forever. He had told them that when he was five.)

They marched into the arena then to face the champion of Sandiki.

Who had been champion for eleven years, since he was twenty-four. He was very graceful and wide and stood six feet in height, only half a foot less than Fezzik.

Fezzik didn't stand a chance.

He was too clumsy; he kept falling down or getting his holds on backward so they weren't holds at all. The champion of Sandiki toyed with him. Fezzik kept getting thrown down or falling down or tumbling down or stumbling down. He always got up and tried again, but the champion of Sandiki was much too fast for him, and too clever, and much, much too experienced. The crowd laughed and ate baklava and enjoyed the whole spectacle.

Until Fezzik got his arms around the champion of Sandiki.

The crowd grew very quiet then.

Fezzik lifted him up.

No noise.

Fezzik squeezed.

And squeezed.

"That's enough now," Fezzik's father said.

Fezzik laid the other man down. "Thank you," he said. "You are a wonderful fighter and I was lucky."

The ex-champion of Sandiki kind of grunted.

"Raise your hands, you're the winner," his mother reminded.

Fezzik stood there in the middle of the ring with his hands raised.

"Booooo," said the crowd.

"Animal."

"Ape!"

"Go-*rilla*!"

"BOOOOOOOOOOOOO!!!"

They did not linger long in Sandiki. As a matter of fact, it wasn't very safe from then on to linger long anywhere. They fought the champion of Ispir. "BOOOOOOOOOOOO!!!" The champion of Simal. "BOOOOOOOOOOOO!!!" They fought in Bolu. They fought in Zile.

"BOOOOOOOOOOOO!!!"

"I don't care what anybody says," Fezzik's mother told him one winter afternoon. "You're my son and you're wonderful." It was gray and dark and they were hotfooting it out of Constantinople just as fast as they could because Fezzik had just demolished their champion before most of the crowd was even seated.

"I'm not wonderful," Fezzik said. "They're right to insult me. I'm too big. Whenever I fight, it looks like I'm picking on somebody."

"Maybe," Fezzik's father began a little hesitantly; "maybe,

Fezzik, if you'd just possibly kind of sort of lose a few fights, they might not yell at us so much."

The wife whirled on the husband. "The boy is eleven and already you want him to throw fights?"

"Nothing like that, no, don't get all excited, but maybe if he'd even look like he was suffering a little, they'd let up on us."

"I'm suffering," Fezzik said. (He was, he was.)

"Let it show a little more."

"I'll try, Daddy."

"That's a good boy."

"I can't help being strong; it's not my fault. I don't even exercise."

"I think it's time to head for Greece," Fezzik's father said then. "We've beaten everyone in Turkey who'll fight us and athletics began in Greece. No one appreciates talent like the Greeks."

"I just hate it when they go 'BOOOOOOOOOOO!!!'" Fezzik said. (He did. Now his private picture of hell was being left alone with everybody going "BOOOOOOOOOOO" at him forever.)

"They'll love you in Greece," Fezzik's mother said.

They fought in Greece.

"AARRRGGGGH!!!" (AARRRGGGGH!!! was Greek for BOOOOO-OOOOO!!!)

Bulgaria.

Yugoslavia.

Czechoslovakia. Romania.

"BOOOOOOOOOOO!!!"

They tried the Orient. The jujitsu champion of Korea. The karate champion of Siam. The kung fu champion of all India.

"SSSSSSSSSSSSSS!!!" (See note on AARRRGGGGH!!!)

In Mongolia his parents died. "We've done everything we can for you, Fezzik, good luck," they said, and they were gone. It was a terrible thing, a plague that swept everything before it. Fezzik would have died too, only naturally he never got sick. Alone, he continued on, across the Gobi Desert, hitching rides sometimes with passing caravans. And it was there that he learned how to make them stop BOOOOOOOOOOO!!!ing.

Fight groups.

It all began in a caravan on the Gobi when the caravan head said, "I'll bet my camel drivers can take you." There were only three of them, so Fezzik said. "Fine," he'd try, and he did, and he won, naturally.

And everybody seemed happy.

Fezzik was thrilled. He never fought just one person again if it was possible. For a while he traveled from place to place battling gangs for local charities, but his business head was never much and, besides, doing things alone was even less appealing to him now that he was into his late teens than it had been before.

He joined a traveling circus. All the other performers grumbled at him because, they said, he was eating more than his share of the food. So he stayed pretty much to himself except when it came to his work.

But then, one night, when Fezzik had just turned twenty, he got the shock of his life: the BOOOOOOOOOOO!!!ing was back again. He could not believe it. He had just squeezed half a dozen men into submission, cracked the heads of half a dozen more. *What did they want from him?*

The truth was simply this: he had gotten too strong. He would never measure himself, but everybody whispered he must be over seven feet tall, and he would never step on a scale, but people claimed he weighed four hundred. And not only that, he was quick now. All the years of experience had made him almost inhuman. He knew all the tricks, could counter all the holds.

"Animal."

"Ape!"

"Go-*rilla*!"

"BOOOOOOOOOOOO!!!"

That night, alone in his tent, Fezzik wept. He was a freak. (Speak—he still loved rhymes.) A two-eyed Cyclops. (Eye drops—like the tears that were dropping now, dropping from his half-closed eyes.) By the next morning, he had gotten control of himself: at least he still had his circus friends around him.

That week the circus fired him. The crowds were BOOOOOOOOOOO!!!ing them now too, and the fat lady threatened to walk out and the midgets were fuming and that was it for Fezzik.

This was in the middle of Greenland, and, as everybody knows, Greenland then as now was the loneliest place on the Earth. In Greenland, there is one person for every twenty square miles of real estate. Probably the circus was pretty stupid taking a booking there, but that wasn't the point.

The point was that Fezzik was alone.

In the loneliest place in the world.

Just sitting there on a rock watching the circus pull away.

He was still sitting there the next day when Vizzini the Sicilian found him. Vizzini flattered him, promised to keep the BOOOOOOOOOOOs away. Vizzini needed Fezzik. But not half as much as Fezzik needed Vizzini. As long as Vizzini was around, you couldn't be alone. Whatever Vizzini said, Fezzik did. And if that meant crushing the head of the man in black . . .

So be it.

*   *   *

BUT NOT BY ambush. Not the coward's way. Nothing unsportsmanlike. His parents had always taught him to go by the rules. Fezzik stood in shadow, the great rock tight in his great hand. He could hear the footsteps of the man in black coming nearer. Nearer.

Fezzik leaped from hiding and threw the rock with incredible power and perfect accuracy. It smashed into a boulder a foot away from the face of the man in black. "I did that on purpose," Fezzik said then, picking up another rock, holding it ready. "I didn't have to miss."

"I believe you," the man in black said.

They stood facing each other on the narrow mountain path.

"Now what happens?" asked the man in black.

"We face each other as God intended," Fezzik said. "No tricks, no weapons, skill against skill alone."

"You mean you'll put down your rock and I'll put down my sword and we'll try to kill each other like civilized people, is that it?"

"If you'd rather, I can kill you now," Fezzik said gently, and he raised the rock to throw. "I'm giving you a chance."

"So you are and I accept it," said the man in black, and he began to take off his sword and scabbard. "Although, frankly, I think the odds are slightly in your favor at hand fighting."

"I tell you what I tell everybody," Fezzik explained. "I cannot help being the biggest and strongest; it's not my fault."

"I'm not blaming you," said the man in black.

"Let's get to it then," Fezzik said, and he dropped his rock and got into fighting position, watching as the man in black slowly moved toward him. For a moment, Fezzik felt almost wistful. This was clearly a good fellow, even if he had killed Inigo. He didn't complain or try and beg or bribe. He just accepted his fate. No complaining, nothing like that. Obviously a criminal of character. (Was he a criminal, though, Fezzik wondered. Surely the mask would indicate that. Or was it worse than that: was he disfigured? His face burned away by acid perhaps? Or perhaps born hideous?)

"Why do you wear a mask and hood?" Fezzik asked.

"I think everybody will in the near future" was the man in black's reply. "They're terribly comfortable."

They faced each other on the mountain path. There was a moment's pause. Then they engaged. Fezzik let the man in black fiddle around for a bit, tested the man's strength, which was considerable for someone who wasn't a giant. He let the man in black feint and dodge and try a hold here, a hold there. Then, when he was quite sure the man in black would not go to his maker embarrassed, Fezzik locked his arms tight around.

Fezzik lifted.

And squeezed.

And squeezed.

Then he took the remains of the man in black, snapped him one way, snapped him the other, cracked him with one hand in the neck, with the other at the spine base, locked his legs up, rolled his limp arms around them, and tossed the entire bundle of what had once been human into a nearby crevice.

That was the theory, anyway.

In fact, what happened was this:

Fezzik lifted.

And squeezed.

And the man in black slipped free.

Hmmm, thought Fezzik, that certainly was a surprise. I thought for sure I had him. "You're very quick," Fezzik complimented.

"And a good thing too," said the man in black.

Then they engaged again. This time Fezzik did not give the man in black a chance to fiddle. He just grabbed him, swung him around his head once, twice, smashed his skull against the nearest boulder, pounded him, pummeled him, gave him a final squeeze for good measure and tossed the remains of what once had been alive into a nearby crevice.

Those were his intentions, anyway.

In actuality, he never even got through the grabbing part with much success. Because no sooner had Fezzik's great hands reached out than the man in black dropped and spun and twisted and was loose and free and still quite alive.

I don't understand a thing that's happening, Fezzik thought. Could I be losing my strength? Could there be a mountain disease that takes your strength? There was a desert disease that took my parents' strength. That must be it, I must have caught a plague, but if that is it, why isn't he weak? No, I must still be strong, it has to be something else, now what could it be?

Suddenly he knew. He had not fought against one man in so long he had all but forgotten how. He had been fighting groups and gangs and bunches for so many years, that the idea of having but a single opponent was slow in making itself known to him. Because you fought them entirely differently. When there were twelve against you, you made certain moves, tried certain holds, acted in certain ways. When there was but one, you had to completely readjust yourself. Quickly now, Fezzik went back through time. How had he fought the champion of Sandiki? He flashed through that fight in his mind, then reminded himself of all the other victories against other champions, the men from Ispir and Simal and Bolu and Zile. He remembered fleeing Constantinople because he had beaten their champion so quickly. So easily. Yes, Fezzik thought. Of course. And suddenly he readjusted his style to what it once had been.

But by that time the man in black had him by the throat!

The man in black was riding him, and his arms were locked across Fezzik's windpipe, one in front, one behind. Fezzik reached back but the man in black was hard to grasp. Fezzik could not get his arms around to his back and dislodge the enemy. Fezzik ran at a boulder and, at the last moment, spun around so that the man in black received the main force of the charge. It was a terrible jolt; Fezzik knew it was.

But the grip on his windpipe grew ever tighter.

Fezzik charged the boulder again, again spun, and again he knew the power of the blow the man in black had taken. But still the grip remained. Fezzik clawed at the man in black's arms. He pounded his giant fists against them.

By now he had no air.

Fezzik continued to struggle. He could feel a hollowness in his legs now; he could see the world beginning to pale. But he did not give up. He was the mighty Fezzik, lover of rhymes, and you did not give up, no matter what. Now the hollowness was in his arms and the world was snowing.

Fezzik went to his knees.

He pounded still, but feebly. He fought still, but his blows would not have harmed a child. No air. There was no more air. There was no more anything, not for Fezzik, not in this world. I am beaten, I am going to die, he thought just before he fell onto the mountain path.

He was only half wrong.

There is an instant between unconsciousness and death, and as the giant pitched onto the rocky path, that instant happened, and just before it happened, the man in black let go. He staggered to his feet and leaned against a boulder until he could walk. Fezzik lay sprawled, faintly breathing. The man in black looked around for a rope to secure the giant, gave up the search almost as soon as he'd begun. What good were ropes against strength like this. He would simply snap them. The man in black made his way back to where he'd dropped his sword. He put it back on.

Two down and (the hardest) one to go . . .

*　　　*　　　*

VIZZINI WAS WAITING for him.

Indeed, he had set out a little picnic spread. From the knapsack that he always carried, he had taken a small handkerchief and on it he had placed two wine goblets. In the center was a small leather wine holder and, beside it, some cheese and some apples. The spot could not have been lovelier: a high point of the mountain path with a splendid view all the way back to Florin Channel. Buttercup lay helpless beside the picnic, gagged and tied and blindfolded. Vizzini held his long knife against her white throat.

"Welcome," Vizzini called when the man in black was almost upon them.

The man in black stopped and surveyed the situation.

"You've beaten my Turk," Vizzini said.

"It would seem so."

"And now it is down to you. And it is down to me."

"So that would seem too," the man in black said, edging just a half-step closer to the hunchback's long knife.

With a smile the hunchback pushed the knife harder against Buttercup's throat. It was about to bring blood. "If you wish her dead, by all means keep moving," Vizzini said.

The man in black froze.

"Better," Vizzini nodded.

No sound now beneath the moonlight.

"I understand completely what you are trying to do," the Sicilian said finally, "and I want it quite clear that I resent your behavior. You are trying to kidnap what I have rightfully stolen, and I think it quite ungentlemanly."

"Let me explain—" the man in black began, starting to edge forward.

"You're killing her!" the Sicilian screamed, shoving harder with the knife. A drop of blood appeared now at Buttercup's throat, red against white.

The man in black retreated. "Let me explain," he said again, but from a distance.

Again the hunchback interrupted. "There is nothing you can tell me I do not already know. I have not had the schooling equal to some, but for knowledge outside of books, there is no one in the world close to me. People say I read minds, but that is not, in all honesty, true. I merely predict the truth using logic and wisdom, and I say you are a kidnapper, admit it."

"I will admit that, as a ransom item, she has value; nothing more."

"I have been instructed to do certain things to her. It is very important that I follow my instructions. If I do this properly, I will be in demand for life. And my instructions do not include ransom, they include death. So your explanations are meaningless; we cannot do business together. You wish to keep her alive for ransom, whereas it is terribly important to me that she stop breathing in the very near future."

"Has it occurred to you that I have gone to great effort and expense, as well as personal sacrifice, to reach this point," the man in black replied. "And that if I fail now, I might get very angry. And if she stops breathing in the very near future, it is entirely possible that you will catch the same fatal illness?"

"I have no doubt you could kill me. Any man who can get by Inigo and Fezzik would have no trouble disposing of me. However, has it occurred to you that if you did that, then neither of us would get what we want—you having lost your ransom item, me my life."

"We are at an impasse then," said the man in black.

"I fear so," said the Sicilian. "I cannot compete with you physically, and you are no match for my brains."

"You are that smart?"

"There are no words to contain all my wisdom. I am so cunning, crafty and clever, so filled with deceit, guile and chicanery, such a knave, so shrewd, cagey as well as calculating, as diabolical as I am vulpine, as tricky as I am untrustworthy . . . well, I told you there were not words invented yet to explain how great my brain is, but let me put it this way: the world is several million years old and several billion people have at one time or another trod upon it, but I, Vizzini the Sicilian, am, speaking with pure candor and modesty, the slickest, sleekest, sliest and wiliest fellow who has yet come down the pike."

"In that case," said the man in black, "I challenge you to a battle of wits."

Vizzini had to smile. "For the Princess?"

"You read my mind."

"It just seems that way, I told you. It's merely logic and wisdom. To the death?"

"Correct again."

"I accept," cried Vizzini. "Begin the battle!"

"Pour the wine," said the man in black.

Vizzini filled the two goblets with deep-red liquid.

The man in black pulled from his dark clothing a small packet and handed it to the hunchback. "Open it and inhale, but be careful not to touch."

Vizzini took the packet and followed instructions. "I smell nothing."

The man in black took the packet again. "What you do not smell is called iocane powder. It is odorless, tasteless and dissolves immediately in any kind of liquid. It also happens to be the deadliest poison known to man."

Vizzini was beginning to get excited.

"I don't suppose you'd hand me the goblets," said the man in black.

Vizzini shook his head. "Take them yourself. My long knife does not leave her throat."

The man in black reached down for the goblets. He took them and turned away.

Vizzini cackled aloud in anticipation.

The man in black busied himself a long moment. Then he turned again with a goblet in each hand. Very carefully, he put the goblet in his right hand in front of Vizzini and put the goblet in his left hand across the kerchief from the hunchback. He sat down in front of the left-hand goblet, and dropped the empty iocane packet by the cheese.

"Your guess," he said. "Where is the poison?"

"Guess?" Vizzini cried. "I don't guess. I think. I ponder. I deduce. Then I decide. But I never guess."

"The battle of wits has begun," said the man in black. "It ends when you decide and we drink the wine and find out who is right and who is dead. We both drink, need I add, and swallow, naturally, at precisely the same time."

"It's all so simple," said the hunchback. "All I have to do is deduce, from what I know of you, the way your mind works. Are you the kind of man who would put the poison into his own glass, or into the glass of his enemy?"

"You're stalling," said the man in black.

"I'm relishing is what I'm doing," answered the Sicilian. "No one has challenged my mind in years and I love it. . . . By the way, may I smell both goblets?"

"Be my guest. Just be sure you put them down the same way you found them."

The Sicilian sniffed his own glass; then he reached across the kerchief for the goblet of the man in black and sniffed that. "As you said, odorless."

"As I also said, you're stalling."

The Sicilian smiled and stared at the wine goblets. "Now a great fool," he began, "would place the wine in his own goblet, because he would know that only another great fool would reach first for what he was given. I am clearly not a great fool, so I will clearly not reach for your wine."

"That's your final choice?"

"No. Because you knew I was not a great fool, so you would know that I would never fall for such a trick. You would count on it. So I will clearly not reach for mine either."

"Keep going," said the man in black.

"I intend to." The Sicilian reflected a moment. "We have now decided the poisoned cup is most likely in front of you. But the poison is powder made from iocane and iocane comes only from Australia and Australia, as everyone knows, is peopled with criminals and criminals are used to having people not trust them, as I don't trust you, which means I can clearly not choose the wine in front of you."

The man in black was starting to get nervous.

"But, again, you must have suspected I knew the origins of iocane, so you would have known I knew about the criminals and criminal behavior, and therefore I can clearly not choose the wine in front of me."

"Truly you have a dizzying intellect," whispered the man in black.

"You have beaten my Turk, which means you are exceptionally strong, and exceptionally strong men are convinced that they are too powerful ever to die, too powerful even for iocane poison, so you could have put it in your cup, trusting on your strength to save you; thus I can clearly not choose the wine in front of you."

The man in black was very nervous now.

"But you also bested my Spaniard, which means you must have studied, because he studied many years for his excellence, and if you can study, you are clearly more than simply strong; you are aware of how mortal we all are, and you do not wish to die, so you would have kept the poison as far from yourself as possible; therefore I can clearly not choose the wine in front of me."

"You're just trying to make me give something away with all this chatter," said the man in black angrily. "Well it won't work. You'll learn nothing from me, that I promise you."

"I have already learned everything from you," said the Sicilian. "I know where the poison is."

"Only a genius could have deduced as much."

"How fortunate for me that I happen to be one," said the hunchback, growing more and more amused now.

"You cannot frighten me," said the man in black, but there was fear all through his voice.

"Shall we drink then?"

"Pick, choose, quit dragging it out, you don't know, you couldn't know."

The Sicilian only smiled at the outburst. Then a strange look crossed his features and he pointed off behind the man in black. "What in the world can that be?" he asked.

The man in black turned around and looked. "I don't see anything."

"Oh, well, I could have sworn I saw something, no matter." The Sicilian began to laugh.

"I don't understand what's so funny," said the man in black.

"Tell me in a minute," said the hunchback. "But first let's drink."

And he picked up his own wine goblet.

The man in black picked up the one in front of him.

They drank.

"You guessed wrong," said the man in black.

"You only *think* I guessed wrong," said the Sicilian, his laughter ringing louder. "That's what's so funny. I switched glasses when your back was turned."

There was nothing for the man in black to say.

"Fool!" cried the hunchback. "You fell victim to one of the classic blunders. The most famous is 'Never get involved in a land war in Asia,' but only slightly less well known is this: 'Never go in against a Sicilian when death is on the line.' "

He was quite cheery until the iocane powder took effect.

The man in black stepped quickly over the corpse, then roughly ripped the blindfold from the Princess's eyes.

"I heard everything that happ—" Buttercup began, and then she said "Oh" because she had never been next to a dead man before. "You killed him," she whispered finally.

"I let him die laughing," said the man in black. "Pray I do as much for you." He lifted her, slashed her bonds away, put her on her feet, started to pull her along.

"Please," Buttercup said. "Give me a moment to gather myself." The man in black released his grip.

Buttercup rubbed her wrists, stopped, massaged her ankles. She took a final look at the Sicilian. "To think," she murmured, "all that time it was your cup that was poisoned."

"They were both poisoned," said the man in black. "I've spent the past two years building up immunity to iocane powder."

Buttercup looked up at him. He was terrifying to her, masked and hooded and dangerous; his voice was strained, rough. "Who are you?" she asked.

"I am no one to be trifled with," replied the man in black. "That is all you ever need to know." And with that he yanked her upright.

"You've had your moment." Again he pulled her after him, and this time she could do nothing but follow.

They moved along the mountain path. The moonlight was very bright, and there were rocks everywhere, and to Buttercup it all looked dead and yellow, like the moon. She had just spent several hours with three men who were openly planning to kill her. So why, she wondered, was she more frightened now than then? Who was the horrid hooded figure to strike fear in her so? What could be worse than dying? "I will pay you a great deal of money to release me," she managed to say.

The man in black glanced at her. "You are rich, then?"

"I will be," Buttercup said. "Whatever you want for ransom, I promise I'll get it for you if you'll let me go."

The man in black just laughed.

"I was not speaking in jest."

"You promise? *You?* I should release you on *your* promise? What is that worth? The vow of a woman? Oh, that is very funny, Highness. Spoken in jest or not." They proceeded along the mountain path to an open space. The man in black stopped then. There were a million stars fighting for prominence and for a moment he seemed to be intent on nothing less than studying them all, as Buttercup watched his eyes flick from constellation to constellation behind his mask.

Then, with no warning, he spun off the path, heading into wild terrain, pulling her behind him.

She stumbled; he pulled her to her feet; again she fell; again he righted her.

"I cannot move this quickly."

"You can! And you will! Or you will suffer greatly. Do you think I could make you suffer greatly?"

Buttercup nodded.

"Then *run!*" cried the man in black, and he broke into a run himself, flying across rocks in the moonlight, pulling the Princess behind him.

She did her best to keep up. She was frightened as to what he would do to her, so she dared not fall again.

After five minutes, the man in black stopped dead. "Catch your breath," he commanded.

Buttercup nodded, gasped in air, tried to quiet her heart. But then they were off again, with no warning, dashing across the mountainous terrain, heading . . .

"Where . . . do you take me?" Buttercup gasped, when he again gave her a chance to rest.

"Surely even someone as arrogant as you cannot expect me to give an answer."

"It does not matter if you tell or not. He will find you."

" 'He,' Highness?"

"Prince Humperdinck. There is no greater hunter. He can track a falcon on a cloudy day; he can find you."

"You have confidence that your dearest love will save you, do you?"

"I never said he was my dearest love, and yes, he will save me; that I know."

"You admit you do not love your husband-to-be? Fancy. An honest woman. You're a rare specimen, Highness."

"The Prince and I have never from the beginning lied to each other. He knows I do not love him."

"Are not capable of love is what you mean."

"I'm very capable of love," Buttercup said.

"Hold your tongue, I think."

"I have loved more deeply than a killer like you can possibly imagine."

He slapped her.

"That is the penalty for lying, Highness. Where I come from, when a woman lies, she is reprimanded."

"But I spoke the truth, I did, I—" Buttercup saw his hand rise a second time, so she stopped quickly, fell dead silent.

Then they began to run again.

They did not speak for hours. They just ran, and then, as if he could guess when she was spent, he would stop, release her hand. She would try to catch her breath for the next dash she was sure would come. Without a sound, he would grab her and off they would go.

It was close to dawn when they first saw the Armada.

They were running along the edge of a towering ravine. They seemed almost to be at the top of the world. When they stopped, Buttercup sank down to rest. The man in black stood silently over her. "Your love comes, not alone," he said then.

Buttercup did not understand.

The man in black pointed back the way they had come.

Buttercup stared, and as she did, the waters of Florin Channel seemed as filled with light as the sky was filled with stars.

"He must have ordered every ship in Florin after you," the man in black said. "Such a sight I have never seen." He stared at all the lanterns on all the ships as they moved.

"You can never escape him," Buttercup said. "If you release me, I promise that you will come to no harm."

"You are much too generous; I could never accept such an offer."

"I offered you your life, that was generous enough."

"*Highness!*" said the man in black, and his hands were suddenly at her throat. "If there is talk of life to be done, let me do it."

"You would not kill me. You did not steal me from murderers to murder me yourself."

"Wise as well as loving," said the man in black. He jerked her to her feet, and they ran along the edge of the great ravine. It was hundreds of feet deep, and filled with rocks and trees and lifting shadows. Abruptly, the man in black stopped, stared back at the Armada. "To be honest," he said, "I had not expected quite so many."

"You can never predict my Prince; that is why he is the greatest hunter."

"I wonder," said the man in black, "will he stay in one group or will he divide, some to search the coastline, some to follow your path on land? What do you think?"

"I only know he will find me. And if you have not given me my freedom first, he will not treat you gently."

"Surely he must have discussed things with you? The thrill of the hunt. What has he done in the past with many ships?"

"We do not discuss hunting, that I can assure you."

"Not hunting, not love, what do you talk about?"

"We do not see all that much of each other."

"Tender couple."

Buttercup could feel the upset coming. "We are always very honest with each other. Not everyone can say as much."

"May I please tell you something, Highness? You're very cold—"

"I'm not—"

"—very cold and very young, and if you live, I think you'll turn to hoarfrost—"

"*Why do you pick at me?* I have come to terms with my life, and that is my affair—I am not cold, I swear, but I have decided certain things, it is best for me to ignore emotion; I have not been happy dealing with it—" Her heart was a secret garden and the walls were very high. "I loved once," Buttercup said after a moment. "It worked out badly."

"Another rich man? Yes, and he left you for a richer woman."

"No. Poor. Poor and it killed him."

"Were you sorry? Did you feel pain? Admit that you felt nothing—"

"Do not mock my grief! *I died that day*."

The Armada began to fire signal cannons. The explosions echoed through the mountains. The man in black stared as the ships began to change formation.

And while he was watching the ships, Buttercup shoved him with all her strength remaining.

For a moment, the man in black teetered at the ravine edge. His arms spun like windmills fighting for balance. They swung and gripped the air and then he began his slide.

Down went the man in black.

Stumbling and torn and reaching out to stop his descent, but the ravine was too steep, and nothing could be done.

Down, down.

Rolling over rocks, spinning, out of all control.

Buttercup stared at what she had done.

Finally he rested far below her, silent and without motion. *"You can die too for all I care,"* she said, and then she turned away.

Words followed her. Whispered from far, weak and warm and familiar. "As . . . you . . . wish . . ."

Dawn in the mountains. Buttercup turned back to the source of the sound and stared down as, in first light, the man in black struggled to remove his mask.

"Oh, my sweet Westley," Buttercup said. "What have I done to you now?"

From the bottom of the ravine, there came only silence.

Buttercup hesitated not a moment. Down she went after him, keeping her feet as best she could, and as she began, she thought she heard him crying out to her over and over, but she could not make sense of his words, because inside her now there was the thunder of walls crumbling, and that was noise enough.

Besides, her balance quickly was gone and the ravine had her. She fell fast and she fell hard, but what did that matter, since she would have gladly dropped a thousand feet onto a bed of nails if Westley had been waiting at the bottom.

Down, down.

Tossed and spinning, crashing, torn, out of all control, she rolled and twisted and plunged, cartwheeling toward what was left of her beloved. . . .

* * *

FROM HIS POSITION at the point of the Armada, Prince Humperdinck stared up at the Cliffs of Insanity. This was just like any other hunt. He made himself think away the quarry. It did not matter if you were after an antelope or a bride-to-be; the procedures held. You gathered evidence. Then you acted. You studied, then you performed. If you studied too little, the chances were strong that your actions would also be too late. You had to take time. And so, frozen in thought, he continued to stare up the sheer face of the Cliffs.

Obviously, someone had recently climbed them. There were foot scratchings all the way up a straight line, which meant, most certainly, a rope, an arm-over-arm climb up a thousand-foot rope with occasional foot kicks for balance. To make such a climb required both strength and planning, so the Prince made those marks in his brain: my enemy is strong; my enemy is not impulsive.

Now his eyes reached a point perhaps three hundred feet from the top. Here it began to get interesting. Now the foot scratchings were deeper, more frequent, and they followed no direct ascending line. Either someone left the rope three hundred feet from the top intentionally, which made no sense, or the rope was cut while that someone was still three hundred feet from safety. For clearly, this last part of the climb was made up the rock face itself. But who had such talent? And why had he been called to exercise it at such a deadly time, seven hundred feet above disaster?

"I must examine the tops of the Cliffs of Insanity," the Prince said, without bothering to turn.

From behind him, Count Rugen only said, "Done," and awaited further instructions.

"Send half the Armada south along the coastline, the other north. They should meet by twilight near the Fire Swamp. Our ship will sail to the first landing possibility, and you will follow me with your soldiers. Ready the whites."

Count Rugen signaled the cannoneer, and the Prince's instructions boomed along the Cliffs. Within minutes, the Armada had begun to split, with only the Prince's giant ship sailing alone closest to the coastline, looking for a landing possibility.

"There!" the Prince ordered, some time later, and his ship began maneuvering into the cove for a safe place to anchor. That took time, but not much, because the Captain was skilled and, more than that, the Prince was quick to lose patience and no one dared risk that.

Humperdinck jumped from ship to shore, a plank was lowered, and the whites were led to ground. Of all his accomplishments, none pleased the Prince as did these horses. Someday he would have an army of them, but getting the bloodlines perfect was a slow business. He now had four whites and they were identical. Snowy, tireless giants. Twenty hands high. On flatland, nothing could catch them, and even on hills and rocky terrain, there was nothing short of Araby close to their equal. The Prince, when rushed, rode all four, bareback, the only way he ever rode, riding one, leading three, changing beasts in mid-stride, so that no single animal had to bear his bulk to the tiring point.

Now he mounted and was gone.

It took him considerably less than an hour to reach the edge of the Cliffs of Insanity. He dismounted, went to his knees, commenced his study of the terrain. There had been a rope tied around a giant oak. The bark at the base was broken and scraped, so probably whoever first reached the top untied the rope and whoever was on the rope at that moment was three hundred feet from the peak and somehow survived the climb.

A great jumble of footprints caused him trouble. It was hard to ascertain what had gone on. Perhaps a conference, because two sets of footprints seemed to lead off while one remained pacing the cliff edge. Then there were two on the cliff edge. Humperdinck examined the prints until he was certain of two things: (1) a fencing match had taken place, (2) the combatants were both masters. The stride length, the quickness of the foot feints, all clearly revealed to his unfailing eye, made him reassess his second conclusion. They were at least masters. Probably better.

Then he closed his eyes and concentrated on smelling out the blood. Surely, in a match of such ferocity, blood must have been spilled. Now it was a matter of giving his entire body over to his sense of smell. The Prince had worked at this for many years, ever since a wounded tigress had surprised him from a tree limb while he was tracking her. He had let his eyes follow the blood hunt then, and it had almost killed him. Now he trusted only his olfactories. If there was blood within a hundred yards, he would find it.

He opened his eyes, moved without hesitation toward a group of large boulders until he found the blood drops. There were few of them, and they were dry. But less than three hours old. Humperdinck smiled. When you had the whites under you, three hours was a finger snap.

He retraced the duel then, for it confused him. It seemed to range from cliff edge and back, then return to the cliff edge. And sometimes the left foot seemed to be leading, sometimes the right, which made no logical sense at all. Clearly swordsmen were changing hands, but why would a master do that unless his good arm was wounded to the point of uselessness, and that clearly had not happened, because a wound of that depth would have left blood spoors and there was simply not enough blood in the area to indicate that.

Strange, strange. Humperdinck continued his wanderings. Stranger still, the battle could not have ended in death. He knelt by the outline of a body. Clearly, a man had lain unconscious here. But again, no blood.

"There was a mighty duel," Prince Humperdinck said, directing his comment toward Count Rugen, who had finally caught up, together with a contingent of a hundred mounted men-at-arms. "My guess would be . . ." And for a moment the Prince paused, following footsteps. "Would be that whoever fell here, ran off there," and he pointed one way, "and that whoever was the victor ran off along the mountain path in almost precisely the opposite direction. It is also my opinion that the victor was following the path taken by the Princess."

"Shall we follow them both?" the Count asked.

"I think not," Prince Humperdinck replied. "Whoever is gone is of minimal importance, since whoever has the Princess is the whoever we're after. And because we don't know the nature of the trap we might be being led into, we need all the arms we have in one band. Clearly, this has been planned by countrymen of Guilder, and nothing must ever be put past them."

"You think this is a trap, then?" the Count asked.

"I always think everything is a trap until proven otherwise," the Prince answered. "Which is why I'm still alive."

And with that, he was back aboard a white and galloping.

When he reached the mountain path where the hand fight happened, the Prince did not even bother dismounting. Everything that could be seen was quite visible from horseback.

"Someone has beaten a giant," he said, when the Count was close enough. "The giant has run away, do you see?"

The Count, of course, saw nothing but rock and mountain path. "I would not think to doubt you."

"And look there!" cried the Prince, because now he saw, for the first time, in the rubble of the mountain path, the footsteps of a woman. "The Princess is alive!"

And again the whites were thundering across the mountain.

When the Count caught up with him again, the Prince was kneeling over the still body of a hunchback. The Count dismounted. "Smell this," the Prince said, and he handed up a goblet.

"Nothing," the Count said. "No odor at all."

"Iocane," the Prince replied. "I would bet my life on it. I know of nothing else that kills so silently." He stood up then. "The Princess was still alive; her footprints follow the path." He shouted at the hundred mounted men: "There will be great suffering in Guilder if she dies!" On foot now, he ran along the mountain path, following the footsteps that he alone could see. And when those footsteps left the path for wilder terrain, he followed still. Strung out behind him, the Count and all the soldiers did their best to keep up. Men stumbled, horses fell, even the Count tripped from time to time. Prince Humperdinck never even broke stride. He ran steadily, mechanically, his barrel legs pumping like a metronome.

It was two hours after dawn when he reached the steep ravine.

"Odd," he said to the Count, who was tiring badly.

The Count continued only to breathe deeply.

"Two bodies fell to the bottom, and they did not come back up."

"That is odd," the Count managed.

"No, *that* isn't what's odd," the Prince corrected. "Clearly, the kidnapper did not come back up because the climb was too steep, and our cannons must have let him know that they were closely pursued. His decision, which I applaud, was to make better time running along the ravine floor."

The Count waited for the Prince to continue.

"It's just odd that a man who is a master fencer, a defeater of giants, an expert in the use of iocane powder, would not know what this ravine opens into."

"And what is that?" asked the Count.

"The Fire Swamp," said Prince Humperdinck.

"Then we have him," said the Count.

"Precisely so." It was a well-documented trait of his to smile only just before the kill; his smile was very much in evidence now. . . .

*   *   *

WESTLEY, INDEED, HAD not the least idea that he was racing dead into the Fire Swamp. He knew only, once Buttercup was down at the ravine bottom beside him, that to climb out would take, as Prince Humperdinck had assumed, too much time. Westley noted only that the ravine bottom was flat rock and heading in the general direction he wanted to follow. So he and Buttercup fled along, both of them very much aware that gigantic forces were following them, and, undoubtedly, cutting into their lead.

The ravine grew increasingly sheer as they went along, and Westley soon realized that whereas once he probably could have helped her through the climb, now there was simply no way of doing so. He had made his choice and there was no changing possible: wherever the ravine led was their destination, and that, quite simply, was that.

(At this point in the story, my wife wants it known that she feels violently cheated, not being allowed the scene of reconciliation on the ravine floor between the lovers. My reply to her—

*   *   *

 This is me, and I'm not trying to be confusing, but the above paragraph that I'm cutting into now is verbatim Morgenstern; he was continually referring to his wife in the unabridged book, saying that she loved the next section or she thought that, all in all, the book was extraordinarily brilliant. Mrs. Morgenstern was rarely anything but supportive to her husband, unlike some wives I could mention (sorry about that, Helen), but here's the thing: I got rid of almost all the intrusions when he told us what she thought. I didn't think the device added a whole lot, and, besides, he was always complimenting himself through her and today we know that hyping something too much does more harm than good, as any defeated political candidate will tell you when he pays his television bills. The thing of it is, I left this particular reference in because, for once, I totally happen to agree with Mrs. Morgenstern. I think it was unfair not to show the reunion. So I wrote one of my own, what I felt Buttercup and Westley might have said, but Hiram, my editor, felt that made me just as unfair as Morgenstern here. If you're going to abridge a book in the author's own words, you can't go around sticking your own in. That was Hiram's point, and we really went round and round, arguing over, I guess, a period of a month, in person, through letters, on the phone. Finally we compromised to this extent: this, what you're reading in the regular type, is

strict Morgenstern. Verbatim. Cut, yes; changed, no. But I got Hiram to agree that Harcourt would at least print up my scene—Ballantine has agreed to do the same—it's all of three pages; big deal—and if any of you want to see what it came out like, drop a note or a postcard to Urban del Rey at Ballantine Books, 201 East 50th Street, New York City, and just mention you'd like the reunion scene. Don't forget to include your return address; you'd be stunned at how many people send in for things and don't put their return address down. The publishers agreed to spring for the postage costs, so your total expense is the note or card or whatever. It would really upset me if I turned out to be the only modern American writer who gave the impression that he was with a generous publishing house (they all stink—sorry about that, Mr. Jovanovich), so let me just add here that the reason they are so generous in paying this giant postage bill is because they fully expect nobody to write in. So please, if you have the least interest at all or even if you don't, write in for my reunion scene. You don't have to read it—I'm not asking that—but I would love to cost those publishing geniuses a few dollars, because, let's face it, they're not spending much on advertising my books. Let me just repeat the address for you, ZIP code and all:

Urban del Rey
Ballantine Books
1540 Broadway
New York, New York 10036
or visit us at: delreybooks.com/promo/princessbride

and just ask for your copy of the reunion scene. This has gone on longer than I planned, so I'm going to repeat the Morgenstern paragraph I interrupted; it'll read better. Over and out.

*   *   *

(AT THIS POINT in the story, my wife wants it known that she feels violently cheated, not being allowed the scene of reconciliation on the ravine floor between the lovers. My reply to her is simply this: (a) each of God's beings, from the lowliest on up, is entitled to at least a few moments of genuine privacy. (b) What actually was spoken, while moving enough to those involved at the actual time, flattens like toothpaste when transferred to paper for later reading: "my dove," "my only," "bliss, bliss," et cetera. (c) Nothing of importance in an expository way was related, because every time Buttercup began "Tell me about yourself," Westley quickly cut her off with "Later, beloved; now is not the time." However, it should be noted, in fairness to all, that (1) he did weep; (2) her eyes did not remain precisely dry; (3) there was more than one embrace; and (4) both parties admitted that, without any qualifications whatsoever, they were more than a little glad to see each other. Besides, (5) within a quarter of an hour, they were arguing. It began quite innocently, the two of them kneeling, facing each other, Westley holding her perfect face in his quick hands. "When I left you," he whispered, "you were already more beautiful than anything I dared to dream. In our years apart, my imaginings did their best to improve on your perfection. At night, your face was forever behind my eyes. And now I see that that vision who kept me company in my loneliness was a hag compared to the beauty now before me."

"Enough about my beauty," Buttercup said. "Everybody always talks about how beautiful I am. I've got a mind, Westley. Talk about that."

"Throughout eternity I shall do that very thing," he told her. "But now we haven't time." He made it to his feet. The ravine fall had shaken and battered him, but all his bones survived the trip uncracked. He helped her to her feet.

"Westley?" Buttercup said then. "Just before I started down

after you, while I was still up there, I could hear you saying something but the words were indistinct."

"I've forgotten whatever it was."

"Terrible liar."

He smiled at her and kissed her cheek. "It's not important, believe me; the past has a way of being past."

"We must not begin with secrets from each other." She meant it. He could tell that. "Trust me," he tried.

"I do. So tell me your words or I shall be given reason not to."

Westley sighed. "What I was trying to get through to you, beloved sweet; what I was, as a matter of accurate fact, shouting with everything I had left, was: 'Whatever you do, stay up there! Don't come down here! Please!' "

"You didn't want to see me."

"Of course I wanted to see you. I just didn't want to see you *down here.*"

"Why ever not?"

"Because now, my precious, we're more or less kind of trapped. I can't climb out of here and bring you with me without it taking all day. I can get out myself, most likely, without it taking all day, but with the addition of your lovely bulk, it's not about to happen."

"Nonsense; you climbed the Cliffs of Insanity, and this isn't nearly that steep."

"And it took a little out of me too, let me tell you. And after that little effort, I tangled with a fella who knew a little something about fencing. And after that, I spent a few happy moments grappling with a giant. And after that, I had to outfake a Sicilian to death when any mistake meant it was a knife in the throat for you. And after that I've run my lungs out a couple of hours. And after that I was pushed two hundred feet down a rock ravine. I'm tired,

Buttercup; do you understand tired? I've put in a night, is what I'm trying to get through to you."

"I'm not stupid, you know."

"Quit bragging."

"Stop being rude."

"When was the last time you read a book? The truth now. And picture books don't count—I mean something with print in it."

Buttercup walked away from him. "There're other things to read than print," she said, "and the Princess of Hammersmith is displeased with you and is thinking seriously of going home." With no more words, she whirled into his arms then, saying, "Oh, Westley, I didn't mean that, I didn't, I didn't, not a single syllabub of it."

Now Westley knew that she meant to say "not a single syllable of it," because a syllabub was something you ate, with cream and wine mixed in together to form the base. But he also knew an apology when he heard one. So he held her very close, and shut his loving eyes, and only whispered, "I knew it was false, believe me, every single syllabub."

And that out of the way, they started running as fast as they could along the flat-rock floor of the ravine.

*　　　*　　　*

WESTLEY, NATURALLY ENOUGH, was considerably ahead of Buttercup with the realization that they were heading into the Fire Swamp. Whether it was a touch of sulphur riding a breeze or a flick of yellow flame far ahead in the daylight, he could not say for sure. But once he realized what was about to happen, he began as casually as possible to find a way to avoid it. A quick glance up the sheer ravine sides ruled out any possibility of his getting Buttercup past the climb. He dropped to the ground, as he had been doing every few minutes, to test the speed of their trackers. Now, he guessed them to be less than half an hour behind and gaining.

He rose and ran with her, faster, neither of them spending breath in conversation. It was only a matter of time before she understood what they were about to be into, so he decided to beat back her panic in any way possible. "I think we can slow down a bit now," he told her, slowing down a bit. "They're still well behind."

Buttercup took a deep breath of relief.

Westley made a show of checking their surroundings. Then he gave her his best smile. "With any luck at all," he said, "we should soon be safely in the Fire Swamp."

Buttercup heard his speech, of course. But she did not, she did not, take it well. . . .

*   *   *

A FEW WORDS now on two related subjects: (1) fire swamps in general and (2) the Florin/Guilder Fire Swamp in particular.

(1) Fire swamps are, of course, entirely misnamed. As to why this has happened, no one knows, though probably the colorful quality of the two words together is enough. Simply, there are swamps which contain a large percentage of sulphur and other gas bubbles that burst continually into flame. They are covered with lush giant trees that shadow the ground, making the flame bursts seem particularly dramatic. Because they are dark, they are almost always quite moist, thereby attracting the standard insect and alligator community that prefers a moist climate. In other words, a fire swamp is just a swamp, period; the rest is embroidery.

(2) The Florin/Guilder Fire Swamp did and does have some particular odd characteristics: (a) the existence of Snow Sand and (b) the presence of the R.O.U.S., about which, a bit more later.

Snow Sand is usually, again incorrectly, identified with lightning sand. Nothing could be less accurate. Lightning sand is moist and basically destroys by drowning. Snow Sand is as powdery as anything short of talcum, and destroys by suffocation.

Most particularly though, the Florin/Guilder Fire Swamp was used to frighten children. There was not a child in either country that at one time or another was not, when misbehaving very badly, threatened with abandonment in the Fire Swamp. "Do that one more time, you're going to the Fire Swamp" is as common as "Clean your plate; people are starving in China." And so, as children grew, so did the danger of the Fire Swamp in their enlarging imaginations. No one, of course, ever actually went into the Fire Swamp, although, every year or so, a diseased R.O.U.S. might wander out to die, and its discovery would only add to the myth and the horror. The largest known fire swamp is, of course, within a day's drive of Perth. It is impenetrable and over twenty-five miles square. The one between Florin and Guilder was barely a third that size. No one had been able to discover if it was impenetrable or not.

Buttercup stared at the Fire Swamp. As a child, she had once spent an entire nightmared year convinced that she was going to die there. Now she could not move another step. The giant trees blackened the ground ahead of her. From every part came the sudden flames. "You cannot ask it of me," she said.

"I must."

"I once dreamed I would die here."

"So did I, so did we all. Were you eight that year? I was."

"Eight. Six. I can't remember."

Westley took her hand.

She could not move. "Must we?"

Westley nodded.

"Why?"

"Now is not the time." He pulled her gently.

She still could not move.

Westley took her in his arms. "Child; sweet child. I have a knife. I have my sword. I did not come across the world to lose you now."

Buttercup was searching somewhere for a sufficiency of courage. Evidently, she found it in his eyes.

At any rate, hand in hand, they moved into the shadows of the Fire Swamp.

*   *   *

PRINCE HUMPERDINCK JUST stared. He sat astride a white, studying the footsteps down on the floor of the ravine. There was simply no other conclusion: the kidnapper had dragged his Princess into it.

Count Rugen sat alongside. "Did they actually go in?"

The Prince nodded.

Praying the answer would be "no," the Count asked, "Do you think we should follow them?"

The Prince shook his head. "They'll either live or die in there. If they die, I have no wish to join them. If they live, I'll greet them on the other side."

"It's too far around," the Count said.

"Not for my whites."

"We'll follow as best we can," the Count said. He stared again at the Fire Swamp. "He must be very desperate, or very frightened, or very stupid, or very brave."

"Very all four I should think," the Prince replied. . . .

*   *   *

WESTLEY LED THE way. Buttercup stayed just behind, and they made, from the outset, very good time. The main thing, she realized, was to forget your childhood dreams, for the Fire Swamp *was* bad, but it wasn't *that* bad. The odor of the escaping gases, which at first seemed almost totally punishing, soon diminished through familiarity. The sudden bursts of flame were easily avoided because, just before they struck, there was a deep kind of popping sound clearly coming from the vicinity where the flames would then appear.

Westley carried his sword in his right hand, his long knife in his left, waiting for the first R.O.U.S., but none appeared. He had cut a very long piece of strong vine and coiled it over one shoulder and was busy working on it as they moved. "What we'll do once I've got this properly done is," he told her, moving steadily on beneath the giant trees, "we'll attach ourselves to each other, so that way, no matter what the darkness, we'll be close. Actually, I think that's more precaution than necessary, because, to tell you the truth, I'm almost disappointed; this place is bad, all right, but it's not *that* bad. Don't you agree?"

Buttercup wanted to, totally, and she would have too; only by then, the Snow Sand had her.

Westley turned only in time to see her disappear.

Buttercup had simply let her attention wander for a moment, the ground seemed solid enough, and she had no idea what Snow Sand looked like anyway; but once her front foot began to sink in, she could not pull back, and even before she could scream, she was gone. It was like falling through a cloud. The sand was the finest in the world, and there was no bulk to it whatsoever, and, at first, no unpleasantness. She was just falling, gently, through this soft powdery mass, falling farther and farther from anything resembling life, but she could not allow herself to panic. Westley had instructed her on how to behave if this happened, and she followed his words now: she spread her arms and spread her fingers and forced herself into the position resembling that of a dead-man's float in swimming, all this because Westley had told her to because the more she could spread herself, the slower she would sink. And the slower she sank, the quicker he could dive down after her and catch her. Buttercup's ears were now caked with Snow Sand all the way in, and her nose was filled with Snow Sand, both nostrils, and she knew if she opened her eyes a million tiny fine bits of Snow Sand would seep behind her eyelids, and now she was beginning to panic badly. How long had she been falling? Hours, it seemed, and she was having pain in holding her breath. "You must hold it till I find you," he had said; "you must go into a dead-man's float and you must close your eyes and hold your breath and I'll come get you and we'll both have a wonderful story for our grandchildren." Buttercup continued to sink. The weight of the sand began to brutalize her shoulders. The small of her back began to ache. It was agony keeping her arms outstretched and her fingers spread when it was all so useless. The Snow Sand was heavier and heavier on her now as she sank always down. And was it bottomless, as they thought when they were children? Did you just sink forever until the sand ate away at you and then did your poor bones continue the trip forever down? No, surely there had to somewhere be a resting place. A resting place, Buttercup thought. What a wonderful thing. I'm so tired, so tired, and I want to rest, and, *"Westley, come save me!"* she screamed. Or started to. Because in order to scream you had to open your mouth, so all she really got out was the first sound of the first word: "Wuh." After that the Snow Sand was down into her throat and she was done.

Westley had made a terrific start. Before she had even entirely disappeared, he had dropped his sword and long knife and had gotten the vine coil from his shoulder. It took him next to no time to knot one end around a giant tree, and, holding tight to the free end, he simply dove headlong into the Snow Sand, kicking his feet as he sank, for greater speed. There was no question in his mind of failure. He knew he would find her and he knew she would be up-set and hysterical and possibly even brain tumbled. But alive. And that was, in the end, the only fact of lasting import. The Snow Sand had his ears and nose blocked, and he hoped she had not panicked, had remembered to spread-eagle her body, so that he could catch her quickly with his headlong dive. If she remembered, it wouldn't be that hard—the same, really, as rescuing a drowning swimmer in murky water. They floated slowly down, you dove straight down, you kicked, you pulled with your free arm, you gained on them, you grabbed them, you brought them to the surface, and the only real problem then would be convincing your grandchildren that such a thing had actually happened and was not just another family fable. He was still concerning his mind with the infants yet unborn when something happened he had not counted on: the vine was not long enough. He hung suspended for a moment, holding to the end of it as it stretched straight up through the Snow Sand to the security of the giant tree. To release the vine was truly mad-ness. There was no possibility of forcing your body all the way back up to the surface. A few feet of ascension was possible if you kicked wildly, but no more. So if he let go of the vine and did not find her within a finger snap, it was all up for both of them. Westley let go of the vine without a qualm, because he had come too far to fail now; failure was not even a problem to be considered. Down he sank then and within a finger snap he had his hand around her wrist. Westley screamed then himself, in horror and surprise, and the Snow Sand gouged at his throat, for what he had grabbed was a skeleton wrist, bone only, no flesh left at all. That happened in Snow Sand. Once the skeleton was picked clean, it would begin, often, to float, like seaweed in a quiet tide, shifting this way and that, sometimes surfacing, more often just journeying through the Snow Sand for eternity. Westley threw the wrist away and reached out blindly with both hands now, scrabbling wildly to touch some part of her, because failure was not a problem; failure is not a problem, he told himself; it is not a problem to be considered, so forget failure; just keep busy and find her, and he found her. Her foot, more precisely, and pulled it to him and then his arm was around her perfect waist and he began to kick, kick with any strength left, needing now to rise the few yards to the end of the vine. The idea that it might be difficult finding a single vine strand in a small sea of Snow Sand never bothered him. Failure was not a problem; he would simply have to kick and when he had kicked hard enough he would rise and when he had risen enough he would reach out for the vine and when he reached out it would be there and when it was there he would tie her to it and with his last breath he would pull them both up to life.

Which is exactly what happened.

She remained unconscious for a very long time. Westley busied himself as best he could, cleansing the Snow Sand from ears and nose and mouth and, most delicate of all, from beneath the lids of her eyes. The length of her quietness disturbed him vaguely; it was almost as if she knew she had died and was afraid to find out for a fact that it was true. He held her in his arms, rocked her slowly. Eventually she was blinking.

For a time she looked around and around. "We lived, then?" she managed finally.

"We're a hardy breed."

"What a wonderful surprise."

"No need—" He was going to say "No need for worry," but her panic struck too quickly. It was a normal enough reaction, and he did not try to block it but, rather, held her firmly and let the hysteria run its course. She shuddered for a time as if she fully intended to fly apart. But that was the worst. From there, it was but a few minutes to quiet sobbing. Then she was Buttercup again.

Westley stood, buckled on his sword, replaced his long knife. "Come," he said. "We have far to go."

"Not until you tell me," she replied. "Why must we endure this?"

"Now is not the time." Westley held out his hand.

"It *is* the time." She stayed where she was, on the ground.

Westley sighed. She meant it. "All right," he said finally. "I'll explain. But we must keep moving."

Buttercup waited.

"We must get through the Fire Swamp," Westley began, "for one good and simple reason." Once he had started talking, Buttercup stood, following close behind him as he went on. "I had always intended getting to the far side; I had not, I must admit, expected to go through. Around, was my intention, but the ravine forced me to change."

"The good and simple reason," Buttercup prompted.

"On the far end of the Fire Swamp is the mouth of Giant Eel Bay. And anchored far out in the deepest waters of that bay is the great ship *Revenge*. The *Revenge* is the sole property of the Dread Pirate Roberts."

"The man who killed you?" Buttercup said. "That man? The one who broke my heart? The Dread Pirate Roberts took your life, that was the story I was told."

"Quite correct," Westley said. "And that ship is our destination."

"You know the Dread Pirate Roberts? You are friendly with such a man?"

"It's a little more than that," Westley said. "I don't expect you to quite grasp this all at once; just believe it's true. You see, I *am* the Dread Pirate Roberts."

"I fail to see how that is possible, since he has been marauding for twenty years and you only left me three years ago."

"I myself am often surprised at life's little quirks," Westley admitted.

"Did he, in fact, capture you when you were sailing for the Carolinas?"

"He did. His ship *Revenge* captured the ship I was on, *The Queen's Pride,* and we were all to be put to death."

"But Roberts did not kill you."

"Clearly."

"Why?"

"I cannot say for sure, but I think it is because I asked him please not to. The 'please,' I suspect, aroused his interest. I didn't beg or offer bribery, as the others were doing. At any rate, he held off with his sword long enough to ask, 'Why should I make an exception of you?' and I explained my mission, how I had to get to America to get money to reunite me with the most beautiful woman ever reared by man, namely you. 'I doubt that she is as beautiful as you imagine,' he said, and he raised his sword again. 'Hair the color of autumn,' I said, 'and skin like wintry cream.' 'Wintry cream, eh?' he said. He was interested now, at least a bit, so I went on describing the rest of you, and at the end, I knew I had him convinced of the truth of my affection for you. 'I'll tell you, Westley,' he said then, 'I feel genuinely sorry about this, but if I make an exception in your case, news will get out that the Dread Pirate Roberts has gone soft and that will mark the beginning of my downfall, for once they stop fearing you, piracy becomes nothing but work, work, work all the time, and I am far too old for such a life.' 'I swear I will never tell, not even my beloved,' I said; 'and if you will let me live, I will be your personal valet and slave for five full years, and if I ever once complain or cause you anger, you may chop my head off then and there and I will die with praise for your fairness on my lips.' I knew I had him thinking. 'Go below,' he said. 'I'll most likely kill you tomorrow.' " Westley stopped talking for a moment, and pretended to clear his throat, because he had spotted the first R.O.U.S. following behind them. There seemed no need yet to alert her, so he just continued to clear his throat and hurry along between the flame bursts.

"What happened tomorrow?" Buttercup urged. "Go on."

"Well, you know what an industrious fellow I am; you remember how I liked to learn and how I'd already trained myself to work twenty hours a day. I decided to learn what I could about piracy in the time left allotted me, since it would at least keep my mind off my coming slaughter. So I helped the cook and I cleaned the hold and, in general, did whatever was asked of me, hoping that my energies might be favorably noted by the Dread Pirate Roberts himself. 'Well, I've come to kill you,' he said the next morning, and I said, 'Thank you for the extra time; it's been most fascinating; I've learned such a great deal,' and he said, 'Overnight? What could you learn in that time?' and I said, 'That no one had ever explained to your cook the difference between table salt and cayenne pepper.' 'Things have been a bit fiery this trip,' he admitted. 'Go on, what else?' and I explained that there would have been more room in the hold if boxes had been stacked differently, and then he noticed that I had completely reorganized things down there and, fortunately for me, there *was* more room, and finally he said, 'Very well, you can be my valet for a day. I've never had a valet before; probably I won't like it, so I'll kill you in the morning.' Every night for the next year he always said something like that to me: 'Thank you for everything, Westley, good night now, I'll probably kill you in the morning.'

"By the end of that year, of course, we were more than valet and master. He was a pudgy little man, not at all fierce, as you would expect the Dread Pirate Roberts to be, and I like to think he was as fond of me as I of him. By then, I had learned really quite a great deal about sailing and hand fighting and fencing and throwing the long knife and had never been in as excellent physical condition. At the end of one year, my captain said to me, 'Enough of this valet business, Westley, from now on you are my second-in-command,' and I said, 'Thank you, sir, but I could never be a pirate,' and he said, 'You want to get back to that autumn-haired creature of yours, don't you?' and I didn't even have to bother answering that. 'A good year or two of piracy and you'll be rich and back you go,' and I said, 'Your men have been with you for years and they aren't rich,' and he said, 'That's because they are not the captain. I am going to retire soon, Westley, and the *Revenge* will be yours.' I must admit, beloved, I weakened a bit there, but we reached no final decision. Instead, he agreed to let me assist him in the next few captures and see how I liked it. Which I did." There was now another R.O.U.S. following them. Flanking them as they moved.

Buttercup saw them now. "Westley—"

"Shhh. It's all right. I'm watching them. Shall I finish? Will it take your mind off them?"

"You helped him with the next few captures," Buttercup said. "To see if you liked it."

Westley dodged a sudden burst of flame, shielded Buttercup from the heat. "Not only did I like it, but it turned out I was talented, as well. So talented that Roberts said to me one April morning, 'Westley, the next ship is yours; let's see how you do.' That afternoon we spotted a fat Spanish beauty, loaded for Madrid. I sailed up close. They were in a panic. 'Who is it?' their captain cried. 'Westley,' I told him. 'Never heard of you,' he answered, and with that they opened fire.

"Disaster. They had no fear of me at all. I was so flustered I did everything wrong, and soon they got away. I was, do I have to add, disheartened. Roberts called me to his cabin. I slunk in like a whipped boy. 'Buck up,' he told me, and then he closed the door and we were quite alone. 'What I am about to tell you I have never said before and you must guard it closely.' I of course said I would. 'I am not the Dread Pirate Roberts,' he said, 'my name is Ryan. I inherited this ship from the previous Dread Pirate Roberts just as you will inherit it from me. The man I inherited from was not the real Dread Pirate Roberts either; his name was Cummberbund. The real original Dread Pirate Roberts has been retired fifteen years and has been living like a king in Patagonia.' I confessed my confusion. 'It's really very simple,' Ryan explained. 'After several years, the original Roberts was so rich he wanted to retire. Clooney was his friend and first mate, so he gave the ship to Clooney, who had an identical experience to yours: the first ship he attempted to board nearly blew him out of the water. So Roberts, realizing the name was the thing that inspired the necessary fear, sailed the *Revenge* to port, changed crews entirely, and Clooney told everyone he was the Dread Pirate Roberts, and who was to know he was not? When Clooney retired rich, he passed the name to Cummberbund, Cummberbund to me, and I, Felix Raymond Ryan, of Boodle, outside Liverpool, now dub thee, Westley, the Dread Pirate Roberts. All we need is to land, take on some new young pirates. I will sail along for a few days as Ryan, your first mate, and will tell everyone about my years with you, the Dread Pirate Roberts. Then you will let me off when they are all believers, and the waters of the world are yours.' " Westley smiled at Buttercup. "So now you know. And you should also realize why it is foolish to be afraid."

"But I am afraid."

"It will all be happy at the end. Consider: a little over three years ago, you were a milkmaid and I was a farm boy. Now you are almost a queen and I rule uncontested on the water. Surely, such individuals were never intended to die in a Fire Swamp."

"How can you be sure?"

"Well, because we're together, hand in hand, in love."

"Oh yes," Buttercup said. "I keep forgetting that."

Both her words and her tone were a trifle standoffish, something Westley surely would have noticed had not a R.O.U.S. attacked him from the tree branch, sinking its giant teeth into his unprotected shoulder, forcing him to earth in a very unexpected spurt of blood. The other two that had been following launched their attack then too, ignoring Buttercup, driving forward with all their hungry strength to Westley's bleeding shoulder.

(Any discussion of the R.O.U.S.—Rodents of Unusual Size— must begin with the South American Capybara, which has been known to reach a weight of 150 pounds. They are nothing but water hogs, however, and present very little danger. The largest pure rat is probably the Tasmanian, which has actually been weighed at one hundred pounds. But they have little agility, tending to sloth when they reach full growth, and most Tasmanian herdsmen have learned with ease to avoid them. The Fire Swamp R.O.U.S.s were a pure rat strain, weighed usually eighty pounds, and had the speed of wolfhounds. They were also carnivorous, and capable of frenzy.)

The rats struggled with each other to reach Westley's wound. Their enormous front teeth tore at the unprotected flesh of his left shoulder, and he had no idea if Buttercup was already half devoured; he only knew that if he didn't do something desperate right then and right there she soon would be.

So he intentionally rolled his body into a spurt of flame.

His clothes began to burn—that he expected—but, more important, the rats shied away from the heat and the flames for just an instant, but that was enough for him to reach and throw his long knife into the heart of the nearest beast.

The other two turned instantly on their own kind and began eating it while it was still screaming.

Westley had his sword by then, and with two quick thrusts, the trio of rats was disposed of. *"Hurry!"* he shouted to Buttercup, who stood frozen where she had been when the first rat landed. "Bandages, bandages," Westley cried. "Make me some bandages or we die," and, with that, he rolled onto the ground, tore off his burning clothes and set to work caking mud onto the deep wound in his shoulder. "They're like sharks, blood creatures; it's blood they thrive on." He smeared more and more mud into his wound. "We must stop my bleeding and we must cover the wound so they do not smell it. If they don't smell the blood, we'll survive. If they do, we're for it, so help me, *please.*" Buttercup ripped her clothes into patches and ties, and they worked at the wound, caking the blood with mud from the floor of the Fire Swamp, then bandaging and re-bandaging over it.

"We'll know soon enough," Westley said, because two more rats were watching them. Westley stood, sword in hand. "If they charge, they smell it," he whispered.

The giant rats stood watching.

"Come," Westley whispered.

Two more giant rats joined the first pair.

Without warning, Westley's sword flashed, and the nearest rat was bleeding. The other three contented themselves with that for a while.

Westley took Buttercup's hand and again they started to move.

"How bad are you?" she said.

"I am in something close to agony but we can talk about that later. Hurry now." They hurried. They had been in the Fire Swamp for one hour, and it turned out to be the easiest one they had of the six it took to cross it. But they crossed it. Alive and together. Hand very much in hand.

It was nearly dusk when they at last saw the great ship *Revenge* far out in the deepest part of the bay. Westley, still within the confines of the Fire Swamp, sank, beaten, to his knees.

For between him and his ship were more than a few inconveniences. From the north sailed in half the great Armada. From the south now, the other half. A hundred mounted horsemen, armored and armed. In front of them the Count. And out alone in front of all, the four whites with the Prince astride the leader. Westley stood. "We took too long in crossing. The fault is mine."

"I accept your surrender," the Prince said.

Westley held Buttercup's hand. "No one is surrendering," he said.

"You're acting silly now," the Prince replied. "I credit you with bravery. Don't make yourself a fool."

"What is so foolish about winning?" Westley wanted to know. "It's my opinion that in order to capture us, you will have to come into the Fire Swamp. We have spent many hours here now; we know where the Snow Sand waits. I doubt that you or your men will be any too anxious to follow us in here. And by morning we will have slipped away."

"I doubt that somehow," said the Prince, and he gestured out to sea. Half the Armada had begun to give chase to the great ship *Revenge*. And the *Revenge*, alone, was sailing, as it had to do, away. "Surrender," the Prince said.

"It will not happen."

"SURRENDER!" the Prince shouted.

"DEATH FIRST!" Westley roared.

". . . will you promise not to hurt him . . . ?" Buttercup whispered.

"What was that?" the Prince said.

"What was that?" Westley said.

Buttercup took a step forward and said, "If we surrender, freely and without struggle, if life returns to what it was one dusk ago, will you swear not to hurt this man?"

Prince Humperdinck raised his right hand: "I swear on the grave of my soon-to-be-dead father and the soul of my already-dead mother that I shall not hurt this man, and if I do, may I never hunt again though I live a thousand years."

Buttercup turned to Westley. "There," she said. "You can't ask for more than that, and that is the truth."

"The truth," said Westley, "is that you would rather live with your Prince than die with your love."

"I would rather live than die, I admit it."

"We were talking of love, madam." There was a long pause. Then Buttercup said it:

"I can live without love."

And with that she left Westley alone.

Prince Humperdinck watched her as she began the long cross to him. "When we are out of sight," he said to Count Rugen, "take that man in black and put him in the fifth level of the Zoo of Death."

The Count nodded. "For a moment, I believed you when you swore."

"I spoke truth; I never lie," the Prince replied. "I said *I* would not hurt him. But I never for a moment said he would not suffer pain. *You* will do the actual tormenting; I will only spectate." He opened his arms then for his Princess.

"He belongs to the ship *Revenge*," Buttercup said. "He is—" she began, about to tell Westley's story, but that was not for her to repeat—"a simple sailor and I have known him since I was a child. Will you arrange that?"

"Must I swear again?"

"No need," Buttercup said, because she knew, as did everyone, that the Prince was more forthright than any Florinese.

"Come along, my Princess." He took her hand.

Buttercup went away with him.

Westley watched it all. He stood silently at the edge of the Fire Swamp. It was darker now, but the flame spurts behind him outlined his face. He was glazed with fatigue. He had been bitten, cut, gone without rest, had assaulted the Cliffs of Insanity, had saved and taken lives. He had risked his world, and now it was walking away from him, hand in hand with a ruffian prince.

Then Buttercup was gone, out of sight.

Westley took a breath. He was aware of the score of soldiers starting to surround him, and probably he could have made a few of them perspire for their victory.

But for what point?

Westley sagged.

"Come, sir." Count Rugen approached. "We must get you safely to your ship."

"We are both men of action," Westley replied. "Lies do not become us."

"Well spoken," said the Count, and with one sudden swing, he clubbed Westley into insensitivity.

Westley fell like a beaten stone, his last conscious thought being of the Count's right hand; it was six-fingered, and Westley could never quite remember having encountered that deformity before. . . .

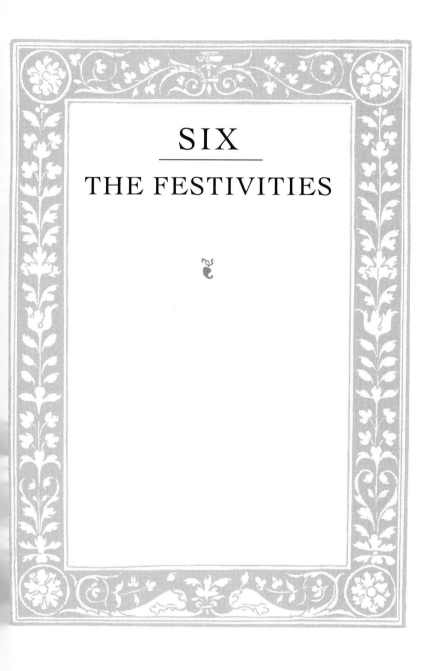

SIX

THE FESTIVITIES

THIS is one of those chapters again where Professor Bongiorno of Columbia, the Florinese guru, claims that Morgenstern's satiric genius is at its fullest flower. (That's the way this guy talks: 'fullest flower,' 'delicious drolleries'—on and on.)

This festivities chapter is mostly detailed descriptions of guess what? Bingo! The festivities. It's like eighty-nine days till the nuptials and every high muckamuck in Florin has to give a 'do' for the couple, and what Morgenstern fills his pages with is how the various richies of the time entertained. What kind of parties, what kind of food, who did the decorations, how did the seating arrangements get settled, all that kind of thing.

The only interesting part, but it's not worth going through forty-four pages for, is that Prince Humperdinck gets more and more interested and mannerly toward Buttercup, cutting down even a little on his hunting activities. And, more important, because of the foiling of the kidnapping attempt, three things happen: (1) everyone is pretty well convinced that the plot was engineered by Guilder, so relations between the countries are more than a little strained; (2) Buttercup is just adored by everybody because the rumors are all over that she acted very brave and even came through the Fire Swamp alive and (3) Prince Humperdinck is, at last, in his own land, a hero. He was never popular, what with his hunting fetish and leaving the country to kind of rot once his old man got senile, but the way he foiled the *kidnapping made everybody realize that this was some brave fella and they were lucky to have him next in line to lead them.*

Anyhow, these forty-four pages cover just about the first month of party giving. And it's not till the end of that, that, for my money, things get going again. Buttercup is in bed, pooped, it's late, the end of another long party, and as she waits for sleep, she wonders what sea Westley is riding on, and the giant and the Spaniard, whatever happened to them? So eventually, in three quick flashbacks, Morgenstern returns to what I think is the story.

*　　　　*　　　　*

WHEN INIGO REGAINED consciousness, it was still night on the Cliffs of Insanity. Far below, the waters of Florin Channel pounded. Inigo stirred, blinked, tried to rub his eyes, couldn't.

His arms were tied together around a tree.

Inigo blinked again, banishing cobwebs. He had gone on his knees to the man in black, ready for death. Clearly, the victor had other notions. Inigo looked around as best he could, and there it was, the six-fingered sword, glittering in the moonlight like lost magic. Inigo stretched his right leg as far as it would go and managed to touch the handle. Then it was simply a matter of inching the weapon close enough to be graspable by one hand, and then it was an even simpler task to slash his bindings. He was dizzy when he stood, and he rubbed his head behind his ear, where the man in black had struck him. A lump, sizable, to be sure, but not a major problem.

The major problem was what to do now?

Vizzini had strict instructions for occasions such as this, when a plan went wrong: *Go back to the beginning.* Back to the beginning and wait for Vizzini, then regroup, replan, start again. Inigo had even made a little rhyme out of it for Fezzik so the giant would not have problems remembering what to do in time of trouble: *"Fool, fool, back to the beginning is the rule."*

Inigo knew precisely where the beginning was. They had gotten the job in Florin City itself, the Thieves Quarter. Vizzini had made the arrangements alone, as he always did. He had met with their employer, had accepted the job, had planned it, all in the Thieves Quarter. So the Thieves Quarter was clearly the place to go.

Only, Inigo hated it there. Everybody was so dangerous, big, mean and muscular, and so what if he was the greatest fencer in the world, who'd know it to look at him? He looked like a skinny Spanish guy it might be fun to rob. You couldn't walk around with a sign saying, "Be careful, this is the greatest fencer since the death of the Wizard of Corsica. Do not burgle."

Besides, and here Inigo felt deep pain, he wasn't that great a fencer, not any more, he couldn't be, hadn't he just been beaten? Once, true, he had been a titan, but now, now—

*   *   *

What happens here that you aren't going to read is the six-page soliloquy from Inigo in which Morgenstern, through Inigo, reflects on the anguish of fleeting glory. The reason for the soliloquy here is that Morgenstern's previous book had gotten bombed by the critics and also hadn't sold beans. (Aside—did you know that Robert Browning's first book of poems didn't sell one copy? True. Even his mother didn't buy it at her local bookstore. Have you ever heard anything more humiliating? How would you like to have been Browning and it's your first book and you have these secret hopes that now, now, you'll be somebody. Established, Important. And you give it a week before you ask the publisher how things are going, because you don't want to seem pushy or anything. And then maybe you drop by, and it was probably all very English and understated in those days, and you're Browning and you chitchat around a bit, before you drop the biggie: 'Oh, by the way, any notions yet on how my poems might be doing?' And then his editor, who has been dreading this moment, probably says, 'Well, you know how it is with poetry these days; nothing's taking off like it used to, requires a bit of time for the word to get around.' And then finally, somebody had to say it. 'None, Bob. Sorry, Bob, no, we haven't yet had one authenticated sale. We thought for a bit that Hatchards had a potential buyer down by Piccadilly, but it didn't quite work out. Sorry, Bob; of course we'll keep you posted in the event of a break-through.' End of Aside.)

Anyway, Inigo finishes his speech to the Cliffs and spends the next few hours finding a fisherman who sails him back to Florin City.

* * *

THE THIEVES QUARTER was worse than he remembered. Always, before, Fezzik had been with him, and they made rhymes, and Fezzik was enough to keep any thief away.

Inigo moved panicked up the dark streets, desperately afraid. Why this giant fear? *What was he afraid of?*

He sat on a filthy stoop and pondered. Around him there were cries in the night and, from the alehouses, vulgar laughter. He was afraid, he realized then, because as he sat there, gripping the six-fingered sword for confidence, he was suddenly back to what he had been before Vizzini had found him.

A failure.

A man without point, with no attachment to tomorrow. Inigo had not touched brandy in years. Now he felt his fingers fumbling for money. Now he heard his footsteps running toward the nearest alehouse. Now he saw his money on the counter. Now he felt the brandy bottle in his hands.

Back to the stoop he ran. He opened the bottle. He smelled the rough brandy. He took a sip. He coughed. He took a swallow. He coughed again. He gulped it down and coughed and gulped some more and half began a smile.

His fears were starting to leave him.

After all, why should he have even been afraid? He was Inigo Montoya (the bottle was half gone now), son of the great Domingo Montoya, so what was there in the world worth fearing? (Now all the brandy was gone.) How dare fear approach a wizard such as Inigo Montoya? Well, never again. (Into the second bottle.) Never never never never again.

He sat alone and confident and strong. His life was straight and fine. He had money enough for brandy, and if you had that, you had the world.

The stoop was wretched and bleak. Inigo slumped there, quite contented, clutching the bottle in his once-trembling hands. Existence was really very simple when you did what you were told. And nothing could be simpler or better than what he had in store.

All he had to do was wait and drink until Vizzini came. . . .

* * *

FEZZIK HAD NO idea how long he was unconscious. He only knew, as he staggered to his feet on the mountain path, that his throat was very sore where the man in black had strangled him.

What to do?

The plans had all gone wrong. Fezzik closed his eyes, trying to think—there was a proper place to go when plans went wrong, but he couldn't quite remember it. Inigo had even made a rhyme up for him so he wouldn't forget, and now, even with that, he was so stupid he had forgotten. Was that it? Was it "Stupid, stupid, go and wait for Vizzini with Cupid"? That rhymed, but where was the

Cupid? "Dummy, dummy, go out now and fill your tummy." That rhymed too, but what kind of instructions were those?

What to do, what to do?

"Dunce, dunce, use your brains and do it right for once"? No help. Nothing was any help. He never had done anything right, not in his whole life, until Vizzini came, and without another thought, Fezzik ran off into the night after the Sicilian.

Vizzini was napping when he got there. He had been drinking wine and dozed off. Fezzik dropped to his knees and put his hands in prayer position. "Vizzini, I'm sorry," he began.

Vizzini napped on.

Fezzik shook him gently.

Vizzini did not wake.

Not so gently this time.

Nothing.

"Oh I see, you're dead," Fezzik said. He stood up. "He's dead, Vizzini is," he said softly. And then, with not a bit of help from his brain, a great scream of panic burst from his throat into the night: *"Inigo!"* and he whirled back down the mountain path, because if Inigo was alive, it would be all right; it wouldn't be the same, no, it could never be that without Vizzini to order them and insult them as only he could, but at least there would be time for poetry, and when Fezzik reached the Cliffs of Insanity he said, "Inigo, Inigo, here I am" to the rocks and "I'm here, Inigo; it's your Fezzik" to the trees and "Inigo, INIGO, ANSWER ME PLEASE" all over until there was no other conclusion to draw but that just as there was now no Vizzini, so there was also no Inigo, and that was hard.

It was, in point of fact, too hard for Fezzik, so he began to run, crying out, "Be with you in a minute, Inigo," and "Right behind you, Inigo" and "Hey, Inigo, wait up" (wait up, straight up which was the way he ran, and wouldn't there be fun with rhymes once he and Inigo were together again), but after an hour or so of shouting his throat gave out because he had, after all, been strangled almost to death in the very recent past. On he ran, on and on and on until finally he reached a tiny village and found, just outside town, some nice rocks that formed kind of a cave, almost big enough for him to stretch out in. He sat with his back against a rock and his hands around his knees and his throat hurting until the village boys found him. They held their breath and crept as close as they dared. Fezzik hoped they would go away, so he froze, pretending to be off with Inigo and Inigo would say "barrel" and Fezzik right quick would come back "carol" and maybe they would sing a little something until Inigo said "serenade" and you couldn't stump Fezzik with one that easy because of "centigrade" and then Inigo would make a word about the weather and Fezzik would rhyme it and that was how it went until the village boys stopped being afraid of him. Fezzik could tell that because they were creeping very close to him now and all of a sudden yelling their lungs out and making crazy faces. He didn't really blame them; he looked like the kind of person you did that to, mocked. His clothes were torn and his throat was gone and his eyes were wild and he probably would have yelled too if he'd been their age.

It was only when they found him funny that he found it, though he did not know the word, degrading. No more yelling. Just laughter now. Laughter, Fezzik thought, and then he thought giraffeter, because that's all he was to them, some huge funny thing that couldn't make much noise. Laughter, giraffeter, from now to hereafter.

Fezzik huddled up in his cave and tried looking on the bright side. At least they weren't throwing things at him.

Not yet, anyway.

*   *   *

WESTLEY AWOKE CHAINED in a giant cage. His shoulder was beginning to fester from the gnawing and digging that the R.O.U.S.s had done into his flesh. He ignored his discomfort, momentarily, to try and adjust to his surroundings.

He was certainly underground. It was not the lack of windows that made that sure; more the dankness. From somewhere above him now, he could hear animal sounds: an occasional lion roar, the yelp of the cheetah.

Shortly after his return to consciousness, the albino appeared, bloodless, with skin as pale as dying birch. The candlelight that served to illuminate the cage made the albino seem totally like a creature who had never seen the sun. The albino held a tray which carried many things, bandages and food, healing powders and brandy.

"Where are we?" from Westley.

A shrug from the albino.

"Who are you?"

Shrug.

That was almost the entire extent of the fellow's conversation. Westley asked question after question while the albino tended and redressed his wound, then fed him food that was warm and surprisingly good and plentiful.

Shrug.

Shrug.

"Who knows I'm here?"

Shrug.

"Lie, but tell me something—*give an answer.* Who knows I'm here?"

Whispered: "I know. They know."

"They?"

Shrug.

"The Prince and the Count, you mean?"

Nod.

"And that is all?"

Nod.

"When I was brought in I was half conscious. The Count was giving the orders, but three soldiers were carrying me. They know too."

Shake. Whispered: "Knew."

"They're dead, that's what you're saying?"

Shrug.

"Am I to die then?"

Shrug.

Westley lay back on the floor of the giant underground cage watching as the albino silently reloaded the tray, glided from sight. If the soldiers were dead, surely it was not unreasonable to assume that he would eventually follow. But if they wanted his erasure, surely it was also not unreasonable to assume that they had not the least intention of doing it immediately, else why tend his wounds, why return his strength with good warm food? No, his death would be a while yet. But in the meantime, considering the personalities of his captors, it was finally not unreasonable to assume that they would do their best to make him suffer.

Greatly.

Westley closed his eyes. There was pain coming and he had to be ready for it. He had to prepare his brain, he had to get his mind controlled and safe from their efforts, so that they could not break him. He would not let them break him. He would hold together against anything and all. If only they gave him sufficient time to make ready, he knew he could defeat pain. It turned out they gave him sufficient time (it was months before the Machine was ready).

But they broke him anyway.

*   *   *

AT THE END of the thirtieth day of festivities, with sixty days more of partying to enjoy, Buttercup was genuinely concerned that she might lack the strength to endure. Smile, smile, hold hands, bow and thank, over and over. She was simply exhausted from one month; how was she to survive twice that?

It turned out, because of the King's health, to be both easy and sad. For with fifty-five days to go, Lotharon began to weaken terribly.

Prince Humperdinck ordered new doctors brought in. (There was still the last miracle man alive, Max, but since they had fired him long before, bringing him back on the case now was simply not deemed wise; if he was incompetent then, when Lotharon was only desperately ill, how could he suddenly be a cure-all now, with Lotharon dying?) The new doctors all agreed on various tried-and-true medications, and within forty-eight hours of their coming on the case, the King was dead.

The wedding date of course, was unchanged—it wasn't every day a country had a five hundredth anniversary—but all the festivities were either curtailed entirely or vastly cut down. And Prince Humperdinck became, forty-five days before the wedding, King of Florin, and that changed everything, because, before, he had taken nothing but his hunting seriously, and now he had to learn, learn *everything*, learn to run a country, and he buried himself in books and wise men and how did you tax this and when should you tax that and foreign entanglements and who could be trusted and how far and with what? And before her lovely eyes, Humperdinck changed from a man of fear and action to one of frenzied wisdom, because he had to get it all straight *now* before any other country dared interfere with the future of Florin, so the wedding, when it actually took place, was a tiny thing and brief, sandwiched in between a ministers' meeting and a treasury crisis, and Buttercup spent her first afternoon as queen wandering around the castle not knowing what in the world to do with herself. It wasn't until King Humperdinck walked out on the balcony with her to greet the gigantic throng that had spent the day in patient waiting that she realized it *had* happened, she *was* the Queen, her life, for whatever it was worth, belonged now to the people.

They stood together on the castle balcony, accepting the cheers, the cries, the endless thunderous "hip hips," until Buttercup said, "Please, may I walk once more among them?" and the King said with a nod that she might and down she went again, as on the day of the wedding announcement, radiant and alone, and again the people swept apart to let her pass, weeping and cheering and bowing and—

—and then one person booed.

On the balcony watching it all Humperdinck reacted instantly, gesturing soldiers into the area where the sound had come from, dispatching more troops quickly down to surround the Queen, and like clockwork Buttercup was safe, the booer apprehended and led away.

"Hold a moment," Buttercup said, still shaken by the unexpectedness of what had happened. The soldier who held the booer stopped. "Bring her to me," Buttercup said, and in a moment the booer was right there, eye to eye.

It was an ancient woman, withered and bent, and Buttercup thought of all the faces that had gone by in her lifetime, but this one she could not remember. "Have we met?" the Queen asked.

The old one shook her head.

"Then why? Why on this day? Why do you insult the Queen?"

"Because you are not worthy of cheers," the old woman said, and suddenly she was yelling, *"You had love in your hands and you gave it up for gold!"* She turned to the crowd. *"It is true what I tell you—there was love alongside her in the Fire Swamp and she dropped it from her fingers like garbage, and that is what she is, the Queen of Garbage."*

"I had given my word to the Prince—" Buttercup began, but the old woman would not be quieted.

"Ask her how she got through the Fire Swamp? Ask her if she did it alone? She threw love away to be the Queen of Grime, the Queen of Muck—I am old and life means nothing to me, so I am the only person in all this crowd to dare to tell truth, and truth says bow to the Queen of Feculence if you want to, but not I. Cheer the Queen of Slime and Ordure if you want to, but not I. Rave over the beauty of the Queen of Cesspools, but not I. Not I!" She was advancing on Buttercup now.

"Take her away," Buttercup ordered.

But the soldiers could not stop her, and the old woman kept coming on, her voice getting louder and louder and Louder! and LOUDER! and *LOUDER* and LOUDER! and—

Buttercup woke up screaming.

She was in her bed. Alone. Safe. The wedding was still sixty days away.

But her nightmares had begun.

The next night she dreamed of giving birth to their first child and

*   *   *

 Interruption, and hey, how about giving old Morgenstern credit for a major league fake-out there. I mean, didn't you think for a while at least that they really were married? I did.

It's one of my biggest memories of my father reading. I had pneumonia, remember, but I was a little better now, and madly caught up

in the book, and one thing you know when you're ten is that, no matter what, there's gonna be a happy ending. They can sweat all they want to scare you, the authors, but back of it all you know, you just have no doubt, *that in the long run justice is going to win out. And Westley and Buttercup — well, they had their troubles, sure, but they were going to get married and live happily ever after. I would have bet the family fortune if I'd found a sucker big enough to take me on.*

Well, when my father got through with that sentence where the wedding was sandwiched between the ministers' meeting and the treasury whatever, I said, 'You read that wrong.'

My father's this little bald barber — remember that too? And kind of illiterate. Well, you just don't challenge a guy who has trouble reading and say he's read something incorrectly, because that's really threatening. 'I'm doing the reading,' he said.

'I know that but you got it wrong. She didn't marry that rotten Humperdinck. She marries Westley.'

'It says right here,' my father began, a little huffy, and he starts going over it again.

'You must have skipped a page then. Something. Get it right, huh?'

By now he was more than a tiny bit upset. 'I skipped nothing. I read the words. The words are there, I read them, good night,' and off he went.

'Hey please, no,' I called after him, but he's stubborn, and, next thing, my mother was in saying, 'Your father says his throat is too sore; I told him not to read so much,' and she tucked and fluffed me and no matter how I battled, it was over. No more story till the next day.

I spent that whole night thinking Buttercup married Humperdinck. It just rocked me. How can I explain it, but the world didn't work that way. Good got attracted to good, evil you flushed down the john and that was that. But their marriage — I couldn't make it jibe. God, did I work at it. First I thought that probably Buttercup had *this fantastic effect on Humperdinck and turned him into a kind of Westley, or maybe Westley and Humperdinck turned out to be long-lost brothers and Humperdinck was so happy to get his brother back he said, 'Look, Westley, I didn't realize who you were when I married her so what I'll do is I'll divorce her and you marry her and that way we'll all be happy.' To this day I don't think I was ever more creative.*

But it didn't take. Something was wrong and I couldn't lose it. Suddenly there was this discontent gnawing away until it had a place big enough to settle in and then it curled up and stayed there and it's still inside me lurking as I write this now.

The next night, when my father went back to reading and the marriage turned out to have been Buttercup's dream, I screamed 'I knew it, all along I knew it,' and my father said, 'So you're happy now, it's all right now, we can please continue?' and I said 'Go' and he did.

But I wasn't happy. Oh my ears were happy, I guess, my story sense was happy, my heart too, but in my, I suppose you have to call it 'soul', there was that damn discontent, shaking its dark head.

All this was never explained to me till I was in my teens and there was this great woman who lived in my home town, Edith Neisser, dead now, and she wrote terrific books about how we screw up our children — Brothers and Sisters *was one of her books,* The Eldest Child *was another. Published by Harper. Edith doesn't need the plug, seeing, like I said, as she's no longer with us, but if there are any amongst you who are worried that maybe you're not being perfect parents, pick up one of Edith's books while there's still time. I knew her 'cause her kid Ed got his haircuts from my pop, and she was this writer and by my teens I knew, secretly, that was the life for me too, except I couldn't tell anybody. It was too embarrassing — barber's sons, if they hustled, maybe got to be IBM salesmen, but writers? No way. Don't ask me how, but eventually Edith discovered my shhhhhh ambition and from then on, sometimes, we would talk. And I remem-*

ber once we were having iced tea on the Neisser porch and talking and just outside the porch was their badminton court and I was watching some kids play badminton and Ed had just shellacked me, and as I left the court for the porch, he said, 'Don't worry, it'll all work out, you'll get me next time' and I nodded, and then Ed said, 'And if you don't, you'll beat me at something else.'

I went to the porch and sipped iced tea and Edith was reading this book and she didn't put it down when she said, 'That's not necessarily true, you know.'

I said, 'How do you mean?'

And that's when she put her book down. And looked at me. And said it: 'Life isn't fair, Bill. We tell our children that it is, but it's a terrible thing to do. It's not only a lie, it's a cruel lie. Life is not fair, and it never has been, and it's never going to be.'

Would you believe that for me right then it was like one of those comic books where the light bulb goes on over Mandrake the Magician's head? 'It isn't!' I said, so loud I really startled her. 'You're right. It's not fair.' I was so happy if I'd known how to dance, I'd have started dancing. 'Isn't that great, isn't it just terrific?' I think along about here Edith must have thought I was well on my way toward being bonkers.

But it meant so much to me to have it said and out and free and flying—that was the discontent I endured the night my father stopped reading, I realized right then. That was the reconciliation I was trying to make and couldn't.

And that's what I think this book's about. All those Columbia experts can spiel all they want about the delicious satire; they're crazy. This book says 'life isn't fair' and I'm telling you, one and all, you better believe it. I got a fat spoiled son—he's not gonna nab Miss Rheingold. And he's always gonna be fat, even if he gets skinny he'll still be fat and he'll still be spoiled and life will never be enough to make him happy, and that's my fault maybe—make it all my fault, if you want—the point is, we're not created equal, for the rich they sing, life isn't fair. I got a cold wife; she's brilliant, she's stimulating, she's terrific; there's no love; that's okay too, just so long as we don't keep expecting everything to somehow even out for us before we die.

Look. (Grownups skip this paragraph.) I'm not about to tell you this book has a tragic ending, I already said in the very first line how it was my favorite in all the world. But there's a lot of bad stuff coming up, torture you've already been prepared for, but there's worse. There's death coming up, and you better understand this: some of the wrong people die. *Be ready for it. This isn't Curious George Uses the Potty. Nobody warned me and it was my own fault (you'll see what I mean in a little) and that was my mistake, so I'm not letting it happen to you. The wrong people die, some of them, and the reason is this; life is not fair. Forget all the garbage your parents put out. Remember Morgenstern. You'll be a lot happier.*

Okay. Enough. Back to the next. Nightmare time.

*   *   *

THE NEXT NIGHT she dreamed of giving birth to their first child and it was a girl, a beautiful little girl, and Buttercup said, "I'm sorry it wasn't a boy; I know you need an heir," and Humperdinck said, "Beloved sweet, don't concern yourself with that; just look at the glorious child God has given us" and then he left and Buttercup held the child to her perfect breast and the child said, "Your milk is sour" and Buttercup said, "Oh, I'm sorry," and she shifted to the other breast and the child said, "No, this is sour too," and Buttercup said, "I don't know what to do" and the baby said, "You always know what to do, you always know exactly what to do, you always do exactly what's right for you, and the rest of the world can go hang," and Buttercup said, "You mean Westley" and the baby said, "Of course I mean Westley," and Buttercup explained patiently, "I thought he was dead, you see; I'd given my word to your father" and the baby said, "I'm dying now; there's no love in your milk, your milk has killed me" and then the child stiffened and cracked and turned in Buttercup's hands to nothing but dry dust and Buttercup screamed and screamed; even when she was awake again, with fifty-nine days to go till her marriage, she was still screaming.

The third nightmare came quickly the following evening, and again it was a baby—this time a son, a marvelous strong boy—and Humperdinck said, "Beloved, it's a boy" and Buttercup said, "I didn't fail you, thank heavens" and then he was gone and Buttercup called out, "May I see my son now" and all the doctors scurried around outside her royal room, but the boy was not brought in. "What seems to be the trouble?" Buttercup called out and the chief doctor said, "I don't quite understand, but he doesn't want to see you" and Buttercup said, "Tell him I am his mother and I am the Queen and I command his presence" and then he was there, just as handsome a baby boy as anyone could wish for. "Close it," Buttercup said, and the doctors closed the door. The baby stood in the corner as far from her bed as he could. "Come here, darling," Buttercup said. "Why? Are you going to kill me too?" "I'm your mother and I love you, now come here; I've never killed anybody." "You killed Westley, did you see his face in the Fire Swamp? When you walked away and left him? That's what I call killing." "When you're older, you'll understand things, now I'm not going to tell you again—come here." "Murderer," the baby shouted. *"Murderer!"* but by then she was out of bed and she had him in her arms and was saying, "Stop that, stop it this instant; I love you," and he said, "Your love is poison; it kills," and he died in her arms and she started to cry. Even when she was awake again, with fifty-eight days to go till her marriage, she was still crying.

The next night she simply refused to go to sleep. Instead, she walked and read and did needlework and drank cup after cup of steaming tea from the Indies. She felt sick with weariness, of course, but such was her fear of what she might dream that she preferred any waking discomfort to whatever sleep might have to offer, and at dawn her mother was pregnant—no, more than pregnant; her mother was having a baby—and as Buttercup stood there in the corner of the room, she watched herself being born and her father gasped at her beauty and so did her mother and the midwife was the first to show concern. The midwife was a sweet woman, known throughout the village for her love of babies, and she said, "Look—trouble—" and the father said, "What trouble? Where before did you ever see such beauty?" and the midwife said, "Don't you understand why she was given such beauty? It's because she has no heart, here, listen; the baby is alive but there is no beat" and she held Buttercup's chest against the father's ear and the father could only nod and say, "We must find a miracle man to place a heart inside" but the midwife said, "That would be wrong, I think; I've heard before of creatures like this, the heartless ones, and as they grow bigger they get more and more beautiful and behind them is nothing but broken bodies and shattered souls, and these without hearts are anguish bringers, and my advice would be, since you're both still young, to have another child, a different child, and be rid of this one now, but, of course, the final decision is up to you" and the father said to the mother, "Well?" and the mother said, "Since the midwife is the kindest person in the village, she must know a monster when she sees one; let's get to it," so Buttercup's father and Buttercup's mother put their hands to the baby's throat and the baby began to gasp. Even when Buttercup was awake again, at dawn, with fifty-seven days to go till her marriage, she could not stop gasping.

From then on, the nightmares became simply too frightening.

When there were fifty days to go, Buttercup knocked, one night, on the door to Prince Humperdinck's chambers. She entered when he bid her to. "I see trouble," he said. "You look very ill." And so she did. Beautiful, of course. Still that. But in no way well.

Buttercup did not see quite how to begin.

He ushered her into a chair. He got her water. She sipped at it, staring dead ahead. He put the glass to one side.

"At your convenience, Princess," he said.

"It comes to this," Buttercup began. "In the Fire Swamp, I made the worst mistake in all the world. I love Westley. I always have. It seems I always will. I did not know this when you came to me. Please believe what I am about to say: when you said that I must marry you or face death, I answered, 'Kill me.' I meant that. I mean this now too: if you say I must marry you in fifty days, I will be dead by morning."

The Prince was literally stunned.

After a long moment, he knelt by Buttercup's chair and, in his gentlest voice, started to speak: "I admit that when we first became engaged, there was to be no love involved. That was as much my choice as yours, though the notion may have come from you. But surely you must have noticed, in this last month of parties and festivities, a certain warming of my attitude."

"I have. You have been both sweet and noble."

"Thank you. Having said that, I hope you appreciate how difficult this next sentence is for me to say: I would die myself rather than cause you unhappiness by standing in the way of your marrying the man you love."

Buttercup wanted almost to weep with gratitude. She said: "I will bless you all my days for your kindness." Then she stood. "So it's settled. Our wedding is off."

He stood too. "Except for perhaps one thing."

"That being?"

"Have you considered the possibility that he might not now want any longer to marry you?"

Until that moment, she had not.

"You were, I hate to remind you, not altogether gentle with his emotions in the Fire Swamp. Forgive me for saying that, beloved, but you did leave him in the lurch, in a manner of speaking."

Buttercup sat down hard, her turn now to be stunned.

Humperdinck knelt again beside her. "This Westley of yours, this sailor boy; he has pride?"

Buttercup managed to whisper, "More than any man alive, I sometimes think."

"Well consider, then, dearest. Here he is, off sailing somewhere with the Dread Pirate Roberts; he has had a month to survive the emotional scars you dealt him. What if he wants now to remain single? Or, worse, what if he has found another?"

Buttercup was now even beyond whispering.

"I think, sweetest child, that we should strike a bargain, you and I: if Westley wants to marry you still, bless you both. If, for reasons unpleasant to mention, his pride will not let him, then you will marry me, as planned, and be the Queen of Florin."

"He couldn't be married. I'm sure. Not my Westley." She looked at the Prince. "But how can I find out?"

"What about this: you write him a letter, telling him everything. We'll make four copies. I'll take my four fastest ships and order them off in all directions. The Dread Pirate Roberts is not often more than a month's sail from Florin. Whichever of my ships finds him will run the white flag of truce, deliver your letter, and Westley can decide. If 'no,' he can speak that message to my captain. If 'yes,' my captain will sail him here to you, and I will have to content myself somehow with a lesser bride."

"I think—I'm not *sure*—but I definitely *think*, that this is the most generous decision I have yet heard."

"Do me this favor then in return: until we know Westley's intentions, one way or another, let us continue as we have, so the festivities will not be halted. And if I seem too fond of you, remember that I cannot help myself."

"Agreed," Buttercup said, going to the door, but not before she kissed his cheek.

He followed her. "Off with you now and write your letter," and he returned the kiss, smiling with his eyes at her until the corridor curved her from his sight. There was no doubt whatsoever in his mind that he was going to seem too fond of her in the days ahead. Because when she died of murder on their wedding night, it was crucial that all Florin realize the depth of his love, the epochal size of his loss, since then no one would dare hesitate to follow him in the revenge war he was to launch against Guilder.

At first, when he hired the Sicilian, he was convinced it was best that someone else do her in, all the while making it appear the work of soldiers from Guilder. And when the man in black had somehow materialized to spoil his plans, the Prince came close to going insane with rage. But now his basically optimistic nature had reasserted itself: everything always worked out for the best. The people were infatuated with Buttercup now as they had never been before her kidnapping. And when he announced from his castle balcony that she had been murdered—he already saw the scene in his mind: he would arrive just too late to save her from strangling but soon enough to see the Guilderian soldiers leaping from the window of his bedroom to the soft ground below—when he made that speech to the masses on the five hundredth anniversary of his country, well, there wouldn't be a dry eye in the Square. And although he was just the least bit perturbed, since he had never actually killed a woman before with his bare hands, there was a first time for everything. Besides, if you wanted something done right, you did it yourself.

*   *   *

THAT NIGHT, THEY began to torture Westley. Count Rugen did the actual pain inducing; the Prince simply sat by, asking questions out loud, inwardly admiring the Count's skill.

The Count really cared about pain. The whys behind the screams interested him fully as much as the anguish itself. And whereas the Prince spent his life in physically following the hunt, Count Rugen read and studied anything he could get his hands on dealing with the subject of Distress.

"All right now," the Prince said to Westley, who lay in the great fifth-level cage; "before we begin, I want you to answer me this: have you any complaints about your treatment thus far?"

"None whatever," Westley replied, and in truth he had none. Oh, he might have preferred being unchained a bit now and then, but if you were to be a captive, you couldn't ask for more than he had been given. The albino's medical ministrations had been precise, and his shoulder was fine again; the food the albino brought had always been hot and nourishing, the wine and brandy wonderfully warming against the dankness of the underground cage.

"You feel fit, then?" the Prince went on.

"I assume my legs are a little stiff from being chained, but other than that, yes."

"Good. Then I promise you this as God himself is my witness: answer the next question and I will set you free this night. But you must answer it honestly, fully, withholding nothing. If you lie, I will know. And then I'll loose the Count on you."

"I have nothing to hide," Westley said. "Ask away."

"Who hired you to kidnap the Princess? It was someone from Guilder. We found fabric indicating as much on the Princess's horse. Tell me that man's name and you are free. Speak."

"No one hired me," Westley said. "I was working strictly freelance. And I didn't kidnap her; I saved her from others who were doing that very thing."

"You seem a reasonable fellow, and my Princess claims to have known you many years, so I will give you, on her account, one last and final chance: the name of the man in Guilder who hired you. Tell me or face torture."

"No one hired me, I swear."

The Count set fire to Westley's hands. Nothing permanent or disabling; he just dipped Westley's hands in oil and brought a candle close enough to set things bubbling. When Westley had screamed "NO ONE—NO ONE—NO ONE—ON MY LIFE!" a sufficient number of times, the Count dipped Westley's hands in water, and he and the Prince left via the underground entrance, leaving the medication to the albino, who was always nearby during the torturing times, but never visible enough to be distracting.

"I feel quite invigorated," the Count said as he and the Prince began to ascend the underground staircase. "It's a perfect question. He was telling the truth, clearly; we both know that."

The Prince nodded. The Count was privy to all his innermost plans for the revenge war.

"I'm fascinated to see what happens," the Count went on. "Which pain will be least endurable? The physical, or the mental anguish of having freedom offered if the truth is told, then telling it and being thought a liar."

"I think the physical," said the Prince.

"I think you're wrong," said the Count.

Actually, they were both wrong; Westley suffered not at all throughout. His screaming was totally a performance to please them; he had been practicing his defenses for a month now, and he was more than ready. The minute the Count brought the candle close, Westley raised his eyes to the ceiling, dropped his eyelids over them, and in a state of deep and steady concentration, he took his brain away. Buttercup was what he thought of. Her autumn hair, her perfect skin, and he brought her very close beside him, and had her whisper in his ear throughout the burning: "I love you. I love you. I only left you in the Fire Swamp to test your love for me. Is it as great as mine for you? Can two such loves exist on one planet at one time? Is there that much room, beloved Westley? . . ."

The albino bandaged his fingers.

Westley lay still.

For the first time, the albino started things. Whispered: "You better tell them."

From Westley, a shrug.

Whispered: "They never stop. Not once they start. Tell them what they want to know and have done with it."

Shrug.

Whispered: "The Machine is nearly ready. They are testing it on animals now."

Shrug.

Whispered: "It's for your own good I tell you these things."

"My own good? What good? They're going to kill me anyway."

From the albino: nod.

*   *   *

THE PRINCE FOUND Buttercup waiting unhappily outside his chamber doors.

"It's my letter," she began. "I cannot make it right."

"Come in, come in," the Prince said gently. "Maybe we can help you." She sat down in the same chair as before. "All right, I'll close my eyes and listen; read to me."

" 'Westley, my passion, my sweet, my only, my own. Come back, come back. I shall kill myself otherwise. Yours in torment, Buttercup.' " She looked at Humperdinck. "Well? Do you think I'm throwing myself at him?"

"It does seem a bit forward," the Prince admitted. "It doesn't leave him a great deal of room to maneuver."

"Will you help me to improve it, please?"

"I'll do what I can, sweet lady, but first it might help if I knew just a bit about him. Is he really so wonderful, this Westley of yours?"

"Not so much wonderful as perfect," she replied. "Kind of flawless. More or less magnificent. Without blemish. Rather on the ideal side." She looked at the Prince. "Am I being helpful?"

"I think emotions are clouding your objectivity just a bit. Do you actually think that there is nothing the fellow can't do?"

Buttercup thought for a while. "It's not so much that there's nothing he can't do; it's more that he can do it all better than anybody else can do it."

The Prince chuckled and smiled. "In other words, for example, you mean if he wanted to hunt, he could outhunt, again for example, someone such as myself."

"Oh, I would think if he wanted to, he could, quite easily, but he happens not to like hunting, at least to my knowledge, though maybe he does; I don't know. I never knew he was so interested in mountain climbing but he scaled the Cliffs of Insanity under most adverse conditions, and everyone agrees that that is not the easiest thing in the world to accomplish."

"Well, why don't we just begin our letter with 'Divine Westley,' and appeal to his sense of modesty," the Prince suggested.

Buttercup began to write, stopped. "Does 'divine' begin *de* or *di*?"

"*Di,* I believe, amazing creature," the Prince replied, smiling gently as Buttercup commenced the letter. They composed it in four hours, and many many times she said, "I could never get through this without you" and the Prince was always most modest, asking little helpful personal questions about Westley as often as was possible without drawing attention to it, and in this way, well before dawn, she told him, smiling as she remembered, of Westley's early fears of Spinning Ticks.

And that night, in the fifth-level cage, the Prince asked, as he was to always ask, "Tell me the name of the man in Guilder who hired you to kidnap the Princess and I promise you immediate freedom" and Westley replied, as he was always to reply, "No one, no one; I was alone" and the Count, who had spent the day getting the Spinners ready, placed them carefully on Westley's skin and Westley closed his eyes and begged and pleaded and after an hour or so the Prince and Count left, the albino remaining behind with the chore of burning the Spinners and then pulling them free from Westley, lest they accidentally poison him, and on the way up the underground stairs to ground level the Prince said, just for conversation's sake, "Much better, don't you think?"

The Count, oddly, said nothing.

Which was vaguely irritating to Humperdinck because, to tell the absolute truth, torture was never all that high on his scale of passions, and he would just as soon have disposed of Westley right then.

If only Buttercup would admit that he, Humperdinck, was the better man.

But she would not! She simply would not! All she ever talked about was Westley. All she ever asked about was news of Westley. Days went by, weeks went by, party after party went by, and all Florin was moved by the spectacle of their great hunting Prince at last so clearly and wonderfully in love, but when they were alone, all she ever said was, "I wonder where could Westley be? What could be taking him so long? How can I live until he comes?"

Maddening. So each night, the Count's discomforts, which made Westley writhe and twist, were really sort of all right. The Prince would manage an hour or so of spectating before he and the Count would leave, the Count still oddly silent. And down below, tending the wounds, the albino would whisper: "Tell them. *Please.* They will only add to your suffering."

Westley could barely suppress his smile.

He had felt no pain, not once, none. He had closed his eyes and taken his brain away. That was the secret. If you could take your brain away from the present and send it to where it could contemplate skin like wintry cream; well, let them enjoy themselves.

His revenge time would come.

Westley was living now most of all for Buttercup. But there was no denying that there was one more thing he wanted too.

His time . . .

* * *

PRINCE HUMPERDINCK SIMPLY had no time. There seemed to be not one decision in all of Florin that one way or another didn't eventually come heavily to rest upon his shoulders. Not only was he getting married, his country was having its five hundredth anniversary. Not only was he noodling around in his mind the best ways to get a war going, he also had to constantly have affection shining from his eyes. Every detail had to be met, and met correctly.

His father was just no help at all, refusing either to expire or stop mumbling *(you thought his father was dead but that was in the fake-out, don't forget—Morgenstern was just edging into the nightmare sequence, so don't be confused)* and start making sense. Queen Bella simply hovered around him, translating here and there, and it was with a shock that Prince Humperdinck realized, just twelve days before his wedding day, that he had neglected to set in motion the crucial Guilder section of his plan, so he called Yellin to the castle late one night.

Yellin was Chief of All Enforcement in Florin City, a job he had inherited from his father. (The albino keeper at the Zoo was Yellin's first cousin, and together they formed the only pair of non-nobles the Prince could come close to trusting.)

"Your Highness," Yellin said. He was small, but crafty, with darting eyes and slippery hands.

Prince Humperdinck came out from behind his desk. He moved close to Yellin and looked carefully around before saying, softly, "I have heard, from unimpeachable sources, that many men of Guilder have, of late, begun to infiltrate our Thieves Quarter. They are disguised as Florinese, and I am worried."

"I have heard nothing of such a thing," Yellin said.

"A prince has spies everywhere."

"I understand," said Yellin. "And you think, since the evidence points that they tried to kidnap your fiancée once, such a thing might happen again?"

"It's a possibility."

"I'll close off the Thieves Quarter then," Yellin said. "No one will enter and no one will leave."

"Not good enough," said the Prince. "I want the Thieves Quarter emptied and every villain jailed until I am safely on my honeymoon." Yellin did not nod quickly enough, so the Prince said, "State your problem."

"My men are not always too happy at the thought of entering the Thieves Quarter. Many of the thieves resist change."

"Root them out. Form a brute squad. But get it done."

"It takes at least a week to get a decent brute squad going," Yellin said. "But that is time enough." He bowed, and started to leave.

And that was when the scream began.

Yellin had heard many things in his life, but nothing quite so eerie as this: he was a brave man, but this sound frightened him. It was not human, but he could not guess the throat of the beast it came from. (It was actually a wild dog, on the first level of the Zoo, but no wild dog had ever shrieked like that before. But then, no wild dog had ever been put in the Machine.)

The sound grew in anguish, and it filled the night sky as it spread across the castle grounds, over the walls, even into the Great Square beyond.

It would not stop. It simply hung now below the sky, an audible reminder of the existence of agony. In the Great Square, half a dozen children screamed back at the night, trying to blot out the sound. Some wept, some only ran for home.

Then it began to lessen in volume. Now it was hard to hear in the Great Square, now it was gone. Now it was hard to hear on the castle walls, now it was gone from the castle walls. It shrunk across the grounds toward the first level of the Zoo of Death, where Count Rugen sat fiddling with some knobs. The wild dog died. Count Rugen rose, and it was all he could do to bury his own shriek of triumph.

He left the Zoo and ran toward Prince Humperdinck's chambers.

Yellin was just going when the Count got there. The Prince was seated now, behind his desk. When Yellin was gone and they were alone, the Count bowed to his majesty: "The Machine," he said at last, "works."

*　　　　*　　　　*

PRINCE HUMPERDINCK TOOK a while before answering. It was a ticklish situation, granted he was the boss, the Count merely an underling, still, no one in all Florin had Rugen's skills. As an inventor, he had, obviously, at last, rid the Machine of all defects. As an architect, he had been crucial in the safety factors involved in the Zoo of Death, and it had undeniably been Rugen who had arranged for the only survivable entrance being the underground fifth-level one. He was also supportive to the Prince in all endeavors of hunting and battle, and you didn't give a follower like that a quick "Get away, boy, you bother me." So the Prince indeed took a while.

"Look, Ty," he said finally. "I'm just thrilled you smoothed all the bugs out of the Machine; I never for a minute doubted you'd get it right eventually. And I'm really anxious as can be to see it working. But how can I put this? I can't keep my head above water one minute to the next: it's not just the parties and the goo-gooing with what's-her-name, I've got to decide how long the Five Hundredth Anniversary Parade is going to be and where does it start and when does it start and which nobleman gets to march in front of which other nobleman so that everyone's still speaking to me at the end of it, plus I've got a wife to murder and a country to frame for it, plus I've got to get the war going once that's all happened, and all this is stuff I've got to do myself. Here's what it all comes down to: I'm just swamped, Ty. So how about if you go to work on Westley and tell me how it goes, and when I get the time, I'll come watch and I'm sure it'll be just wonderful, but for now, what I'd like is a little breathing room, no hard feelings?"

Count Rugen smiled. "None." And there weren't any. He always felt better when he could dole out pain alone. You could concentrate much more deeply when you were alone with agony.

"I knew you'd understand, Ty."

There was a knock on the door and Buttercup stuck her head in. "Any news?" she said.

The Prince smiled at her and sadly shook his head. "Honey, I promised to tell you the second I hear a thing."

"It's only twelve days, though."

"Plenty of time, dulcet darling, now don't worry yourself."

"I'll leave you," Buttercup said.

"I was going too," the Count said. "May I walk you to your quarters?"

Buttercup nodded, and down the corridors they wandered till they reached her suite. "Good night," Buttercup said quickly; ever since that day he had first come to her father's farm, she had always been afraid whenever the Count came near.

"I'm sure he'll come," the Count said; he was privy to all the Prince's plans, and Buttercup was well aware of this. "I don't know your fellow well, but he impressed me greatly. Any man who can find his way through the Fire Swamp can find his way to Florin Castle before your wedding day."

Buttercup nodded.

"He seemed so strong, so remarkably powerful," the Count went on, his voice warm and lulling. "I only wondered if he possessed true sensitivity, as some men of great might, as you know, do not. For example, I wonder: is he capable of tears?"

"Westley would never cry," Buttercup answered, opening her chamber door. "Except for the death of a loved one." And with that she closed the Count away and, alone, went to her bed and knelt. Westley, she thought then. Do come please; I have begged you in my thoughts now these many weeks and still no word. Back when we were on the farm, I thought I loved you, but that was not love. When I saw your face behind the mask on the ravine floor, I thought I loved you, but that was again nothing more than deep infatuation. Beloved: I think I love you now, and I pray you only give me the chance to spend my life in constant proving. I could spend my life in the Fire Swamp and sing from morn till night if you were by me. I could spend eternity sinking down through Snow Sand if my hand held your hand. My preference would be to last eternity with you beside me on a cloud, but hell would also be a lark if Westley was with me. . . .

She went on that way, silent hour after silent hour; she had done nothing else for thirty-eight evenings now, and each time, her ardor deepened, her thoughts became more pure. Westley. Westley. Flying across the seven seas to claim her.

For his part, and quite without knowing, Westley was spending his evenings in much the same fashion. After the torture was done, when the albino had finished tending his slashes or burns or breaks, when he was alone in the giant cage, he sent his brain to Buttercup, and there it dwelled.

He understood her so well. In his mind, he realized that moment he left her on the farm when she swore love, certainly she meant it, but she was barely eighteen. What did she know of the depth of the heart? Then again, when he had removed his black mask and she had tumbled to him, surprise had been operating, stunned astonishment as much as emotion. But just as he knew that the sun was obliged to rise each morning in the east, no matter how much a western arisal might have pleased it, so he knew that Buttercup was obliged to spend her love on him. Gold was inviting, and so was royalty, but they could not match the fever in his heart, and sooner or later she would have to catch it. She had less choice than the sun.

So when the Count appeared with the Machine, Westley was not particularly perturbed. As a matter of fact, he had no idea what the Count was bringing with him into the giant cage. As a matter of absolute fact, the Count was bringing nothing; it was the albino who was doing the actual work, making trip after trip with thing after thing.

That was what it really looked like to Westley: things. Little soft rimmed cups of various sizes and a wheel, most likely, and another object that could turn out to be either a lever or a stick; it was hard to tell.

"A good good evening to you," the Count began.

He had never, to Westley's memory, shown such excitement. Westley made a very weak nod in return. Actually, he felt about as well as ever, but it didn't do to let that kind of news get around.

"Feeling a bit under the weather?" the Count asked.

Westley made another feeble nod.

The albino scurried in and out, bringing more things: wirelike extensions, stringy and endless.

"That will be all," the Count said finally.

Nod.

Gone.

"This is the Machine," the Count said when they were alone. "I've spent eleven years constructing it. As you can tell, I'm rather excited and proud."

Westley managed an affirmative blink.

"I'll be putting it together for a while." And with that, he got busy.

Westley watched the construction with a good deal of interest and, logically enough, curiosity.

"You heard that scream a bit earlier on this evening?"

Another affirmative blink.

"That was a wild dog. This machine caused the sound." It was a very complex job the Count was doing, but the six fingers on his right hand never for a moment seemed in doubt as to just what to do. "I'm very interested in pain," the Count said, "as I'm sure you've gathered these past months. In an intellectual way, actually. I've written, of course, for the more learned journals on the subject. Articles mostly. At the present I'm engaged in writing a book. My book. *The* book, I hope. The definitive work on pain, at least as we know it now."

Westley found the whole thing fascinating. He made a little groan.

"I think pain is the most underrated emotion available to us," the Count said. "The Serpent, to my interpretation, was pain. Pain has been with us always, and it always irritates me when people say 'as important as life and death' because the proper phrase, to my mind, should be, 'as important as pain and death.'" The Count fell silent for a time then, as he began and completed a series of complex adjustments. "One of my theories," he said somewhat later, "is that pain involves anticipation. Nothing original, I admit, but I'm going to demonstrate to you what I mean: I will not, underline *not*, use the Machine on you this evening. I could. It's ready and tested. But instead I will simply erect it and leave it beside you, for you to stare at the next twenty-four hours, wondering just what it is and how it works and can it really be as dreadful as all that." He tightened some things here, loosened some more over there, tugged and patted and shaped.

The Machine looked so silly Westley was tempted to giggle. Instead, he groaned again.

"I'll leave you to your imagination, then," the Count said, and he looked at Westley. "But I want you to know one thing before to-morrow night happens to you, and I mean it: you are the strongest, the most brilliant and brave, the most altogether worthy creature it has ever been my privilege to meet, and I feel almost sad that, for the purposes of my book and future pain scholars, I must destroy you."

"Thank . . . you . . ." Westley breathed softly.

The Count went to the cage door and said over his shoulder, "And you can stop all your performing about how weak and beaten you are; you haven't fooled me for a month. You're practically as strong now as on the day you entered the Fire Swamp. I know your secret, if that's any consolation to you."

". . . secret?" Hushed, strained.

"You've been taking your brain away," the Count cried. "You haven't felt the least discomfort in all these months. You raise your eyes and drop your eyelids and then you're off, probably with—I don't know—her, most likely. Good night now. Try and sleep. I doubt you'll be able to. Anticipation, remember?" With a wave, he mounted the underground stairs.

Westley could feel the sudden pressure of his heart.

Soon the albino came, knelt by Westley's ear. Whispered: "I've been watching you all these days. You deserve better than what's coming. I'm needed. No one else feeds the beasts as I do. I'm safe. They won't hurt me. I'll kill you if you'd like. That would foil them. I've got some good poison. I beg you. I've seen the Machine. I was there when the wild dog screamed. Please let me kill you. You'll thank me, I swear."

"I must live."

Whispered: "But—"

Interruption: "They will not reach me. I am all right. I am fine. I am alive, and I will stay that way." He said the words loud, and he said them with passion. But for the first time in a long time, there was terror. . . .

*   *   *

"WELL, COULD YOU sleep?" the Count asked the next night upon his arrival in the cage.

"Quite honestly, no," Westley replied in his normal voice.

"I'm glad you're being honest with me; I'll be honest with you; no more charades between us," the Count said, putting down a number of notebooks and quill pens and ink bottles. "I must carefully track your reactions," he explained.

"In the name of science?"

The Count nodded. "If my experiments are valid, my name will last beyond my body. It's immortality I'm after, to be quite honest." He adjusted a few knobs on the Machine. "I suppose you're naturally curious as to how this works."

"I have spent the night pondering and I know no more than when I started. It appears to be a great conglomeration of soft rimmed cups of infinitely varied sizes, together with a wheel and a dial and a lever, and what it does is beyond me."

"Also glue," added the Count, pointing to a small tub of thick stuff. "To keep the cups attached." And with that, he set to work, taking cup after cup, touching the soft rims with glue, and setting them against Westley's skin. "Eventually I'll have to put one on your tongue too," the Count said, "but I'll save that for last in case you have any questions."

"This certainly isn't the easiest thing to get set up, is it?"

"I'll be able to fix that in later models," the Count said; "at least those are my present plans," and he kept right on putting cup after cup on Westley's skin until every inch of exposed surface was covered. "So much for the outside," the Count said then. "This next is a bit more delicate; try not to move."

"I'm chained hand, head and foot," Westley said. "How much movement do you think I'm capable of?"

"Are you really as brave as you sound, or are you a little frightened? The truth, please. This is for posterity, remember."

"I'm a little frightened," Westley replied.

The Count jotted that down, along with the time. Then he got down to the fine work, and soon there were tiny tiny soft rimmed cups on the insides of Westley's nostrils, against his eardrums, under his eyelids, above and below his tongue, and before the Count arose, Westley was covered inside and out with the things. "Now all I do," the Count said very loudly, hoping Westley could hear, "is get the wheel going to its fastest spin so that I have more than enough power to operate. And the dial can be set from one to twenty and, this being the first time, I will set it at the lowest setting, which is one. And then all I need do is push the lever forward, and we should, if I haven't gummed it up, be in full operation."

But Westley, as the lever moved, took his brain away, and when the Machine began, Westley was stroking her autumn-colored hair and touching her skin of wintry cream and—and—and then his world exploded—because the cups, the cups were everywhere, and before, they had punished his body but left his brain, only not the Machine; the Machine reached everywhere—his eyes were not his to control and his ears could not hear her gentle loving whisper and his brain slid away, slid far from love into the deep fault of despair, hit hard, fell again, down through the house of agony into the county of pain. Inside and out, Westley's world was ripping apart and he could do nothing but crack along with it.

The Count turned off the Machine then, and as he picked up his notebooks he said, "As you no doubt know, the concept of the suction pump is centuries old—well, basically, that's all this is, except instead of water, I'm sucking life; I've just sucked away one year of your life. Later I'll set the dial higher, certainly to two or three, perhaps even to five. Theoretically, five should be five times more severe than what you've just endured, so please be specific in your answers. Tell me now, honestly: how do you feel?"

In humiliation, and suffering, and frustration, and anger, and anguish so great it was dizzying, Westley cried like a baby.

"Interesting," said the Count, and carefully noted it down.

*   *   *

IT TOOK YELLIN a week to get his enforcers together in sufficient number, together with an adequate brute squad. And so, five days before the wedding, he stood at the head of his company awaiting the speech of the Prince. This was in the castle courtyard, and when the Prince appeared, the Count was, as usual, with him, although, not as usual, the Count seemed preoccupied. Which, of course, he was, though Yellin had no way of knowing that. The Count had sucked ten years from Westley this past week, and, with the life of sixty-five that was average for a Florinese male, the victim had approximately thirty years remaining, assuming he was about twenty-five when they started experimenting. But how best to go about dividing that? The Count was simply in a quandary. So many possibilities, but which would prove, scientifically, most interesting? The Count sighed; life was never easy.

"You are here," the Prince began, "because there may be another plot against my beloved. I charge each and every one of you with being her personal protector. I want the Thieves Quarter empty and all the inhabitants jailed twenty-four hours before my wedding. Only then will I rest easy. Gentlemen, I beg you: think of this mission as being an affair of the heart, and I know you will not fail." With that he pivoted and, followed by the Count, hurried from the courtyard, leaving Yellin in command.

The conquest of the Thieves Quarter began immediately. Yellin worked long and hard at it each day, but the Thieves Quarter was a mile square, so there was much to do. Most of the criminals had been through unjust and illegal roundups before, so they offered little resistance. They knew the jails were not celled enough for all of them, so if it meant a few days' incarceration, what did it matter?

There was, however, a second group of criminals, those who realized that capture meant, for various past performances, death, and these, without exception, resisted. In general, Yellin, through adroit handling of the Brute Squad, was able to bring these bad fellows, eventually, under control.

Still, thirty-six hours before the sunset wedding, there were half a dozen holdouts left in the Thieves Quarter. Yellin arose at dawn and, tired and confused—not one of the captured criminals seemed to come from Guilder—he gathered the best of the Brute Squad and led them into the Thieves Quarter for what simply had to be the final foray.

Yellin went immediately to Falkbridge's Alehouse, first sending all save two Brutes off on various tasks, keeping a noisy one and a quiet one for his own needs. He knocked on Falkbridge's door and waited. Falkbridge was by far the most powerful man in the Thieves Quarter. He seemed almost to own half of it and there wasn't a crime of any dimension he wasn't behind. He always avoided arrest, and everyone except Yellin thought Falkbridge must be bribing somebody. Yellin *knew* he was bribing somebody, since every month, rain or shine, Falkbridge came to Yellin's house and gave him a satchel full of money.

"Who?" Falkbridge called from inside the alehouse.

"The Chief of All Enforcement in Florin City, accompanied by Brutes," Yellin replied. Completeness was one of his virtues.

"Oh." Falkbridge opened the door. For a power, he was very unimposing, short and chubby. "Come in."

Yellin entered, leaving the two Brutes in the doorway. "Get ready and be quick," Yellin said.

"Hey, Yellin, it's me," Falkbridge said softly.

"I know, I know," Yellin said softly right back. "But please, do me a favor, get ready."

"Pretend I did. I'll stay in the alehouse, I promise. I got enough food; no one will ever know."

"The Prince is without mercy," Yellin said. "If I let you stay and I'm found out, that's it for me."

"I been paying you twenty years to stay out of jail. You're a rich man just so I don't have to go to jail. Where's the logic of me paying you and no advantages?"

"I'll make it up to you. I'll get you the best cell in Florin City. Don't you trust me?"

"How can I trust a man I pay twenty years to stay out of jail when all of a sudden, the minute a little extra pressure's on, he says 'go to jail'? I'm not going."

"You!" Yellin signaled to the noisy one.

The Brute started running forward.

"Put this man in the wagon immediately," Yellin said.

Falkbridge was starting to explain when the noisy one clubbed him across the neck.

"Not so hard!" Yellin cried.

The noisy one picked up Falkbridge, tried dusting his clothes.

"Is he alive?" Yellin asked.

"See, I didn't know you wanted him breathing in the wagon; I thought you only wanted him in the wagon breathing or not, so—"

"Enough," Yellin interrupted and, upset, he hurried out of the alehouse while the noisy one brought Falkbridge. "Is that everyone then?" Yellin asked as various Brutes were visible leaving the Thieves Quarter pulling various wagons.

"I think there's still the fencer with the brandy," the noisy one began. "See, they tried getting him out yesterday but—"

"I can't be bothered with a drunk; I'm an important man, get him out of here and do it now, both of you; take the wagon with you, and be quick! This quarter must be locked and deserted by sundown or the Prince will be mad at me, and I don't like it much when the Prince is mad at me."

"We're going, we're going," the noisy one replied, and he hurried off, letting the quiet one bring the wagon with Falkbridge inside. "They tried getting this fencer yesterday, some of the standard enforcers, but it seems he has certain sword skills that made them wary, but I think I have a trick that will work." The quiet one hurried along behind, dragging the wagon. They rounded a corner, and from around another corner just up ahead, a kind of drunken mumbling was starting to get louder.

"I'm getting very bored, Vizzini" came from out of sight. "Three months is a long time to wait, especially for a passionate Spaniard." Much louder now: *"And I am very passionate, Vizzini, and you are nothing but a tardy Sicilian.* So if you're not here in ninety more days, I'm done with you. You hear? *Done!"* Much softer now: "I didn't mean that, Vizzini, I just love my filthy stoop, take your time. . . ."

The noisy Brute slowed. "That kind of talk goes on all day; ignore it, and keep the wagon out of sight." The quiet one pushed the wagon almost to the corner and stopped it. "Stay with the wagon," the noisy one added, and then whispered, "Here comes my trick." With that he walked alone around the corner and stared ahead at the skinny fellow sitting clutching the brandy bottle on the stoop. "Ho there, friend," the noisy one said.

"I'm not moving: keep your 'ho there,'" said the brandy drinker.

"Hear me through, please: I have been sent by Prince Humperdinck himself, who is in need of entertainment. Tomorrow is our country's five hundredth anniversary and the dozen greatest tumblers and fencers and entertainers are at this very moment competing. The finest pair will compete personally tomorrow for the new bride and groom. Now, as to why I'm here: yesterday, some of my friends tried rousting you and they said, later, that you resisted with some splendid swordwork. So, if you would like, I, at great personal sacrifice, will rush you to the fencing contest, where, if you are as good as I am told, you might have yet the honor of entertaining the Royal Couple tomorrow. Do you think you could win such a competition?"

"Breezing."

"Then hurry while there's still time to enter."

The Spaniard managed to stand. He unsheathed his sword and flashed it a few times across the morning.

The noisy one took a few quick steps backward and said, "No time to waste; come along now."

Then the drunk started yelling: "I'm—waiting—for—Vizzini—"

"Meanie."

"I'm—not—mean, I'm—just—following—the—rule—"

"Cruel."

"Not—cruel, not—mean; can't you understand I'm . . ." and here his voice trailed off for a moment as he squinted. Then, quietly, he said, "Fezzik?"

From behind the noisy one, the quiet one said, "Who says-ik?"

Inigo took a step from his stoop, trying desperately to make his eyes focus through the brandy. " 'Says-ik'? Is that a joke you made?"

The quiet one said, "Played."

Inigo gave a cry and started staggering forward: *"Fezzik, it's you!"*

"TRUE!" And he reached out, grabbed Inigo just before he stumbled, brought him back to an upright position.

"Hold him just like that," the noisy Brute said, and he moved in quickly, right arm raised, as he had done to Falkbridge.

S

P

L

A

T

!

Fezzik dumped the noisy Brute into the wagon beside Falk-bridge, covered them both with a soiled blanket, then hurried back to Inigo, whom he had left leaning propped against a building.

"It's just so good to see you," Fezzik said then.

"Oh, it is . . . it . . . is, but . . ." Inigo's voice was winding steadily down now. "I'm too weak for surprises" were the last sounds he got out before he fainted from fatigue and brandy and no food and bad sleep and lots of other things, none of them nutritious.

Fezzik hoisted him up with one arm, took the wagon in the other, and hurried back to Falkbridge's house. He carried Inigo inside, placed him upstairs on Falkbridge's feather bed, then hurried away to the entrance of the Thieves Quarter, dragging the wagon behind him. He made very sure that the dirty blanket covered both the victims, and outside the entrance the Brute Squad held a boot count of those they had removed. The total came out right, and, by eleven in the morning, the great walled Thieves Quarter was officially empty and padlocked.

Released from active duty, Fezzik followed the wall around to a quiet place and waited. He was alone. Walls were never any problem for him, not so long as his arms worked, and he quickly scaled this one and hurried back through the quiet streets to Falkbridge's house. He made some tea, carried it upstairs, force-fed Inigo. Within a few moments, Inigo was blinking under his own power.

"It's just so good to see you," Fezzik said then.

"Oh, it is, it is," Inigo agreed, "and I'm sorry for fainting, but I have done nothing for ninety days but wait for Vizzini and drink brandy, and a surprise like seeing you, well, that was just too much for me on an empty stomach. But I'm fine now."

"Good," Fezzik said. "Vizzini is dead."

"He is, eh? Dead, you say ... Vizz ..." and then he fainted again.

Fezzik began berating himself. "Oh, you stupid, if there's a right way and a wrong way, trust you to find the dumb way; fool, fool, back to the beginning was the rule." Fezzik really felt idiotic then because, after months of forgetting, now that he didn't need to remember any more, he remembered. He hurried downstairs and made some tea and brought some crackers and honey and fed Inigo again.

When Inigo blinked, Fezzik said, "Rest."

"Thank you, my friend; no more fainting." And he closed his eyes and slept for an hour.

Fezzik busied himself in Falkbridge's kitchen. He really didn't know how to prepare a proper meal, but he could heat and he could cool and he could sniff the good meat from the rotted, so it wasn't too great a task to finally end up with something that once looked like roast beef and another thing that could have been a potato.

The unexpected smell of hot food brought Inigo around, and he lay in bed, eating every bite Fezzik fed him. "I never realized I was in such terrible condition," Inigo said, chewing away.

"Shhh, you'll be fine now," Fezzik said, cutting another piece of meat, putting it into Inigo's mouth.

Inigo chewed it carefully down. "First you appearing so suddenly and then, on top of that, the business of Vizzini. It was too much for me."

"It would have been too much for anybody; just rest." Fezzik began to cut another piece of meat.

"I feel such a baby, so helpless," Inigo said, taking the next bite, chewing away.

"You'll be as strong as ever by sundown," Fezzik promised, getting the next piece of meat ready. "The six-fingered man is named Count Rugen and he's here right now in Florin City."

"Interesting," Inigo managed this time before he fainted again.

Fezzik stood over the still figure. "Well it *is* so good to see you," he said, "and it's been such a long time and I've just got so much news."

Inigo only lay there.

Fezzik hurried to Falkbridge's tub and plugged it up and after a lot of work he got it filled with steaming water and then he dunked Inigo in, holding him down with one hand, holding Inigo's mouth shut with the other, and when the brandy began to sweat from the Spaniard's body, Fezzik emptied the tub and filled it again, with icy water this time, and back he plunged Inigo, and when that water began to warm a bit back he filled the tub with steaming stuff and back went Inigo and now the brandy was really oozing from his pores and that was how it went, hour after hour, hot to icy cold to steaming hot and then some tea and then some toast and then some steaming hot again and more icy cold and then a nap and then more toast and less tea but the longest steamer yet and this time there wasn't much brandy left inside and one final icy cold and then a two-hour sleep until by midafternoon, they sat downstairs in Falkbridge's kitchen, and now, at last, for the first time in ninety days, Inigo's eyes were almost bright. His hands did shake, but not all that noticeably, and perhaps the Inigo of before the brandy would have bested this fellow now in sixty minutes of solid fencing. But not too many other masters in the world would have survived for five.

"Tell me briefly now: while I've been here with the brandy, you have been where?"

"Well, I spent some time in a fishing village and then I wandered a bit, and then a few weeks ago I found myself in Guilder and the talk there was of the coming wedding and perhaps a coming war and I remembered Buttercup when I carried her up the Cliffs of Insanity; she was so pretty and soft and I had never been so near perfume before that I thought it might be nice to see her wedding celebrations, so I came here, but my money was gone, and then they were forming a brute squad and needed giants and I went to apply and they beat me with clubs to see if I was strong enough and when the clubs broke they decided I was. I've been a Brute First Class all this past week; it's very good pay."

Inigo nodded. "All right, again, and this time *please* be brief, from the beginning: the man in black. Did he get by you?"

"Yes. Fairly too. Strength against strength. I was too slow and out of practice."

"Then it was he that killed Vizzini?"

"That is my belief."

"Did he use his sword or his strength?"

Fezzik tried to remember. "There weren't any sword wounds and Vizzini didn't seem broken. There were just these two goblets and Vizzini dead. Poison is my guess."

"Why would Vizzini take poison?"

Fezzik hadn't the least idea.

"But he was definitely dead?"

Fezzik was positive.

Inigo began to pace the kitchen, his movements quick and sharp, the way his movements were before. "All right, Vizzini is dead, enough of that. Tell me *briefly* where the six-fingered Rugen is so I may kill him."

"That may not be so easy, Inigo, because the Count is with the Prince, and the Prince is in his castle, and he is pledged not to leave it till after his wedding, for he fears another sneak attack from Guilder, and all the entrances but the main one are sealed for safety and the main doors are guarded by twenty men."

"Hmmm," Inigo said, pacing faster now. "If you fought five and I fenced five, that would mean ten gone, which would be bad because that would also mean ten left and they would kill us. *But,*" and now he picked up his pace even more, "if you should take six and I took eight, that would mean fourteen beaten, which would not be as bad but still bad enough, since the six remaining would kill us." And now he whirled on Fezzik. "How many could you handle at the most?"

"Well, some of them are from the Brute Squad, so I don't think more than eight."

"Leaving me twelve, which is not impossible, but not the best way to spend your first evening after three months on brandy." And suddenly Inigo's body sagged and in his eyes, bright a moment ago, now there was moisture.

"What has happened?" Fezzik cried.

"Oh, my friend, my friend, I need Vizzini. I am not a planner. I follow. Tell me what to do and no man alive does it better. But my mind is like fine wine; it travels badly. I go from thought to thought but not with logic, and I forget things, and help me, Fezzik, what am I to do?"

Fezzik wanted to cry now too. "I'm the stupidest fellow that was ever born; you know that. I couldn't remember to come back here even after you made up that special lovely rhyme for me."

"I need Vizzini."

"But Vizzini is dead."

And then Inigo was up again, blazing about the kitchen, and for the first time his fingers were snapping with excitement: "I don't need Vizzini; I need his master: *I need the man in black!* Look—he bested me with steel, my greatness; he bested you with strength; yours. He must have outplanned and outthought Vizzini and he will tell me how to break through the castle and kill the six-fingered beast. If you have the least notion where the man in black is at this moment, relate, *quickly,* the answer."

"He sails the seven seas with the Dread Pirate Roberts."

"Why would he do a thing like that?"

"Because he is a sailor for the Dread Pirate Roberts."

"A sailor? *A common sailor?* A common ordinary seaman bests the great Inigo Montoya with the sword? In-con-ceiv-a-ble. He must *be* the Dread Pirate Roberts. Otherwise it makes no sense."

"In any event, he is sailing far away. Count Rugen says so and the Prince himself gave the order. The Prince wants no pirates around, what with all the trouble he is having with Guilder—remember, they kidnapped the Princess once, they might try—"

"Fezzik, *we* kidnapped the Princess once. You never were strong on memory, but even you should recall that *we* put the Guilder uniform pieces under the Princess's saddle. Vizzini did it because he was under orders to do it. Someone wanted Guilder to look guilty and who but a noble would want that and what noble more than the war-loving Prince himself? We never knew who hired Vizzini. I guess Humperdinck. And as for the Count's word on the man in black's whereabouts, since the Count is the same man who slaughtered my father, we can rest assured that he is certainly a terrific fellow." He started for the door. "Come. We have much to do."

Fezzik followed him through the darkening streets of the Thieves Quarter. "You'll explain things to me as we go along?" Fezzik asked.

"I'll explain them to you now. . . ." His bladelike body knifed on through the quiet streets, Fezzik hurrying alongside. "(a) I need to reach Count Rugen to at last avenge my father; (b) I cannot plan on how to reach Count Rugen; (c) Vizzini could have planned it for me but, (c prime) Vizzini is unavailable; however, (d) the man in black outplanned Vizzini, so, therefore, (e) the man in black can get me to Count Rugen."

"But I told you, Prince Humperdinck, after he captured him, gave orders for all to hear that the man in black was to be returned safely to his ship. Everyone in Florin knows this to be so."

"(a) Prince Humperdinck had some plans to kill his fiancée and hired us to carry them out but (b) the man in black ruined Prince Humperdinck's plans; however, eventually, (c) Prince Humperdinck managed to capture the man in black, and, as everybody in all Florin City also knows, Prince Humperdinck has a terrible temper, so, therefore, (d) if a man has a terrible temper, what could be more fun than losing it against the very fellow who spoiled your plans to kill your fiancée?" They had reached the Thieves Quarter wall now. Inigo jumped on Fezzik's shoulders and Fezzik started to climb. "Conclusion (1)," Inigo continued, not missing a beat, "since the Prince is in Florin City taking out his temper on the man in black, the man in black must also be in Florin City. Conclusion (2), the man in black must not be too happy with his present situation. Conclusion (3), I am in Florin City and need a planner to avenge my father, while he is in Florin City and needs a rescuer to salvage his future, and when people have equal needs of each other, conclusion (4 and final) deals are made."

Fezzik reached the top of the wall and started carefully climbing down the other side. "I understand everything," he said.

"You understand nothing, but it really doesn't matter, since what you mean is, you're glad to see me, just as I'm glad to see you because no more loneliness."

"That's what I mean," said Fezzik.

*   *   *

IT WAS DUSK when they began their search blindly through all of Florin City. Dusk, a day before the wedding. Count Rugen was about to begin his nightly experiments at that dusk, gathering up his notebooks from his room, filled with all his jottings. Five levels underground, behind high castle walls, locked and chained and silent, Westley waited beside the Machine. In a way, he still looked like Westley, except, of course, that he had been broken. Twenty years of his life had been sucked away. Twenty were left. Pain was anticipation. Soon the Count would come again. Against any wishes he had left, Westley went on crying.

*   *   *

IT WAS DUSK when Buttercup went to see the Prince. She knocked loudly, waited, knocked again. She could hear him shouting inside, and if it had not been so important, she would never have knocked the third time, but she did, and the door was yanked open, and the look of anger on his face immediately changed to the sweetest smile. "Beloved," he said. "Come in. A moment more is all I need." And he turned back to Yellin. "Look at her, Yellin. My bride-to-be. Has any man ever been so blessed?"

Yellin shook his head.

"Am I wrong, do you think, to go to any lengths, then, to protect her?"

Yellin shook his head again. The Prince was driving him crazy with his stories of the Guilder infiltration. Yellin had every spy he'd ever used working day and night and not one of them had come up with anything about Guilder. And yet the Prince insisted. Inwardly, Yellin sighed. It was beyond him; he was simply an enforcer, not a prince. In fact, the only remotely disturbing news he'd heard since he'd closed the Thieves Quarter that morning was within the hour, when someone told him of a rumor that the ship of the Dread Pirate Roberts had perhaps been seen sailing all the way into Florin Channel itself. But such a thing, Yellin knew from long experience, was, simply, rumor.

"I'll tell you, they are everywhere, these Guilders," the Prince went on. "And since you seem unable to stop them, I wish to change some plans. All the gates have been sealed to my castle except the front one, yes?"

"Yes. And twenty men guard it."

"Add eighty more. I want a hundred men. Clear?"

"A hundred men it will be. Every Brute available."

"Inside the castle I'm quite safe. I have my own supplies, food, stables, enough. As long as they cannot get at me, I will survive. These, then, are the new and final plans—jot them down. All five-hundredth-anniversary arrangements are canceled until after the wedding. The wedding is tomorrow sunset. My bride and I will ride my whites to Florin Channel surrounded by all your enforcers.

There we will board a ship and begin our long-awaited honeymoon surrounded by every ship in the Florin Armada—"

"Every ship but four," Buttercup corrected.

He blinked at her a moment in silence. Then he said, blowing her a kiss, but discreetly, so Yellin couldn't see, "Yes yes, how forgetful I am, every ship but four." He turned back to Yellin.

But in his blink, in that following silence, Buttercup had seen it all.

"Those ships will stay with us until I deem it safe to release them. Of course, Guilder could attack then, but that is a chance we must risk. Let me think if there's anything else." The Prince loved giving orders, especially the kind he knew would never need carrying out. Also, Yellin was a slow jotter, and that only added to the fun. "Excused," the Prince said finally.

With a bow, Yellin was gone.

"The four ships were never sent," Buttercup said, when they were alone. "Don't bother lying to me any more."

"Whatever was done was done for your own good, sweet pudding."

"Somehow, I do not think so."

"You're nervous, I'm nervous; we're getting married tomorrow, we've got a right to be."

"You couldn't be more wrong, you know; I'm very calm." And in truth, she did seem that way. "It doesn't matter whether you sent the ships or not. Westley will come for me. There is a God; I know that. And there is love; I know that too; so Westley will save me."

"You're a silly girl, now go to your room."

"Yes, I am a silly girl and, yes again, I will go to my room, and you are a coward with a heart filled with nothing but fear."

The Prince had to laugh. "The greatest hunter in the world and you say I am a coward?"

"I do, I do indeed. I'm getting much smarter as I age. I say you are a coward and you are; I think you hunt only to reassure yourself that you are not what you are: the weakest thing to ever walk the Earth. He will come for me and then we will be gone, and you will be helpless for all your hunting, because Westley and I are joined by the bond of love and you cannot track that, not with a thousand bloodhounds, and you cannot break it, not with a thousand swords."

Humperdinck screamed toward her then, ripping at her autumn hair, yanking her from her feet and down the long curving corridor to her room, where he tore that door open and threw her inside and locked her there and started running for the underground entrance to the Zoo of Death—

*   *   *

My father stopped reading.

'Go on,' I said.

'Lost my place,' he said and I waited there, still weak with pneumonia and wet with fear until he started reading again. 'Inigo allowed Fezzik to open the door—' 'Hey,' I said. 'Hold it, that's not right, you skipped,' and then I quick caught my tongue because we'd just had that scene when I got all upset about Buttercup marrying Humperdinck when I'd accused him of skipping, and I didn't want any repeat of that. 'Daddy,' I said, 'I don't mean anything or anything, but wasn't the Prince sort of running toward the Zoo and then the next thing you said was about Inigo, and maybe, I mean, shouldn't there be a page or like that in between?'

My father started to close the book.

'I'm not fighting; please, don't close it.'

'It is not for that,' he said, and then he looked at me for a long time. 'Billy,' he said (he almost never called me that; I loved it when he did; anybody else I hated it, but when the barber did it, I don't know, I just melted), 'Billy, do you trust me?'

'What is that? Of course I do.'

'Billy, you got pneumonia; you're taking this book very serious, I know, because we already fought once about it.'

'I'm not fighting any more—'

'Listen to me—I never lied to you yet, did I? Okay. Trust me. I don't want to read you the rest of this chapter and I want you to say it's all right.'

'Why? What happens in the rest of this chapter?'

'If I tell you, I could accomplish the same by reading. Just say okay.'

'I can't say that until I know what happens.'

'But—'

'Tell me what happens and I'll tell you if it's okay and I promise if I don't want to hear it, you can skip on to Inigo.'

'You won't do me this favor?'

'I'll sneak out of bed when you're asleep; I don't care where you hide the book, I'll find it and I'll read the rest of the chapter myself, so you might as well tell me.'

'Billy, please?'

'I gotcha; you might as well admit it.'

My father sighed this terrible sound.

I knew I had him beaten then.

'Westley dies,' my father said.

I said, 'What do you mean, "Westley dies"? You mean dies?'

My father nodded. 'Prince Humperdinck kills him.'

'He's only faking though, right?'

My father shook his head, closed the book all the way.

'Aw shit,' I said and I started to cry.

'I'm sorry,' my father said. 'I'll leave you alone,' and he left me.

'Who gets Humperdinck?' *I screamed after him.*

He stopped in the hall. 'I don't understand.'

'Who kills Prince Humperdinck? *At the end, somebody's got to get him. Is it Fezzik? Who?'*

'Nobody kills him. He lives.'

'You mean he wins, Daddy? Jesus, what did you read me this thing for?' and I buried my head in my pillow and I never cried like that again, not once to this day. I could feel almost my heart emptying into my pillow. I guess the most amazing thing about crying though is that when you're in it, you think it'll go on forever but it never really lasts half what you think. Not in terms of real time. In terms of real emotions, it's worse than you think, but not by the clock. When my father came back, it couldn't have been even an hour later.

'So,' he said, 'shall we go on tonight or not?'

'Shoot,' I told him. Eyes dry, no catch in throat, nothing. 'Fire when ready.'

'With Inigo?'

'Let's hear the murder,' I said. I knew I wasn't about to bawl again. Like Buttercup's, my heart was now a secret garden and the walls were very high.

*　　　*　　　*

HUMPERDINCK SCREAMED TOWARD her then, ripping at her autumn hair, yanking her from her feet and down the long curving corridor to her room, where he tore that door open and threw her inside and locked her there and started running for the underground entrance to the Zoo of Death and down he plunged, giant stride after giant stride, and when he threw the door of the fifth-level cage open, even Count Rugen was startled at the purity of whatever the emotion was that was reflected in the Prince's eyes. The Prince moved to Westley. "She loves you," the Prince cried. "She loves you still and you love her, so think of that—think of this too: in all this world, you might have been happy, genuinely happy. Not one couple in a century has that chance, not really, no matter what the storybooks say, but you could have had it, and so, I would think, no one will ever suffer a loss as great as you" and with that he grabbed the dial and pushed it all the way forward and the Count cried, "Not to twenty!" but by then it was too late; the death scream had started.

*   *   *

IT WAS MUCH worse than the scream of the wild dog. In the first place, the dial for the wild dog had only been set at six, whereas this was more than triple that. And so, naturally enough, it was more than three times as long. And more than three times as loud. But none of this really was why it was worse.

It was the scream from a human throat that made the difference.

In her chamber, Buttercup heard it, and it frightened her, but she had not the least idea what it was.

By the main door of the castle, Yellin heard it, and it also frightened him, though he couldn't imagine what it was either.

All the hundred Brutes and fighters flanked by the main door heard it too, and, to a man, they were bothered by it, and they talked it over for quite a while, but none of them had any sound notions as to what it might have been.

The Great Square was filled with common people excited about the coming wedding and anniversary, and they all heard it too, and no one even made the pretense of not being scared, but, again, none of them knew at all what it might have been.

The death scream rose higher in the night.

All the streets leading into the Square were also filled with citizens, all trying to crowd into the Square, and they heard it, but once they admitted they were petrified, they gave up trying to guess what it might have been.

Inigo knew immediately.

In the tiny alley that he and Fezzik were trying to force their way through, he stopped, remembering. The alley led to the streets that led to the Square, and the alley was jammed too.

"I don't like that sound," Fezzik said, his skin, for the moment, cold.

Inigo grabbed the giant and the words began pouring out: "Fezzik—Fezzik—that is the sound of Ultimate Suffering—I know that sound—that was the sound in my heart when Count Rugen slaughtered my father and I saw him fall—the man in black makes it now—"

"You think that's him?"

"Who else has cause for Ultimate Suffering this celebration night?" And with that, he started to follow the sound.

But the crowds were in his way, and he was strong but he was thin and he cried, "Fezzik—Fezzik—we must track that sound, we must trace it to its source, and I cannot move, so you must lead me. Fly, Fezzik; this is Inigo begging you—make a path—*please!*"

Well, Fezzik had rarely had anyone beg him for anything, least of all Inigo, and when something like that happened, you did what you could, so Fezzik, without waiting, began to push. Forward. Lots of people. Fezzik pushed harder. Lots of people began to move. Out of Fezzik's way. Fast.

The death scream was starting to fade now, fading in the clouds.

"Fezzik!" said Inigo. "All your power, NOW."

Down the alley Fezzik ran, people screaming and diving to get out of his way, and in his footsteps Inigo kept pace, and at the end of the alley was a street and the scream was fainter now but Fezzik turned left and into the middle of the street he went and he owned it, no one was in his way, nothing dared block his way, and the scream was getting just so hard to hear, so with all his might Fezzik roared, "QUIET!" and the street was suddenly hushed and Fezzik pounded along, Inigo right behind, and the scream was still there, still faintly there, and into the Great Square itself and the castle beyond before the scream was gone. . . .

*   *   *

WESTLEY LAY DEAD by the Machine. The Prince kept the dial by the twenty mark long long after it was necessary, until the Count said, "Done."

The Prince left without another look at Westley. He took the secret underground stairs four at a time. "She actually called me a coward," he said, and then he was gone from sight.

Count Rugen started taking notes. Then he threw his quill pen down. He tested Westley briefly, then he shook his head. Death was not of any intellectual interest to him at all; when you were dead, you couldn't react to pain. The Count said, "Dispose of the body," because, even though he couldn't see the albino, he knew the albino was there. It was really a shame, he realized as he mounted the stairs after the Prince. You just didn't come across victims like Westley every day of the year.

When they were gone, the albino came out, pulled the cups from the corpse, decided to burn the body on the garbage pyre back behind the castle. Which meant a wheelbarrow. He hurried up the underground stairs, came out the secret entrance, moved quickly to the main tool shed; all the wheelbarrows were buried back at the rear wall, behind the hoes and rakes and hedge trimmers. The albino made a hissing sound of displeasure and began to pick his way past all the other equipment. This kind of thing always seemed to happen to him when he was in a hurry. The albino hissed again, extra work, extra work, all the time. Wouldn't you just know it?

He finally got the barrow out and was just passing the false and deadly supposed main entrance to the Zoo when "I'm having the devil's own trouble tracking that scream" was spoken to him, and the albino whirled to find, there, *there* in the castle grounds, a blade-thin stranger with a sword in his hand. The sword suddenly flicked its way to the albino's throat. "Where is the man in black?" the swordsman said then. He had a giant scar slanting down each cheek and seemed like no one to trifle with.

Whispered: "I know no man in black."

"Did the scream come from that place?" The fellow indicated the main entrance.

Nod.

"And the throat it came from? I need this man, so be quick!"

Whispered: "Westley."

Inigo reasoned: "A sailor? Brought here by Rugen?"

Nod.

"And I reach him where?"

The albino hesitated, then pointed to the deadly entrance. Whispered: "He is on the bottom level. Five levels down."

"Then I have no more need for you. Quiet him a while, Fezzik."

From behind him, the albino was aware of a giant shadow moving. Funny, he thought—the last thing he remembered—I thought that was a tree.

Inigo was on fire now. There was no stopping him. Fezzik hesitated by the main door. "Why would he tell the truth?"

"He's a zookeeper threatened with death. Why would he lie?"

"That doesn't follow."

"*I don't care!*" Inigo said sharply, and, in fact, he didn't. He knew in his heart the man in black was down there. There was no other reason for Fezzik to find him, for Fezzik to know of Rugen, for everything to be coming together after so many years of waiting. If there was a God, then there was a man in black waiting. Inigo knew that. He *knew* it. And, of course, he was absolutely right. But again, of course, there were many things he did not know. That the man in black was dead, for one. That the entrance they were taking was the wrong one, for another, a false one, set up to foil those, like himself, who did not belong. There were spitting cobras down there, though what would actually come at him would be worse. These things he did not know either.

But his father had to be revenged. And the man in black would figure out how. That was enough for Inigo.

And so, with an urgency that would soon turn to deep regret, he and Fezzik approached the Zoo of Death.

SEVEN

THE WEDDING

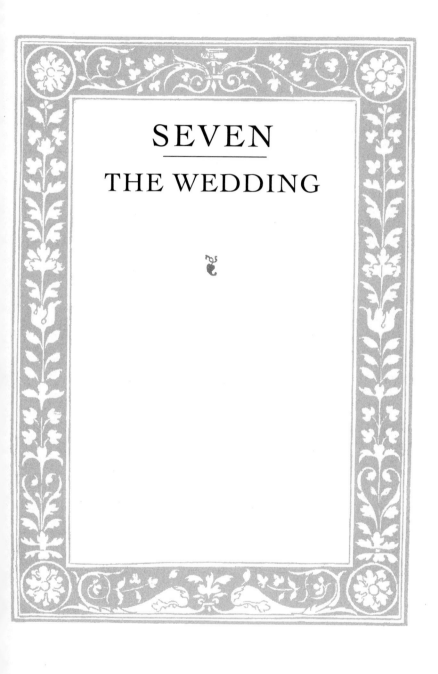

INGO allowed Fezzik to open the door, not because he wished to hide behind the giant's strength but, rather, because the giant's strength was crucial to their entering: someone would have to force the thick door from its hinges, and that was right up Fezzik's alley.

"It's open," Fezzik said, simply turning the knob, peering inside.

"Open?" Inigo hesitated. "Close it then. There must be something wrong. Why would something as valuable as the Prince's private zoo be left unlocked?"

"It smells of animals something awful in there," Fezzik said. "Did I get a whiff!"

"Let me think," Inigo said; "I'll figure it out," and he tried to do his best, but it made no sense. You didn't leave diamonds lying around on the breakfast table and you kept the Zoo of Death shut and bolted. So there had to be a reason; it was just a matter of exercising your brain power and the answer would be there. (The answer to why the door happened to be unlocked was really this: it was always unlocked. And the reason for that was really this: safety. No one who had entered via the front door had ever survived to exit again. The idea basically belonged to Count Rugen, who helped the Prince architect the place. The Prince selected the location—the farthest corner of the castle grounds, away from everything, so the roars wouldn't bother the servants—but the

Count designed the entrance. The real entrance was by a giant tree, where a root lifted and revealed a staircase and down you went until you arrived at the fifth level. The false entrance, called the real entrance, took you down the levels the ordinary way, first to second, second to third, or, actually, second to death.)

"Yes," Inigo said finally.

"You figured it out?"

"The reason the door was unlocked is simply this: the albino would have locked it, he would never have been so stupid as not to, *but,* Fezzik, my friend, we got to *him* before he got to *it.* Clearly, once he was done with his wheelbarrowing, he would have begun locking and bolting. It's quite all right; you can stop worrying; let's go."

"I just feel so safe with you," Fezzik said, and he pulled the door open a second time. As he did it, he noticed that not only was the door unlocked, it didn't even have a place for a lock, and he wondered should he mention that to Inigo, but decided against it, because Inigo would have to wait and figure some more and they had done enough of that already, because, although he said he felt safe with Inigo, in truth he was very frightened. He had heard odd things about this place, and lions didn't bother him, and who cared about gorillas; they were nothing. It was the creepers that made him squeamish. And the slitherers. And the stingers. And the ... and the everything, Fezzik decided, to be truthful and honest. Spiders and snakes and bugs and bats and you name it—he just wasn't very fond of any of them. "Still smells of animals," he said, and he held the door open for Inigo, and together, stride for stride, they entered the Zoo of Death, the great door shutting silently behind them.

"Quite a bizarre place," Inigo said, moving past several large cages in which were cheetahs and hummingbirds and other swift things. At the end of the hall was another door with a sign above it saying, "To Level Two." They opened that door and saw a flight of stairs leading very steeply down. "Careful," Inigo said; "stay close to me and watch your balance."

They started down toward the second level.

"If I tell you something, will you promise not to laugh at me or mock me or be mean to me?" Fezzik asked.

"My word," Inigo nodded.

"I'm just scared to pieces," Fezzik said.

"Be sure it ceases," Inigo said right back.

"Oh, that's a wonderful rhyme—"

"Some other time," Inigo said, making another, feeling quite bright about the whole thing, sensing the pleasure in having Fezzik visibly relax as they descended, so he smiled and clapped Fezzik on his great shoulder for the good fellow he was. But deep, deep inside, Inigo's stomach was knotting. He was absolutely appalled and astonished that a man of unlimited strength and power would be scared to pieces; until Fezzik spoke, Inigo was positive that *he* was the only one who was genuinely scared to pieces, and the fact that they both were did not bode well if panic time came. Someone would have to keep his wits, and he had assumed automatically that since Fezzik had so few, he would find retaining them not all that difficult. No good, Inigo realized. Well, he would simply have to do his best to avoid panic situations and that was that.

The staircase was straight, and very long, but eventually they reached the end of it. Another door. Fezzik gave it a push. It opened. Another corridor lined with cages, big ones though, and inside, great baying hippos and a twenty-foot alligator thrashing angrily in shallow water.

"We must hurry," Inigo said, picking up the pace; "much as we might like to dawdle," and he half ran toward a sign that said, "To

Level Three." Inigo opened the door and looked down and Fezzik peered over his shoulder. "Hmmm," Inigo said.

This staircase was different. It was not nearly as steep, and it curved halfway, so that whatever was near the bottom of it was quite out of sight as they stood at the top preparing to go down. There were strange candles burning high on the walls out of reach. The shadows they made were very long and very thin.

"Well, I'm certainly glad I wasn't brought up here," Inigo said, trying for a joke.

"Fear," Fezzik said, the rhyme out before he could stop it.

Inigo exploded. "Really! If you can't maintain control, I'm going to send you right back up and you can just wait there *all by yourself*."

"Don't leave me; I mean, don't make me leave you. Please. I meant to say 'beer'; I don't know how the *f* got in there."

"I'm really losing patience with you; come along," Inigo said, and he started down the curving stairs, Fezzik following, and as the door closed behind them, two things happened:

(1) The door, quite clearly, locked.

(2) Out went the candles on the high walls.

"DON'T BE FRIGHTENED!" Inigo screamed.

"I'M NOT, I'M NOT!" Fezzik screamed right back. And then, above his heartbeat, he managed, "What are we going to do?"

"S-s-s-simple," said Inigo after a while.

"Are you frightened too?" asked Fezzik in the darkness.

"Not ... remotely," Inigo said with great care. "And before, I meant to say 'easy'; I don't know how the 's-s-s-s-' got in there. Look: we can't go back and we certainly don't want to stay here, so we just must keep on going as we were before these little things happened. Down. Down is our direction, Fezzik, but I can tell you're a bit edgy about all this, *so,* out of the goodness of my heart, I will let you walk down not behind me, and not in front of me, but right next to me, on the same step, stride for stride, and you put an arm around my shoulder, because that will probably make you feel better, and I, so as not to make you feel foolish, will put an arm around your shoulder, and thus, safe, protected, together, we will descend."

"Will you draw your sword with your free hand?"

"I already have. Will you make a fist with yours?"

"It's clenched."

"Then let's look on the bright side: we're having an adventure, Fezzik, and most people live and die without being as lucky as we are."

They moved down one step. Then another. Then two, then three, as they got the hang of it.

"Why do you think they locked the door behind us?" Fezzik asked as they moved.

"To add spice to our trip, I suspect," replied Inigo. It was certainly one of his weaker answers, but the best he could come up with.

"Here's where the turn starts," said Fezzik, and they slowed, making the sharp turn without stumbling, continuing on down. "And they took away the candles for the same reason—spice?"

"Most likely. Don't squeeze me quite so hard—"

"Don't *you* squeeze *me* quite so hard—"

By then they knew they were for it.

There has been, for many years, a running battle among jungle zoologists as to just which of the giant snakes is the biggest. The anaconda men are forever trumpeting the Orinoco specimen that weighed well over five hundred pounds, while the python people never fail to reply by pointing out that the African Rock found outside Zambesi measured thirty-four feet, seven inches. The argument, of course, is silly, because "biggest" is a vague word, having no value whatever in arguments, if one is serious.

But any serious snake enthusiast would admit, whatever his schooling, that the Arabian Garstini, though shorter than the python and lighter than the anaconda, was quicker and more ravenous than either, and this specimen of Prince Humperdinck's was not only remarkable for its speed and agility, it was also kept in a permanent state just verging on the outskirts of starvation, so the first coil came like lightning as it dropped from above them and pinioned their hands so the fist and sword were useless and the second coil imprisoned their arms and "Do something—" Inigo cried.

"I can't—I'm caught—you do something—"

"Fight it, Fezzik—"

"It's too strong for me—"

"Nothing is too strong for you—"

The third coil was done now, around the upper shoulders, and the fourth coil, the final coil, involved the throat, and Inigo whispered in terror, because he could hear the beast's breathing now, could actually feel its breath, "Fight it . . . I'm . . . I'm . . ."

Fezzik trembled with fear and whispered, "Forgive me, Inigo."

"Oh, Fezzik . . . Fezzik . . ."

"What . . . ?"

"I had such rhymes for you. . . ."

"What rhymes? . . ."

Silence.

The fourth coil was finished.

"Inigo, what rhymes?"

Silence.

Snake breath.

"Inigo, I want to know the rhymes before I die—Inigo, I really want to know—*Inigo, tell me the rhymes,*" Fezzik said, and by now he was very frustrated and, more than that, he was spectacularly angry and one arm came clear of one coil and that made it a bit less of a chore to fight free of the second coil and that meant he could take that arm and bring it to the aid of the other arm and now he was yelling it out, *"You're not going anywhere until I know those rhymes"* and the sound of his own voice was really very impressive, deep and resonant, and who was this snake anyway, getting in the path of Fezzik when there were rhymes to learn, and by this time not only were both arms free of the bottom three coils but he was furious at the interruption and his hands grabbed toward the snake breath, and he didn't know if snakes had necks or not but whatever it was that you called the part that was under its mouth, that was the part he had between his great hands and he gave it a smash against the wall and the snake hissed and spit but the fourth coil was looser, so Fezzik smashed it again and a third time and then he brought his hands back a bit for leverage and he began to whip the beast against the walls like a native washerwoman beating a skirt against rocks, and when the snake was dead, Inigo said, "Actually, I had no specific rhymes in mind; I just had to do something to get you into action."

Fezzik was panting terribly from his labors. "You lied to me is what you're saying. My only friend in all my life turns out to be a liar." He started tromping down the stairs, Inigo stumbling after him.

Fezzik reached the door at the bottom and threw it open and slammed it, with Inigo just managing to slip inside before the door crashed shut.

It locked immediately.

At the end of this corridor, the "To Level Four" sign was clearly visible, and Fezzik hurried toward it. Inigo pursued him, hurrying past the poisoners, the spitting cobras and Gaboon vipers and, perhaps most quickly lethal of all, the lovely tropical stonefish from the ocean outside India.

"I apologize," Inigo said. "One lie in all these years, that's not such a terrible average when you consider it saved our lives."

"There's such a thing as principle" was all Fezzik would answer, and he opened the door that led to the fourth level. "My father made me promise never to lie, and not once in my life have I even been tempted," and he started down the stairs.

"Stop!" Inigo said. "At least examine where we're going."

It was a straight staircase, but completely dark. The opening at the far end was invisible. "It can't be as bad as where we've been," Fezzik snapped, and down he went.

In a way, he was right. For Inigo, bats were never the ultimate nightmare. Oh, he was afraid of them, like everybody else, and he would run and scream if they came near; in his mind, though, hell was not bat-infested. But Fezzik was a Turkish boy, and people claim the fruit bat from Indonesia is the biggest in the world; try telling that to a Turk sometime. Try telling that to anyone who has heard his mother scream, *"Here come the king bats!"* followed by the poisonous fluttering of wings.

"HERE COME THE KING BATS!" Fezzik screamed, and he was, quite literally, as he stood halfway down the dark steps, paralyzed with fear, and behind him now, doing his best to fight the darkness, came Inigo, and he had never heard that tone before, not from Fezzik, and Inigo didn't want bats in his hair either, but it wasn't worth that kind of fright, so he started to say "What's so terrible about king bats" but "What" was all he had time for before Fezzik cried, "Rabies! Rabies!" and that was all Inigo needed to know, and he yelled, "Down, Fezzik," and Fezzik still couldn't move, so Inigo felt for him in the darkness as the fluttering grew louder and with all his strength he slammed the giant on the shoulder hollering *"Down"* and this time Fezzik went to his knees obediently, but that wasn't enough, not nearly, so Inigo slammed him again crying, "Flat, flat, all the way down," until Fezzik lay on the black stairs shaking and Inigo knelt above him, the great six-fingered sword flying into his hands, and this was it, this was a test to see how far down the ninety days of brandy had taken him, how much of the great Inigo Montoya remained, for, yes, he had studied fencing, true, he had spent half his life and more learning the Agrippa attack and the Bonetti defense and of course he had studied his Thibault, but he had also, one desperate time, spent a summer with the only Scot who ever understood swords, the crippled MacPherson, and it was MacPherson who scoffed at everything Inigo knew, it was MacPherson who said, "Thibault, Thibault is fine if you fight in a ballroom, but what if you meet your enemy on terrain that is tilted and you are below him," and for a week, Inigo studied all the moves from below, and then MacPherson put him on a hill in the upper position, and when those moves were mastered, MacPherson kept right on, for he was a cripple, his legs stopped at the knee, and so he had a special feel for adversity. "And what if your enemy blinds you?" MacPherson once said. "He throws acid in your eyes and now he drives in for the kill; what do you do? Tell me that, Spaniard, *survive that, Spaniard.*" And now, waiting for the charge of the king bats, Inigo flung his mind back toward the MacPherson moves, and you had to depend on your ears, you found his heart from his sounds, and now, as he waited, above him Inigo could feel the king bats massing, while below him Fezzik trembled like a kitten in cold water.

"Be still!" Inigo commanded, and that was the last sound he made, because he needed his ears now, and he tilted his head toward the flutter, the great sword firm in his right hand, the deadly point circling slowly in the air. Inigo had never seen a king bat, knew nothing of them; how fast were they, how did they come at you, at what angle, and how many made each charge? The flutter was dead above him now, ten feet perhaps, perhaps more, and could bats see in the night? Did they have that weapon too? "Come on!" Inigo was about to say, but there was no need, because with a rush of wings he had expected and a high long shriek he had not, the first king bat swooped down at him.

Inigo waited, waited, the flutter was off to the left, and that was wrong, because he knew where he was and so did the beasts, so that meant they must have been preparing something for him, a cut, a sudden turn, and with all control left to his brain he kept his sword just as it was, circling slowly, not following the sound until the fluttering stopped and the king bat veered in silence toward Inigo's face.

The six-fingered sword drove through like butter.

The death sound of the king bat was close to human, only a bit higher pitched and shorter, and Inigo was only briefly interested because now there was a double flutter; they were coming at him from two sides and one right, one left, and MacPherson told him always move from strength to weakness, so Inigo stabbed first to the right, then drove left, and two more almost human sounds came and went. The sword was heavy now, three dead beasts changed the balance, and Inigo wanted to clear the weapon, but now another flutter, a single one, and no veering this time, straight and deadly for his face and he ducked and was lucky; the sword moved up and into the heart of the lethal thing and now there were four skewered on the sword of legend, and Inigo knew he was not about to lose this fight and from his throat came the words, "I am Inigo Montoya and still the Wizard; come for me," and when he heard three of them fluttering, he wished he had been just a bit more modest but it was too late for that, so he needed surprise, and he took it, shifting position against the beasts, standing straight, taking their dives long before they expected it, and now there were seven king bats and his sword was completely out of balance and that would have been a bad thing, a dangerous thing, except for one important aspect: there was silence now in the darkness. The fluttering was done.

"Some giant you are," Inigo said then, and he stepped over Fezzik and hurried down the rest of the darkened stairs.

Fezzik got up and lumbered after him, saying, "Inigo, listen, I made a mistake before, you didn't lie to me, you tricked me, and father always said tricking was fine, so I'm not mad at you any more, and is that all right with you? It's all right with me."

They turned the knob on the door at the bottom of the black stairs and stepped onto the fourth level.

Inigo looked at him. "You mean you'll forgive me completely for saving your life if I completely forgive you for saving mine?"

"You're my friend, my only one."

"Pathetic, that's what we are," Inigo said.

"Athletic."

"That's very good," Inigo said, so Fezzik knew they were fine again. They started toward the sign that said, "To Level Five," passing strange cages. "This is the worst yet," Inigo said, and then he jumped back, because behind a pale glass case, a blood eagle was actually eating what looked like an arm. And on the other side there was a great black pool, and whatever was in it was dark and many armed and the water seemed to get sucked toward the center of the pool where the mouth of the thing was. "Hurry," Inigo said, and he found himself trembling at the thought of being dropped into the black pool.

They opened the door and looked down toward the fifth level.

Stunning.

In the first place, the door they opened had no lock, so it could not trap them. And in the second place the stairs were all brightly lit. And in the third place the stairs were absolutely straight. And in the fourth place, it wasn't a long flight at all.

And in the main place, there was nothing inside. It was bright and clean and totally, without the least doubt, empty.

"I don't believe it for a minute," Inigo said, and, holding his sword at the ready, he took the first step down. "Stay by the door— the candles will go out any second."

He took a second step down.

The candles stayed bright.

A third step. The fourth. There were only about a dozen steps in all, and he took two more, stopping in the middle. Each step was perhaps a foot in width, so he was six feet from Fezzik, six feet from the large, ornate green-handled door that opened onto the final level. "Fezzik?"

From the upper door: "What?"

"I'm frightened."

"It looks all right though."

"No. It's supposed to; that's to fool us. Whatever we've gotten by before, this must be worse."

"But there's nothing to see, Inigo."

Inigo nodded. "That's why I'm so frightened." He took another step down toward the final, ornate green-handled door. Another. Four steps to go. Four feet to go.

Forty-eight inches from death.

Inigo took another step. He was trembling now; almost out of control.

"Why are you shaking?" Fezzik from the top.

"Death is here. Death is here." He took another step down.

Twenty-four inches to dying.

"Can I come join you now?"

Inigo shook his head. "No point in your dying too."

"But it's empty."

"No. Death is here." Now he was out of control. "If I could see it, I could fight it."

Fezzik didn't know what to do.

"I'm Inigo Montoya the Wizard; come for me!" He turned around and around, sword ready, studying the brightly lit staircase.

"Now you're scaring me," Fezzik said, and he let the door close behind him and started down the stairs.

Inigo started up after him, saying "No." They met on the sixth step.

Seventy-two inches from death now.

The green speckled recluse doesn't destroy as quickly as the stonefish. And many think the mamba brings more suffering, what with the ulcerating and all. But gram for gram, nothing in the universe comes close to the green speckled recluse; among other spiders, compared with the green speckled recluse, the black widow was a rag doll. Prince Humperdinck's recluse lived behind the ornate green handle on the bottom door. She rarely moved, unless the handle turned. Then she struck like lightning.

On the sixth stair, Fezzik put his arm around Inigo's shoulder. "We'll go down together, step by step. There's nothing here, Inigo."

To the fifth step. "There has to be."

"Why?"

"Because the Prince is a fiend. And Rugen is his twin in misery. And this is their masterpiece." They moved to the fourth step.

"That's wonderful thinking, Inigo," Fezzik said, loud and calmly; but, inside, he was starting to go to pieces. Because here he was, in this nice bright place, and his one friend in all the world was cracking from the strain. And if you were Fezzik, and you hadn't much brain power, and you found yourself four stories underground in a Zoo of Death looking for a man in black that you really didn't think was down there, and the only friend you had in all the world was going quickly mad, what did you do?

Three steps now.

If you were Fezzik, you panicked, because if Inigo went mad, that meant the leader of this whole expedition was you, and if you were Fezzik, you knew the last thing in the world you could ever be was a leader. So Fezzik did what he always did in a panic situation.

He bolted.

He just yelled and jumped for the door and slammed it open with his body, never even bothering with the niceties of turning that pretty green handle, and as the door gave behind his strength he kept right on running until he came to the giant cage and there, inside and still, lay the man in black. Fezzik stopped then, relieved greatly, because seeing that silent body meant one thing: Inigo was right, and if Inigo was right, he couldn't be crazy, and if he wasn't crazy, then Fezzik didn't have to lead anybody anywhere. And when that thought reached his brain, Fezzik smiled.

Inigo, for his part, was startled at Fezzik's strange behavior. He saw no reason for it whatsoever, and was about to call after Fezzik when he saw a tiny green speckled spider scurrying down from the door handle, so he stepped on it with his boot as he hurried to the cage.

Fezzik was already inside the place, kneeling over the body.

"Don't say it," Inigo said, entering.

Fezzik tried not to, but it was on his face. "Dead."

Inigo examined the body. He had seen a lot of corpses in his time. "Dead." Then he sat down miserably on the floor and put his arms around his knees and rocked back and forth like a baby, back and forth, back and forth and back.

It was too unfair. You expected unfairness if you breathed, but this went beyond that. He, Inigo, no thinker, had thought—hadn't he found the man in black? He, Inigo, frightened of beasts and crawlers and anything that stung, had brought them down the Zoo unharmed. He had said good-by to caution and stretched himself far beyond any boundaries he ever dreamed he possessed. And now, after such effort, after being reunited with Fezzik on this day of days for this one purpose, to find the man to help him find a plan to help him revenge his dead Domingo—gone. All was gone. Hope? Gone. Future? Gone. All the driving forces of his life. Gone. Snuffed out. Beaten. Dead.

"I am Inigo Montoya, the son of Domingo Montoya, and I do not accept it." He sprang to his feet, started up the underground stairs, stopping only long enough to snap commands. "Come, come along. Bring the body." He searched through his pockets for a moment, but they were empty, from the brandy. "Have you got any money, Fezzik?"

"Some. They pay well on the Brute Squad."

"Well I just hope it's enough to buy a miracle, that's all."

*   *   *

WHEN THE KNOCKING started on his hut door, Max almost didn't answer it. "Go away," he almost said, because lately it was only kids come to mock him. Except this was a little past the time for kids being up—it was almost midnight—and besides, the knocking was both loud and, at the same time, rat-a-tatty, as if the brain was saying to the fist, "Hurry it up; I want to see a little action."

So Max opened the door a peek's worth. "I don't know you."

"Aren't you Miracle Max that worked all those years for the King?" this skinny guy said.

"I got fired, didn't you hear? That's a painful subject, you shouldn't have brought it up, good night, next time learn a little manners," and he closed the hut door.

Ra-a-tat—rat-a-*tattt*.

"Get away, I'm telling you, or I call the Brute Squad."

"I'm on the Brute Squad," this other voice said from outside the door, a big deep voice you wanted to stay friendly with.

"We need a miracle; it's very important," the skinny guy said from outside.

"I'm retired," Max said, "anyway, you wouldn't want someone the King got rid of, would you? I might kill whoever you want me to miracle."

"He's already dead," the skinny guy said.

"He is, huh?" Max said, a little interest in his voice now. He opened the door a peek's worth again. "I'm good at dead."

"Please," the skinny guy said.

"Bring him in. I'm making no promises," Miracle Max answered after some thought.

This huge guy and this skinny guy brought in this big guy and put him on the hut floor. Max poked the corpse. "Not so stiff as some," he said.

The skinny guy said, "We have money."

"Then go get some great genius specialist, why don't you? Why waste time messing around with me, a guy who the King fired." It almost killed him when it happened. For the first two years, he wished it had. His teeth fell out from gnashing; he pulled the few loyal tufts from his scalp in wild anger.

"You're the only miracle man left alive in Florin," the skinny guy said.

"Oh, so *that's* why you come to me? One of you said, 'What'll we do with this corpse?' And the other one said, 'Let's take a flyer on that miracle man the King fired,' and the first one probably said, 'What've we got to lose; he can't kill a corpse' and the other one probably said—"

"You were a wonderful miracle man," the skinny guy said. "It was all politics that got you fired."

"Don't insult me and say wonderful—I was *great*—I *am* great—there was never—*never*, you hear me, sonny, a miracle man could match me—half the miracle techniques I invented—and then they fired me. . . ." Suddenly his voice trailed off. He was very old and weak and the effort at passionate speech had drained him.

"Sir, please, sit down—" the skinny guy said.

"Don't 'sir' me, sonny," Miracle Max said. He was tough when he was young and he was still tough. "I got work to do. I was feeding my witch when you came in; I got to finish that now," and he lifted the hut trap door and took the ladder down into the cellar, locking the trap door behind him. When that was done, he put his finger to his lips and ran to the old woman cooking hot chocolate over the coals. Max had married Valerie back a million years ago, it seemed like, at Miracle School, where she worked as a potion ladler. She wasn't, of course, a witch, but when Max started practice, every miracle man had to have one, so, since Valerie didn't mind, he called her a witch in public and she learned enough of the witch trade to pass herself off as one under pressure. "Listen! Listen!" Max whispered, gesturing repeatedly toward the hut above. "Upstairs you'll never guess what I got—a giant and a spick."

"A giant on a stick?" Valerie said, clutching her heart; her hearing wasn't what it once was.

"Spick! Spick! A Spanish fella. Scars and everything, a very tough cookie."

"Let them steal what they want; what do we have worth fighting over?"

"They don't want to *steal*, they want to *buy*. Me. They got a corpse up there and they want a miracle."

"You were always good at dead," Valerie said. She hadn't seen him trying so hard not to seem excited since the firing had all but done him in. She very carefully kept her own excitement under control. If only he would work again. Her Max was such a genius, they'd all come back, every patient. Max would be honored again and they could move out of the hut. In the old days, the hut was where they tried experiments. Now it was home. "You had nothing else pressing on for the evening, why not take the case?"

"I could, I admit that, no question, but suppose I did? You know human nature; they'd probably try getting out without paying. How can I force a giant to pay if he doesn't want to? Who needs that kinda grief? I'll send them on their way and you bring me up a nice cup of chocolate. Besides, I was halfway through an article on eagles' claws that was very well written."

"Get the money in advance. Go. Demand. If they say no, out with them. If they say yes, bring the money down to me, I'll feed it to the frog, they'll never find it even if they change their mind and try to rob it back."

Max started back up the ladder. "What should I ask for? I haven't done a miracle—it's what, three years now? Prices may have skyrocketed. Fifty, you think? If they got fifty, I'll consider. If not, out they go."

"Right," Valerie agreed, and the minute Max had shut the trap door, she clambered silently up the ladder and pressed her ear to the ceiling.

"Sir, we're in a terrible rush, so—" this one voice said.

"Don't you hurry me, sonny, you hurry a miracle man, you get rotten miracles, that what you want?"

"You'll do it, then?"

"I didn't say I'd do it, sonny, don't try pressuring a miracle man, not this one; you try pressuring me, out you go, how much money you got?"

"Give me your money, Fezzik?" the same voice said again.

"Here's all I've got," this great voice boomed. "You count it, Inigo."

There was a pause. "Sixty-five is what we've got," the one called Inigo said.

Valerie was about to clap her hands with joy when Max said, "I never worked for anything that little in my life; you got to be joking, excuse me again; I got to belch my witch; she's done eating by now."

Valerie hurried back to the coals and waited until Max joined her. "No good," he said. "They only got twenty."

Valerie stirred away at the stove. She knew the truth but dreaded having to say it, so she tried another tack. "We're practically out of chocolate powder; twenty could sure be a help at the barterer's tomorrow."

"No chocolate powder?" Max said, visibly upset. Chocolate was one of his favorites, right after cough drops.

"Maybe if it was a good cause you could lower yourself to work for twenty," Valerie said. "Find out why they need the miracle."

"They'd probably lie."

"Use the bellows cram if you're in doubt. Look: I would hate to have it on my conscience if we didn't do a miracle when nice people were involved."

"You're a pushy lady," Max said, but he went back upstairs.

"Okay," he said to the skinny guy. "What's so special I should bring back out of all the hundreds of people pestering me every day for my miracles this particular fella? And, believe me, it better be worth while."

Inigo was about to say "So he can tell me how to kill Count Rugen," but that didn't quite sound like the kind of thing that would strike a cranky miracle man as aiding the general betterment of mankind, so he said, "He's got a wife, he's got fifteen kids, they haven't a shred of food; if he stays dead, they'll starve, so—"

"Oh, sonny, are you a liar," Max said, and he went to the corner and got out a huge bellows. "I'll ask him," Max grunted, lifting the bellows toward Westley.

"He's a corpse; he can't talk," Inigo said.

"We got our ways" was all Max would answer, and he stuck the huge bellows way down into Westley's throat and started to pump. "You see," Max explained as he pumped, "there's different kinds of dead: there's sort of dead, mostly dead, and all dead. This fella here, he's only sort of dead, which means there's still a memory inside, there's still bits of brain. You apply a little pressure here, a little more there, sometimes you get results."

Westley was beginning to swell slightly now from all the pumping.

"What are you doing?" Fezzik said, starting to get upset.

"Never mind, I'm just filling his lungs; I guarantee you it ain't hurting him." He stopped pumping the bellows after a few moments more, and then started shouting into Westley's ear: "WHAT'S SO IMPORTANT? WHAT'S HERE WORTH COMING BACK FOR? WHAT YOU GOT WAITING FOR YOU?" Max carried the bellows back to the corner then and got out a pen and paper. "It takes a while for that to work its way out, so you might as well answer me some questions. How well do you know this guy?"

Inigo didn't much want to answer that, since it might have

sounded strange admitting they'd only met once alive, and then to duel to the death. "How do you mean exactly?" he replied.

"Well, for example," Max said, "was he ticklish or not?"

"Ticklish?" Inigo exploded angrily. "*Ticklish!* Life and death are all around and you talk ticklish!"

"Don't you yell at me," Max exploded right back, "and don't you mock my methods—tickling can be terrific in the proper instances. I had a corpse once, worse than this fella, mostly dead he was, and I tickled him and tickled him; I tickled his toes and I tickled his armpits and his ribs and I got a peacock feather and went after his belly button; I worked all day and I worked all night and the following dawn—*the following dawn, mark me*—this corpse said, 'I just hate that,' and I said, 'Hate what?' and he said, 'Being tickled; I've come all the way back from the dead to ask you to stop,' and I said, 'You mean this that I'm doing now with the peacock feather, it bothers you?' and he said, 'You couldn't guess how much it bothers me,' and of course I just kept on asking him questions about tickling, making him talk back to me, answer me, because, I don't have to tell you, once you get a corpse really caught up in conversation, your battle's half over."

"Tr . . . ooooo . . . luv . . ."

Fezzik grabbed onto Inigo in panic and they both pivoted, staring at the man in black, who was silent again. " 'True love,' he said," Inigo cried. "You heard him—true love is what he wants to come back for. That's certainly worth while."

"Sonny, don't you tell me what's worth while—true love is the best thing in the world, except for cough drops. Everybody knows that."

"Then you'll save him?" Fezzik said.

"Yes, absolutely, I *would* save him, *if* he had said 'true love,' but you misheard, whereas I, being an expert on the bellows cram, will tell you what any qualified tongue man will only be happy to verify—namely, that the *f* sound is the hardest for the corpse to master, and that it therefore comes out *vuh*, and what your friend said was 'to blove,' by which he meant, obviously, 'to bluff'— clearly he is either involved in a shady business deal or a card game and wishes to win, and that is certainly not reason enough for a miracle. I'm sorry, I never change my mind once it's made up, good-by, take your corpse with you."

"Liar! Liar!" shrieked suddenly from the now open trap door.

Miracle Max whirled. "Back, Witch—" he commanded.

"I'm not a witch, I'm your wife—" she was advancing on him now, an ancient tiny fury—"and after what you've just done I don't think I want to be *that* any more—" Miracle Max tried to calm her but she was having none of it. "He said 'true love,' Max—even I could hear it—'true love,' 'true love.' "

"Don't go on," Max said, and now there was pleading coming from somewhere.

Valerie turned toward Inigo. "He is rejecting you because he is afraid—he is afraid he's done, that the miracles are gone from his once majestic fingers—"

"Not true—" Max said.

"You're right," Valerie agreed, "it isn't true—they never were majestic, Max—you were never any good."

"The Ticklish Cure—you were there—you saw—"

"A fluke—"

"All the drowners I returned—"

"Chance—"

"Valerie, we've been married eighty years; how can you do this to me?"

"Because true love is expiring and you haven't got the decency to tell why you don't help—well I do, and I say this, Prince Humperdinck was *right* to fire you—"

"Don't say that name in my hut, Valerie—you made a pledge to me you'd never breathe that name—"

"Prince Humperdinck, Prince Humperdinck, Prince Humperdinck—at least he knows a phony when he sees one—"

Max fled toward the trap door, his hands going to his ears.

"But this is his fiancée's true love," Inigo said then. "If you bring him back to life, he will stop Prince Humperdinck's marriage—"

Max's hands left his ears. "This corpse here—he comes back to life, Prince Humperdinck suffers?"

"Humiliations galore," Inigo said.

"Now *that's* what I call a worth-while reason," Miracle Max said. "Give me the sixty-five; I'm on the case." He knelt beside Westley. "Hmmm," he said.

"What?" Valerie said. She knew that tone.

"While you were doing all that talking, he's slipped from sort of to mostly dead."

Valerie tapped Westley in a couple of places. "Stiffening," she said. "You'll have to work around that."

Max did a few taps himself. "Do you suppose the oracle's still up?"

Valerie looked at the clock. "I don't think so, it's almost one. Besides, I don't trust her all that much any more."

Max nodded. "I know, but it would have been nice to have a little advance hint on whether this is gonna work or not." He rubbed his eyes. "I'm tired going in; I wish I'd known in advance about the job; I'd have napped this afternoon." He shrugged. "Can't be helped, down is down. Get me my Encyclopedia of Spells and the Hex Appendix."

"I thought you knew all about this kind of thing," Inigo said, starting to get upset himself now.

"I'm out of practice, retired; it's been three years, you can't mess around with these resurrection recipes; one little ingredient wrong, the whole thing blows up in your face."

"Here's the hex book and your glasses," Valerie puffed, coming up the basement ladder. As Max began thumbing through, she turned to Inigo and Fezzik, who were hovering. "You can help," she said.

"Anything," Fezzik said.

"Tell us whatever's useful. How long do we have for the miracle? If we work it—"

"*When* we work it," Max said from his hex book. His voice was growing stronger.

"*When* we work it," Valerie went on, "how long does it have to maintain full efficiency? Just exactly what's going to be done?"

"Well, that's hard to predict," Inigo said, "since the first thing we have to do is storm the castle, and you never can be really sure how those things work out."

"An hour pill should be about right," Valerie said. "Either it's going to be plenty or you'll both be dead, so why not say an hour?"

"We'll all three be fighting," Inigo corrected. "And then once we've stormed the castle we have to stop the wedding, steal the Princess and make our escape, allowing space somewhere in there for me to duel Count Rugen."

Visibly Valerie's energy drained. She sat wearily down. "Max," she said, tapping his shoulder. "No good."

He looked up. "Huh?"

"They need a fighting corpse."

Max shut the hex book. "No good," he said.

"But I bought a miracle," Inigo insisted. "I paid you sixty-five."

"Look here—" Valerie thumped Westley's chest—"nothing. You ever hear anything so hollow? The man's life's been sucked away. It'll take months before there's strength again."

"We haven't got months—it's after one now, and the wedding's at six tonight. What parts can we hope to have in working order in seventeen hours?"

"Well," Max said, considering. "Certainly the tongue, absolutely the brain, and, with luck, maybe a little slow walk if you nudge him gently in the right direction."

Inigo looked at Fezzik in despair.

"What can I tell you?" Max said. "You needed a fantasmagoria."

"And you never could have gotten one of those for sixty-five," Valerie added, consolingly.

*   *   *

 *Little cut here, twenty pages maybe. What happens basically is an alternation of scenes—what's going on in the castle, then what's the situation with the miracle man, back and forth, and with every shift he gives the time, sort of 'there were now eleven hours until six o'clock,' that kind of thing. Morgenstern uses the device, mainly, because what he's really interested in, as always, is the satiric antiroyalty stuff and how stupid they were going through with all these old traditions, kissing the sacred ring of Great-grandfather So-and-So, etc.*

There is some action stuff which I cut, which I never did anywhere else, and here's my logic: Inigo and Fezzik have to go through a certain amount of derring-do in order to come up with the proper ingredients for the resurrection pill, stuff like Inigo finding some frog dust while Fezzik is off after holocaust mud, this latter, for example, requiring, first, Fezzik's acquiring a holocaust cloak so he doesn't burn to death gathering the mud, etc. Well, it's my conviction that this is

the same kind of thing as the Wizard of Oz sending Dorothy's friends to the wicked witch's castle for the ruby slippers; it's got the same 'feel,' if you know what I mean, and I didn't want to risk, when the book's building to climax, the reader's saying, 'Oh, this is just like the Oz books.' Here's the kicker, though: Morgenstern's Florinese version came before *Baum wrote* The Wizard of Oz, *so in spite of the fact that he was the originator, he comes out just the other way around. It would be nice if somebody, maybe a Ph.D. candidate on the loose, did a little something for Morgenstern's reputation, because, believe me, if being ignored is suffering, the guy has suffered.*

The other reason I made the cut is this: you just know that the resurrection pill has got to work. You don't spend all this time with a nutty couple like Max and Valerie to have it fail. At least, a whiz like Morgenstern doesn't.

One last thing: Hiram, my editor, felt the Miracle Max section was too Jewish in sound, too contemporary. I really let him have it on that one; it's a very sore point with me, because, just to take one example, there was a line in Butch Cassidy and the Sundance Kid *where Butch said, 'I got vision and the rest of the world wears bifocals,' and one of my genius producers said, 'That line's got to go; I don't put my name on this movie with that line in it,' and I said why and he said, 'They didn't talk like that then; it's anachronistic.' I remember explaining, 'Ben Franklin wore bifocals — Ty Cobb was batting champion of the American League when these guys were around — my mother was alive when these guys were alive and she wore bifocals.' We shook hands and ended enemies but the line stayed in the picture.*

And so here the point is, if Max and Valerie sound Jewish, why shouldn't they? You think a guy named Simon Morgenstern was Irish Catholic? Funny thing — Morgenstern's folks were named Max and Valerie and his father was a doctor. Life imitating art, art imitat-

ing life; I really get those two confused, sort of like I can never remember if claret is Bordeaux wine or Burgundy. They both taste good is the only thing that really matters, I guess, and so does Morgenstern, and we'll pick it up again later, thirteen hours later, to be precise, four in the afternoon, two hours before the wedding.

*   *   *

"You mean, that's it?" Inigo said, appalled.

"That's it," Max nodded proudly. He had not been up this long a stretch since the old days, and he felt terrific.

Valerie was so proud. "Beautiful," she said. She turned to Inigo then. "You sound so disappointed—what did you think a resurrection pill looked like?"

"Not like a lump of clay the size of a golf ball," Inigo answered.

*   *   *

(Me again, last time this chapter: no, that is not anachronistic either; there were golf balls in Scotland seven hundred years ago, and, not only that, remember Inigo had studied with MacPherson the Scot. As a matter of fact, everything Morgenstern wrote is historically accurate; read any decent book on Florinese history.)

*   *   *

"I usually give them a coating of chocolate at the last minute; it makes them look a lot better," Valerie said.

"It must be four o'clock," Max said then. "Better get the chocolate ready, so it'll have time to harden."

Valerie took the lump with her and started down the ladder to the kitchen. "You never did a better job; smile."

"It'll work without a hitch?" Inigo said.

Max nodded very firmly. But he did not smile. There was something in the back of his mind bothering him; he never forgot things, not important things, and he didn't forget this either.

He just didn't remember it in time. . . .

*   *   *

AT 4:45 PRINCE Humperdinck summoned Yellin to his chambers. Yellin came immediately, though he dreaded what was, he knew, about to happen. As a matter of fact, Yellin already had his resignation written and in an envelope in his pocket. "Your Highness," Yellin began.

"Report," Prince Humperdinck said. He was dressed brilliantly in white, his wedding costume. He still looked like a mighty barrel, but brighter.

"All of your wishes have been carried out, Highness. Personally I have attended to each detail." He was very tired, Yellin was, and his nerves long past frayed.

"Specify," said the Prince. He was seventy-five minutes away from his first female murder, and he wondered if he could get his fingers to her throat before even the start of a scream. He had been practicing on giant sausages all the afternoon and had the movements down pretty pat, but then, giant sausages weren't necks and all the wishing in the world wouldn't make them so.

"All passages to the castle itself have been resealed this very morning, save the main gate. That is now the only way in, and the only way out. I have changed the lock to the main gate. There is only one key to the new lock and I keep it wherever I am. When I am outside with the one hundred troops, the key is in the outside lock and no one can leave the castle from the inside. When I am with you, as I am now, the key is in the inside lock, and no one may enter from the outside."

"Follow," said the Prince, and he moved to the large window of his chamber. He pointed outside. Below the window was a lovely planted garden. Beyond that the Prince's private stables. Beyond that, naturally, the outside castle wall. "That is how they will come," he said. "Over the wall, through my stables, past my garden, to my window, throttle the Queen and back the way they came before we know it."

"They?" Yellin said, though he knew the answer.

"The Guilderians, of course."

"But the wall where you suggest is the highest wall surrounding all of Florin Castle—it is fifty feet high at that point—so that would seem the least likely point of attack." He was trying desperately to keep himself under control.

"All the more reason why they should choose this spot; besides, the world knows that the Guiderians are unsurpassed as climbers."

Yellin had never heard that. He had always thought the Swiss were the ones who were unsurpassed as climbers. "Highness," he said, in one last attempt, "I have not yet, from a single spy, heard a single word about a single plot against the Princess."

"I have it on unimpeachable authority that there will be an attempt made to strangle the Princess this very night."

"In that case," Yellin said, and he dropped to one knee and held out the envelope, "I must resign." It was a difficult decision—the Yellins had headed enforcement in Florin for generations, and they took their work more than seriously. "I am not doing a capable job, sire; please forgive me and believe me when I say that my failures were those of the body and mind and not of the heart."

Prince Humperdinck found himself, quite suddenly, in a genuine pickle, for once the war was finished, he needed someone to stay in Guilder and run it, since he couldn't be in two places at once, and the only men he trusted were Yellin and the Count, and the Count would never take the job, being obsessed, as he was these days, with finishing his stupid Pain Primer. "I do *not* accept your resignation, you *are* doing a capable job, there is *no* plot, *I* shall slaughter the Queen myself this very evening, *you* shall run Guilder for me after the war, now get back on your feet."

Yellin didn't know what to say. "Thank you" seemed so inadequate, but it was all he could come up with.

"Once the wedding is done with I shall send her here to make ready while I shall, with boots carefully procured in advance, make tracks leading from the wall to the bedroom and returning then from the bedroom to the wall. Since you are in charge of law enforcement, I expect you will not take long to verify my fears that the prints could only be made by the boots of Guilderian soldiers. Once we have that, we'll need a royal proclamation or two, my father can resign as being unfit for battle, and you, dear Yellin, will soon be living in Guilder Castle."

Yellin knew a dismissal speech when he heard one. "I leave with no thought in my heart but to serve you."

"Thank you," Humperdinck said, pleased, because, after all, loyalty was one thing you couldn't buy. And in that mood, he said to Yellin by the door, "And, oh, if you see the albino, tell him he may stand in the back for my wedding; it's quite all right with me."

"I will, Highness," Yellin said, adding, "but I don't know where my cousin is—I went looking for him less than an hour ago and he was nowhere to be found."

The Prince understood important news when he heard it because he wasn't the greatest hunter in the world for nothing and, even more, because if there was one thing you could say about the albino it was that he was *always* to be found. "My God, you don't suppose there *is* a plot, do you? It's a perfect time; the country celebrates; if Guilder were about to be five hundred years old, I know I'd attack them."

"I will rush to the gate and fight, to the death if necessary," Yellin said.

"Good man," the Prince called after him. If there was an attack, it would come at the busiest time, during the wedding, so he would have to move that up. State affairs went slowly, but, still, he had authority. Six o'clock was out. He would be married no later than half past five or know the reason why.

*   *   *

AT FIVE O'CLOCK, Max and Valerie were in the basement sipping coffee. "You better get right to bed," Valerie said; "you look all troubled. You can't stay up all night as if you were a pup."

"I'm not tired," Max said. "But you're right about the other."

"Tell Mama." Valerie crossed to him, stroked where his hair had been.

"It's just I been remembering, about the pill."

"It was a beautiful pill, honey. Feel proud."

"I think I messed up the amounts, though. Didn't they want an hour? When I doubled the recipe, I didn't do enough. I don't think it'll work over forty minutes."

Valerie moved into his lap. "Let's be honest with each other; sure, you're a genius, but even a genius gets rusty. You were three years out of practice. Forty minutes'll be plenty."

"I suppose you're right. Anyway, what can we do about it? Down is down."

"The pressures you been under, if it works at all, it'll be a miracle."

Max had to agree with her. "A fantasmagoria." He nodded.

*　　　*　　　*

THE MAN IN black was nearly stiff when Fezzik reached the wall. It was almost five o'clock and Fezzik had been carrying the corpse the whole way from Miracle Max's, back street to back street, alleyway to alleyway, and it was one of the hardest things he had ever done. Not taxing. He wasn't even winded. But if the pill was just what it looked like, a chocolate lump, then he, Fezzik, was going to have a lifetime of bad dreams of bodies growing stiff between his fingers.

When he at last was in the wall shadow, he said to Inigo, "What now?"

"We've got to see if it's still safe. There might be a trap waiting." It was the same part of the wall that led, shortly, to the Zoo, in the farther corner of the castle grounds. But if the albino's body had been discovered, then who knew what was waiting for them?

"Should I go up then?" Fezzik asked.

"We'll both do it," Inigo replied. "Lean him against the wall and help me." Fezzik tilted the man in black so he was in no danger of falling and waited while Inigo jumped onto his shoulders. Then Fezzik did the climbing. Any crack in the wall was enough for his fingers; the least imperfection was all he needed. He climbed quickly, familiar with it now, and after a moment, Inigo was able to grab hold of the top and say, "All right; go on back down," so Fezzik returned to the man in black and waited.

Inigo crept along the wall top in dead silence. Far across he could see the castle entrance and the armed soldiers flanking it. And closer at hand was the Zoo. And off in the deepest brush in the farthest corner of the wall, he could make out the still body of the albino. Nothing had changed at all. They were, at least so far, safe. He gestured down to Fezzik, who scissored the man in black between his legs, began the arm climb noiselessly.

When they were all together on the wall top, Inigo stretched out the dead man and then hurried along until he could get a better view of the main gate. The walk from the outer wall to the main castle gate was slanted sightly down, not much of an incline, but a steady one. There must be—Inigo did a quick count—at least a hundred men standing at the ready. And the time must be—he estimated closely—five after five now, perhaps close to ten. Fifty minutes till the wedding. Inigo turned then and hurried back to Fezzik. "I think we should give him the pill," he said. "It must be around forty-five minutes till the ceremony."

"That means he's only got fifteen minutes to escape with," Fezzik said. "I think we should wait until at least five-thirty. Half before, half after."

"No," Inigo said. "We're going to stop the wedding before it happens—that's the best way, at least to my mind. Before they're all set. In the hustle and bustle beforehand, that's when we should strike."

Fezzik had no further rebuttal.

"Anyway," Inigo said, "we don't know how long it takes to swallow something like this."

"I could never get it down myself. I know that."

"We'll have to force-feed him," Inigo said, unwrapping the chocolate-colored lump. "Like a stuffed goose. Put our hands around his neck and kind of push it down into whatever comes next."

"I'm with you, Inigo," Fezzik said. "Just tell me what to do."

"Let's get him in a sitting position, I think, don't you? I always find it's easier swallowing sitting up than lying down."

"We'll have to really work at it," Fezzik said. "He's completely stiff by now. I don't think he'll bend easy at all."

"You can make him," Inigo said. "I always have confidence in you, Fezzik."

"Thank you," Fezzik said. "Just don't ever leave me alone." He pulled the corpse between them and tried to make him bend in half, but the man in black was so stiff Fezzik really had to perspire to get him at right angles. "How long do you think we'll have to wait before we know if the miracle's on or not?"

"Your guess is as good as mine," Inigo said. "Get his mouth as wide open as you can and tilt his head back a little and we'll just drop it in and see."

Fezzik worked at the dead man's mouth a while, got it the way Inigo said, tilted the neck perfect the first time, and Inigo knelt directly above the cavity, dropped the pill down, and as it hit the throat he heard, "Couldn't beat me alone, you dastards; well, I beat you each apart, I'll beat you both together."

"You're alive!" Fezzik cried.

The man in black sat immobile, like a ventriloquist's dummy, just his mouth moving. "That is perhaps the most childishly obvious remark I have ever come across, but what can you expect from a strangler. Why won't my arms move?"

"You've been dead," Inigo explained.

"And we're not strangling you," Fezzik explained, "we were just getting the pill down."

"The resurrection pill," Inigo explained. "I bought it from Miracle Max and it works for sixty minutes."

"What happens after sixty minutes? Do I die again?" (It wasn't sixty minutes; he just thought it was. Actually it was forty; only they had used up one already in conversation, so it was down to thirty-nine.)

"We don't know. Probably you just collapse and need tending for a year or however long it takes to get your strength back."

"I wish I could remember what it was like when I was dead," the man in black said. "I'd write it all down. I could make a fortune on a book like that. I can't move my legs either."

"That will come. It's supposed to. Max said the tongue and the brain were shoo-ins and probably you'll be able to move, but slowly."

"The last thing I remember was dying, so why am I on this wall? Are we enemies? Have you got names? I'm the Dread Pirate Roberts, but you can call me 'Westley.' "

"Fezzik."

"Inigo Montoya of Spain. Let me tell you what's been going on—" He stopped and shook his head. "No," he said. "There's too much, it would take too long, let me distill it for you: the wedding is at six, which leaves us probably now something over half an hour to get in, steal the girl, and get out; but not before I kill Count Rugen."

"What are our liabilities?"

"There is but one working castle gate and it is guarded by perhaps a hundred men."

"Hmmm," Westley said, not as unhappy as he might have been ordinarily, because just then he began to be able to wiggle his toes.

"And our assets?"

"Your brains, Fezzik's strength, my steel."

Westley stopped wiggling his toes. "That's *all*? That's it? Everything? The grand total?"

Inigo tried to explain. "We've been operating under a terrible time pressure from the very beginning. Just yesterday morning, for example, I was a hopeless drunk and Fezzik toiled for the Brute Squad."

"It's impossible," Westley cried.

"*I am Inigo Montoya and I do not accept defeat*—you will think of something; I have complete confidence in you."

"She's going to marry Humperdinck and I'm *helpless*," Westley said in blind despair. "Lay me down again. Leave me alone."

"You're giving in too easily, we fought monsters to reach you, we risked everything because you have the brains to conquer problems. I have complete and absolute total confidence that you—"

"I want to die," Westley whispered, and he closed his eyes. "If I had a month to plan, maybe I might come up with something, but this . . ." His head rocked from side to side. "I'm sorry. Leave me."

"You just moved your own head," Fezzik said, doing his best to be cheery. "Doesn't that up your spirits?"

"My brains, your strength and his steel against a hundred troops? And you think a little head-jiggle is supposed to make me happy? Why didn't you leave me to death? This is worse. Lying here helpless while my true love marries my murderer."

"I just know once you're over your emotional outbursts, you'll come up with—"

"I mean if we even had a wheelbarrow, that would be something," Westley said.

"Where did we put that wheelbarrow the albino had?" Inigo asked.

"Over by the albino, I think," Fezzik replied.

"Maybe we can get a wheelbarrow," Inigo said.

"Well why didn't you list that among our assets in the first place?" Westley said, sitting up, staring out at the massed troops in the distance.

"You just sat up," Fezzik said, still trying to be cheery.

Westley continued to stare at the troops and the incline leading down toward them. He shook his head. "What I'd give for a holocaust cloak," he said then.

"There we can't help you," Inigo said.

"Will this do?" Fezzik wondered, pulling out his holocaust cloak.

"Where . . . ?" Inigo began.

"While you were after frog dust—" Fezzik answered. "It fit so nicely I just tucked it away and kept it."

Westley got to his feet then. "All right. I'll need a sword eventually."

"Why?" Inigo asked. "You can barely lift one."

"True," Westley agreed. "But that is hardly common knowledge. Hear me now; there may be problems once we're inside—"

"I'll say there may be problems," Inigo cut in. "How do we stop the wedding? Once we do, how do I find the Count? Once I do, where will I find you again? Once we're together, how do we escape? Once we escape—"

"Don't pester him with so many questions," Fezzik said. "Take it easy; he's been dead."

"Right, right, sorry," Inigo said.

The man in back was moving verrrrrry slowly now along the top of the wall. By himself. Fezzik and Inigo followed him through the darkness in the direction of the wheelbarrow. There was no denying the fact that there was a certain excitement in the air.

*   *   *

BUTTERCUP, FOR HER part, felt no excitement whatsoever. She had, in fact, never remembered such a wonderful feeling of calm. Her Westley was coming; that was her world. Ever since the Prince had dragged her to her room she had spent the intervening hours thinking of ways to make Westley happy. There was no way he could miss stopping her wedding. That was the only thought that could survive the trip across her conscious mind.

So when she heard the wedding was to be moved up, she wasn't the least upset. Westley was always prepared for contingencies, and if he could rescue her at six, he could just as happily rescue her at half past five.

Actually, Prince Humperdinck got things going even faster than he had hoped. It was 5:23 when he and his bride-to-be were kneeling before the aged Archdean of Florin. It was 5:24 when the Archdean started to speak.

And 5:25 when the screaming started outside the main gate.

Buttercup only smiled softly. Here comes my Westley now, was all she thought.

*   *   *

IT WAS NOT, in point of fact, her Westley that was causing the commotion out front. Westley was doing all he could to simply walk straight down the incline toward the main gate without help. Ahead of him, Inigo struggled with the heavy wheelbarrow. The reason for its weight was that Fezzik stood in it, arms wide, eyes blazing, voice booming in terrible rage: "I AM THE DREAD PIRATE ROBERTS AND THERE WILL BE NO SURVIVORS." He said that over and over, his voice echoing and reverberating as his rage increased. He was, standing there, gliding down through the darkness, quite an imposing figure, seeming, all in all, probably close to ten feet tall, with voice to match. But even that was not the cause of the screaming.

*   *   *

YELLIN, FROM HIS position by the gate, was reasonably upset at the roaring giant gliding down toward them through the darkness.

Not that he doubted his hundred men could dispatch the giant; the upsetting thing was that, of course, the giant would be aware of that too, and logically there must somewhere in the dimness out there be any number of giant helpers. Other pirates, anything. Who could tell? Still, his men held together remarkably staunchly.

It was only when the giant got halfway down the incline that he suddenly, happily, burst into flame and continued his trip saying, "NO SURVIVORS, NO SURVIVORS!" in a manner that could only indicate deadly sincerity.

It was seeing him happily burning and advancing that started the Brute Squad to screaming. And once that happened, why, everybody panicked and ran. . . .

EIGHT

HONEYMOON

NCE the panic was well under way, Yellin realized he had next to no chance of bringing things immediately under control. Besides, the giant was terribly close now, and the roar of "NO SUR-VIVORS" made it very hard to do any solid thinking, but fortunately he had the sense to grab the one and only key to the castle and hide it on his person.

Fortunately too, Westley had the sense to look for such behavior. "Give me the key," Westley said to Yellin, once Inigo had his sword securely pressuring Yellin's Adam's apple.

"I have no key," Yellin replied. "I swear on the grave of my parents; may my mother's soul forever sizzle in torment if I am lying."

"Tear his arms off," Westley said to Fezzik, who was sizzling a bit himself now, because there was a limit as to just how long a holocaust cloak was really good for, and he wanted to strip a bit, but before he did that, he reached for Yellin's arms.

"This key you mean?" Yellin said, and he dropped it, and after Inigo had taken his sword, they let him run away.

"Open the gate," Westley said to Fezzik.

"I'm so hot," Fezzik said, "can I please take this thing off first?" and after Westley's nod, he pulled the flaming cloak away and left it on the ground, then unlocked the gate and pulled the door open enough for them to slip through.

"Lock it and keep the key, Fezzik," Westley said. "It must be after 5:30 by now; half an hour left to stop the wedding."

"What do we do after we win?" Fezzik said, working with the key, forcing the great lock to close. "Where should we meet? I'm the kind of fellow who needs instructions."

Before Westley could answer, Inigo cried out and readied his sword. Count Rugen and four palace guards were rounding a corner and running toward them. The time was then 5:34.

*   *   *

THE WEDDING ITSELF did not end until 5:31, and Humperdinck had to use all of his persuasive abilities to get even that much accomplished. As the screaming from outside the gate burst all bounds of propriety, the Prince interrupted the Archdean with gentlest manner and said, "Holiness, my love is simply overpowering my ability to wait—please skip on down to the end of the service."

The time was then 5:27.

"Humperdinck and Buttercup," the Archdean said, "I am very old and my thoughts on marriage are few, but I feel I must give them to you on this most happy of days." (The Archdean could hear absolutely nothing, and had been so afflicted since he was eighty-five or so. The only actual change that had come over him in the past years was that, for some reason, his impediment had gotten worse. "Mawidge," he said. "Vewy old." Unless you paid strict attention to his title and past accomplishments, it was very hard to take him seriously.)

"Mawidge—" the Archdean began.

"Again, Holiness, I interrupt in the name of love. Please hurry along as best you can to the end."

"Mawidge is a dweam wiffin a dweam."

Buttercup was paying little attention to the goings on. Westley must be racing down the corridors now. He always ran so beautifully. Even back on the farm, long before she knew her heart, it was good to watch him run.

Count Rugen was the only other person in the room, and the commotion at the gate had him on edge. Outside the door he had his four best swordsmen, so no one could enter the tiny chapel, but, still, there were a lot of people screaming where the Brute Squad should have been. The four guards were the only ones left inside the castle, for the Prince needed no spectators to the events that were soon to happen. If only the idiot cleric would speed things along. It was already 5:29.

"The dweam of wuv wapped wiffin the gweater dweam of ever-wasting west. Eternity is our fwiend, wemember that, and wuv wiw fowwow you fowever."

It was 5:30 when the Prince stood up and approached the Arch-dean firmly. "Man and wife," he shouted. "*Man and wife.* Say that!"

"I'm not there yet," the Archdean answered.

"You just arrived," the Prince replied. "Now!"

Buttercup could picture Westley rounding the final corner. There were four guards outside waiting. At ten seconds per guard, she began figuring, but then stopped, because numbers had always been her enemy. She looked down at her hands. Oh, I hope he still thinks I'm pretty, she thought; those nightmares took a lot out of me.

"Man and wife, you're man and wife," the Archdean said.

"Thank you, Holiness," the Prince said, whirling toward Rugen. "Stop that commotion!" he commanded, and before his words were finished, the Count was running for the chapel door.

It was 5:31.

*   *   *

IT TOOK A full three minutes for the Count and the guards to reach the gate, and when they did, the Count could not believe it—he had seen Westley killed, and now there was Westley. And with a giant and a strangely scarred swarthy fellow. Something about the twin scars banked deep into his memory, but now was not the time for reminiscing. "Kill them," he said to the fencers, "but leave the middle-sized one until I tell you" and the four guards drew their swords—

—but too late; too late and too slow, because as Fezzik moved in front of Westley, Inigo attacked, the great blade blinding, and the fourth guard was dead before the first one had had sufficient time to hit the floor.

Inigo stood still a moment, panting. Then he made a half turn in the direction of Count Rugen and executed a quick and well-formed bow. "Hello," he said. "My name is Inigo Montoya. You killed my father. Prepare to die."

And in reply, the Count did a genuinely remarkable and unexpected thing: he turned and ran. It was now 5:37.

*   *   *

KING LOTHARON AND Queen Bella arrived at the wedding chapel in time to see Count Rugen leading the four guards in a charge down the corridor.

"Are we too early?" Queen Bella said, as they entered the wedding chapel and found Buttercup and Humperdinck and the Archdean.

"There is much going on," the Prince said. "All, in due time, will come matchlessly clear. But I fear there is a strong possibility that, at this very moment, the Guilderians are attacking. I need time alone in the garden to formulate my battle plans, so could I prevail upon you two to personally escort Buttercup to my bedchamber?"

His request was, naturally, granted. The Prince hurried off then, and, after one stop to unlock a closet and remove several pairs of boots that had once belonged to Guilderian soldiers, he hurried outside.

Buttercup, for her part, walked very slowly and peacefully between the old King and Queen. There was no need ever to worry, not with Westley there to stop her wedding and take her away forever. The truth of her situation did not take genuine effect until she was halfway to Humperdinck's room.

There was no Westley.

No sweet Westley. He had not seen fit to come for her.

She gave a terrible sigh. Not so much of sadness as of farewell. Once she got to Humperdinck's room, it would all be done. He had a splendid collection of swords and cutlery.

She had never seriously contemplated suicide before. Oh, of course she'd thought about it; every girl does from time to time. But never seriously. To her quiet surprise, she found it was going to be the easiest thing in the world. She reached the Prince's chamber, said good night to the Royal Family, and went directly to the wall display of weaponry. The time was then 5:46.

*   *   *

INIGO, AT 5:37, was so startled at the Count's cowardice that for a moment he simply stood there. Then he gave chase and, of course, he was faster, but the Count made it through a doorway, slammed and locked it, and Inigo was helpless to budge the thing. "Fezzik," he called out desperately, "Fezzik, break it down."

But Fezzik was with Westley. That was his job, to stay and protect Westley, and though they were still within view of Inigo, Fezzik could do nothing; Westley had already started to walk. Slowly. Weakly. But he was, under his own power, walking.

"Charge it," Fezzik replied. "Slam your shoulder hard. It will give for you."

Inigo charged the door. He slammed and slammed his shoulder, but he was thin, the door otherwise. "He's getting away from me," Inigo said.

"But Westley is helpless," Fezzik reminded him.

"Fezzik, I *need* you," Inigo screamed.

"I'll only be a minute," Fezzik said, because there were some things you did, no matter what, and when a friend needed help, you helped him.

Westley nodded, kept on walking, still slowly, still weak, but still able to move.

"Hurry," Inigo urged.

Fezzik hurried. He lumbered to the locked door, threw his bulk against it hard.

The door held.

"Please," Inigo urged.

"I'll get it, I'll get it," Fezzik promised, and he took a few steps back this time, then drove his shoulder against the wood.

The door gave some. A little. But not enough.

Fezzik backed away from it now. With a roar he charged across the corridor and when he was close he left the castle floor with both feet and the door splintered.

"Thank you, thank you," Inigo said, already halfway through the broken door.

"What do I do now though?" Fezzik called.

"Back to Westley," Inigo answered, in full flight now, beginning chasing through a series of rooms.

"Stupid," Fezzik punished himself with, and he turned and re-joined Westley. Only Westley was no longer there. Fezzik could feel the panic starting inside him. There were half a dozen possible corridors. "Which which which?" Fezzik said, trying to figure it out, trying for once in his life to do something right. "You'll pick the wrong one, knowing you," he said out loud, and then he took a corridor and started hurrying along it as fast as he could.

He did pick the wrong one.

Westley was alone now.

*   *   *

INIGO WAS GAINING. He could see, instant to instant, flashes of the fleeing noble in the next room, and when he reached that place, the Count would have made it into the room beyond. But each time, Inigo was gaining. By 5:40, he felt confident he would, after a chase of twenty-five years, be alone in a room with his revenge.

*   *   *

BY 5:48, BUTTERCUP felt quite sure she would be dead. It was still a minute before that as she stood staring at the Prince's knives. The most lethal looked to be the one most used, the Florinese dagger. Pointed at one end, it entered easily, growing into a triangular shape by the hilt. For quicker bleeding, it was said. They were made in varying sizes, and the Prince's looked to be one of the largest, being wrist thick where it joined the handle. She pulled it from the wall, put it to her heart.

"There are always too few perfect breasts in this world; leave yours alone," she heard. And there was Westley on the bed. It was 5:48, and she knew that she would never die.

Westley, for his part, assumed he had till 6:15 for his hour to be up. That was, of course, when an hour was up, only he didn't have an hour; only forty minutes. Till 5:55, actually. Seven minutes more. But, as has been said, he had no way of knowing that.

*   *   *

AND INIGO HAD no way of knowing that Count Rugen had a Florinese dagger. Or that he was expert with the thing. It took

Inigo until 5:41 before he actually cornered the Count. In a billiard room. "Hello," he was about to say. "My name is Inigo Montoya; you killed my father; prepare to die." What he actually got out was somewhat less: "Hello, my name is Ini—"

And then the dagger rearranged his insides. The force of the throw sent him staggering backward into the wall. The rush of blood weakened him so quickly he could not keep his feet. "Domingo, Domingo," he whispered, and then he was, at forty-two minutes after five, lost on his knees. . . .

*   *   *

BUTTERCUP WAS BAFFLED by Westley's behavior. She rushed to him, expecting to be met halfway in a wild embrace. Instead, he only smiled at her and remained where he was, lying on the Prince's pillows, a sword beside his body.

Buttercup continued the journey alone and fell onto her very one and darling Westley.

"Gently," he said.

"At a time like this that's all you can think to say? 'Gently'?"

"*Gently,*" Westley repeated, not so gently this time.

She got off him. "Are you angry at me for getting married?" she wondered.

"You are not married," he said, softly. Strange his voice was. "Not in my church or any other."

"But this old man did pronounce—"

"Widows happen. Every day—don't they, Your Highness?" And now his voice was stronger as he addressed the Prince, who entered, muddy boots in hand.

Prince Humperdinck dove for his weapons, and a sword flashed in his thick hands. "To the death," he said, advancing.

Westley gave a soft shake of his head. "No," he corrected. "To the pain."

It was an odd phrase, and for the moment it brought the Prince up short. Besides, why was the fellow just lying there? Where was the trap? "I don't think I quite understand that."

Westley lay without moving but he was smiling more deeply now. "I'll be only too delighted to explain." It was 5:50 now. Twenty-five minutes of safety left. (There were five. He did not know that. How could he know that?) Slowly, carefully, he began to talk. . . .

* * *

INIGO WAS TALKING too. It was still 5:42 when he whispered, "I'm . . . sorry . . . Father. . . ."

Count Rugen heard the words but nothing really connected until he saw the sword still held in Inigo's hand. "You're that little Spanish brat I taught a lesson to," he said, coming closer now, examining the scars. "It's simply incredible. Have you been chasing me all these years only to fail now? I think that's the worst thing I ever heard of; how marvelous."

Inigo could say nothing. The blood fauceted from his stomach.

Count Rugen drew his sword.

". . . sorry, Father . . . I'm sorry. . . ."

'I DON'T WANT YOUR "SORRY"! MY NAME IS DOMINGO MONTOYA AND I DIED FOR THAT SWORD AND YOU CAN KEEP YOUR "SORRY." IF YOU WERE GOING TO FAIL, WHY DIDN'T YOU DIE YEARS AGO AND LET ME REST IN PEACE?' And then MacPherson was after him too— 'Spaniards! I never should have tried to teach a Spaniard; they're dumb, they forget, what do you do with a wound? How many times did I teach you—*what do you do with a wound*?'

"Cover it . . ." Inigo said, and he pulled the knife from his body and stuffed his left fist into the bleeding.

Inigo's eyes began to focus again, not well, not perfectly, but enough to see the Count's blade as it approached his heart, and Inigo couldn't do much with the attack, parry it vaguely, push the point of the blade into his left shoulder where it did no unendurable harm.

Count Rugen was a bit surprised that his point had been deflected, but there was nothing wrong with piercing a helpless man's shoulder. There was no hurry when you had him.

MacPherson was screaming again—'Spaniards! Give me a Polack anytime; at least the Polacks remember to use the wall when they have one; only the Spaniards would forget to use a wall—'

Slowly, inch by inch, Inigo forced his body up the wall, using his legs just for pushing, letting the wall do all the supporting that was necessary.

Count Rugen struck again, but for any number of reasons, most probably because he hadn't expected the other man's movement, he missed the heart and had to be content with driving his blade through the Spaniard's left arm.

Inigo didn't mind. He didn't even feel it. His right arm was where his interest lay, and he squeezed the handle and there was strength in his hand, enough to flick out at the enemy, and Count Rugen hadn't expected that either, so he gave a little involuntary cry and took a step back to reassess the situation.

Power was flowing up from Inigo's heart to his right shoulder and down from his shoulder to his fingers and then into the great six-fingered sword and he pushed off from the wall then, with a whispered, ". . . hello . . . my name is . . . Inigo Montoya; you killed . . . my father; prepare to die."

And they crossed swords.

The Count went for the quick kill, the inverse Bonetti.

No chance.

"Hello . . . my name is Inigo Montoya; you killed my father . . . prepare to die. . . ."

Again they crossed, and the Count moved into a Morozzo defense, because the blood was still streaming.

Inigo shoved his fist deeper into himself. "Hello, my name is Inigo Montoya; you killed my father; prepare to die."

The Count retreated around the billiard table.

Inigo slipped in his own blood.

The Count continued to retreat, waiting, waiting.

"Hello, my name is Inigo Montoya; you killed my father; prepare to die." He dug with his fist and he didn't want to think what he was touching and pushing and holding into place but for the first time he felt able to try a move, so the six-fingered sword flashed forward—

—and there was a cut down one side of Count Rugen's cheek—

—another flash—

—another cut, parallel, bleeding—

"Hello, my name is Inigo Montoya; you killed my father; prepare to die."

"Stop saying that!" The Count was beginning to experience a decline of nerve.

Inigo drove for the Count's left shoulder, as the Count had wounded his. Then he went through the Count's left arm, at the same spot the Count had penetrated his. "Hello." Stronger now. "Hello! HELLO. MY NAME IS INIGO MONTOYA. YOU KILLED MY FATHER. PREPARE TO DIE!"

"No—"

"Offer me money—"

"Everything," the Count said.

"Power too. Promise me that."

"All I have and more. Please."

"Offer me anything I ask for."

"Yes. Yes. Say it."

"I WANT DOMINGO MONTOYA, YOU SON OF A BITCH," and the six-fingered sword flashed again.

The Count screamed.

"That was just to the left of your heart." Inigo struck again.

Another scream.

"That was below your heart. Can you guess what I'm doing?"

"Cutting my heart out."

"You took mine when I was ten; I want yours now. We are lovers of justice, you and I—what could be more just than that?"

The Count screamed one final time and then fell dead of fear.

Inigo looked down at him. The Count's frozen face was petrified and ashen and the blood still poured down the parallel cuts. His eyes bulged wide, full of horror and pain. It was glorious. If you like that kind of thing.

Inigo loved it.

It was 5:50 when he staggered from the room, heading he knew not where or for how long, but hoping only that whoever had been guiding him lately would not desert him now. . . .

*   *   *

"I'M GOING TO tell you something once and then whether you die or not is strictly up to you," Westley said, lying pleasantly on the bed. Across the room, the Prince held the sword high. "What I'm going to tell you is this: drop your sword, and if you do, then I will leave with this baggage here"—he glanced at Buttercup—"and you will be tied up but not fatally, and will soon be free to go about your business. And if you choose to fight, well, then, we will not both leave alive."

"I expect to breathe a while," the Prince said. "I think you are bluffing—you have been prisoner for months and I myself killed you less than a day ago, so I doubt that you have much might left in your arm."

"Possibly true," Westley agreed, "and when the moment comes, remember that: I *might* indeed be bluffing. I could, in fact be lying right here because I lack the strength to stand. All that, weigh carefully."

"You are only alive now because you said 'to the pain.' I want that phrase explained."

"My pleasure." It was 5:52 now. Three minutes left. He thought he had eighteen. He took a long pause, then started speaking. "Surely, you must have guessed I am no ordinary sailor. I am, in fact, Roberts himself."

"I am, in fact, not the least surprised or awed."

"To the pain means this: if we duel and you win, death for me. If we duel and I win, *life* for you. But life on my terms."

"Meaning?" It could all still be a trap. His body was at the ready.

"There are those who credit you with skill as a hunter, though I find that doubtful."

The Prince smiled. The fellow was baiting him. Why?

"And if you hunt well, then surely, when you tracked your lady, you must have begun at the Cliffs of Insanity. A duel was fought there and if you noted the movements and the strides, you would know that those were masters battling. They were. Remember this: I *won* that fight. And I am a pirate. We have our special tricks with swords."

It was 5:53. "I am not unfamiliar with steel."

"The first thing you lose will be your feet," Westley said. "The left, then the right. Below the ankle. You will have stumps available to use within six months. Then your hands, at the wrist. They heal somewhat quicker. Five months is a fair average." And now Westley was beginning to be aware of strange changes in his body and he began talking faster, faster and louder. "Next your nose. No smell of dawn for you. Followed by your tongue. Deeply cut away. Not even a stump left. And then your left eye—"

"And then my right eye and then my ears, and shall we get on with it?" the Prince said. It was 5:54.

"*Wrong!*" Westley's voice rang across the room. "Your ears you keep, so that every shriek of every child at seeing your hideousness will be yours to cherish—every babe that weeps in fear at your approach, every woman that cries 'Dear God, what is that thing?' will reverberate forever with your perfect ears. That is what 'to the pain' means. It means that I leave you to live in anguish, in humiliation, in freakish misery until you can stand it no more; so there you have it, pig, there you know, you miserable vomitous mass, and I say this now, and live or die, it's up to you: *Drop your sword!*"

The sword crashed to the floor.

It was 5:55.

Westley's eyes rolled up into his head and his body crumpled and half pitched from the bed and the Prince saw that and went to the floor, grabbing for his sword, standing, starting to bring it high, when Westley cried out: "Now you *will* suffer: *to the pain!*" His eyes were open again.

Open and blazing.

"I'm sorry; I meant nothing, I didn't; look," and the Prince dropped his sword a second time.

"Tie him," Westley said to Buttercup. "Be quick about it—use the curtain sashes; they look enough to hold him—"

"You'd do it so much better," Buttercup replied. "I'll get the sashes, but I really think you should do the actual tying."

"Woman," Westley roared, "you are the property of the Dread Pirate Roberts and you . . . do . . . what . . . you're . . . told!"

Buttercup gathered the sashes and did what she could with tying up her husband.

Humperdinck lay flat while she did it. He seemed strangely happy. "I wasn't afraid of you," he said to Westley. "I dropped my sword because it will be so much more pleasure for me to hunt you down."

"You think so, do you? I doubt you'll find us."

"I'll conquer Guilder and then I'll come for you. The corner you least expect, when you round it, you will find me waiting."

"*I am the King of the Sea*—I await you with pleasure." He called out to Buttercup. "Is he tied yet?"

"Sort of."

There was movement at the doorway and then Inigo was there. Buttercup cried out at the blood. Inigo ignored her, looked around. "Where's Fezzik?"

"Isn't he with you?" Westley said.

Inigo leaned for a moment against the nearest wall, gathering strength. Then he said, "Help him up," to Buttercup.

"Westley?" Buttercup replied. "Why does he need me to help him?"

"Because he has no strength, now do what you're told," Inigo said, and then suddenly on the floor, the Prince began struggling mightily with the sashes and he was tied, and tied well, but power and anger were both on his side.

"You *were* bluffing; I was right the first time," Humperdinck said, and Inigo said, "That was not a clever thing of me to let slip; I'm sorry," and Westley said, "Did you at least win your battle?" and Inigo said, "I did," and Westley said, "Let us try to find some place to defend ourselves; at least perhaps we can go together," and Buttercup said, "I'll help you up, poor darling," and Fezzik said, "Oh, Inigo, I need you, please, Inigo; I'm lost and miserable and frightened and I just need to see a friendly face."

They moved slowly to the window.

Wandering lost and forlorn through the Prince's garden was Fezzik, leading the four giant whites.

"Here," Inigo whispered.

"*Three* friendly faces," Fezzik said, kind of bouncing up and down on his heels, which he always did when things were looking up. "Oh, Inigo, I just ruined everything and I got so lost and when I stumbled into the stables and found these pretty horses I thought four was how many of them there were and four was how many of us there were too, if we found the lady—hello, lady—and I thought, Why not take them along with me in case we all ever run into each other." He stopped a moment, considering. "And I guess we did."

Inigo was terribly excited. "Fezzik, you thought for yourself," he said.

Fezzik considered that a moment too. "Does that mean you're not mad at me for getting lost?"

"If we only had a ladder—" Buttercup began.

"Oh, you don't need a ladder to get down here," Fezzik said; "it's only twenty feet, I'll catch you, only do it one at a time, please; there's not enough light, so if you all come at once I might miss."

So while Humperdinck struggled, they jumped, one at a time, and Fezzik caught them gently and put them on the whites, and he still had the key so they could get out the front gate, and except for the fact that Yellin had regrouped the Brute Squad, they would have gotten out without any trouble at all. As it was, when Fezzik unlocked the gate, they saw nothing but armed Brutes in formation, Yellin at their lead. And no one smiling.

Westley shook his head. "I am dry of notions."

"Child's play," of all people, Buttercup said, and she led the group toward Yellin. "The Count is dead; the Prince is in grave danger. Hurry now and you may yet save him. All of you. Go."

Not a Brute moved.

"They obey me," Yellin said. "And I am in charge of enforcement, and—"

"And *I*," Buttercup said. *"I,"* she repeated, standing up in the saddle, a creature of infinite beauty and eyes that were starting to grow frightening, *"I,"* she said for the third and last time, "am

the

QUEEEEEEEEEEEEN."

There was no doubting her sincerity. Or power. Or capability for vengeance. She stared imperiously across the Brute Squad.

"Save Humperdinck," one Brute said, and with that they all dashed into the castle.

"Save Humperdinck," Yellin said, the last one left, but clearly his heart wasn't in it.

"Actually, that was something of a fib," Buttercup said as they began to ride for freedom, "seeing as Lotharon hasn't officially resigned, but I thought 'I am the Queen' sounded better than 'I am the Princess.' "

"All I can say is, I'm impressed," Westley told her.

Buttercup shrugged. "I've been going to royalty school three years now; *some*thing had to rub off." She looked at Westley. "You all right? I was worried about you back on the bed there. Your eyes rolled up into your head and everything."

"I suppose I was dying again, so I asked the Lord of Permanent Affection for the strength to live the day. Clearly, the answer came in the affirmative."

"I didn't know there was such a Fellow," Buttercup said.

"Neither did I, in truth, but if He didn't exist, I didn't much want to either."

The four great horses seemed almost to fly toward Florin Channel.

"It appears to me as if we're doomed, then," Buttercup said.

Westley looked at her. "Doomed, madam?"

"To be together. Until one of us dies."

"I've done that already, and I haven't the slightest intention of ever doing it again," Westley said.

Buttercup looked at him. "Don't we sort of have to sometime?"

"Not if we promise to outlive each other, and I make that promise now."

Buttercup looked at him. "Oh my Westley, so do I."

*   *   *

'And they lived happily ever after,' my father said.

'Wow,' I said.

He looked at me. 'You're not pleased?'

'No, no, it's just, it came so quick, the ending, it surprised me. I thought there'd be a little more, is all. I mean, was the pirate ship waiting or was that just a rumor like it said?'

'Complain to Mr. Morgenstern. "And they lived happily ever after" is how it ends.'

The truth was, my father was fibbing. I spent my whole life thinking it ended that way, up until I did this abridgement. Then I glanced at the last page. This is how Morgenstern ends it.

*   *   *

BUTTERCUP LOOKED AT him. "Oh my Westley, so do I."

From behind them suddenly, closer than they imagined, they could hear the roar of Humperdinck: "Stop them! Cut them off!"

They were, admittedly, startled, but there was no reason for worry: they were on the fastest horses in the kingdom, and the lead was already theirs.

However, this was before Inigo's wound reopened; and Westley relapsed again; and Fezzik took the wrong turn; and Buttercup's horse threw a shoe. And the night behind them was filled with the crescendoing sound of pursuit. . . .

*   *   *

 That's Morgenstern's ending, a 'Lady or the Tiger?' type effect (this was before 'The Lady or the Tiger?,' remember). Now, he was a satirist, so he left it that way, and my father was, I guess I realized too late, a romantic, so he ended it another way.

Well, I'm an abridger, so I'm entitled to a few ideas of my own. Did they make it? Was the pirate ship there? You can answer it for yourself, but, for me, I say yes it was. And yes, they got away. And got their strength back and had lots of adventures and more than their share of laughs.

But that doesn't mean I think they had a happy ending either. Because, in my opinion anyway, they squabbled a lot, and Buttercup lost her looks eventually, and one day Fezzik lost a fight and some hotshot kid whipped Inigo with a sword and Westley was never able to really sleep sound because of Humperdinck maybe being on the trail.

I'm not trying to make this a downer, understand. I mean, I really do think that love is the best thing in the world, except for cough drops. But I also have to say, for the umpty-umpth time, that life isn't fair. It's just fairer than death, that's all.

*New York City
February, 1973*

BUTTERCUP'S
BABY

AN EXPLANATION

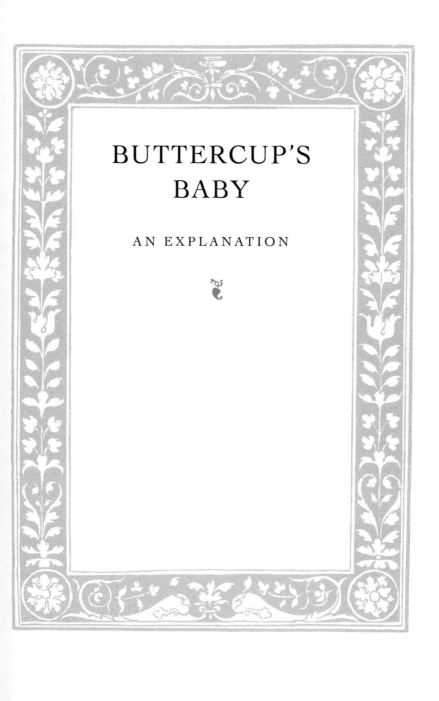

OU'RE probably wondering why I only abridged the first chapter. The answer is simple: *I was not allowed to do more.* The following explanation is kind of personal, and I'm sorry for putting you through it. Some of this—more than some, a lot—was painful when it happened, still is as I write it down for you. I don't come out all that well a lot of the time, but that can't be helped. Morgenstern was always honest with his audience. I don't think I can be any less with you . . .

*   *   *

MY TROUBLES BEGAN twenty-five years ago with the reunion scene.

You remember, in my abridgement of *The Princess Bride,* when Buttercup and Westley have been reunited just before the Fire Swamp, I stuck my two cents in and said I thought Morgenstern had cheated his readers by not including a reunion scene for the lovers so I'd written my own version and send in if you want a copy? (Page 171–72 in this edition.)

My late great editor Hiram Haydn felt I was wrong, that if you abridge someone you can't suddenly start using your own words. But I *liked* my reunion scene a lot. So, to humor me, he let me stick that note in the book about sending in for it.

No one—please believe this—*no one* thought anyone would actually request my version. But Harcourt, the original hardcover publisher, got deluged, and later Ballantine, the paperback publisher, got deluged even more. I loved that. Publishers having to spend money. My reunion scene was poised for mailing—but not one was ever sent.

What follows is the explanatory letter I wrote that *was* mailed to the tens of thousands of people who had written in over the years asking for the scene.

Dear Reader,

Thank you for sending in and no, this is not the reunion scene, because of a certain roadblock named Kermit Shog.

As soon as bound books were ready, I got a call from my lawyer, Charley—(you may not remember, but Charley's the one I called from California to go down in the blizzard and buy *The Princess Bride* from the used-book dealer). Anyway, he usually begins with Talmudic humor, wisdom jokes, only this time he just says, "Bill, I think you better get down here," and before I'm even allowed a "why?" he adds, "Right away if you can."

Panicked, I zoom down, wondering who could have died, did I flunk my tax audit, what? His secretary lets me into his office and Charley says, "This is Mr. Shog, Bill."

And there he is, sitting in the corner, hands on his briefcase, looking exactly like an oily version of Peter Lorre. I really expected him to say, "Give me the Falcon, you must, or I will be forced to keeel you."

"Mr. Shog is a lawyer," Charley goes on. And then this next was said underlined: *"He represents the Morgenstern estate."*

Who knew? Who could have dreamed such a thing existed, an estate of a man dead at least a million years that no one ever heard of over here anyway? "Perhaps you will give me the Falcon now," Mr. Shog said. That's not true. What he said was, "Perhaps you will like a few words with your client alone now," and Charley nodded and out he went and once he was done I said, "Charley, my God, I never figured—" and he said, "Did Harcourt?" and I said, "Not that they ever mentioned," and he said, "Ooch," the grunting sound lawyers make when they know they've backed a loser. "What does he want?" I said. "A meeting with Mr. Jovanovich," Charley answered . . .

It turned out that Kermit Shog did not *just* want a meeting with William Jovanovich, the brilliant man who ran the firm. He also wanted amazing amounts of money and he *also* wanted the unabridged *The Princess Bride* version printed with a huge first printing (100,000), and, of course, the idea of little me sending out the reunion scene died that day.

But the lawsuits began. Over the years, a grand total of thirteen—only eleven directly concerning me. It was horrible, but the one good thing was that the copyright on Morgenstern ran out in '78. So I told everyone who sent in for the reunion scene that their names were being put on a list and kept and once '78 rolled around, *voila* . . . but I was wrong again. Here is part of the next note I sent out to all people requesting the reunion scene.

I'm really sorry about this but you know the story that ends, "Disregard previous wire, letter follows?" Well, you've got to disregard the business about the Morgenstern copyright running out in '78. That was a definitely a boo-boo but Mr. Shog, being Florinese, has trouble, naturally, with our numbering system. The copyright runs out in *'87*, not '78.

Worse, he died. Mr. Shog, I mean. (Don't ask how you could tell. It was easy. One morning he just stopped sweating, so there it was.) What makes it worse is that the whole affair is now in the hands of his kid, named—wait for it—Mandrake Shog. Mandrake moves with all the verve and speed of a lizard flaked out on a riverbank.

The only good thing that's happened in this whole mess is I finally got a shot at reading some of *Buttercup's Baby*. Up at Columbia, they feel it's definitely superior to *The Princess Bride* in satirical content. Personally, I don't have the emotional attachment to it, but it's a helluva story, no question.

It's funny, looking back, but at the time I had really zero interest in *Buttercup's Baby*.

Many reasons, but among them this: *I was writing my own novels then.* To make sense of that, I suppose I ought to tell you what I did with *The Princess Bride*. I know the book cover just says "abridged by" and, yes, I jumped from "good part" to "good part." But it was really a good deal more than that.

Morgenstern's *The Princess Bride* is a thousand-page manuscript. I got it down to three hundred. But I didn't just cut out his satiric interludes. I made elisions constantly. And there was all kinds of stuff, some of it wonderful, I got rid of. Example: Westley's terrible childhood and how he came to be the Farm Boy. Example: How the King and Queen went to Miracle Max because they knew they had somehow given birth to a monster (Humperdinck), and could Max change that? Max's failure is what led to his firing, which in turn, caused his crisis in confidence. (His wife, Valerie, refers to it when she says to Inigo: "He is afraid he's done, that the miracles are gone from his once majestic fingers . . ." (p. 278 in this version.)

I felt all this, exciting and moving as a lot of it is, to be off the spine of the story. *I* went with true love and high adventure and I think I was right to do that. And I think the results have proved that. Morgenstern *never* had any audience for his book—except in Florin, of course. I brought it to people everywhere and, with the movie, to a wider audience still. So, sure, I abridged it.

But, I'm sorry, I *shaped* it. *I also brought it to life.* I don't know what you want to call that, but whatever I did, it's sure *something*.

*   *   *

SO *BUTTERCUP'S BABY* was just not for me at that time. The workload was one thing. It would have meant thousands of hours of labor. But that was nothing compared to the constant attacks by the Shogs. Lawsuit after awful lawsuit, and each time I had to defend myself, had to give depositions, which I frankly found hateful because they were all attacks on my honesty.

I had had, then, enough of Mr. Morgenstern for awhile.

I didn't actually read *Buttercup's Baby*, either. I happened to be at Columbia University one afternoon—I gave my papers to Columbia—and some Florinese kid stopped by, handed me a rough translation to glance at. The full title of the book is this: *Buttercup's Baby: S. Morgenstern's Glorious Examination of Courage Matched Against the Death of the Heart.* Had a great opening page, a real shocker, but that was mostly what I remember. It was just another book to me then, you see. It had not become lodged in my heart.

Yet.

*   *   *

SO WHAT CHANGED things?

To tell you the truth, and I might as well, my life the last dozen years has been, how can I put it, what's the reverse of giddy? Oh, I've written plenty of screenplays and some nonfiction, but I haven't written a novel, and please remember that that's painful for me because in my heart that's what I am, a novelist, a novelist who happens to write screenplays. (I hate it when I sometimes meet people and they say, "Well, when's the next book coming out?" and I always make a smile and lie that I'm on the homestretch now.) And the movies I've been involved with—except for *Misery*—have all brought their share of disappointment.

I live alone here in New York, in a nice hotel, room service twenty-four hours, all that's great, but I feel, sometimes, that whatever I wrote once that maybe had some quality, well, maybe those days are gone.

But to balance the bad, there was always my son, Jason.

You all remember how when he was ten he was this humorless blimp, this waddler? Well that was his *thin* phase. Helen and I used to fight about it all the time.

He had just passed three hundred biggies when he turned fifteen. I had come home from work early, hollered my presence, was heading for the wine closet when I heard this heartbreaking sound—

—sobbing—

—coming from the kid's room. I took a breath, went to his door, knocked. Jason and I were not close at this point. The truth is, he didn't care for me all that much. He barely acknowledged my existence, pissed on the movies I wrote, never dreamed of opening any of the books. It killed me, of course, but I never let on.

"Jason?" I said from just outside his door.

The awful sobbing continued.

"What is it?"

"You can't help—no one can help—nothing can help—" And then this forlorn *wahhhhhh* . . .

I knew the last person he wanted to see was me. But I had to go in. "I promise I won't tell anybody."

He came rolling into my arms, his face fiery, distorted. "Oh,

Daddy, I'm ugly and I've got no friends and all the girls laugh at me and make fun because I'm so fat."

I had to blink back tears myself—because it was all true, y'see. I was trapped there in that moment. I didn't know if he wanted to hear the truth from me or not. Finally I had to say it. "Who cares?" I told him. "*I* love you."

He grabbed me so hard. "Poppa," he managed, "Poppa," the first blessed time he ever called me that, his hot tears fresh on my skin.

That was our turning point.

For the past twenty years, no one could have asked for a better son. More than that, Jason's the best friend I have in the world. But our real clincher happened the next day.

I took him down to the Strand Bookstore, on Broadway and 12th Street, where I go a lot, research mostly, and we were about to enter when he stopped and pointed to a photograph in the window, the front cover of a book of photographs.

"I wonder who that is?" Jason said, staring.

"He's an Austrian bodybuilder, trying to make it as an actor. I met him when I was in L.A. last. He wants to be Fezzik if *The Princess Bride* ever happens." (This was the late '70s now, twenty years back. Schwarzenegger was nothing then, but when *The Princess Bride* did finally happen, he was such a huge star we couldn't afford him in our budget.) "I liked him. Very bright young guy."

Jason could not take his eyes off the picture.

Then I said what I guess turned out to be the magic words: *"He was pudgy once too."*

Jason looked at me then. "I don't think so," he said.

I didn't think so either, but it didn't hurt to say it.

"It came up in conversation." I said. "He said he thought he had gone as far in the bodybuilding world as he could. What drove him was he didn't like the way he looked when he was young." An aside

about Arnold, which I bet you didn't know: he was friends with Andre the Giant. (I guess strong guys all know each other.) Following is
a story he told me. I used it in the obit I wrote when Andre, alas, died.

Andre once invited Schwarzenegger to a wrestling arena in
Mexico where he was performing in front of 25,000 screaming
fans, and after he'd pinned his opponent, he gestured for
Schwarzenegger to come into the ring.

So through the noise, Schwarzenegger climbs up. Andre
says, "Take off your shirt, they are all crazy for you to take off
your shirt, I speak Spanish." So Schwarzenegger, embarrassed, does what Andre tells him. Off comes his jacket, his
shirt, his undershirt, and he begins striking poses. And then
Andre goes to the locker room while Schwarzenegger goes
back to his friends.

And it had all been a practical joke. God knows what the
crowd was screaming for, but it wasn't for Schwarzenegger to
semistrip and pose: "Nobody gave a s—— if I took my shirt
off or not, but I fell for it. Andre could do that to you."

"I wonder how much that picture book is?" Jason said then.
(We're still outside of the Strand, remember, and we didn't know
it, but the earth has moved.)

Are you surprised to learn I bought it for him?

This is what happened to Jason in the next two years: he went
from 308 to 230. He went from five-foot-six-and-a-half to six-foot-
three. He had always been tops in his class at Dalton, but now,
ripped and gorgeous, he was popular too.

This is what happened to Jason in the years after that. College,
Medical School, the decision to be a shrink like his mom. (Except
Jason's speciality is sex therapy.) *New York* magazine rated him

tops in the city and he also met this lovely lady Wall-Streeter, Peggy Henderson, and they got happily married.

And and and had a son.

I went to the hospital as soon as he was born. "We're calling him Arnold," Peggy told me, holding him in her arms.

"Perfect," I said. The truth is, obviously, I was hoping they might remember me too, somehow. But down was down.

"That's right," Jason said. "William Arnold." And he took Willy and put him in my arms.

High point of my life.

*   *   *

FOR THOSE OF you who have not yet thrown the book across the room in frustration, let me explain that this all really does have to do with why only the first chapter of *Buttercup's Baby*. And I promise to get there so fast you won't believe it.

OK. Willy the kid. Jason and Peggy live only two blocks away and I am careful not to drive them nuts, but I never had a grandson before. Not a toy at Zitomer's escaped me. Not a cough from him didn't keep me up all night going through my health encyclopedias.

I could refuse him, obviously, nothing.

Which is why my behavior in the park was so odd. Gorgeous spring day, Peggy and Jason holding hands up ahead, me and seven-year-old Willy tossing a Wiffle ball back and forth a step behind. We already go to some weekend Knick games together. (I've had season tickets since Hubie Brown was sent down to earth to destroy me.)

"We have a request," Jason began things.

"Guess what we finished last night?" Peggy went on. "*The Princess Bride*. We took turns reading it out loud."

Trying for casual, I asked the youngster what he thought of the entire enterprise.

"It was good," Willy replied, " 'cept for the end."

"I don't like the end all that much, either," I said. "Blame Mr. Morgenstern."

"No, no," Peggy explained. "He didn't dislike the ending. He didn't like *that it ended.*"

Pause. We walked in silence.

"I told him about the sequel, Poppa," Jason said then.

Peggy nodded. "He got really excited."

And then my Willy said the words: "Read it to me?"

I knew at that moment I was losing it. I remember exactly my fear—what if I couldn't bring it to life this time? What if I failed? Failed us both?

"That's the request, Dad. Willy wants you to read him *Buttercup's Baby*. We all want you to do it."

"Well it's too bad about what 'we' all want, isn't it," I started, my voice too loud. "It's sure too bad 'we' can't have everything, isn't it? You all better get used to disappointment," and before I did anything even worse, I looked at my watch, gestured that I had to go, took off, went home, stayed there, didn't answer the phone, had early Chinese sent in from Pig Heaven, started drinking, was gone by midnight.

And woke before dawn with a dream, so vivid; I went out to my terrace, paced, started trying to figure out the dream, and more than that, I guess, my life and how had I screwed it up.

It was a memory of that second pneumonia, and Helen was reading the screenplay of the movie to me—only this time she was young and wonderful, and she was also crying.

On the terrace I knew why—we are all the writers of our own

dreams—she was *me*, she was *me* crying for *me*, for what I had become. And then I remembered she wasn't reading *The Princess Bride*, she was reading about Fezzik and the madman on the mountain, the start of *Buttercup's Baby*, and I realized that twice I had almost died and Morgenstern had come to save me and now here he was again, saving me again, because I knew this, standing there looking out at the city as the sun rose: I would be a *real* writer once more, not just some schmuck with an Underwood, as screenwriters are still thought of Out There.

I didn't think I was ready to go from zero to sixty, to start a novel from scratch. I didn't feel confident that I could make everything up, as I had done for my thirty novel-writing years.

Let me explain what I was *not* ready to do.

Take Szell, the Nazi dentist in *Marathon Man* (Olivier in the movie, and wasn't he great? Remember the "is it safe" scene with the dental tools?). There is this street in Manhattan, 47th between Fifth and Sixth, and I was walking along it one day, decades back, on my way somewhere, can't remember, doesn't matter, but that block is called the "diamond district." It is filled with an amazing number of diamond shops, most of them run by Jews, and on a lot of them, you could see they still had their concentration camp numbers. I thought that day what a great scene it might be if I could have a Nazi walking on that street.

Which Nazi I didn't know, but probably I started doing some mild research, reading and asking people, and I finally came across the most brilliant of them all, Mengele—the double doctor, Ph.D. and M.D.—then thought to be living in Argentina, the guy who did the heartless experiments on twins.

OK, great, I've got my guy—but why does he risk everything to come to 47th street? I knew this much: it couldn't be to go to the prom. The most wanted man on earth had to have an unshakable reason.

Years go by, with Mengele stuck in the corner of my head and gradually Babe started to appear, the marathon man of the title. Then I caught a break: I read about a surgeon who had invented a heart sleeve operation, somewhere, maybe Cleveland, but I could put him in New York.

Yesss. Mengele came to America, to New York, because he *had* to, to save his life.

Brilliant.

I am flying for the next little while because I have solved my most difficult problem and then it hits me—*fool!*—what kind of a villain is it who's so *frail he needs heart surgery*? My God, if someone chased him he might keel over from the effort.

Obviously, a couple of years later I figured out some things and wrote the book and wrote the movie and the scene that still works best, along with the dental scene, is Szell wandering among the Jews.

On the terrace that morning I knew I wasn't ready to take on that kind of trip. But this shaping of *Buttercup's Baby* was a perfect middle step for me. Bringing it to life as I had *The Princess Bride* would give me the confidence to at last go back to being what I once was.

So I would do the abridgment of the sequel and then do my own novel and ride off into the frigging sunset, thank you very much. Once offices opened for the day I called Charley (still my lawyer) and told him that I wanted more than anything on earth to abridge the sequel and was there any way he thought the Morgenstern estate would put an end to hostilities?

He said the most amazing thing: "*They* contacted *me* today. The Shogs. Kermit's daughter did. She's a young lawyer for the firm, sounded nice and bright, and let me quote her: *'We want to settle for peace with your Mr. Goldman.'*"

Tennessee said it best: "Sometimes there's God so quickly."

*   *   *

I MET KARLOFF Shog the next morning for breakfast in the dining room of the Carlyle Hotel, none prettier in all New York. Charley set it up and decided not to be there, no point, this was a "look-like" where we would both try on our charm and see if we could do business.

So I sat waiting for her to appear. With a name like Karloff Shog, I figured a mustache was a sure bet and don't even think about her armpits. (In case you don't know—and you don't know, nobody knows stuff like this—Karloff is the most popular girl's name in Florin. Make of that what you will.)

This dreamboat walks in. Mid-thirties, dressed to kill, long loose blonde hair, gorgeous. She comes right over and she holds out her hand. "Hi, Carly Shog, this is so great meeting you, you look just like the pictures on your books, only, may I say, younger."

"You may say that as loudly and as often as you want." I tend to be a little thick-tongued when sweet young things are around, so that was pretty smooth for me. The nutty thing is, at that moment, when we had met on earth for all of ten seconds, *I thought she wanted me.* "Want" in the sense of "desire." And if you know me at all, you know I don't think anybody *ever* wants me. Not wants in the sense of desire anyway. "What brings you to America?"

'We're doing a lot of legal stuff in the States now. I just moved here." Now a pause. "Thank God." She looked at me. "I can tell you've never been in Florin." I said I hadn't. "It's a little inbred. I mean, in Florin if you marry your first cousin, that's considered good." Another pause. "An attempt at humor. Sorry."

I have dated some terrific women since Helen left me a decade past. But this one here, this blue-eyed lawyer with the body and the brains, on any list, was special. She reached across the table then, took my hand—

—Let me run that by you again: *she* took *my* hand!

And looked into my eyes and said, "I'm just so glad our legal troubles are done."

"It's been awful," I agreed. "I was only sued once before in my whole life." (It's true.) "And that was by an actor so it doesn't really count."

Need I tell you her laugh was bell-like? Then, to only improve her bank account came this: "You won't believe me, but I've read every novel you've ever written. Including the Harry Longbaugh." (*No Way to Treat A Lady* was first published under a pseudonym, Harry Longbaugh, the real name of the Sundance Kid.)

I am so in love at this point it is ri*dic*ulous. "The lawsuits your guys filed—you'll drop them?"

"Of course. All thirteen. That's what we're going to do for you, and all we want from you is your goodwill."

"Goodwill?" If I'd have had an engagement ring with me, it would've been hers.

"Yes. It's so important that *Buttercup's Baby* be published. Here in America."

I signaled for coffee and a waiter poured us some. We fiddled with sweetener and low-fat milk and all that other yummy stuff we do to our stomachs these days. We sipped silently. And we looked at each other. Then I said the nuttiest thing: "How old are you, Carly?"

"How old do you want me to be? I know all about you. I know you were born at Michael Reese Hospital in Chicago on August 12th, 1931. Pretty good?"

I nodded.

She opened her purse then. "All you have to know is this, Bill. I broke up with my boyfriend when I left Florin City. And he was fifty-five. I have a thing for ..." And here she paused, smiled so sweetly. "... for *vigorous* older men."

Mark Antony was never this smitten.

She reached into her purse, handed me a piece of paper. "This is just legal boilerplate. Have your lawyer check it out, then sign it and mail it back to me."

"What is it?"

"It's called settling for peace. *We* agree to drop all the lawsuits. *You* agree that we did nothing wrong, and that you wish us the best on all future projects."

"I do *more* than wish you well. I'm going to kill myself doing *Buttercup's Baby*."

"Of course you would," she said then, and do you know the most important six words in the last thirty years in World Culture? I'll tell you what they are. Peter Benchley came up with them when he was walking along a beach and the words were these: *"What if the shark got territorial?"* Because out of that came the novel *Jaws*, and then the movie *Jaws*, and nothing's really been the same since.

Well, Carly Shog's next six words weren't *that* important. Except, of course, to me. Before she said them I asked her, "Why did you say 'Of course you *would*?' You meant 'of course you *will*.' *I'm* doing *Buttercup's Baby*."

That moment, waiting for her to speak, looking at the glorious lady, at her pale blue eyes, I remember thinking something weird is going on, something bad, even. But in no paranoid nightmare could I have come up with what she said next:

"Stephen King is doing the abridgment."

*   *   *

HERE'S WHAT I did not say: "What's the punch line?" Here's another: "You're killing me." Or: "He'll laugh right in your face." Try: "You rotten bitch." While I was busy saying nothing, Carly went smartly on.

"Here's what we get when you sign that letter: safety. See, you're nowhere near King in terms of sales, no one is, we don't have to go there. But a lot of people connect you with Morgenstern because of the movie and what we *don't* want is people wondering why you decided not to do the sequel. Good will is very important, and we can't have you running around claiming betrayal. I wrote this. I think you can live with it."

Here's what she put down: "I'm so excited Stephen King has come on board. Frankly, I'm exhausted as far as Mr. Morgenstern is concerned. So I wish everyone the best. And I don't know about you, but I can't wait to read *Buttercup's Baby*."

I looked at her a moment before I spoke. She looked like Bela Lugosi now. "He won't do it. King. I know him a little, and there's no reason on earth he'd get dragged into something like this."

"Steve doesn't feel he's getting 'dragged into' anything. He's genuinely excited. We talk every day. Will, 'til everything's finalized."

"I don't believe you. I don't know what you're after but find another buyer." I stood up.

"His name wasn't always King," Carly said then. "He has ancestors who lived in Florin City way back when. He still visits in the summertime."

I sat back down.

"Does he know about me?"

"Bill, of course. And I told him just what the peace settlement says—that you're exhausted. That's easy enough to believe. My God, you haven't written a novel in well over a decade."

She now strongly resembled Leatherface from *The Texas Chainsaw Massacre*. "I'll see you in court," I said, tossing some money on the table, walking out. A stupid and hollow thing to say. She could keep pressuring me with the lawsuits. No question, she had all the cards.

All but one.

*　　　*　　　*

LATE THE NEXT morning I was sitting in the airport in Bangor, Maine. I knew King basically from *Misery*, a screenplay I wrote from one of his best and favorite novels. I'd come up to Bangor a couple of times, just your basic research, chatting with him, a few questions I thought could be better answered in person than over the phone. We had a sneak for him when the movie was done and Rob Reiner, the director, and I paced the lobby while it was on, hoping he'd like it. It meant a lot to us to please him. Rob's career really took off with *Stand By Me*, another work by King (a novella called *The Body*).

We could tell as soon as we saw him walking out that he was happy about what we'd done with his baby. He loved Kathy Bates especially. (Not alone in that; she won the Oscar for Best Actress.) It's funny but what I remember even more was the moment before it started when he left us to take his seat: the look on his face was so hopeful. Like a kid. I commented on that to Rob who said, "I think he's as vulnerable now as when he started—which is how he's managed to stay Stephen King."

I don't think everyone realizes what a phenomenon he is. It's not just the hundreds of millions of books sold—it's that he has arguably been the hottest writer in the world for *so long. Carrie* came out in '74—a quarter century sitting closest to the fire.

I saw him through the window now. Jeans, lumberjack shirt, shambling walk. King's a lot bigger than you think. And remarkably unpretentious.

We sat in a private corner of the waiting room—I hadn't eaten since the legendary lunch the day before with the Fiend of Florin. And I'd been up half the night getting everything all set, just how to say it rationally, novelist to novelist, storyteller to storyteller, and the way it went in my head I wasn't even halfway through before he said, "Bill, that bitch lied to me, she said you *didn't want to do it*. I only said I'd get involved because she talked to a bunch of relatives I still have back there and they put pressure on me but I felt dragged into the damn thing from the beginning."

The silence went on. King looked me. Waiting. I knew I was making him nervous, just sitting there, but I couldn't figure how to start. All I knew was I didn't want to embarrass him. Or, worse, humiliate myself.

Finally he asked, "How's Kathy? I liked her in *Titanic*."

He's giving you a way to start, I told myself. So talk about Kathy Bates. You've got a great Kathy Bates story, tell him. "I don't see her much, but did I ever tell you how she got the *misery* part? It's a great story."

King shook his head.

"I wrote the part for her. I'd seen her on stage for years—she's one of the great actresses but she'd never gotten her break in films—and before I started I was talking with Rob and I said, 'I'm going to write Annie Wilkes for Kathy Bates.' And Rob said, 'Oh, good. She's great. We'll use her.'"

"Then what?" King asked.

"That was it. The most sought after female role that year and it went to this unknown. I loved being part of that. Changing a life."

"Great story, all right," King said, trying to sound enthusiastic. But I knew his heart wasn't in it.

"No!" I said, way too loud, but I was not in the best of shape, as readers of these pages will have sensed. "No," I repeated, more conversationally. "That's not the story. *Here's* the great story."

King waited.

"Okay. So Rob calls her in. Just Kathy and Rob in the room and she has never come close to a lead in a movie and Rob just lets it fly: 'You've got the part.' Kathy sits there for a moment before she says this: 'The part. I've got it.' Rob nods, repeats the news. 'You've got it.' Now there's another pause before Kathy comes out with this: 'The Annie part. Annie Wilkes. That part?' Rob nods again. 'Annie Wilkes. The lead.' Now a little faster from Kathy: 'And I've got it and it's all set and everything.' 'All set,' from Rob. Now she leans forward a little. 'Let me just get this straight—I am playing Annie Wilkes, the lead, in *Misery*?' 'Yup,' says Reiner. And Kathy goes on: 'It's done and everything, I mean, I am definitely playing Annie, and that's set and done and everything, no mistakes or anything?' And Rob says, 'It is so set you wouldn't believe it.' And then there is a moment of silence in the room. And then she says this: *'Can I tell my mother?'* "

King just loved it. (I do too. It's one of my all-time favorite sweet Hollywood stories.) He laughed and smiled and looked at me questioningly, and I raised my right hand and said, "All true, word of honor," and I could feel myself, at last, relaxing. I knew I could do it now, talk to him, convince him not to do the sequel, because, after all, I had done *The Princess Bride* and, even on this earth, fair was occasionally fair, and he said, "I really liked the movie." I said, "I did too, not just Kathy but how about Jimmy Caan?" Then he said, "I meant *The Princess Bride*."

"Thanks. So do I," and I was about to go on when I realized something. Something just awful. *He hadn't mentioned the novel,* just the movie. But, my God, he had to like it, I was just being paranoid.

"I wish I felt the same about the novel," he said, and I could see it pained him to say it.

The most popular storyteller of the century tells you that you suck as a storyteller. I would like to report I handled the whole thing with maturity. But, alas, what I said, like a total jerk, was, "Yeah? Well, a lot of people liked it just fine, thank you very much."

Suddenly he was leaning in toward me. "Bill, the way you caught his style was fine, but, the fact is, I don't like a lot of what you did with the abridgement. For example, Chapter Four—*you cut out seventy pages on Buttercup's training.* How could you do that? There was wonderful stuff in there. You *must* have seen the Royalty School. It's one of the great buildings left in all of Europe. Buttercup's curriculum is amazing. How could you leave it out?"

"I was mostly interested in the story, you know, the plot." And that's when I broke it to him. "I never went there. To Florin. What was so important about going?"

"*What was so important?* You flew up here just to check out things for a screenplay adaptation."

I didn't say anything then because I could feel this terrible wind coming and I knew it would blow me away.

"That's why *I* want to do *Buttercup's Baby,*" he said. "Get things right this time."

I was dead in the water. I stood, thanked him for his time, started out, devastated.

"I'm really sorry," he said.

I made a smile. Not the easiest thing for me to pull off at that moment, but I liked King, didn't want him of all people to see me fall apart.

He called after me: "Bill—wait—I just had an idea. Listen—I'll do the abridgement and *you can do the screenplay*. I'll make that a deal-breaker in my contract." King was trying to be helpful, I understood that, but right there in the airport I told him about my dad reading to me and Jason not liking it and me realizing how I had only been read the good parts and now Jason was me and he had this kid, Willy, this wonderful child named after me, and Willy wanted me to read it to him and none of this abridgement business would have happened if I hadn't started it and what would he do if he ever lost it, his power, storytelling, as I'd lost mine, and how would he like to spend the rest of his life writing perfect parts for perfectly horrible people who happen to be movie stars this week, with all that power—

—and I was what I most didn't want to ever be, humiliated, so I left him there, forcing myself not to run out the door, gone . . .

*   *   *

THE PLANE BACK to New York left in three hours and I grabbed a cab, hid in Bangor 'til it was time, cabbed back to the airport.

Late. Weather problems.

I sat on a bench in the airport, leaned back, closed my eyes until King asked, "You had to come all the way to Maine to have a nervous breakdown?" He was sitting alongside me. "You did make one good point, and I've thought a lot about it—none of this abridgement business would have happened except your dad kept skipping stuff. So in a way you're very much right, it is your baby, you began it."

Pause.

Then he said it.

"Try the first chapter."

He could tell from my expression that I didn't quite understand what he meant. I guess I was like Kathy talking to Rob. "Look, this is the twenty-fifth anniversary year of *The Princess Bride*, right? *Your* version." It was. "Well, probably your publisher will want to do something, maybe reprint it in hardcover." I nodded. We'd already talked about that. "Well, abridge the first chapter of *Buttercup's Baby*. Include it if you want. You probably ought to write an introduction to the chapter, explaining why you're not doing the whole book. I'll call the Shogs, tell them my decision. They won't like it but they'll go along. They've been wanting to be in business with me for years. Florinese rights to my stuff are coming due in the next couple of years."

For a moment then he hesitated, and I wondered if he was changing his mind. I just waited, hoping not. Next he shook his head, and there was a look on his face that might have said "Am I nuts to do this?" Then these wonderful words: *"Bill, I expect you to really try this time."*

"I'll research the hell out of it," I told him. (And have I ever.) "But what happens after I publish the chapter?"

"Let's go one step at a time," he answered. "You write it, I'll read it, Morgenstern's public will read it. I'll send a bunch of copies to all my cousins in Florin, see what they think." He stood, looked at me. "I guess the most important thing is really Morgenstern. He was a master and it would be nice if we could please *him*, don't you think?"

"That would be best of all," I said, God's truth.

We shook hands, said good-bye, he started away, glanced back. "You haven't read *Buttercup's Baby* yet, have you?"

"Not yet."

"It's a pretty amazing story."

"What are you saying? That even *I* can't screw it up?"

"You got that right," Stephen King said, and he smiled . . .

*   *   *

I LEFT FOR Florin immediately. (I didn't get *to* Florin immediately, of course—Florin Air's scheduling geniuses saw to that. I took the Air France night flight to Brussels, where you connect with InterItalia, which lets you out in Guilder, and then just the short hop to Florin City.) I'd made out a list of places to see. Royalty School, obviously, because King put such emphasis on it, the Cliffs of Insanity—I phoned ahead and made a booking, the place is insane with visitors now—the forest where the Battle of the Trees took place, on and on. King had given me a list of friends and scholars who he thought might prove helpful. One wonderful cousin ran the best restaurant in Florin, a blessing, because Florin, as you may know, is the root vegetable capital of Europe, good for their farmers, but rutabaga is their national dish and you can get sick of it pretty fast unless a skillful cook is around.

It was odd, those first days, looking at real places that I thought were made up when I was a kid. I was worried that they might not live up to my fantasies. (Some of them didn't, most of them did.)

The Thieves Quarter where Fezzik reunited with Inigo, I saw that, and the room where Inigo finally *finally* killed Count Rugen— it's on the castle tour. Buttercup's farm has been kept pretty much intact, but what can I tell you, it's a farm. And of course the Fire Swamp is still as deadly as ever, no one's allowed in, but I did see the spot not that far away where local scholars believe that Buttercup and Westley held each other after she pushed him off the cliff. (It's where the reunion scene took place, and let me tell you, it was strange, me standing there, looking at that patch of ground.)

You still can't get to One Tree Island by boat because of the surrounding whirlpool, so I rented a helicopter, wandered. (One Tree is where they went to get their strength back.) It's where Buttercup and Westley first made love, where poor Waverly was born.

Probably I shouldn't call her "poor" Waverly, she had a great time for awhile, parents who loved her, the world's greatest fencer as her guard, the world's strongest man as her baby-sitter. Can't ask for a whole lot more.

Of course, everything changed with the kidnapping, but I better shut up now, before I get ahead of the story . . .

BUTTERCUP'S BABY

S. MORGENSTERN'S GLORIOUS

EXAMINATION OF COURAGE

MATCHED AGAINST

THE DEATH OF THE HEART

ABRIDGED BY

WILLIAM GOLDMAN

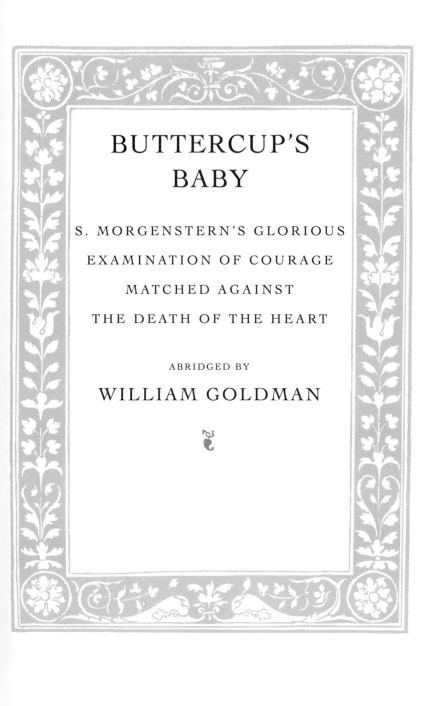

ONE

FEZZIK DIES

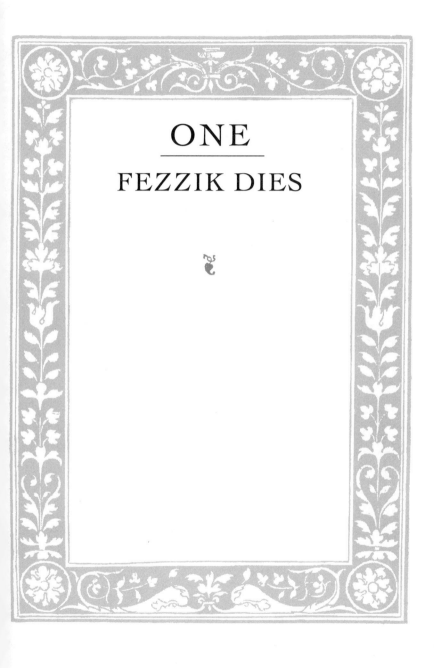

1. FEZZIK

EZZIK chased the madman up the mountain, the madman who carried the most precious thing, for Fezzik, ever to be on earth, the kid herself, Buttercup's Baby.

"Chased" was perhaps the wrong word. "Lumbered after" might have been more accurate. However you wanted to put it, the news was not good, because Fezzik, try as he might, was falling farther and farther behind. There were two reasons. The first: size. They were fifteen thousand feet in the air, the rise was sheer, and Fezzik had terrible trouble finding footholds that might make him secure. His huge clumpy feet would touch here or there, seeking sanctuary, but it took too much time.

And the madman used that time to his advantage, increasing his lead, occasionally glancing down with his skinless face, to see how much farther Fezzik had fallen behind. Even to Fezzik, his plan was clear: get to the crest, run across the plateau, start down the far side, leave Fezzik helpless, still trying for the ascent.

The second reason for Fezzik's lack of success was this: fear. Or, to be more specific, fears. Being the biggest and strongest, no one realized he also had feelings. Just because he could uproot trees, people didn't want to know that the little squirmy bugs that lived in the roots spooked him. Just because he had defeated the wrestling champions of seventy-three countries, people didn't believe that his mother had to keep candles burning all night long when he was (comparatively speaking) little. Of course, the idea of public speaking was beyond thought. But Fezzik would rather have spent the rest of his years in constant speechmaking than face what was staring at him now. The possibility of

F

A

L

L

I

N

G

With nothing but rocks to crush his body at the end.

True, he had climbed the Cliffs of Insanity, but that was different. He'd had a rope to hold on to so he knew which way to go, and he'd had Vizzini insulting him, which always made the time pass more pleasantly.

If only the madman possessed some other baggage, Fezzik would have stopped and crept back down to safety. If only it was all the silver in Persia or a pill that you only took once and you weren't a giant anymore.

Easy to stop the chase then.

But this was Waverly, his blessing, and though he knew in his great heart he would lose this pursuit, knew he would somehow slip, Fezzik lumbered on.

He glanced up. She was rolled in the blanket she had been kidnapped in—and how long ago was that now? Fezzik chose not to remember because the kidnapping had been his fault. He had allowed it somehow—it had happened on his watch. Fezzik blinked back quick tears of remorse. Her body was still. The madman probably gave her some potion. To make her easier to carry.

Above him, the madman stopped, pushed, kicked out—

—and giant rocks were coming down toward him.

Fezzik did his best to get out of their way, but he was too slow. The rocks grazed his feet, knocking them loose from their holds, and now he, Fezzik the Turk, was swinging high in space, holding on by just the strength of a few fingers.

The madman cried out with delight, then climbed on, rounded a mountain corner, was gone.

Fezzik hung in space. So very afraid.

The winds picked at his body.

His left hand began to cramp so Fezzik took it out of the hold, reached a yard up to a better one.

He hung there, thinking, and what he thought was not how very afraid he was but that he had just gone up three entire feet, using only his hands. Could he do that again? He reached up another yard, found another hold. This is all very interesting, he told himself. I actually went up *without using my feet*. I went up faster than before, *without using my feet*.

Hmmm.

And then suddenly he was *moving*. Just using his hands to reach, grab, then the next, reach, grab, and never mind using all fours, just use the upper twos—

—and then he was moving *fast*.

Fezzik *flew* up the mountain now. Somewhere on the other side was the madman, probably taking his time, feeling sure that Fezzik was gone. Fezzik increased his speed, up to the crest, then to the plateau, racing across it with enormous strides, and when the madman got there with the babe, Fezzik was waiting.

"I would like the child," Fezzik said softly.

"Of course you would." The madman had no mouth. The sound came from somewhere inside his skinless face. He still held Waverly's body.

Fezzik took a step nearer.

"*I can breathe fire,*" the madman said.

Fezzik knew that it was true. But he was unafraid.

Another step closer.

"*I can change shape,*" the madman said, louder now, and Fezzik knew that it was true. But he also knew this: fear had entered the heart of his enemy.

"These are my final words," Fezzik said. "When I tell you to give me the child, you will give me the child."

"*I will use all my magic on you!*"

"You can try," Fezzik said softly. "But even though you have no face, I can see how frightened you are. You are frightened that I will hurt you." He paused. "And I will." He paused again. "Badly."

The fear inside the madman was pulsing now.

Fezzik's great hands reached toward the blanket. "Give me the child," he said, and the madman started to do that very thing, but then, instead, he flipped his hands so that Waverly rolled out of her blanket, spun high into the mountain air—

—the momentum carried her over the edge where the two men were standing, and as she spun, her eyes fluttered open, and she looked around wildly, saw Fezzik, reached out toward him as she fell from sight, said the word she alone called him: "Shade."

Fezzik had no choice. He dove into space after her, gave up his life for the child . . .

*   *   *

Well, what do you think?

It's exciting, I'll give Morgenstern that. A "grabber," as TV guys say. But this is a novel, *you have time to develop plot and character, no one's changing the channel here. So I'm not nuts about it. I also don't like calling Chapter 1 "Fezzik Dies."*

Do you believe that Morgenstern's really going to kill Fezzik? I sure don't, not for a New York minute. Forget that he's my favorite. But think what he did for Buttercup and Westley: he let himself get set on fire, just before the castle storming; he found the four white horses they all rode to freedom on; and don't think for a minute Inigo would have made it down through the Zoo of Death without Fezzik right there with him, so in a way, he saved Westley.

And, I'm sorry, you don't knock off someone like that. It's wrong. *Just to get your story off with a bang.*

In other words, I disapprove of this opening. There are, in fact, a number of things I'm not happy with in this chapter. But you know the reasons I have to go along.

And I'm also not sure I should be including this next section about Inigo. I had a big fight with my publisher, Peter Gethers. He's against putting it in, finds it confusing. Before I give my reasons, I think you better have a chance to see for yourself what we're arguing about.

*   *   *

2. INIGO

INIGO WAS IN Despair.

Hard to find on the map (this was after maps) not because cartographers didn't know of its existence, but because when they visited to measure its precise dimensions, they became so depressed they began to drink and question everything, most notably why would anyone want to be something as stupid as a cartographer? It required constant travel, no one ever knew your name, and, most of all, since wars were always changing boundaries, why bother? There grew up, then, a gentleman's agreement among mapmakers of the period to keep the place as secret as possible, lest tourists flock there and die. (Should you insist on paying a visit, it's closer to the Baltic states than most places.)

Everything about Despair was depressing. Nothing grew in the ground and what fell from the skies did not provoke much happy conversation. The entire country was damp and dank, and why the locals all did not flee was not only a good question, it was the only question. Locals talked about nothing else. "Why don't we move?" husbands would say each day to wives, and wives would answer, "God, I don't know, let's," and children would jump and shout, "Hooray hooray, we're out of here," but then nothing would happen. Bindibus live in more hideous conditions but they don't travel a lot either. There was a certain comfort in knowing that no matter how bad things were, they couldn't get worse. "We have endured everything," the locals would tell themselves. "Whereas if we pick up and go, say, to Paris, we would get gout and be insulted by Parisians all day."

Inigo, however, had a warm spot for the place. For it was here, years and years ago, that he had won his first fencing championship. He had arrived shortly before the tournament was to begin, and he had come with a heavy heart. Tears always behind his eyes. He could not shake his mood, because of what had just happened to him in Italy, on his first visit there. A journey he had begun with such hopes . . .

*   *   *

BY THE TIME he turned twenty, Inigo Montoya of Arabella, Spain, had spent his last eight years wandering the world. He had not yet begun the hunt for the six-fingered man who had killed his beloved father, Domingo. He was not ready and would not be until the great swordmaker, Yeste, pronounced him so. Yeste, his father's dearest friend, would never send him out if there were flaws. Flaws would not only bring death but, far worse, humiliation.

Inigo knew one thing and that only: when he finally found his tormenter, when he was at last able to face him and say, "Hello, my name is Inigo Montoya, you killed my father, prepare to die," there could be no question in his mind of defeat. The six-fingered man was a master. And so, preparing for such a master, Inigo had wandered the world. Getting stronger as he grew, learning from whoever could teach him mysteries that needed solving. Lately, he had begun to specialize. His talents were past phenomenal, but still not good enough to get the blessing of Yeste.

He had recently been to Iceland, to spend months with Ardnock, the great frozen terrain expert. Inigo had already mastered fighting from below and from above, fighting from trees, from rocks, in rapids. But what if the six-fingered man was from the far north, and they battled on frost, or freshly watered ice? And what if Inigo, helpless and slipping, lost his balance, lost the battle, lost everything?

After Iceland, he spent half a year on the equator, studying with Atumba, the master of heat, because what if the six-fingered man came from a steaming country, and what if they battled in the heat of the hottest day, temperature at 150, and what if the grip of his sword went wet for a moment in his hand?

Now, having just turned twenty, he was in Italy, to see Piccoli, the tiny ancient, the acknowledged king of the mind. (Piccoli was from the most famous line of great Italian teachers—another branch was centered in Venice and taught singing to every famous Italian tenor whose name ends in a vowel.) Inigo knew he would not be able to think when his death battle came. His mind had to be a spring day, and his movements had to come on their own, his spins and twists and thrusts all had to leap unbidden.

Piccoli lived in a small stone house, in the employ of Count Cardinale, the strange and secret man who controlled most of the country. Piccoli had heard of Inigo because although Yeste was the greatest and most famous maker of swords, there were rumors that when he was confronted with a task that was too much even for him, he would go to the town of Arabella, high in the hills above Toledo, to the hovel of one Domingo Montoya, a widower who lived with a young son.

It was there that the six-fingered sword had been forged.

Could it truly be the wonder of his world? Piccoli had heard of it for a decade, yearned to see it dance before he died. The greatest weapon since Excalibur and where was it now? Gone with the child Montoya from the house of Yeste. And where was that child?

Piccoli had spent his entire long life training his mind, so that he had the ability to sit for a day in the middle of a mad battle and know nothing of the screams and slaughter going on around him. When he was in his mind, he was as if dead. And every morning at dawn he would go into his mind and stay there 'til noon. No power could disturb him.

He had gone into his mind at dawn, one day, there to stay 'til the sun was highest—but on this one morning, at eight o'clock, a strangeness.

He was in his mind as he always was at six and at seven and at half-past seven, and at quarter 'til eight, and ten 'til, and five and four and three—

—and then Piccoli was pierced by something so dazzling even he had to open his eyes—

—to see a young man approaching, tall, blade-thin, muscular, spring-legged, who was handsome enough but would have been more than that, save for the two scars that paralleled his cheeks—

—who held such glory in his hands, the sun was dancing there.

Piccoli could not breathe as the young man approached. "I want to see Mr. Piccoli, please."

"I wish to see your sword."

Piccoli trembled as he took it in his tiny hands. "What could you possibly want from me?" He could not take his eyes off the weapon. "You have the world here."

Inigo told him.

"You want me to teach you to control your mind?" Piccoli asked.

Inigo nodded. "I have come from very far."

"A waste, I fear. You are young. The young have not the patience. They are stupid. They think their bodies will save them."

"Let me learn."

"Pointless. Go wage your battle without me."

"*I beg you.*"

Piccoli sighed. "All right. Let me show you how stupid you are. Answer my queries: *"what on all the earth do you want more than anything?"*

"Why, to kill the six-fingered man, of course."

And with that Piccoli started screaming: "Wrong, wrong! Listen—*see what I say.*" His voice grew soft, seductive. "The six-fingered man has his sword in his hand—he thrusts—see what I say, Montoya, watch the sword. He has thrust the sword toward your father, now the sword is entering your father's heart, Domingo's heart is shredded and you are ten and standing there, you are helpless, do you remember that moment? I command you, *remember that moment!*"

Inigo could not stop his sudden tears.

"Now you are watching him fall. Look—*look at him—watch Domingo die—*"

Inigo began sobbing out of all control.

"*Tell me what you feel—*"

Inigo was barely able to speak the word: "Pain . . . "

"Yes, right, of course, pain, killing pain. *That's* what you should want more than anything, an end to your pain."

" . . . yes . . . "

"That pain is with you, every moment every day?"

" . . . yes . . . "

"If you think of ending your pain, you will kill the six-fingered man. But if you only think revenge, he will kill you, because he has already taken the thing on earth you treasured most, and he will know that, and when you battle he will say things, he will taunt you, he will talk about your pathetic father and he will laugh at your love for a failure like Domingo, and you will scream in rage and your revenge will take control and you will attack blindly—and then he will cut you to pieces."

Inigo saw it all, and it was true. He saw himself charging and heard himself screaming and then he felt the six-fingered man's sword as it entered his body, drove through his heart. "Please, do not let me lose to him," he finally managed to say.

Piccoli looked at the shattered young man before him. He gently returned the six-fingered sword. "Go dry your tears, Montoya," he said at last. "We start your training in the morning . . . "

*   *   *

IT WAS SAVAGE work. Inigo had never imagined it would be anything less, but Piccoli was merciless beyond human reckoning. For eight years Inigo had sprinted two hours each day, to make his legs muscular and strong. Now, with Piccoli he could not sprint at all. For eight years he had squeezed apple-size rocks two hours a day, so his wrists might deliver the death blow from any and all positions. Now, rock squeezing was banned. For eight years he had never skipped and dodged less than two hours a day so his legs would be quick. Now, no skipping, no dodging.

Inigo's body, so lash-strong, so whippet-quick, the body he had shaped for lethal combat, the body that was the envy of most men. That body? Piccoli *hated* it. "Your body is your enemy while you are with me," Piccoli explained. "We must weaken it for now. It is the only way you can grow your mind. As long as you think you can fight your way out of trouble, you will never be able to fight your way out of trouble."

For eight years Inigo had gotten by on four hours' sleep. Now, that was *all* he did. Sleep. Doze. Rest. Snooze. He catnapped under orders, siestaed constantly. It seemed to him he was grabbing forty winks every time eighty winks had gone by. And while resting, he had to think about his mind.

Weeks passed. He was sleeping twelve hours a day at first, then fifteen. Piccoli's goal was a fat twenty, and Inigo knew the torture would never stop until his goal was reached. He did nothing but lie there and think about this mind.

His only job was to think about his mind. Get acquainted with it, learn its ways.

His sole exercise was fifteen minutes each day while the sun went down. Piccoli would send him outside, the sword in hand. And nod. Just once. And Inigo would flash in the dying light, the sword alive, and his body would leap and duck and the shadows moved like ghosts. Piccoli was very old, but once he had seen Bastia and this was Bastia again, alive again on earth.

One more nod from the tiny ancient head and back to rest. To bed. To lie there and think about his mind.

And it went that way until the day Piccoli had to go to the village for provisions. Inigo was alone in the stone house, and then there were soft footsteps approaching, and a soft voice, enquiring for the owner, and then Inigo was alone no longer. He looked toward the figure framed in the doorway, stood. And spoke these most remarkable and unexpected words:

"I cannot marry you."

She looked at him. "Have we met, sire?"

"In my dreams."

"And we decided not to marry? What strange dreams from such a young fellow."

"No younger than you."

"You work for Piccoli?"

Inigo shook his head. "Mostly I *sleep* for Piccoli. Come closer?"

"I have no choice."

"You work in the castle?"

"I have lived there all my life. My mother too."

"Inigo Montoya of Spain. You . . . ?" He waited for her name. He knew it would be a wondrous name, a name he would remember forever.

"Giulietta, sire."

"Do you think me strange, Giulietta?"

"I'd be pretty dopey if I didn't," Giulietta said. Before adding, "sire."

"Do you feel your heart at this moment? I feel mine."

"I'd be pretty dopey if I didn't," Giulietta said. Her black eyes studied his face so closely before she said, "I think you better tell me of your dreams."

Inigo began. He told of the slaughter and his scars, and how, when he had healed he had begun his quest. And how wandering through the world, town to city to village, alone, always that, sometimes he made up companions since there were none really for company.

And when he was perhaps thirteen, there was a someone always waiting for him at the end of the day. As he grew up and older, she grew older, too, the girl, and she would be there, always there, and they would eat scraps together for dinner and sleep in haylofts in each other's arms, and her black eyes were so kind when they looked at him. "As your eyes are kind now, as you look at me, and her black hair tumbled down as I can see yours now, tumbling down, and you have kept me blessed company all these years, Giulietta, and I love you and I will forever, but I cannot, and I hope you understand, because my quest comes first, above all else, even with what I see in your eyes, I cannot marry you."

She was so obviously touched. Inigo knew that. Inigo saw that he had moved her deeply. He waited for her reply.

Finally Giulietta said, "Do you tell that story often? I'll bet the village girls go *nuts* over you." She turned toward the door then. "Go try it on them." And she was gone.

The next morning before he went into his mind, she was back. "Let me get this thing straight, Inigo—we had *scraps* for dinner? *I'm* in *your* fantasy and the best you can come up with is *scraps*?" She turned toward the door then. "You have no chance of winning my heart."

Inigo went back into his mind.

The next noon she poked him awake. "Let me get this straight, Inigo—we slept in *haylofts*? You couldn't even come up with a clean room at an inn? Do you know how scratchy haylofts are?" She turned toward the door then. "You have less chance of winning my heart today than you had yesterday."

Inigo went back into his mind.

The next dusk she stood in the doorway. It was just before his fifteen minutes of movement, and she said, "How do I know you're going to find this six-fingered man? And how do I know you can beat him? What if I took some kind of weird pity on you and waited and then he won?"

"That is my nightmare. That is why I study."

She pointed at his sword. "Are you any good with that thing?"

Inigo went outside and danced with the six-fingered sword in the dying light. He tried hard to be particularly dazzling and ended with a special flourish taught him years before by MacPherson in Scotland. It involved a spin and a sword toss and ended with a bow.

"Impressive stuff, Inigo, I admit it," she said when he was done. "But what happens after you find this guy and run him through? How are you going to earn a living? Doing stunts like *that*? What do you expect me to do, play the tambourine and gather the crowd? You have so little chance of winning my heart, there is no point to our ever seeing each other again. Good-by."

Watching her leave there was no question: Inigo's heart was aching . . .

*   *   *

SHE DID NOT return 'til the night of the Ball. Inigo could not help but hear the music pouring out of the castle down through the night. Musicians had been practicing for days. Suddenly Giulietta was there, beckoning. "It's so beautiful," she whispered. "I thought you might want to see. I can sneak you in, but you must do exactly what I say—it will go badly if we are found out."

They raced through the long shadows, paused only briefly outside the kitchen—then she nodded and they were inside and she pointed left to show that was their way, then right, and he followed 'til the ballroom itself stood before them.

It was a sight beyond his conceiving. A room of such size, such elegance, with flowers to fill a forest and musicians playing softly. Inigo stared—and kept staring—until he heard a gasp and Giulietta whispered, "Oh, no, *the Count is here*. I must go, get behind the door."

Inigo slipped behind the door, wondering how horrible the punishment was for sneaking into a castle, for peering in rooms only the mighty should behold. He closed his eyes and made a silent prayer that the Count would never see him.

He opened his eyes to nightmare: the Count was staring at him. An old, old man. Dressed in such magnificence. With a look of such disdain. And a voice *of shattering power.*

"You," he began, his rage already building, *"are a thief!"*

"I have never stolen—" Inigo started to say.

"Who are you?"

Inigo could not get the words out. "Ummmm . . . Montoya. Inigo Montoya of Arabella, Spain."

"A Spaniard? In my house? I shall have to fumigate!" And then the Count came close. *"How did you get in here?"*

"Someone brought me. But I will never reveal her name. Punish me, do anything you will with me, but her name will always be a secret from you." Then he gasped as Giulietta stood in a distant doorway. He gestured for her to run, but the Count's turn was too fast and he saw. "Do nothing to her," Inigo cried out. "She has lived here all her life as did her mother before her."

"Her mother was my wife," the Count roared, loudest of all. *"You pathetic excuse for a money-grubbing fool, you disgrace to the face of the world."* And with a shriek of disgust he turned and was gone.

Giulietta was beside Inigo then, so excited. "Daddy likes you," she said.

*　　*　　*

THEY DANCED THROUGH the night. They held each other as lovers do. Inigo, with all of his study of movement, swirled like a light-footed dream and Giulietta had been trained since childhood for such things, and the musicians had played for fat dukes and grotesque merchants but now, looking at this dark couple hardly touching ground, they realized their music had to match the dancers.

Even today, all the servants in the Castle Cardinale remember the sound of that music.

Of course, before the spinning and the holding, there were a few minor points that needed a bit of ironing out.

"Daddy likes you," Giulietta said, watching as her father stormed away.

"Time out," Inigo said. "If you're his daughter, that makes you a Countess. And if you are a Countess that makes you a liar, because you said you were a servant. And if you're a liar, I cannot trust you, because there is no excuse for lying, especially when you knew of my dreams and my love. And so I must say farewell." He started to go.

"One thing?" This from Giulietta.

"More lies?"

"You judge. Yes, I am a Countess. Yes, I lied. It is not all that easy being me. I do not expect sympathy but you must hear my side. I am one of the richest women on earth. In the eyes of many men, one of the more attractive. I am also, please believe me, and I know it sounds arrogant, but I am also wise and tender and kind. I did not dress as a servant girl to fool you. I always dress as a servant girl. To try and find truth. Every eligible noble for a thousand miles has come to the castle. To ask my father for my hand. They say they want my happiness, but they only want my money. And all I want is love."

Inigo said nothing.

She took a step so she was closer. Then another so she was beside him. Then she whispered quickly, "When you came here with your dream, you won my heart. But I had to wait. To think. And now I have thought." She gestured for the musicians to play even more beautifully. "This is *our* party. *We* are the only guests. I did all this to please you, and if you do not kiss my mouth, Inigo Montoya of Spain, I will more than likely die."

How could he not obey her?

They danced through the night. Ohhh, how they danced. Inigo and Giulietta. And they embraced. And he kissed her mouth and her tumbling hair. And Inigo felt, for the first time since the dying, such happiness. It had fled from him, happiness, and when you spend years without, you forget that no blessing compares . . .

*   *   *

 Guess what? It stops there. Bang, the little riff on happiness, end of section.

*I call this the "Unexplained Inigo Fragment."
And what Peter objected to, as well as the fact that he finds it confusing, is simply this:* nothing happens.

He's right, in a strictly narrative way. But I feel that here, for the first time, Morgenstern shows us the human side of Inigo so we know he's more than just this Spanish Revenge Machine. (Frankly, I wish I had known this part existed before I read The Princess Bride.*) I don't think I could have cared any more deeply than I did, but my God, what poor Inigo gave up to honor his father! Think about it. We all have fantasies, right?*

You think before I met and married her I carried about this vision of Helen, my genius shrink wife? Of course not. But here Inigo has made this perfect creature for his own heart—and he finds her. And she loves him back.

And they part.

That's an assumption of mine, I know. But since we are told Inigo had a heavy heart when he reached Despair (and he came there from Italy), I have to go that way.

I included this section here for a very simple reason: I think it's Morgenstern at his best. I ran it by King, of course, and he felt I had to include it, since Morgenstern did. He also put me in touch with this professor cousin he has at Florin University—the son of the lady who runs the great restaurant. And this cousin, a Morgenstern expert, feels that the confusion on my part is my fault. That if I'd done sufficient scholarly preparation, I would understand Morgenstern's symbolism, and would therefore know that plenty happens here. Namely, according to this cousin anyway, it is here that Inigo first learns that Humperdinck has set a plan in motion to kidnap Westley and Buttercup's first child, right after it's born. And then Inigo has to race back to One Tree and stop that from happening. King's cousin says this Unexplained Inigo Fragment isn't a fragment at all, but a completed part of the whole of the novel.

I don't get any of that; if you do, great. And while you're at it, decide if you think I was right or not, including it. If you disagree, that's OK. All I know is my heart was pure . . .

*   *   *

3. BUTTERCUP AND WESTLEY

THE FOUR GREAT horses seemed almost to fly toward Florin Channel.

"It appears to me as if we're doomed, then," Buttercup said.

Westley looked at her. "Doomed, Madam?"

"To be together. 'Til one of us dies."

"I've done that already, and I haven't the slightest intention of ever doing it again," Westley said.

Buttercup looked at him. "Don't we sort of have to, sometime?"

"Not if we promise to outlive each other. And I make that promise now."

Buttercup looked at him. "Oh, my Westley, so do I."

From behind them suddenly, closer than they had imagined, they could hear the roar of Humperdinck: "Stop them! Cut them off!" They were, admittedly, startled, but there was no reason for worry: they were on the fastest horses in the kingdom, and the lead was already theirs.

However, this was before Inigo's wound reopened, and Westley relapsed again, and Fezzik took the wrong turn, and Buttercup's horse threw a shoe. And the night behind them was filled with the crescendoing sound of pursuit . . .

*   *   *

You see what he's done here?

This half page above is, of course, the ending of The Princess Bride, *and this will only take a sec, but I'd like to draw attention to what he's doing in the sequel:* playing with time. *Look, I snitched in my explanation that Waverly was going to get kidnapped, forget that. Morgenstern tells you the same in the very opening pages with Fezzik on the mountain.*

OK, so the kidnapping's already happened. Then in the Unexplained Inigo Fragment, he tells us that the kidnapping's about to happen *(at least according to King's cousin he does). Now here, he goes back to* before *Buttercup and Westley have even safely gotten away from Humperdinck.*

I think it's interesting, but some of you may find it confusing. Willy, my grandchild, did. I was reading it out loud to him (and how great a feeling was that, sports fans) when he said, "Wait a sec," so I did. And he said, "How can Inigo hear about the kidnapping and the next sentence practically, it's Princess Bride *all over again?" I explained it was the way Morgenstern chose to tell* this *particular story. Then he said this: "Can you do that?"*

I sure hope so.

*   *   *

HOWEVER, THIS WAS before Inigo's wound reopened,—*me again, and no, that was not a typo, I just thought it would make the transition easier if I repeated the last paragraph, go right on now*— and Westley relapsed again, and Fezzik took the wrong turn, and

Buttercup's horse threw a shoe. And the night behind them was filled with the crescendoing sound of pursuit . . .

Fezzik's mistake came first. He was in the lead, a position he tried to avoid whenever possible, but here he had no choice, since Inigo was losing strength with each stride and the lovers, well, they just sopped back and forth to each other about Eternity.

Which meant Fezzik, the ideal friend, the loyal follower, the lover of rhymes, perhaps not the most brilliant of fellows but certainly the most devoted bringer-up of any rears you might mention, found himself facing the most hateful, the most insidious bewilderment ever conceived of by the mind of man—

—*a fork in the road.*

"It's not actually a road (toad)," he reassured himself. "It's more a path (wrath)," "nothing to cause fret (sweat)." They were on their way to Florin Channel where the great pirate ship *Revenge* was waiting to scoop them up and head them all toward happiness. So relax, Fezzik, he told himself, treat the escapade as a lark (hark), a memory that would in the future bring warm smiles. After all, it was not even remotely a large fork.

It was, if you will, petite (sweet). A mere jog in the lane (pain).

Fezzik almost made himself believe that. Then reality took hold—

—because it was *still a fork*—

—something that required *thought, wisdom*, a *plan*—

—and he knew he could screw up something like that anytime.

*　　　*　　　*

Me here, and no, this is not an interruption, just a note to explain I have gone to a lot of extra work to make this perfect, as you know, and I didn't want anyone writing in to point out that "screw up" was anachronistic. It isn't. It's an ancient Turkish wrestling expression, a shorter version of "corkscrew up," a hold that brings pain of such magnitude that death soon follows. To "corkscrew down," of course, has been illegal for centuries. Everywhere.

*   *   *

THE FORK CAME closer.

They were surrounded by trees everywhere, always thickening, and the Brutes behind were clearly gaining, and even though the fork was indeed wee, it had to be there for a reason, and that reason Fezzik believed was that one way led to the Channel and the waiting *Revenge* while the other led elsewhere. And since the sea was their only profitable destination, elsewhere, no matter where else it elsed, was the same as doom.

Fezzik turned quickly to ask Inigo his opinion—but Inigo was bleeding so terribly now, the bouncing of the stallion not being helpful when you have recently been slit inside.

Fezzik instinctively reached back, grabbed his weakening comrade, pulled him onto his horse to see what he might do to save him—

—and while he was reaching, the fork was on them and Fezzik wasn't even watching as his horse took the left turning—which turned out to be, alas, toward Elsewhere.

"Hi," Fezzik said, once he had Inigo in front of him. "Are you excited? I'm as excited as can be." Inigo was too weak for reply. Fezzik studied Inigo's wound, pushed one of Inigo's hands deeper into it, hoping to somehow help stop the bleeding. It was clearly up to him to save Inigo now, and to do that he'd have to get him to a good Blood Clogger. Surely the *Revenge* would employ such a fellow.

From Inigo this: a groan.

"I agree completely," Fezzik said, wondering how the trees could become so much thicker so very quickly. It was amazing. They were almost like a wall now in front of them. "I'm also sure that just past this last wall of trees is Florin Channel and all our dreams will come true."

From Inigo the same, only less of it. Then his fingers managed to clutch Fezzik's great hand. "I go to face my father now . . . but Rugen is dead . . . so it was not a useless life . . . beloved friend . . . tell me I did not fail . . ."

He was losing Inigo now, and as he held the wounded fencer in his arms, Fezzik knew few things but one of them was this: wherever the bottom of the pit was located, surely he was there now.

"Mr. Giant?" he heard then.

Fezzik wondered who Buttercup was talking to, until he realized that they had never actually been introduced. Oh, he had rendered her unconscious, kidnapped her, almost killed her, so you couldn't say they were unacquainted, but none of it was truly a formal how-do-you-do.

"Fezzik, Princess."

"Mr. Fezzik," she cried out louder than necessary, but it was because at that moment her horse threw a shoe.

"Just Fezzik is fine, I'll know you mean me," he told her, watching her face in the moonlight. Never had he seen an equal. No one had. Except at the moment, she was not at her best—since not only was her horse behaving erratically, there was such pain behind her eyes. "What is wrong, Highness? Tell me so that I might help."

"My Westley has stopped breathing."

Wrong as usual, Fezzik realized, the pit is bottomless. He instinctively reached back, grabbed his breathless leader, pulled him onto his horse to see what he might do to save him—

—and while he was doing the reaching, his overburdened horse stopped. Had to. For there was now a wall of trees blocking any progress—

—and Inigo would not stop bleeding—

—and Westley would not start breathing—

—and Buttercup would not stop staring at him, her face lit with the hope that of all the creatures left stomping the earth, he, Fezzik, was the only one that could save her beloved and thereby stop her heart from shredding.

Fezzik at this heroic moment knew what he wanted most to do: suck his thumb forever. But since that was out of the question, he did the next best thing. He made a poem.

> Fezzik's in trouble, bubble bubble,
> His brain is just not in the pink.
> His mind is rubble, rub-a-dub double,
> Because everyone needs him to think.

Great work, no question, considering he was carrying two almost corpses on his stopped horse while the Princess was weeping, hoping for a miracle. Hmm. Fezzik went for a different rhyme scheme, hopeful it would jog something useful.

> Great-armed Fezzik, blocked by trees,
> Forget that she is crying.
> Though lost (and that it's *all your fault*)
> Forget that two are dying.

> Mighty Fezzik, strong of brawn
> Who most around think brainless,
> All you have to do is spawn
> A plan that will be painless.

> Fezzik the fearless, Fezzik the wise,
> Fezzik the wonder of the age,
> Fezzik who—

The "who" is lost to time now.

Because it was at that moment of poetic inspiration that Prince Humperdinck's razor-sharp, metal-tipped arrow ripped through Fezzik's clothing on its way to his great heart . . .

*   *   *

ONCE HE REALIZED they had taken the left turning, Prince Humperdinck knew they were his. He turned to Yellin, the Chief Enforcer of Florin, a finger to his lips. Yellin raised a hand and the fifty trailing members of the Brute Squad slowed.

The moon's perfect yellow dusted the thickening trees. Humperdinck could not help but stare at their beauty. Only the trees of Florin could interrupt, however briefly, a blood hunt. Was there anyplace on earth with such trees, Humperdinck wondered? No; resoundingly *no*. They ranked among the treasures of the universe.

During the Prince's contemplative moment, Yellin gestured for the Brute Squad to get into their attack groups: the knifers here, the stranglers there, the crushers in between.

The Prince rounded the last small turning—and there in front of him, so beautifully framed by the perfect trees, was the death tableau. His weeping runaway bride, the two still men on the buckling horse, held there in the arms of the giant. "Damn," he told himself. "If only I'd brought the Royal Sketcher." Well, he would just have to hold this in memory.

In the Prince's world, the world of scourge and pain, there was still great controversy who to initially attack. Should the nearest be selected? Or should it be the leader? Clearly Westley was that, but at the moment, a frail one at best. And the other still man must have had power, since he had killed Rugen—not the easiest task. It was standard to leave the women for last, they were not expert at blood;

they also whimpered and looked to the Heavens for escape—always good for chuckles around future campfires.

Leaving the giant.

The Prince unsheathed his bow, selected his sharpest metal tip, made the insertion. He was a great archer, but at night, with moonlight and shadow, he was a good deal more. He had not missed a night kill in ever so long.

An inhale for balance.

A final smile to the trees.

Then the pull back, the release, and the arrow was on its straight way. The Prince held his breath until he saw the arrow rip the cloth of the giant, at the heart site.

The giant cried out loud in shock and fell backward off his horse.

As he fell, Yellin led the Brute charge and the Battle of the Trees, brief though it was, was on—the fifty Brutes at full cry charging the three men lying sprawled on the ground, the lone woman trying to somehow hold them all in her arms . . .

As her attackers came eyeball close, Buttercup had this thought: if she had to die, what better way existed than with her true love in her arms and the beauty of her beloved Florinese trees covering her with their branches? Even as a child, nothing pleased her more than the glorious trees at the bottom of her farm, and when her chores for the day were done, that is where she went to wander so happily. What peace they gave. And they would continue to give that peace to her fellow Florinese forever and—

*   *   *

 Time out. Can you believe that last paragraph? Buttercup's about to die and she thinks of foliage? Horrible, horrible. So do not hold your breath waiting for

the stupid Battle of the Trees. I went nuts when I first read this. I'm like you probably, zooming happily along, and Morgenstern was clearly a master of narrative, but right now I bet you are wondering this: what happened?

My God, Fezzik shot in the heart, the two other guys drifting away, Buttercup trying to hold it all together while these FIFTY ARMED BRUTES come charging in—we all want to know what happened, right?

Here is what you are not reading: sixty-five pages on Florinese trees, their history and importance. *(Morgenstern had already started if you noticed—just when he realizes he's got them, Prince Humperdinck does an entire dumb paragraph about trees.) Even his Florinese publishers begged him to cut it. So I don't care what grief those Morgenstern whizzes at Columbia give me, if ever anything needed getting rid of, it was this.*

Want to know why he put it in?

It actually has to do with The Princess Bride. *Or rather, its success in Florin. Morgenstern was suddenly flush so he went right out and bought this country house that was off by itself and abutted this huge government-owned forest preserve. He was, indeed, master of all he surveyed.*

However . . .

He had been misinformed. This lumber company had title and not long after he moved in, guess what, they began sawing down all these trees. Morgenstern went nuts. *(He really did. His entire correspondence with the lumber company is right there in the Morgenstern Museum, just to the left off Florin Square.)*

He couldn't make them stop and in a year or two, his house was all naked and alone and kind of dumb-looking, so he sold it (at a loss, which just killed *him) and moved back into town.*

But from then on, he became the country's best-known tree savior.

(He had his eye on another country place it turns out, similarly secluded, and he wouldn't buy it until he felt he was safe from the lumber interests.)

So what he did here in Buttercup's Baby *was carefully build this huge suspense moment confident that his readers would have to read his tree essay in order to find out who lived and died.*

Briefly now, in terms of narrative, this is what you found out: A) Fezzik survived Humperdinck's metal-tipped arrow because of Miracle Max's holocaust cloak, which Fezzik kept tucked inside his tunic, and the folds of it blunted the arrow's impact, saving his life. B) The pirates from the ship Revenge *were hiding in the trees so when the Brutes were about to slaughter our quartet, they rained down on them like a rage from Heaven and took care of them all in just a couple of minutes, and when Humperdinck and Yellin saw this, they both fled. Then, C) the pirates, headed by Pierre—their number one guy and next in line to become the Dread Pirate Roberts—took the four and scooted out to the* Revenge *with them, hoping everyone would be alive when they all got there.*

Time back in.

*   *   *

AS SOON AS the four were safely aboard, Pierre signaled for the anchor raising and the great pirate ship *Revenge* slipped through the waters of Florin Channel toward open sea. A snap of his fingers brought the Blood Clogger, who set to work on Inigo while Pierre himself, chief medico and second in command, turned his attention to Westley, or as he was known on the ship, the Dread Pirate Roberts. Fezzik and Buttercup stood close by. Buttercup could not stop trembling so she reached out, tried to hold Fezzik's hand, realized the size discrepency, held his thumb instead.

The Clogger ripped off Inigo's shirt, examined the bleeding man.

There were minor sword wounds near each shoulder, but they were nothing. The stomach drew his attention. "A three-sided Florinese dagger," he said to Pierre, then turned to Fezzik. "When?"

"A few hours ago," Fezzik answered. "While we were storming the castle."

"I can clog him," the Clogger said. "But he will have little use for *this*." He indicated the six-fingered sword still clutched in Inigo's right hand. "Not for a very long time." And with that he scurried off, returned in a moment with flour and tomato puree, mixed them expertly, began filling the wound. He looked at Pierre then, nodded in the direction of Westley. "Want me to work on him?"

"This is not a matter of blood. Listen." He pounded on Westley's chest, listened to the awful empty sound. "His life has been sucked away."

"It happened this afternoon," Fezzik said carefully, trying not to upset Buttercup any more. "If you were in town you probably heard his death scream."

"That was *him*?" Pierre cried out. "They did that to my master? Where was this?"

"At the bottom of the Zoo of Death." Fezzik indicated Inigo. "We found him there."

Pierre studied Westley a moment longer before he sagged. "He must have been tortured beyond human endurance." He shook his head. "If only I'd been with you. I would have known what to do. I would have *rushed* him to Miracle Max."

Fezzik started bouncing up and down. "But that's what *we* did. We went straight there. For a resurrection pill."

Energy began to flow back into Pierre's body. "If Max worked on him, then we have hope."

"We have more than hope," Buttercup said. "There is true love."

"Princess," Pierre said, "you work your side of the street and I'll work mine." He looked at Fezzik, thinking. Then this question: "Did Max tell you how dead he was?"

" 'Sort of'. But then he slipped to 'mostly.' "

Pierre nodded. " 'Mostly' is not ideal, but I can work around that. Was it a new resurrection pill, not an old one Max had hanging around?"

"Made fresh today—I had to gather the Holocaust mud," Fezzik said.

Pierre was getting excited now. His eyes blazed at Fezzik. "Last and most important question: *did Valerie have time to do the chocolate coating?*"

"She let me lick the pot," Fezzik said, happy because he knew he was giving the right answer. "It was duh-licious."

*   *   *

Little cut here. (I already said in the introduction that they went to One Tree Island to get their health back so there's not a lot of nail-biting tension in the air concerning Westley's survival at this point.)

What you're not going to read is a six-page sequence in which Pierre—and we all care desperately about spending time with him, right?—does all these wondrous modern Florinese medical things to help Westley. None of which work, natch, because at this point in his life, Morgenstern had a hate on for doctors because he had developed gas (and I'm sorry if this is disgusting to you but I promised King I would research the hell out of it, and I did a lot of legwork before I found that Morgenstern's entire medical record is on view in the Museum, but not everyone can see the personal stuff like this, you have to have some kind of scholarly interest to read it, and even then you can't take it out of the place). I forget where this sentence began, sorry, but anyway, he had gas, couldn't shake it, and gave Pierre this sequence to get his own back. (When nothing worked, by the way, Fezzik picked Westley up and hung him by the feet over the side till his lungs filled with seawater, a famous cure in Turkey—not for death but rather gout, which Fezzik's father suffered from. Westley coughed like crazy but it got him talking again.)

*　　　*　　　*

INIGO WAS STILL unconscious but had stopped bleeding when Westley finally opened his eyes. Middle of the night. Buttercup lay alongside him on the deck while Fezzik watched over them all. Pierre approached, knelt, spoke softly. "I have the worst of all news."

" 'Worst' does not exist," Westley whispered. He studied Buttercup's face. "We are together."

Pierre took a breath, then said it. "You must leave the ship. And you must do so this night."

Before Buttercup could voice her outrage, Westley put a finger to her lips. "Of course. I understand. Humperdinck is after us."

"His entire armada. We can outrun them for awhile, but sooner or later, as long as you are here . . ."

"We are not in the best of shape for travel," Buttercup said. "Give us a few days. My husband is the most powerful man for a thousand miles. No place on earth is safe from him."

"Not possible. Much as I would like to. The crew would panic, as well they should, and I cannot have them losing faith in me."

Westley nodded. Then he was silent. Then he said Fezzik's name. Fezzik waited. "Do you remember the climb up the Cliffs of Insanity?"

"I don't want to go back there," Fezzik said. "I'm afraid of heights."

"Fezzik," Westley said patiently. "I don't want to live there either. Just answer me this. You were carrying three people when you did it, and please think before you answer me: *were you tired?*"

Fezzik waited 'til he was sure he had it right. Then he said, "No."

"Why weren't you? Our lives depend on this, so please take your time."

Fezzik didn't need time. "My arms," he said quietly.

Westley looked at him only a moment more. Then he turned to Pierre. "We will need chains and a small boat." He paused. "Go quickly now. You must get us close to One Tree Island by dawn."

*   *   *

THE *REVENGE MADE* spectacular time, full sail and a favoring wind, and soon they were sailing through a remote part of Florin Sea. Before dawn, the small boat was lowered and the four, all heavily chained to Fezzik now, got in. Neither Westley nor Inigo were capable of much movement. Fezzik took the oars, Westley nodded, and Fezzik began to row.

From the bridge, Pierre said, "I pray to see you again."

"Do," Westley told him.

Buttercup cradled him in her lap. "That was so sweet of him," she said. "He did not seem a man of great religious conviction."

"This will be his first prayer. And it could not be for a more needy group."

"Why do you say that?" Buttercup asked.

"Let us just hold each other," Westley said. "While we can."

"That's fairly ominous of you, don't you think?"

Fezzik listened. Terrified. But he had so many questions he did not know where to begin. So he just rowed. And every so often he smiled down at Inigo. Who every so often was able to smile back.

They were silent then, the four. For what seemed a very long time. The night could not have been prettier. The weather balmy. The waves all but nonexistent. A sweet caressing wind.

Ahhhhhh.

Fezzik rowed on, getting into a fine rhythm, his great arms enjoying the outing. He rowed harder for a moment and, of course, the tiny boat went faster. Then back to normal pace and, of course, the tiny boat slowed. Fezzik enjoyed doing that—it got rid of the monotony; harder, faster, normal, slower, harder, faster, normal. Faster.

Hmm, Fezzik thought, I wonder why that happened?

He rowed harder again and this time the vessel seemed close to flight, and it was then that Fezzik pulled the oars entirely out of the water—

—and the boat careened on faster than before.

Much faster than before. And then in the distance, but approaching quickly, came the *roar*. And Fezzik said, "Oh, Westley, I did something wrong, I'm sorry, I didn't mean to zoom like this. I was just sort of breaking the monotony, faster slower, that kind of thing, and I never meant for this to happen."

"It is not you," Westley replied, keeping his voice as steady as he could so as not to make things worse for his comrades. "The whirlpool has us now."

Inigo blinked awake on the word. "Fezzik . . . row around it."

"We can't do that," Westley said then.

Buttercup spoke all their thoughts then. "Westley, my hero and savior, what's the deal here?"

"I'll be very brief. Humperdinck's armada is after us. We need to disappear and mend. One Tree Island, from all I've heard, may well be the best spot on earth for us."

"And just what makes it so special?" Buttercup asked, louder now, because the small boat was rocketing now and the *roar* was growing loud.

"I can't be specific because I've never been there," Westley explained, half shouting, holding tight to the side so as not to be pulled overboard. "No one has ever been there. It is shrouded by mist with just the top of the single tree visible above the clouds. The mist is caused by the whirlpool. The island is surrounded by the whirlpool. And rocks. No boat can sail through—the rocks crush it or the water sucks it down. Now do you see why it is perfect for us? Humperdinck cannot get there and soon he will lose interest in trying to."

"Let me get this straight," Buttercup said. "The entire armada cannot get to the island but *we* can?"

"That is my belief."

"I don't mean to be pushy about this, but I am not keen on being crushed *or* drowned. Westley, *what in the world do we have that they don't?*"

"We have Fezzik," Westley replied simply.

"We absolutely do," Fezzik shouted, happy that the answer was so easily forthcoming. "He is right here inside my skin."

"But, my darling, what can Fezzik do?"

"Why, swim us through the whirlpool, of course."

No one answered for a moment because at that moment the tiny boat began to crack from the pressure of the water, and the *roar* of the whirlpool began to surround them, which meant it was very close. Westley checked Buttercup's chains and Inigo's as well as his own, making certain they were securely locked around Fezzik. The boat had little left it could do. It had brought them close, but now ahead the rocks became visible and Westley shouted through it all, *"Save us, Fezzik, save us or we die."*

Now Fezzik, as the world knows, had a terrible case of low self-esteem. So he was all for the theory behind Westley's words. Saving people. How wonderful. What in all the world could be better than saving people, especially these three with him now? Nothing. So in theory he should have made ready to dive in.

In practice he just sat in the bottom of the boat and shivered.

"Fezzik, *now!*" Westley shouted.

Fezzik shivered all the worse.

"He needs a rhyme," Inigo explained to Westley. Then to Fezzik: "Fezzik is no *zero*."

Fezzik shivered even more.

"Do you want a hint?" Inigo shrieked as the boat began to splinter. Still the shivering.

"He's a *hero*," Inigo went on.

Fezzik would have none of it, put his head in his hands.

"What could he be afraid of?" Buttercup cried out.

"Fezzik," Westley shouted into Fezzik's ear. "Are you afraid of the sharks?"

Even worse shivering. And a shake of the head.

Now the whirlpool was starting to spin them.

"Is it the sucking squid?"

Still worse. And another shake of the head.

Now the whirlpool began to pull them down.

"Is it the sea monsters?"

More shivering, more shaking.

And Westley, aware that they had next to no chance of survival the way things were going, cried, "Tell me!"

Fezzik buried his head in his hands.

And then from Westley, the loudest shout of all: "Nothing is worse than sea monsters. *What are you so afraid of?*"

Fezzik raised his great head and managed to look at them. "Getting water up my nose," he whispered. "I hate it so much." And then he buried his head again.

The boat was shattering by this time. In the final moments they clung to the remnants and Westley said, "I am too weak for the task, Inigo you do it," and Inigo said, "I am a Spaniard—I do not hold another man's nose," and Buttercup, not for the last time, heard herself say, "You men," and then as the whirlpool had them in its power, she took both of her hands and clamped them over Fezzik's nose.

*　　　*　　　*

THE WHIRLPOOL KNEW from the first it had them, it had not lost a battle in centuries, not since a soldier coming home from the Crusades caught it at a remarkably calm time, managed to slip almost past, was but a few feet from One Tree's shore before exhausted, he collapsed backward and the whirlpool made no mistakes this time, just kept him down at the bottom longer than it had ever kept anyone, before releasing its grip, letting him float up toward where the sharks waited.

The sharks were waiting this day, too, excited, four to shred, and they swam just at the outskirts of the whirlpool, watching as the bodies sank. Fezzik made no resistance whatsoever, did nothing 'til he was certain Buttercup's grip was solid. The whirlpool took them under, sped them down, on their way to the bottom and Fezzik let it happen, hoping only that the others could hold their breaths longer than they ever had, and soon he could feel the bottom of the sea. It was not deep here, whirlpools did not love deep water, and Fezzik bunched his giant body and *shoved* down with his mighty legs, shoved harder than he ever had before. As soon as his body began its upward trajectory, he started with his arms, his great tireless arms, windmilling them with more ferocity than the whirlpool had ever known, and it did what it could—increased its roar, swirled more savagely—but the arms would not stop, nothing could make them stop, and the chains held, and the others were unconscious from the battle, but Fezzik knew, as soon as he surfaced at the far end of the whirlpool, that Inigo had been right with his rhyme, he was definitely not a zero, not this day of days . . .

They were still chained when they reached the shore of One Tree, and they stayed that way for two days, all of them motionless, near dead from wounds and torture and exhaustion. Then they unchained themselves and, staying close together, began to explore their new home.

*   *   *

Me, obviously, and I'm sorry, but you don't want to read ten pages on vegetation. (Morgenstern's tree fixation scores again. His point here is that One Tree being pretty close to Eden is what all of Florin could be if only people didn't chop everything down.) The four get their strength back slowly. Buttercup nurses them and Fezzik takes care of food, cooking and cleaning the fish that was most of their diet. (Buttercup one day has nothing special going on so she makes him a gift for his nose—a clothespin. *Well, Fezzik goes nuts, he's so happy. It fits perfectly, he's never without it, etc., etc., and armed with that, Fezzik becomes the scourge of the area, swimming all over, fighting sharks and sucking squids—tastes like chicken, I thought the more squeamish among you would be glad for that bit of info—bringing his catch of the day back for food.) Anyway, this section ends with the moon high, perfect night, very romantic, all that. Inigo and Fezzik are off in their tents dozing, Buttercup and Westley sitting alone by a flickering fire.*

*   *   *

"YOU KNOW, WE'VE only kissed," Buttercup said, staring at the embers.

"Of course," Westley replied.

Not getting the answer she expected, Buttercup tried again. "We've certainly had more than our share of adventures, no one can deny it. And true love . . . to have that, we must be the most blessed of creatures."

"Surely the most blessed," Westley agreed.

"But," Buttercup said then, trying for frivolity, "thus far, the unalloyed fact that shines out is this: *we have only kissed.*"

"What else is there?" Wesley asked. He touched his lips lightly to her cheek, sighed. "Surely there could be nothing more."

This was somewhat disingenuous on his part, because he had been King of the Sea for several years and, well, things happened.

"Silly lad," she told him, smiling. "I have enough knowledge for us both. Of course I should, considering all those classes in lovemaking I took at Royalty School." She had taken the classes, but since Humperdinck had instructed her professors to teach her nothing whatsoever, Buttercup, though she smiled, was terrified.

"I am anxious for your teachings to begin."

She looked at his perfect face. She thought that, more than anything, she wanted this to go as it had in her heart. But what if she failed? What if she was just another case of big-talk, little-do and eventually he would tire of her, leave her? "I know so much it is hard to be sure just where is the best place to begin. If I go too fast, raise your hand."

He waited and when he saw the helplessness in her eyes he realized he had never loved her quite so much or so deeply. "Will you try not to laugh at me?"

"I would never embarrass a beginner such as yourself. It would be cruelty itself to mock your ignorance when I, of course, am totally wise."

"Do we begin standing up or lying down?"

"A very good question, that," Buttercup said quickly, not having the least notion what else to say. "There is great controversy as to which."

"Well perhaps it would be wise to cover both contingencies. Why don't I get a blanket in case lying down carries the day?" The blanket he brought and spread for them was soft, the pillow softer still.

"If we were to lie down," Westley said, lying down, "would we start close together on the blanket or far apart?"

"Again, great controversy," she replied. "You see, one of the problems with knowing so much is one sees both sides of questions."

"You are very patient with me and I appreciate that." He held out a hand for her. "We could do this: we could *try* lying close together on the blanket and experiment, more or less."

Buttercup took his strong hand. "My professors were all in favor of experimenting."

They were very close on the blanket now. The breeze, seeing this, knowing what they had been through to reach this moment, thought it might be nice to caress them. The stars, seeing this, thought it might be nice if they dimmed for awhile. The moon went along with the whole notion, slipping half behind a cloud. Buttercup still held his hand. She wondered for a moment if it would be wise to stop now, tell truths, try again another evening. She was about to suggest that, but then she looked deeply into his eyes. They were the color of the sea before a storm and what she read in them gave her the strength to continue . . .

*   *   *

 Want a shocker? Willy liked that scene. I remember when my father read The Princess Bride *to me, I hated the kissing stuff. I told him before I read it he might find it a little short on derring-do, so maybe that helped. His only question after was what kind of "things" happened when Westley was King of the Sea? I answered that if Morgenstern had wanted us to know, he would have told us. (He bought it. Phew.)*

Anyway, you will probably not be surprised to learn the obligatory nine months flew by pretty fast and . . .

*   *   *

"I THINK SUNSET would be a lovely time," Buttercup said. "I think he would like that, opening his eyes to the world at that moment. Yes, sunset it shall be."

She was speaking at breakfast to the others, and they all agreed. In point of fact, since none of them had the least experience with birthing, they could hardly argue. And no one could argue with Buttercup's handling of herself. She had blossomed in the nine months since she and Westley first made love, had dealt with her situation with a serenity remarkable in one so young. True, the first months brought a touch of morning sickness, and, yes, it was discomforting. But all she had to do to banish it was look at Westley and tell herself she was bringing another such as he into the universe. And *poof*, the sickness was in retreat.

She knew their firstborn would be a boy. She had a dream the first month that it would be so. The dream recurred two more times. And after that she never doubted. And she behaved throughout as if this were the most normal of human conditions. You swelled, certainly, but that didn't stop you from your regular life, which in her case often consisted of helping Fezzik cook, helping Inigo mend his heart, walking and talking with Westley, discussing their future, where they would settle, what they might do with the rest of their lives considering that the most powerful man on earth was out to kill them.

After the meal, she was ready. Westley had made her a special birthing bed, the softest straw and pillows softer still. It faced west, and he built a nearby fire, and he had kettles boiling with pure water. An hour before sunset, when her contractions were but five minutes apart, he carried her to the bed and set her gently down, and sat alongside her, massaging her. She was so happy, as was he, and by the time the sun was starting to set the contractions were but two minutes apart.

Buttercup stared at the sun and smiled, took his hand and whispered to him, "It's what I always wanted most on earth, bringing your son into life at such a time, with you beside me." They were both so happy, and Westley told her, "We are one heartbeat," and she kissed him softly and said, "And will always be."

During this, Inigo was fencing with shadows, excellent practice if you had no proper opponent to play with. Westley, of course was superb, and they had spent many happy hours slashing away at each other. But now, as sunset ended, Inigo made ready to stop soon and go welcome the baby.

Fezzik usually watched them, or Inigo alone when that was the case. But not this night. He was hiding on the far side of One Tree's one tree, the sky-topper. And he was holding his stomach and trying not to groan and be a bother, but the truth was this: for the strongest man on earth, for a man who earned his living inflicting pain, Fezzik was squeamish. He could handle blood as well as the next fighter, when it came from an opponent. But he had asked Westley and Inigo what was it going to be like, when Buttercup's son was born, and though neither of them were expert, they both indicated there might be some blood as well as other stuff.

Fezzik rolled on the ground as the phrase "other stuff," went though his bean. There was a Turkish word that described such things—*byuk*. Fezzik held his stomach and thought *byuk* over and over. He knew, from looking at the stars overhead, that the boy was shortly to arrive.

But, by midnight, they knew something was wrong.

The contractions were but a minute apart as they looked out at the sun's afterglow—but that is where they stayed. At ten they were still as before, and Buttercup would have handled it quietly, as she had the preceding hours—

—but at midnight her back began to spasm. She could withstand that; Westley was beside her, what were spasms? She was settling in for a long visit with them—

—until the pain crept from her back to her hips, found one leg, then both, set them on fire—

—the blaze in her legs was the beginning of her torment.

Her color faded but she was still Buttercup and she was lit by the glow from the flames. She was still, then, something to see.

It was not 'til dawn that they saw what the pain had done to her.

Westley stayed alongside, rubbed her back, massaged her legs, toweled her perspiring face. He was wonderful.

By noon, they knew something was very much wrong.

Fezzik rumbled over, took a look, ran back and hid in his spot, helpless. Inigo grabbed the six-fingered sword and fought with the breezes until he realized the sun was going down again and they were into the second day.

"I don't want you to worry," Buttercup whispered to her beloved.

"Nothing unusual so far," Westley replied. "From all I've heard, thirty hours is perfectly normal."

"Good, I'm glad to know that."

When the next dawn came and she had clearly begun to weaken, she managed to say, "What else have you heard?" and Westley said, "Everyone agrees on this: the longer the labor, the healthier the baby."

"How lucky we shall be to have a healthy son."

By the second sunset, it was only about survival.

Fezzik sobbed behind the tree as Westley counseled with Inigo. They spoke evenly—but terror was starting to circle about them. "I don't know of such things," Inigo said.

"Nor do I."

"I've heard of a cutting that can save the life. You cut the woman somehow."

"And kill my beloved? I would kill whoever tried."

Just then Buttercup cried out and Westley ran to her, dropped beside her. ". . . I'm sorry to be . . . such a bother . . ."

"What caused the scream?"

Buttercup reached for his hand, held it so tight. ". . . my spine is on fire . . ."

Westley smiled. "How lucky we are. Once that happens with the spine, well, that's a clear signal that our son is about to be born."

"The spine is nothing, not when you get used to it. I have had real pain, when I heard Roberts had killed you. That was hard to deal with. I suffered then. But this—" She tried to snap her fingers but her body was not obeying her. "Nothing."

"Inigo and I were just talking about where to go once we are a family. You remember how before I left your father's farm I was thinking of America? That still seems a good notion to me, what do you think?"

She whispered, "America?"

"Yes, across the ocean somewhere, and do you know when I first loved you?"

". . . tell me . . ."

"Well, we were young and you had just berated me terribly, called me a dullard and a fool as you did in those days: 'Farm Boy, why can't you ever do anything right? Farm Boy, you're hopeless, hopeless and dull and you'll never amount to anything.'"

Buttercup managed a smile. ". . . I was horrible . . ."

"On your *good* days you were horrible, but you could be much worse than that, and when the boys started coming around you were at your worst. One evening when they had all gone away and I was in the barn brushing Horse and you came out, humming and silly and said, 'I can have any boy in the village and lah de dah,' and I went to my hovel and I said to myself, 'That's it, you can keep those idiots for all I care, I am gone,' so I packed my belongings and I started out of the farm and I looked up at your window and I thought, 'You will be so sorry for humiliating me because I will come back here someday with all the wealth of Asia, good-bye forever.' "

". . . you really left me . . .?"

"That was the theory. But the reality was this: I turned and took a step toward the gate and I thought, 'What value has all the wealth of Asia without her smile?' And then I took another step and thought, 'But what if that smile comes and you not here to see it?' I just stood by at your window and I realized I had to be there in case your smile happened. Because I was so helpless when it came to you, I was so besotted by your splendor, I was soooooo ecstatic to be near you even though all you did was insult me. I could never leave."

She smiled the sweetest smile she could manage.

Westley gestured for Inigo to come closer. "I think we've rounded the corner," he whispered.

"I can see that," Inigo whispered back.

But they were living on hope and they both knew they were, and Westley held her so gently as her breathing grew increasingly weak. Inigo patted Westley on the shoulder as one comrade does to another, nodded that all was going to be well. And Westley nodded back. But Inigo in his heart knew this: it was soon to be over.

And behind the tree, Fezzik, alone, gasped, because *he* knew this: he was suddenly not alone anymore. He began to try and fight it, because something was invading him, invading his brain, and the Lord only knew his brain could use a little help, but Fezzik struggled on because when you were invaded, you never knew who was coming along for the ride, a helper or a damager, someone good, or, more terrifying, someone who wished anguish. Fezzik's mother had been invaded the day she met his father, for she was far too shy to approach him and flirt the way Turkish lasses were supposed to do in those days, so she just stood aside while the other village girls swooped him up. And she wanted Fezzik's father, wanted to spend her life with him, she knew that but she was helpless so she scuffed away, leaving the field to the braver girls—but then the invasion came and suddenly Fezzik's mother was brassy, and her temporary new tenant gave her confidence to do wonderful things, so back she went to join the other village flirts, and she outdid them all, with her flaunting smile and the wondrous way her body moved. At least it did that day, and Fezzik's father was smitten with her and even though the invader left that evening, they got married and his mother was so happy and his father only wondered as the years went on, wondered whatever happened to that glorious brazen creature who had won his heart . . .

Fezzik could feel his power going as the invader took control. His last thought was really a prayer: that please, whoever you are, if you harm the child, kill me first.

And by the fire Westley held Buttercup all the more tightly and said words of optimism, and Inigo always replied in the same tone.

Until that awful fiftieth hour of Buttercup's labor when Inigo could lie no more and said the dreaded words: "We've lost her."

Westley looked at her still face and it was true, and he had done nothing to save her. Not once in all of his life, except when he in the Machine, had he ever let tears visit, not even when his beloved parents were tortured in front of him, not once, never, never the one time.

Now he fauceted. He fell across her, and Inigo could only watch helplessly. And Westley wondered what was he going to do until he died, because going on alone was not possible. They had battled the Fire Swamp and survived. If he had known how it was going to end, Westley thought at that moment, he would have let them die there. At least that way they would have been together.

And then, from behind them, there came a sound more strange than any they had come across before, a disembodied sound, as if a corpse were talking, and the sound **boomed** out at them:

"We have the body."

Inigo whirled, then cried out in the night. And Westley, in despair, was so surprised at Inigo's sound he whirled, and he too cried out in the night.

Something was moving toward them out of the darkness.

They both squinted to make sure. Their eyes did not deceive.

Fezzik was moving toward them out of the darkness.

At least something that *looked like* Fezzik was coming toward them. But his eyes were bright, and his pace was quick, and his voice—they had neither ever heard a voice like it. So deep, thunderous, and measured. And the accent was something they had also never heard before. Not until they finally reached America. (Or, more accurately, when the ones left alive got there.)

"Fezzik," Inigo said. "This is not the time."

"We have the body." Fezzik said again. **"We have a fine strapping child inside. She has been kept waiting far too long."**

Now the giant knelt beside the still woman, gestured for Westley to move, put his ear to her, clapped his hands sharply. **"You"** he said, pointing at Inigo, **"bring me soap and water to disinfect my hands."**

"Where did he hear that word?" Westley asked.

"I don't know, but I think I better do it," Inigo said, hurrying to the fire.

And now Fezzik pointed to the great sword. **"Sterilize it in the fire."**

"Why?" Inigo said, bringing Fezzik the soap and towel.

"To make the cut."

"No" Westley said. *"I will not let him give you the sword."*

And now the voice took on a power more frightening than ever. **"This child is a putterer. That is what we call those that linger too long. But this child is more than that—she is in backward. And the umbilical chord is tightening around her throat. Now, if you wish to live your life alone, keep the sword. If you wish a child and wife, do what I tell you."**

"Be at your best," Westley said, and he nodded for Inigo to hand the great sword to the giant.

Fezzik marched it to the fire, sizzled the point red, returned to the lady, knelt. **"The umbilical chord is very tight now. There is little breath left now. There is little time."** And for a moment Fezzik closed his eyes, breathed deep. Then he moved.

And his great hands were so soft, the giant fingers so skilled, and as Westley and Inigo stared, Fezzik's hands did his bidding, and the sword touched Buttercup's skin, and then there was the cut, long but precise, and then there was blood but Fezzik's eyes only blazed more deeply and his fingers waltzed, and he reached inside and gently took her out, took the child out, a girl, Buttercup was wrong, it was a girl, and here at last she came, pink and white like a candy stick—

—here came Waverly . . .

*　　　*　　　*

4. FEZZIK FALLING

SHE WAS CONSIDERABLY below him at the start, twisting and spinning from momentum and wind. Fezzik had never seen the world like this, from this high, fifteen thousand feet with nothing below to break the fall, nothing, but at the far end rock formations.

He called after her but, of course, she could not hear. He stared after her but, of course, he was not gaining. There are scientific laws explaining that bodies fall at the same speed no matter how different the size. But the makers of the laws had never tried explaining Fezzik, because his feet, so useless at finding holds on sheer mountainsides, were unmatched at flutter-kicking in falling air. He cupped his fingers so his hands were perfect hollow mitts and then he set to work, swinging his arms and fluttering his feet so that if you tried to watch them, you couldn't and then Fezzik strained still more—

—and the distance between them began to close. From a hundred feet to half, then half again and when he was that close Fezzik called out to her, his word—

"*Keeeeed!*"

She heard and stared up and when he had her eyes Fezzik made her favorite silly face—the one where his tongue touched the tip of his nose—and she saw it, of course, and then, of course, she laughed out loud with joy.

Because now she knew what all this was, just another of their glorious games that always ended so happily . . .

*   *   *

FROM THE START, they were different. Sometimes when she was very little and dozing and Fezzik was helping Buttercup he would say, "She has to tinkle," and Buttercup would answer, "No, she doesn't, she's just . . ." and then she would stop before she got to "fine" because Waverly had blinked awake soaking wet, and Buttercup would look at Fezzik in those moments with such a look of wonder.

Or sometimes Waverly and Buttercup would be playing happily,

Fezzik watching, always there, watching so close, and Buttercup would say, "Fezzik, why do you look so sad?" and Fezzik would say, "I hate it when she's sick," and that night, a fever would come. He knew when she was hungry, or tired, he knew why she was smiling. And when crankiness was just around the corner.

Which made him, in Buttercup's mind, the perfect baby-sitter, since how could you improve on a sitter who knew what was going to happen? So Fezzik looked after her constantly and when she dozed he would sit between Waverly and the sun, which was why, when she started to talk, she called him "Shade"—because he was that, her shade in those earliest days.

Later, when she learned games, she had but to blink in his direction and he knew, not that she wanted to play, but which game. Westley agreed with Buttercup that although, yes, theirs was an unusual nurse-child relationship, it was a blessing, since it provided her with time to heal and recover, and better yet, time for them to be together. So Fezzik and Waverly learned from each other and enjoyed each other. Occasional spats, of course, but that comes, as Buttercup explained to him one day, with mothering.

"Can Waverly come play in the whirlpool with me?" Fezzik would ask constantly.

Buttercup would hesitate. "It gets her overtired, Fezzik."

"Please, please, please."

Buttercup would give in, of course, and off they would go, stopping first for the clothespin, then into the water, Waverly sitting securely on his head, his hands gripping her feet, and *whoosh*. It was truly magical, watching them, as Inigo and her parents did often. Because Fezzik, having conquered the whirlpool, had befriended it. He would kick up to speed, then swim into the whirl and let it carry them around, with Waverly shrieking and Fezzik keeping balance as they rode the water together, their favorite game, which always ended so happily . . .

*   *   *

FEZZIK WAS CLOSE enough to reach out now, so he did, brought the child into his arms, made another face, took her fears away. "Shade," she said, so happy.

Three thousand feet now.

Next he pulled her close to him.

Two thousand.

He knew as the rocks flew up toward him that he could never save himself. But if he could bundle her next to his body, if he could lie flat in the air and bring her into his arms so his mighty back took the initial assault, there was a good chance she would be shaken, yes, shaken terribly.

But she might live.

He made his body flat against the wind. He pulled her to him with all his sweet strength. "Keed," he whispered finally, "If you ever need shade, think of me."

One final silly face.

One blessed responding laugh.

Fezzik closed his eyes then, thinking only this: thank God I was a giant after all . . .

*   *   *

Willy was quiet when I finished. He gathered up his baseball and his frisbee, hit the elevator button. Dinnertime coming up and I had to get him home. He didn't speak again 'til we were on the street. "No way Fezzik dies, I don't care what the chapter's called."

I nodded. We walked in silence, and you know how Fezzik could tell what was going on with Waverly? Well, I can do that with Willy, at least on my good days, and I knew this great question was coming. "Grandpa?" he said finally.

Do you think I love that? You remember how much money Westley was going to get when he decided to leave Buttercup after she tormented him once too often about the boys in the village? That's how much. "Speak into the microphone," I said, making my hand one.

"Okay—that thing that invaded Fezzik? Here's what I don't get: how did it know to invade him right then? I mean, if it came a day earlier, it would have just had to wait around inside him for twenty-four hours feeling stupid."

I told him I doubted that question had ever been asked on Planet Earth before.

Jason and Peggy were waiting at the door. "It was good, Dad,"" Willy said. "It played around with time a lot."

"We really need another novelist in the family," Jason said, and I laughed and hugged everybody, started back home. It was a gorgeous spring evening so I let the park win me for awhile, just walked in silence, thinking.

First thing that has to be said: Morgenstern hasn't lost a whole lot off his fastball. This is clearly a different piece of work from The Princess Bride, *but he was a much older man when he wrote it.*

And since maybe this is the end of my involvement, a couple of closing thoughts.

Like Willy, I don't believe Fezzik is going to die here. My money is on Morgenstern saving him. He saved him from Humperdinck's arrow with the holocaust cloak, he'll come up with something.

The Unexplained Inigo Fragment. What was that? Couldn't he have given us a couple of hints at least as to why? Will it all make sense later?

Who was the madman on the mountain? Was he born without

skin? How did he get Waverly? Was he the kidnapper or just a member of a gang? And if he was just a member, who was his boss?

And who did invade Fezzik?

A beautiful young couple passed me then. She was pregnant out to here and I wished her a Waverly. And I realized something, and this is it:

We've traveled a long way, you and I, from when Buttercup was only among the twenty most beautiful women on earth (because of her potential), riding Horse and taunting the Farm Boy, and Inigo and Fezzik were brought in to kill her. You've written letters, kept in touch, you'll never know how much I appreciate that. I was on the beach at Malibu once, years back, and I saw this young guy with his arm around his girl and they were both wearing T-shirts that said WESTLEY NEVER DIES.

Loved that.

And you know what? I like these four. Buttercup and Westley, Fezzik and Inigo. They've all suffered, been punished, no silver spoons for this bunch. And I can just feel these terrible forces gathering against them. I just know it's going to get worse for them than it's ever been. Will they all even live? "Death of the heart" the subtitle says. Whose death? And even more important maybe, whose heart? Morgenstern has never given them an easy shot at happiness.

This time I sure hope he lets them get there . . .

Florin City/New York City
April 16, 1998

ABOUT THE AUTHOR

WILLIAM GOLDMAN has been writing books and movies for more than forty years. He has won two Academy Awards (for *Butch Cassidy and the Sundance Kid* and *All the President's Men*), and three Lifetime Achievement awards in screenwriting. His novel *Marathon Man* has made him very famous in dentists' offices around the world.